The Secret Heirs

COLLECTION

July 2019

August 2019

September 2019

October 2019

Secret Heirs: Baby Scandal

RACHAEL THOMAS

KATE HEWITT

ANNIE WEST

MILLS & BOON

First Published in Great Britain 2019
By Mills & Boon, an imprint of HarperCollins *Publishers*
1 London Bridge Street, London, SE1 9GF

SECRET HEIRS: BABY SCANDAL
© 2019 Harlequin Books S.A.

From One Night to Wife © Rachael Thomas 2015
Larenzo's Christmas Baby © Kate Hewitt 2015
A Vow to Secure His Legacy © Annie West 2016

ISBN: 978-0-263-27683-1

MIX
Paper from
responsible sources
FSC® C007454

This book is produced from independently certified FSC™ paper
to ensure responsible forest management.

For more information visit: www.harpercollins.co.uk/green

Printed and bound in Spain by CPI, Barcelona

CHAPTER ONE

Nikos Lazaro Petrakis stood and glared out at the sparkling sea beyond the offices of Xanthippe Shipping, his self-built empire, but he didn't see any of it. The words he'd just read in a text burned into his mind. And memories of the only woman who had stirred longings for things he could never allow himself to want set his body alight.

We need to talk. Meet me on the beach tonight. Serena.

Serena James had almost got through his defensive wall, affecting him far more than he cared to admit. He'd been glad when the excuse to banish her from his life had presented itself. He hadn't heard from her since that night three months ago. She'd walked away from him without looking back, rousing memories he'd rather have forgotten, but her silence since had been a welcome relief.

He pressed his eyes shut against the image of Serena. She had been hard to forget and, judging by the way his mind raced now, he still hadn't achieved that aim. For weeks his body had longed for hers. He'd been able to see her, smell her and feel her warmth if he closed his eyes, letting his thoughts slip back. But he'd held firm to his resolution of no commitments. He'd pushed her away emotionally and physically, but hadn't been able to sever the thread of attraction completely. It remained like a web spun in the early dawn, keeping them inextricably linked.

On his return to Athens he'd thrown himself fiercely into his work and had gone after the cruise company Adonia with a ruthlessness that had made even his PA look at him in question.

He clenched his jaw against the heated memories of his time with Serena, knowing there could only be one reason for her return to Santorini, the island he'd grown up on. His eyes snapped open and he inhaled deeply. There could be no other explanation.

During the summer she had arrived on the island to research her next article, and the passionate romance they'd shared had culminated in reckless and unprotected sex on the beach. Were there now life-changing repercussions? Consequences he hadn't planned on and most definitely didn't want?

Alarm bells began to ring. Why had she had waited so long? Had she done as he'd feared and used her journalistic background and connections to find out more about him? Anger fizzed through him as he stared broodily at the view. Did Serena know he wasn't the fisherman he'd led her to believe he was simply because it had been easier that way?

Her job as a travel writer wasn't in the league of working for the national tabloids, but that didn't mean she wouldn't use a story if it presented itself. He'd been extra-careful that she didn't find out who he really was, having had enough of press speculation over his business dealings, as well as over his constant succession of female companions.

If he'd known Serena's profession before their first amazing night together he might have been able to walk away, instead of being snared by her innocence and drawn in too deep towards something he'd always resisted.

To his sceptical mind there was only one reason she was here on the island, demanding to see him instead of simply calling. After believing she was different from all the other women he'd dated, she'd proved him wrong. She was here to use his wealth in order to secure her future and it couldn't have come at a worse time. His deal for Adonia Cruise Liners could be lost if her story got out.

He swore aggressively, but the words did not ease the suspicion that filled him. Irritated, he marched from the windows to his desk, stabbing at the buttons on the phone. The calm enquiry of his PA cut through the rage of his emotions and he forced them back under control. How could Serena ruffle his equanimity so spectacularly even when she wasn't in his company?

'Organise my plane. I need to go to Santorini this afternoon.'

The Greek words were fluid and assertive as control flooded through him once more, but his anger towards Serena and the situation didn't abate. Suspicion surfaced again. Why had she chosen now to come back? What did she want?

Did she know he was in the final and delicate negotiation stages of acquiring a cruise company? Expanding his shipping beyond freight and into the world of luxury cruises? It would make him CEO of the biggest shipping company in Greece. He didn't need the added complications she might bring with her. Not now—not ever.

Despite the looming deal, his mind was drawn to back to Serena: vivacious, happy and utterly gorgeous. She'd made him want things he couldn't have. The fact that no other man had ever made love to her—that she'd given *him* her virginity—had complicated the issue, and he'd forced himself to say goodbye, turning his back on what they'd briefly shared. Because of his past it was impossible to make an emotional commitment—even if he wanted to. Never again would he be that vulnerable.

Nikos took a deep breath and strode to the window, watching as a large cruise liner docked with an ease belying its size. Beyond that several container ships waited on the horizon, but the familiar sense of fulfilment from seeing the reality of his hard work and dreams out at sea didn't come. Nothing before had ever taken the edge off standing at his window and looking at all he'd achieved, but right now his mind was elsewhere, unable to focus on anything other than the memory of the slender redhead who for two weeks had driven him wild with desire.

He could still see her pale face, and the green eyes that had always sparkled with life like the sea beneath the dazzling sun. Her silky hair, as red as autumn leaves, had begged his fingers to slide through it. Each smile had invited his kisses so tantalisingly.

The last words he'd said to her forged forward in his memory—as did the image of her standing on the beach, dusting sand from her clothes, her face flushed from the passion that had engulfed them so spectacularly that evening. He should have had more control, more restraint, but she'd made that impossible. Just holding her in his arms, feeling her curves against his body and her soft lips beneath his, had been too much temptation.

Had that been what she'd intended? He balled his hands into tight fists of frustration, hearing again his words that night, harsh and unyielding, breathing life into the worst scenario as he'd made his position clear.

'If there are consequences of what has just happened you will *tell me.'*

He'd put stern emphasis on those last words and could

still see her face paling beneath his hard gaze. As she'd looked up at him the desire burning in her eyes had slipped away faster than the setting sun. He'd spoken in a stern and uncompromising tone, but with his past snapping at his heels he'd been unable to think rationally, furious that passion had got the better of him, making him break his cardinal rule of always being in control.

He couldn't blame her for running from him that night. He'd been furious at her—but mostly at himself.

Since the day she'd left he'd yearned for her, wanted her in his arms at night, but he had held firm to the resolute silence that had existed between them. As weeks had turned to months he'd hoped his fear of consequences of their night on the beach was unfounded.

Now, three months after that heated night under the stars, she was back. His heart slammed harder in his chest at the implications of her visit. She might have left it too long to tell him, and almost certainly had ulterior motives, but there was only one reason she was back and he had to face the fact.

She was carrying his child.

Serena's heart thumped hard as she waited on the beach, with the day ebbing faster than the tide. Where was Nikos? Would he come?

The rhythmic rush of the waves over the sand did little to calm her.

During her flight from London thoughts of the amazing two weeks they'd spent together had been overshadowed by her accidental discovery of Nikos's true identity only minutes before she'd boarded the plane. The man she'd fallen in love with was far from the humble fisherman he'd described himself as being all those months ago. She'd been sitting in the departure lounge and Nikos's image had flashed across the news app on her phone, with a story speculating on the Greek shipping billionaire's involvement in an aggressive takeover bid.

Nikos was a shipping billionaire?

She'd chosen to fly out to Santorini believing that he had very little money, but that he at least deserved to be given her news in person. Her shocking discovery, moments before she'd boarded her flight, had changed everything. Angry and betrayed, all she wanted now was to upset Nikos's profitable little world and turn it upside down—just as he'd done hers.

As she stood on the beach the bravado she'd built up during the flight threatened to desert her. He would know exactly why she was here, but it didn't make what she had to tell him any easier—whoever he was. He didn't want 'consequences', as he had so nicely put it, and of that she was certain.

The tiny stirrings of hope she'd allowed to grow…that they might have a future together…had been crushed completely. A man like Nikos—a billionaire—would most certainly wash his hands of her.

Instinctively she placed her palm protectively over her stomach and the new life within. What if Nikos didn't come? She'd wanted him to acknowledge that their passionate holiday affair had resulted in pregnancy. Now she wasn't so sure. Did she want a man like that in her life? In her child's life?

How *could* he have deceived her? She despised liars, having lived in the shadow of lies all her life.

She scoured her memory for that last night on the island. The gentle, loving fisherman she'd fallen in love with had changed drastically, showing a new and unfamiliar side, when he'd realised what might come of their spontaneous lovemaking.

It should have been just a goodbye kiss—one she could keep in her memory when she'd returned to her life in England. She'd known he didn't want more, and had accepted it, wanting to experience love for the first time in the arms of a man who demanded nothing—the man she loved. But they'd both lost control as passion had claimed them, neither caring about anything other than the desire that had raged between them like wildfire, engulfing everything in its path.

A flurry of panic rose up again. She hadn't told anyone yet—not even her family. She couldn't bear to see their reactions, knowing she'd let them down. Her sister knew of her brief romance with Nikos, but she hadn't found the courage to tell her about the baby—not now, with all of Sally's IVF problems.

'Serena.'

She closed her eyes as she heard his voice behind her, deep and heavily accented. She couldn't turn yet. The wretchedness she felt would surely be in her eyes. Either that or her love for him might still shine through, and that was something she just couldn't let him see. Not after the way he'd cut her out of his life because of a mistake in the making, made by both of them.

A *mistake*. She hated that word. She'd lived with it hanging over her all her life. She was one of those—a mistake that had taken her parents by surprise. Forcing them to reconcile their differences and remain married.

'Serena,' he said again, and touched her arm.

She couldn't avoid the moment any longer. Her breath caught in her throat and somersaulting butterflies took flight in her stomach.

She was more nervous than she'd ever been in her life as she turned to face him, desperate to keep her voice calm. 'I had almost given up on you.'

Was that wobbly whisper really her voice? She must stay strong. Her unbalanced emotions couldn't get the better of her—not now. But as she moved back from his touch she questioned if she could go through with this. Was she doing the right thing? Should she even have come here?

Nikos moved closer to her, forcing her to look up at him, and when she did she could hardly suppress a gasp of surprise. His blue eyes, so uncharacteristic for a Greek man, weren't the colour of a summer sky, as she remembered them, but icy cold. He'd changed. This was a very different man from the one she'd fallen in love with. And it wasn't only the smart clothes he now wore instead of the tatty work jeans she'd always seen him in.

He was still tall, dark haired, with angled features, but each angle looked harsher, and his lips were set in a don't-mess-with-me line of rigidity.

'Sorry I had business to attend to.'

'You look...' She paused as she struggled to find the right word, completely taken aback by his unyielding aura. His deceit, and the enormity of what she was about to announce made small talk almost impossible. The next few minutes would affect the rest of her life and she almost faltered, but bravely pushed on. 'You look very smart—very much the businessman.'

His brows lifted in surprise and she thought she saw a hint of anger in the blue depths of his eyes. There was hardly a trace of the man she'd laughed and loved with for the duration of her holiday three months ago—the man she had given much more than just her heart to. This was the real Nikos.

'I may have been brought up a simple fisherman, but that doesn't mean I have to stay that way.'

The sharpness of his words made her blink, and again she took a step backwards, the sand shifting beneath her feet. She glanced around the now deserted beach in a desperate attempt to avoid that stern glare.

He wasn't making it easy for her. It was obvious from his irritation that he knew why she was here—why she'd sought him out after he'd so cruelly ended their two weeks of romance. He was toying with her, forcing her to tell him.

'Do you know why I'm here?'

She hated the way her words trembled, and resisted the urge to hug her arms about herself in an attempt to protect herself from his anger. Whatever else she did, she had to remain strong.

He didn't take his gaze from her face. She stood firm, refusing to be intimidated as his cold words rose above the rush of the waves.

'You should have done this about two months ago.'

Each matter-of-fact word lacerated her heart, almost annihilating the love for him she'd carried in her heart since she'd left the island. Each carefully spoken word proved she had been nothing more than a convenient amusement.

Whatever her dreams of Nikos had been, to him she'd only been a passing fancy—a brief encounter that didn't require commitment, just soft words and passionate kisses. One he thought he could brush aside when it suited him. But things had changed and now he had to acknowledge the situation.

Enraged by his attitude, and all she'd learnt, she faced up to him, the fire of determination scorching through her. 'For the past two and a half months I have been somewhat preoccupied with nausea.'

Each sharp word flew at him like a dagger. The injustice of his accusation was stinging, giving her the strength to stand her ground. After desperately keeping her pregnancy from her family, the strain was too much. He was pushing her almost to breaking point.

'You could have called. I did, after all, ask to be told.'

His blue eyes had become so dark and forbidding they were like the hidden depths of the ocean. Unknown and uninviting.

'*Ask?*' The word rushed from her, wrapped tightly in disbelief. 'You didn't *ask* anything. You *demanded*.'

His eyes hardened, glinting like icicles as the full moon shone on them and fixed her to the spot. 'I was doing the right thing. I asked that you tell me if you became pregnant. I did not demand anything of you. It would only have taken one call, Serena. Why wait so long? Why now?'

'I needed time to think—to decide what I was going to do.' She'd thought herself into circles. Total panic had made any kind of sensible thought impossible, but even then the answer had been the same.

Nikos had no intention of being a father. She would have to bring up her child alone. Such thoughts had driven her mad with fear and panic, as had the conviction that her mother would be devastated. Her daughter falling pregnant after little more than a one-night stand would be too much of a nightmare for her to deal with. And she wasn't a naive teenager, which would only make her mother's reaction worse. She always worried about what other people thought of her—that was why she'd hidden the sham of her marriage behind a facade of happiness.

At twenty-three Serena should have known better. But, having purposely kept any advances at arm's length, she hadn't.

The experience of making love with a man was something she'd planned to share with someone she loved. So when Nikos had sauntered into her life, sweeping her off her feet, she'd known almost from the moment they'd met where it would end. She'd given Nikos, the man she'd fallen instantly in love with, her most precious gift.

In doing so she'd let everyone down. But worse to bear was the pain she would cause her sister.

'To decide what you were going to do?'

She saw his brows quirk together savagely as his gruff voice startled her out of her thoughts.

'Yes—*do*.' He was beginning to exasperate her. He was making her do all the work in this conversation, forcing every word from her when he didn't even have the decency to admit his deceit. Was it a form of punishment?

'And have you thought?'

The powerful aura radiating from him was something she hadn't noticed before, even though they'd spent almost every evening of her time on the island together. Not only did he look different, he acted differently. This Nikos was totally in command, completely intimidating—and, worse than anything else, he was without care or kindness.

She met it head-on with a cold indifference that hid the panic and nerves she really felt.

'Yes, I've thought, Nikos. I've thought of your lies, and of those callous words you threw at me the last time I saw you. I've thought of nothing other than your insistence that I inform you of any *consequences*.'

His mouth was set in a grim line of irritation, but she pushed on. Behind him the sky displayed beautiful oranges and deep purples, and she wondered how such a stunning sunset could play host to this terrible moment.

'It seems I'm now to be punished for not telling you as soon as I knew, but—more fool me—I wanted to tell you personally. Face-to-face. Not in a phone call. And that meant waiting until now—until I felt well enough to travel.'

'Yet you can't.' He moved closer, his words coming out in a provoking growl. 'You can't say it, can you?'

'Oh, I can, Nikos—I *can*.' Fury charged through her

like a tornado. Her heart raced and each breath she took became deeper. He was killing her love, shattering any hope she had harboured. Despite the turmoil her mind was in, the irrational sway of emotions, she flung the words he wanted to hear forcefully at him. 'I'm *pregnant*, Nikos. I'm pregnant with your child.'

'Why have you come all this way, Serena? What exactly do you want from me?'

He stepped closer, towering over her, intimidating. She hated the way her breath caught in her throat, hated the way her body longed for his even as his icy words splintered around her.

'I don't want anything from you. At least not from Nikos the fisherman—but that isn't you, is it?' She lifted her chin, aiming for defiance—which was far from the uncertainty she was fighting so hard to conceal.

His eyes narrowed and he pierced her with a fierce stare. 'How much?'

Serena's mind swam with confusion. What was he talking about? 'How much what?'

She backed away, unable to deal with the close proximity of his body. How had she ever thought coming to the island was a good idea? She'd wanted to tell him face-to-face to convince herself that any hope of more was futile, knowing it would be the only way to prevent that *what if* feeling.

'Money.'

He spat the word at her so venomously she stepped back even further, until the backs of her legs met the large rock she'd been sitting on whilst waiting for him. She'd never thought telling him would be easy, but this was totally unexpected. Did he think she was here just for financial gain?

'I don't want your money.' Her head began to swim and

giddiness threatened, but she couldn't stop now. Not until she'd told him everything. 'All I wanted to do was tell you in person and leave.'

She looked up at him, wishing things were different—that he hadn't lied, that he hadn't said the words that still replayed over and over in her mind. *'You will tell me.'* The insistent way he'd delivered them had left her in no doubt that fathering a child was the last thing he wanted.

She took in a deep and silent breath and thought of her sister, and the heartbreak she and her husband had been through each time IVF had failed. It seemed so unfair to find out that she'd become pregnant so easily when her sister was breaking her heart, wanting a child. It was just too cruel, and it had left her unable to say anything to her family, let alone confide in her sister. The only person she'd told was Nikos. And right now he was making her feel alone and isolated.

Her time with Nikos had been nothing more than a holiday romance—one of many for him, she was sure. But for her it had changed everything—for ever—and he'd just confirmed her worst fear. He was going to turn his back on her *and* his child.

She briefly closed her eyes against the torrent of emotions that coursed through her. Pain induced by Nikos, infused with the ever-present hurt of knowing she'd been an unexpected addition to her family, forcing her parents to stay together. If only Nikos felt something for her everything might be different, but that was evidently a hopeless dream. She should walk away now—for her baby's sake, if not hers.

'You think you can tell me I am about to be a father and then just leave?'

He moved away from her, towards the ebbing tide, and turned to look out at the sea. His broad shoulders were tense, but she was glad she wasn't under his scrutiny any longer.

I don't know what to do. The words screamed inside her head as intense pain stabbed at her heart. She pressed the pads of her fingers to her closed eyes. Going down that line of thought now wouldn't accomplish anything.

Guilt boiled inside her—as if she'd stolen something from her sister. Especially as she knew there wouldn't be any more IVF for her after the last treatment. Her sister and her husband didn't have any savings left.

'How can we raise a child, Nikos?'

Her words were a tremulous whisper as she moved to stand beside him. The rush of the waves suddenly sounded loud on the beach as she looked at his profile. Not for the first time, she wondered who this man was.

Images of the handsome man she'd had an affair with filled her mind as she looked away and out across the sea. The setting sun was almost gone from the sky. But she didn't see its beauty. All she saw was Nikos, the man she'd given her heart to, believing she loved him and that he might love her. During those long, hot days his dark hair had gleamed beneath the sun and his blue eyes had filled with desire each time they'd met.

He had been everything she'd ever dreamed of and more, sweeping her away so fast she'd given up her teenage dreams of waiting to find her true love before discovering the pleasure of intimacy with a man. She didn't regret one moment of that decision. She'd loved Nikos—until he'd looked at her with his condemning eyes on that last night.

He didn't respond and instinctively she reached out to him, touching his arm. As he turned and looked at her she saw his face wore an expression of pain, and she had the unexpected urge to throw herself into his arms, to be held tight and told everything was going to be okay. Because deep down it was what she wanted—what she needed. To be loved by only this man. But the man she loved didn't exist.

Instead she stood as tall and proud as possible, finding strength she hadn't realised she had left. 'We can't, Nikos. Not together.'

'What are you saying, Serena?' Nikos all but stumbled over his words as the implications of what she'd said almost silenced him. The reality of the situation had hit him hard, taking away the ability to speak.

Memories of the day his mother had left and questions from his past rushed forward. He tried hard to prevent them from colliding with the present, but he couldn't shake them off. His father had cursed her, saying he should never have married an English girl, and Nikos had stood alone, ignored and forgotten by each of them. Then his mother had left, her cruel parting words ringing in his ears.

If his father had still been alive he could have found out more about the mother he barely remembered. As a teenager he'd been angry when he'd learnt that her career had been more important than her marriage and her young son. So when she'd made contact on his sixteenth birthday, saying she'd never meant to hurt him, he'd blocked her from his life. He didn't want to open that door again.

He clenched his hands into tight fists. Fury carried through the years raged inside him, but he pushed it back. He had to keep calm.

That letter from his mother had made him vow never to marry. He had no intention of making the same mistake as his parents. But that vow also denied him the possibility of being a father.

Something shifted inside him. *Serena was carrying his child.* He took in a deep, steadying breath. He was going to be a father. Fate had altered his life decision and no matter what Serena did or said he would be a father to his child in every way. His past would not write his child's future. His child would not experience the heartache he'd known and he'd do everything in his power to achieve that.

'Neither of us can give this child what it needs.'

Her voice was soft, with a definite and unyielding firmness. He looked down at her, hardly able to believe what he was hearing. He couldn't comprehend the cool and composed words that had slipped easily from her mouth. She was writing off her child as easily as his mother had done.

An icy-cold chill slipped down his spine and the image of the woman before him combined with that of the fair-haired woman in the tatty photograph he'd kept hidden away since he'd been given it by his grandmother. It was his mother—but as far as he was concerned it was just the woman who'd given birth to him. He'd locked it away, out of sight and out of mind, hating her too much to acknowledge her as his mother.

Serena blinked rapidly and he thought he saw a glimmer of moisture, the smallest hint of tears. He narrowed his eyes, assessing the situation. His breath, deep and hard, almost burned his chest as his heart was pumped full of anger, his mouth filled with the bitter taste of betrayal as he remembered what had sounded like a throwaway comment at the time.

Had she planned this from the very start? She'd seduced him so wickedly with her kisses that last night on the beach that he'd lost all control. Had that been her intention all along?

He furrowed his brow, resisting the need to put distance between them. She'd been a virgin the first time they'd made love, which had shocked him so much that he'd fallen under her spell, wanting to spend more and more time with her, yet unable to allow himself to want her emotionally. Had he been naive to be seduced by her?

'I never planned to be a father, but that doesn't mean I won't be there for my child.'

He clenched his fists against the fear of what those words meant. Could he really be a good father when his own had ignored him so much that his grandparents had been compelled to taken him in?

'I will.'

A spark of something akin to fear mingled with hope showed in her eyes as she moved closer. 'You want to raise the baby with me?'

He shut his heart to the image of a happy family, slamming the door firmly. 'That won't be possible, will it? Not if you have already decided to give it away like a parcel.'

'I haven't decided any such thing.' She glared at him like a wounded animal, wary and untrusting.

'You constantly spoke of your sister—about her longing for a baby. Do you recall what you told me?' The harsh words growled from him, and before she could reply he pressed on. '*"If I could have a baby for her, I would."* Those were your exact words.'

'How can you twist things like that? It's what I wished I could do—not what I planned.'

Disappointment rushed over him like a waterfall. When she'd asked if he wanted to raise the baby with her he'd almost allowed himself to believe it was what she wanted, that it could be possible. How foolish.

'Did you really think you could come here and use the baby—my baby—as a bargaining tool to get money for your sister? Or, worse, give my baby to her?'

She pushed slim fingers through the thickness of her red hair, distracting him momentarily.

'No. That's not how it is. This is *my* baby.'

'It's my baby too, Serena.' Fury thundered in his veins, pulsing around him so fast he couldn't think straight. It was obvious she'd done her homework. She knew who he was. But was she really capable of seducing him, hoping to become pregnant with a baby for her sister? If he was thinking rationally he'd say no, but with such a revelation knocking him sideways he'd believe anything right now.

As she stood there, glaring angrily at him, challenging him on every level, he knew he had to be there for his baby as it grew up. He wanted to give it all he'd never had. But it didn't matter how much money he had, he didn't know if he could do the one thing a father should. Love his child—or anyone.

How could he when he'd never known the love of his parents? And he'd always kept his distance from his grandparents, shunned their love, preferring to stay safe behind his defences even as a young boy. But he had a bond with them. Could he at least bond with his child?

Was he heartless? Was that why his mother had turned her back on him? Why his father had barely looked at him? Was it his fault?

'I will be there for my child.' He watched her for a hint of guilt, any trace of her deceit.

'What's *that* supposed to mean?'

The fury in her voice overflowed, confirming his suspicions.

'Drop the innocent act. You know who I am. For a woman with your journalist's training it must have been all too easy to discover more about the father or your child.' Venom spiked every word as he looked at her, suddenly becoming aware of the waves creeping closer to them. How long had they been discussing this? Hours? Seconds? He didn't know. Only that it would change things and change *him* for ever.

'I have only just looked you up on the internet—in the departure lounge at the airport, to be exact. Because, stupidly, I believed you were an island fisherman, living a simple life. There shouldn't have been anything more to know.' Her furious words were flung at him and her eyes sparked like fireworks. 'You lied to me, used me.'

So the flame-haired temptress had a temper!

'Just as you lied to *me*—using me, the "simple fisherman", as a means to an end.'

'I didn't use you at all.'

'So you *deny* you seduced me in the hope of getting pregnant with a child you planned to give to your sister?'

She gasped in shock, her acting skills well and truly on display. 'Of *course* I do.'

'In that case I won't be upsetting your plans.'

'And what does *that* mean?'

Her temper flared again. Begrudgingly he admired her spirit. She was even more beautiful when the fire of determination rose up within her.

'Only that I have every possible means at my disposal and I *will* be a father to my child, no matter what obstacles you put in my way. I will remove each and every one to get what I want. My child. My heir.'

CHAPTER TWO

SERENA WAS SPEECHLESS. She blinked rapidly as if seeing Nikos for the first time. What did he mean? Her head began to swim as she tried to process what he was saying and she cursed her pregnancy-induced emotions, biting back hard against the urge to dissolve into frustrated tears.

This wasn't going at all to plan. She hadn't expected him to welcome her with open arms—not after his parting words—but the discovery of his deceit and his determination to overrule her was totally unexpected.

'You let me think you were an island fisherman. One who shouldn't have anything more to tell.'

She'd known coming back to Santorini wouldn't give her all she really wanted, but never in all her wildest dreams had she imagined this scenario.

She looked at Nikos again, searching for the man she'd fallen in love with. The man who'd set light to the undiscovered woman inside her, capturing her heart and body.

'Why?' she asked simply.

'It was for the best at the time.' Each word was firm and decisive, his face a mask of composure.

I will remove each and every one to get what I want. My child. My heir.

His words of warning echoed in her head like a haunting melody. It seemed that no matter how much she'd tried to be different from her parents, wanting only to have a happy family, she was heading down the same path.

Her parents had been forced to stay together by an unplanned pregnancy, a mistake. She had grown up carrying the guilt of being that mistake, knowing she had forced her parents to stay together. *She* was the reason they'd fought, the reason they hated each other now. She didn't want her child to suffer the same guilt because of the mistake she and Nikos had made.

'I *am* an island fisherman.'

He stepped towards her, his voice softer now, but instinct told her not to let her guard drop, that trouble was brewing.

'But I am also a businessman. My office is in Piraeus and I live in Athens.'

'So what were you doing on the island? Using the guise of a fisherman to lure women and bolster your ego?' She couldn't stop the words from rushing at him.

He glared at her. 'Fishing was my grandfather's trade, his business. I help out with the fleet that he started. And knowing your background I wasn't going to disclose anything personal to you.'

'My background?' She was completely at a loss as to what he meant.

'You *are* a journalist, are you not?'

She tried hard to process what he was telling her, but couldn't understand why he'd kept the truth from her. Was it really because she had studied journalism? Did he really fear that? Or was it simply that he hadn't wanted her to know who he was?

'Why did you feel the need to hide it from me, Nikos?' She couldn't imagine the life Nikos really led. It was too far removed from the man she'd met, the man she'd fallen in love with. He was shattering every dream she'd had of him. 'Why were you even here, masquerading as a fisherman?'

'My life changed when I left the island, and my fortunes with it.' He looked at her, his eyes glacial and hard, his expression unyielding. 'Every year since, I've spent two weeks helping the small fleet of fisherman here on the island. It's a way of staying connected to my grandparents. And you didn't ask questions—which made a change.'

'A change from what?' He wasn't making sense—or was it her jumbled emotions? She was tired. Thinking coherently wasn't easy, but she forced her mind to concentrate.

'From women wanting all they can get from me—financially and emotionally. It appears you are not different after all.'

'You lied—you hid the truth—because you were afraid I'd want more?' The words rushed from her before she could hold them back and his eyes narrowed in response, his mouth setting into an irritated line of hardness.

The stark question he'd fired at her earlier came back, its full meaning now painfully clear.

'How much?'

That was what he'd said when she'd told him she only wanted one thing from him. It hadn't made any sense. Now it hit her. He thought she wanted money from him—or worse still, that she'd deliberately got pregnant to give the baby to Sally.

Sickness rose up and her head spun. What kind of man was he?

'Why didn't you tell me when we were together?' She hurled the question at him, her knees becoming ever weaker with shock as nausea threatened to take over.

'What we shared...' He took her hands in his and she hated the way her pulse leapt at his touch, counteracting all the pain and turmoil of moments before. 'It was something special. But it was never destined to be more than a holiday romance, a passing affair.'

He was right about that, at least. She had wished and hoped for more, but deep down had known it would finish once she'd left the island and returned to her life. What she *hadn't* known was that he too would leave the island and go back to his life. A life he'd kept from her because he'd believed she was after his money or the scoop of a big story.

She pulled her hands from his slowly and shook her head in despair. 'It doesn't mean we can raise a child together, Nikos. Money isn't everything.'

Fury seeped through Nikos's veins like poison, mixing with memories of the day his mother had walked away and left him. Serena's words, although calmly said, screamed inside his head. What was she saying? What plans had she been making for their child whilst he'd been living in ignorance of its existence?

'It still sounds very much as if you are considering giving my baby away.' Incredulity made his tone sharper than a blade.

'That is absurd.'

She met his accusation head-on, looking determined to do battle and defend herself. And he knew for certain that there could only be one reason. He'd exposed her plans before she'd had a chance to knock him sideways with the idea, but all it had done was make him ever more certain that he would be there for his child—not just now and again, but all the time.

'You have more than implied it.'

He clenched his hands into tight fists, resisting the need to reach for her, to hold her arms and force her to look him in the eye and tell him the truth.

'We can't sort this out now—not when you are jumping to such outrageous conclusions.'

She looked at him tempestuously and her green eyes met his, but his usual accuracy in reading a person had deserted him. He couldn't see lies or truth, but he did see something else in them. The same fiery passion he'd seen three months ago—which had been his undoing.

He stepped closer to her…so close he could smell the sweetness of her perfume. He battled with his memories of their time together as the scent of summer flowers invaded his senses, light and floral, evoking more memories he'd do better to bury. But he couldn't. This woman, the only one who'd made him want more than a brief affair, was in reality no better than his mother. Worse, in fact. She wanted to abandon her child, and she expected him to do the same.

'Nikos, we have to be practical. The baby will grow up in England—with me.'

Never. The word resounded in his head. *Never.*

He ignored the pleading edge to her voice, wondering if she thought he'd meekly accept that. Would she really be a mother to his child? Or had she planned all along to give her baby away?

His thoughts returned to his mother with unnerving clarity. Had she been being practical when she'd walked away? Had she given her six-year-old son a thought as she'd left, preferring to escape with her lover, to the bright city lights and her modelling career, instead of remaining on the island with the man she'd married?

Nikos tried to push back the demons that had haunted him since that day. The woman who'd given birth to him didn't know him—just as he didn't know her. He might have passed her on the streets of Athens, or any other city he'd visited for business, and not known. All he knew was that despite her attempts to contact him since he'd turned sixteen he'd written her out of his life.

He looked at Serena, the woman he might have loved if things had been different—if his past hadn't convinced him he was incapable of love or being loved.

'No.'

The word was fired harshly from him like a bullet and, precisely aimed, it found its mark. Serena's eyes widened in surprise and those long lashes blinked rapidly in confusion. Did she *have* to be so beautiful? So compelling even in the heat of this war she'd waged?

'You can't just say no. We haven't sorted anything.'

She looked beseechingly up at him, searching his face, and he took a deep breath as memories of kissing those soft lips avalanched over him. Did she know the effect she was having on him? Did she realise that right at this moment he couldn't think past what they'd had, those passionate moments they'd shared in the summer?

The waves rushed to the shore with a normality that stunned him. Apparently they were not aware of the horrendous situation unfolding on the sand. The lights of the small town glowed like stars around them and he found his past colliding with the present, becoming inseparable.

'How can I trust you not to abandon my child to your sister after what you said?'

His voice was an angry growl, and he fought hard against the rage of emotions that forged through him. All his life he'd carried the hurt of total rejection by the one woman who should have loved him unconditionally.

'I'm not abandoning my child to anyone—not even to you.'

For a moment he thought he saw pain flash in her eyes, thought he saw the agony of it on her face, but it was gone in an instant. Hard lines of determination replaced it.

'Telling me we can't raise this child together after saying your sister is desperate for a baby sounds very much like you are planning just that.'

He moved back from her, not trusting the rage that had become like the rush of a river in flood. All the childhood doubts he'd successfully locked away were now out and running riot.

'How can you even think of doing such a thing?'

'How can you even think *that*?' She gasped out the pained words. 'I want this child. I want to give it everything I possibly can.'

The conviction in her voice struck a raw nerve. 'As do I.'

'Can you really give our child all it needs when you admit you don't want to be a father?'

She moved towards him, her hand momentarily reaching out to him, but he flinched from her touch, his raw emotions making coherent thought difficult.

How could she doubt he would give his child all it needed? The idea of being a father was one that he had always savagely dismissed because it would entail marriage—something he'd proved he'd be unable to commit to—but now he was presented with the reality he knew exactly what he wanted.

'A child needs love.'

Vehemently the words rushed from him, and he was annoyed at her ability to take away his composure, his control. He knew more than most that a child needed love. It was all he'd craved as a young boy. But could he be a father? Could he love his child? His father hadn't been able to and his mother never had. She'd admitted that as she'd left. How could he be any different from them?

Serena laughed—a soft, nervous laugh, but a laugh nonetheless. He bit down hard, clenching his teeth, trying to stop harsh words rushing out.

'Can you really do that, Nikos?'

His silence seemed to answer her question and she ploughed on with her own arguments for being a single parent.

'Can you love a child you don't want?'

'Do not question my ability to be a father,' he growled, hardly able to contain his anger.

'A child needs stability, a loving home. It doesn't matter if it's with one parent or two, so long as it has all it needs.'

Strength sounded in her voice and her face was full of determination as she looked into his eyes, challenging him with everything she had.

'I've already made it clear that is not a problem.' He knew his voice had turned to a low growl, full of anger, but her constant referral to his inability to provide for his child was more than he could take.

'It's your deceit, Nikos, that has made me think you can't.' Her face was stern as she looked at him. 'Your lies haven't changed anything just as your real identity hasn't. I will not allow my baby to become a possession to be bargained over. Least of all by you.'

'After your scheme to get pregnant you are not in a position to make demands on me.'

He felt the reins of control slipping, felt her gaining the moral high ground—especially now haunting images from his childhood were being rapidly unleashed.

'That is *so* far from the truth,' she retaliated hotly, then moved towards him, her voice softening. 'This wasn't planned, at all, and I cannot even *consider* giving away my baby.'

Suddenly he was a young boy again, standing on this very beach, looking out to sea, hoping the next boat that came in would have his mother on board, that she would change her mind and come home. He'd watched and waited for many years, before finally dismissing her from his mind, his thoughts and his heart. She was a cold and heartless woman and he'd accepted the fact that he'd never see her again.

'But you want money?'

'Nikos, this isn't about money. I believed you couldn't afford to raise a child—just as I can't. It doesn't mean I'm not going to try, though. I hadn't planned on having a child, but I am certainly going to be there for him or her—all the time.'

Him or her. Suddenly the child she carried had gained an identity, an image in his mind. It would either be a little girl, with flame-red hair like her mother's, or a little boy with a cheeky smile and plenty of attitude.

Then her words sank into his mind. Had she really thought he couldn't afford to raise his child? The niggling suspicion that she'd known who he really was resurfaced. It wouldn't have been hard for her to source information about him on the internet. His business acumen made him a much talked of man—as did his single status. He didn't believe she'd only just found out.

She reached out for him again and he resisted the urge to draw back, strangely wanting to feel the heat of her touch.

'I am having this baby, Nikos. With or without you.'

He snapped back his arm, suddenly not wanting to be touched by her after all, not wanting the hot sizzle that sparked through him to take over.

That was one thing he had to control: he couldn't desire her.

Serena's heart sank as he pulled away from her. He hated her touch, and the anger in his eyes worried her. Whatever else had gone before, and whatever was to come, they had created a new life together. They had to find a way to give their baby the best. Which meant agreeing on how that was to be done.

Images unwittingly filled her mind. Nikos at her side as she held a baby, its hair as dark as his and with the same deep blue eyes looking up at her.

The image of happiness ripped her heart in two. That kind of happy-ever-after was what she'd wished for herself as a child. She'd wanted nothing more than for her parents to be happy together, and most of all she wished they'd wanted her, their youngest child. Instead she'd had to face the reality that she'd been a sudden and unexpected addition to the family—one that had put pressure on the cracks that had already been showing between her parents.

'Where do you propose the baby grows up?' Nikos moved closer, his barely concealed annoyance clearly evident.

'With *me*.' Desperation echoed in every word and she saw him inhale deeply, holding on to the anger her words had provoked.

'In England?'

The syllables of his words were broken, the sound staccato and harsh. She swallowed as she looked at him—anything else would show a weakness, one he'd exploit fully.

'Yes.'

Serena thought of all the heartache her sister had endured, the number of times she'd hoped for a baby and the number of times her dreams had come crashing down. She had indeed discussed it with Nikos, and couldn't believe he was now using it against her.

It was a really cruel twist of fate that it was *her* who'd fallen pregnant—and from just one night of unprotected sex. But it had been more than that—for her at least. That last evening on the secluded beach they'd walked hand in hand as the sun had set and shared a gentle kiss. It had rekindled the fire of passion they'd experienced in her small hotel room.

She reminded herself that from the outset Nikos had made it clear he didn't consider theirs a lasting romance, but one that would end when she went home. She'd gone along with the idea, feeling secure in the knowledge that she could walk away, that it didn't have to be more. But she'd fallen hopelessly in love with Nikos.

That night, as they'd reached the seclusion of the edge of the beach, surrounded by rocks and caves, he'd kissed her so passionately they hadn't been able to stop. The urgency of their desire had forced them down onto the cool sand, but nothing had prepared her for his reaction afterwards— those cold words of dismissal, the demand that he should know if 'consequences' resulted. Well, they had.

'So *you* would see our child grow up, hear its first words, watch its first steps, while I would be relegated to the background, lucky to catch a glimpse of it before it becomes a teenager?'

His voice brought her rapidly back to the present, and she swallowed down the lump in her throat as tears once again threatened.

The accusation in his tone speared her conscience and she wondered, not for the first time, if she really could do this alone. She'd thought his harsh words on the beach, after they'd made love in such an explosive and spontaneous way, had left her with little choice. He'd as good as told her he had no wish to be a father—that the very idea was abhorrent to him.

'Don't try and make it sound like you *want* this baby, Nikos.' She almost hissed the words at him. 'Not when you told me so coldly that you wanted to know of any "consequences."'

'Being a father is not something I had planned.'

He moved away from her, raking his long tanned fingers through his hair, and she sensed his frustration with every nerve in her body.

'Which is why I will return to England and bring up our baby alone.'

She seized on his declaration before he could say anything else, but thoughts of telling her sister almost choked her. How could she tell a woman who wanted a child so desperately that she had made a mistake? That *she* now had that most desired thing? How could she destroy her sister like that?

Anger sparked from his eyes, making her step back away from him, her footsteps faltering in the sand as she stumbled. Before she knew what had happened she was in his arms. The breath seemed to be sucked from her body as the all too familiar scent of Nikos invaded every part of her, setting free yet more memories.

She bit down on her lower lip, anxiety making her brow furrow and her breathing quicken as she looked up at him. His unusual blue eyes sparked with a fiery mix of anger and desire, making her stomach flutter.

'I might not have planned to be a father, but that doesn't mean I'm going to turn my back on my child.'

His words made her heart beat faster, and again the idea of living happily ever after with him flashed before her. Then it was gone, drowned by the reality of their situation. How could they possibly raise a child together? How could they ever be happy after his cold disregard and his lies to conceal his true identity?

She shook her head. 'It will never work, Nikos. Never.'

His hold on her arm tightened, his fingers pressing into

her as he pulled her close. She could feel his breath on her face and fought hard against the overwhelming need to close her eyes and press her lips to his. It was as if she'd stepped back in time, back to the first moment they had met, to the spark of attraction that had leapt to life between them instantly.

She became aware of her phone ringing inside her small handbag and the magic around them evaporated, disappearing to leave stark reality. He let go of her, stepped back, his eyes hard and narrowed, full of suspicion. As the phone ceased its insistent ring an ominous silence settled around them, one so heavy that even the waves seemed to have quietened, stilling in anticipation of what was to come next.

'I am not allowing my child to be brought up in another country. My child will be raised to know its Greek heritage, its Greek family and most importantly its father.'

Each calmly spoken word caressed her face, and even if he'd spoken in Greek she'd have been sure they were words of passion. But she wasn't fooled—they were words of control.

'So where do *I* fit into that?' She pulled back from him, needing the space to think.

'That is what you must decide.' Again it was said in an almost seductive whisper.

'And if I *want* to go back to England?' The question came out as an unexpected hoarse whisper, the pain of it hurting so much.

'Then you must do so—once the child has been born, here in Greece, where it will remain.'

She gasped in disbelief. 'You can't force me to stay. Or expect me to leave without my baby.'

Who *was* this man? Where had the man she'd fallen

in love with gone? This cold, hard and angry man was a total stranger.

'I'm not forcing you to do anything. The choice is yours.'

'No, Nikos.' She stood tall, strength rising up through her. Although she really didn't want her child to grow up with just one parent. She wanted her baby to have all that onlookers thought *she'd* had: two loving and happy parents.

'We will, of course, have to be married.'

He glared at her, hostility emanating from the blue depths of his eyes, and she was thankful they weren't having this conversation in daylight. She didn't want to see the full force of that hostility. At least now it was masked by the quickly descending darkness.

Her phone began to ring again, and her heart hammered loudly as he glanced down at her bag.

'Perhaps you should answer that.'

'No. I can't.'

It was all she could manage as the full implications of what he'd just said hit home. Was she referring to the phone or to marriage? She had no idea, and the words he'd said raced inside her head, confusing her further.

They would have to be married.

Exasperation mixed with fury and fizzed inside Nikos, threatening to explode as he looked down at Serena. Her gorgeous red hair, blown by the warm wind across her face, had created a veil—one she could partially hide behind as she glared back up at him.

'What do you mean, no?'

Nikos thought of the deal he was about to close for the cruise liner company and the effort he'd put into it. Now, trying to reason with Serena, he realised that the deal was a picnic in the sun compared to the negotiation of *this* deal and what was at stake. His child—something he'd never thought he'd have because he'd never allowed himself to want the impossible. He couldn't turn and walk away now. If he did he'd be worse, far worse, than his mother and father.

'I don't know...' she said, shaking her head.

Damn the woman—she was forcing him to strike a deal for his child.

'Well, you'd better think fast.'

He watched her face, saw the ever-changing expressions, holding her captive with his glare.

'Did you ever consider marriage when we had our romantic fling in the summer? Our holiday affair?'

Her voice was sharp and strong, but it was her pale face that told him she was having as much difficulty with this as he was. So she should. What woman would consider giving away her child? One just like his mother.

'You don't even love me.'

'Love has nothing to do with it.' He moderated his tone, aware of his anger rising once more.

'So why do we have to get married?' The disbelief in her voice was more than clear.

'Marriage has never been on my agenda.'

That much was true. After living in the shadow of his parents' marital breakdown he'd written that idea off as a young man, preferring to enjoy the company of woman without complication and commitment. He only sought the pleasure of a woman's company for fun. Purely carnal. Nothing more. Which was exactly what he'd been doing with Serena during her stay on the island.

'And being a father?'

She dropped the question so lightly between them he almost didn't hear it.

'I *will* be a father to my child.' He evaded her question and the truth that lay buried within him. He wanted to be a father—to have his child grow up in a world of love and happiness—but he was sceptical that such happiness actually existed.

'Make no mistake, Serena. My child will not be shuffled between countries like an unwanted Christmas present.'

CHAPTER THREE

SERENA STEPPED AWAY from Nikos—away from the anger of his words. 'I can't talk about this any more.' She needed to put distance between them. 'Maybe we should have this discussion tomorrow?'

He looked at her, unexpected concern in his eyes. 'Perhaps that is best. When you are more rested you will be able to think rationally. Then you will accept that we should marry—for our baby.'

She bristled with indignation at his comment, sure his ability to use English hadn't compromised his choice of words. She *was* perfectly rational, and she had no intention of marrying someone who didn't love her.

'Nothing will change.'

'Where are you staying?'

Nikos asked the question lightly—a little too lightly—arousing her suspicions as to why he appeared to be giving in so easily.

He couldn't be trusted. He'd proved that with his non-revelation about who he really was. She might not have looked him up on the internet before, but she certainly had now. The uneasy feeling that she was dealing with something much bigger than she'd anticipated filled her with dread. He'd concealed his identity, lied to her. *Why?* What would he have to gain by doing that?

'In the same hotel.'

She spoke softly, trying not to think about the nights they'd spent in her room when she'd stayed there before. Why she'd insisted on the same room she didn't know—romantic notions and memories of being there with the man she'd fallen in love with? Or was it because of the night she'd experienced love with Nikos for the first time?

He'd been gentle and kind then, accepting she was innocent but not knowing just how much. She had been sure he was the man she'd waited for. She'd loved him. She'd wanted him to make love to her because then he hadn't been at all like the Nikos who now openly admitted deceiving her and was virtually forcing her into marriage.

'Then we shall go there now and collect your bags.'

He moved towards her, taking her hand in his. She didn't want to follow, to obey his command, but just the touch of his hand against hers sent a sizzle of heat scorching through her and she knew that, whatever the outcome of her visit to the island, there was still unfinished business between them. Her body still craved his, still imagined his caress, his kisses. Stupid as it was, she still loved him.

The hum of music from the bars and restaurants drifted on the warm night air as the sea became an inky blackness, melting into the star-filled sky. Despite the idyllic setting, the idea of walking hand in hand with Nikos felt anything but romantic. Intimidating, maybe—threatening, definitely—but she was powerless to stop it, unable to resist him.

'Nikos!' she gasped, pulling back against him, suddenly regaining her strength, knowing she had to fight. 'What are you *doing*?'

He stopped and looked down at her. His handsome face was partially in shadow, but his eyes sparked like a warrior's, locking with hers, sending a shiver of excitement and apprehension skittering down her spine.

'Taking control.'

The firmness of his voice, still sexy and accented, hinted at the level of discipline he was currently putting on himself.

'Of what? Me?'

She stood tall, facing him in the darkness, hoping that he wouldn't see how unsure she really was, that her voice sounded strong and defiant.

'Of my child.'

She blinked in shock. Did he think that his playing the role of protector would make her fall in line with his plans? That she would marry him and live happily ever after? How could that ever happen when he didn't want her, let alone love her? If she married him her child would grow up knowing it was the mistake that had forced them together—something she *never* wanted a child of hers to feel.

'You don't need to come back to the hotel to do that.'

She really didn't want to be with him at the moment. She needed to think, to re-evaluate things. Nothing had gone as she'd planned. And it was all down to the revelation of his true identity.

His hand in hers felt unnervingly right, but the whole situation was wrong. Confusion at this newly assertive man was mixed with the ever-present heat of desire, fizzing like a newly popped bottle of champagne, and she didn't want to partake of it right now.

'We'll talk again tomorrow.'

'We *will* talk again tomorrow—in Athens.'

He started to walk again, his hand still tightly holding hers, and although she knew she shouldn't want her hand in his she did. A small sliver of hope entered her heart as the sound of the waves was left behind. She walked with him out onto the street and towards the small family-run hotel she adored so much—just as she'd done when she was there before, when things had been different, much more simple.

Then his words registered.

'Athens?' Serena hadn't realised she'd spoken aloud until he turned to look at her, his vivid blue eyes ever watchful.

'My home is there—and my business. We will be leaving in an hour.'

His expression was harsh, his tone firm, and she was so stunned she couldn't say a word. What had made him think she'd leave with him?

'Give me one good reason why I should go anywhere with you when you've lied to me from the very start?'

She couldn't just go—but if he walked away now would she ever be able to forgive herself in years to come when her child wanted to know where its father was?

'There is only one reason, Serena, and it's a *very* good one. You are carrying my child.'

The lights from the hotel shone on his face, highlighting the sharp angles of his cheekbones, making him look so formidable she could imagine him in a boardroom, dominating and controlling everything.

'A child you don't want.'

She flung the accusation at him, feeling hysteria rise inside her. She was too emotionally drained for this—too tired. After almost a day of travelling she just wanted to rest. No, she *had* to rest. But she also had to resist the urge to give in to him, to allow him to take control. He'd lied to her once and she knew from experience that it would happen again. Hadn't her father lied, time and time again?

'There is nothing to discuss. Get your bags. My plane is waiting.'

Inside she seethed with resentment, but she didn't have

the energy to retaliate. He looked down at her and she desperately tried to put up some resistance. It was hard—and not just because she was so tired. Deep down she wanted to be with Nikos, wished she could find a happy-ever-after with him.

She followed him into the hotel, inwardly doing battle with her desire to go with him. Maybe they could recapture what they'd shared such a short time ago? The bright lights of the small reception area made her blink briefly against the glare and she knew that would never happen.

Nikos spoke in hushed Greek to the owner of the hotel and the reality of what was happening rocketed back at her.

She had to go with him—just to sort things out. He was the father of her child and she owed it to the baby to sort things out amicably. But she also owed it to herself not to let him hurt her again, and to do that she had to remain strong.

He turned to face her, his arm outstretched as he drew her close in a show of affection she hadn't been expecting. It was one she was sure was for the hotel owner's benefit.

'We'll be on the plane soon. You can rest there.'

'Rest…?'

Oh, but he was good. She could see the hotel owner smiling at them, as if he was witnessing love's dream couple reunited. Did he *know* Nikos—the real Nikos?

'You must be exhausted.'

His arm about her shoulder pulled her in closer to him and his lips pressed affectionately and familiarly on her forehead, confusing her already muddled emotions further.

'Let's get your things.'

Unable to do anything but play out the charade he'd started, she allowed herself to be led towards the stairs. The lean length of his body was pressed close to her side, sending a spark of awareness all through her. It was so strong she was glad when they reached her room. She belatedly rummaged in her handbag for the key, remembering the phone calls she'd not answered. She'd have to deal with those soon—but first she had an overbearing Greek to deal with.

'Did you purposely choose the same room?' A hint of seductive mockery played at the corners of his mouth and sparkled in his eyes as he looked at her.

As she entered the room she looked about her. It was much the same as it had been that first night.

'I didn't ask for this room. They must have remembered me.' She smiled at him, briefly forgetting her intentions, and for a moment it was like going back to those nights they'd spent together, teasing and laughing with each other.

She'd been so in love with him, so sure he was *the* man. She had encouraged his kisses, yearned for his touch and craved his body, hers seemingly knowing exactly what to do despite her innocence.

'Is this it? This small case?'

The atmosphere changed as he spoke.

'As I told you, I came to do the decent thing and tell you to your face. I didn't intend to stay long. It was never as if we could start again where we'd left off. Not when you'd made it so clear what your thoughts on being a father were.'

'I did not make any such thing clear.'

He narrowed his eyes and she knew she'd hit a nerve.

'The possibility that those moments on the beach might have made you a father *horrified* you, Nikos. Don't try to deny it.' She fired the words at him, feeling herself emotionally stronger again. She wasn't going to allow him to manipulate her just because he had power and wealth. He might have hidden that from her when they first met, but no way would she let him use it against her now.

'That is untrue and you know it.'

He moved closer to her and her heart rate rushed away like a herd of wild horses.

'*Do* I?' She snapped the question out, desperate to hide the effect he was having on her.

His deep, silky voice, heavily accented, did untold things to the heady desire she was trying to suppress. She couldn't let it show. Whatever else he thought, he *had* to think she was completely indifferent to him.

He moved closer to her, his eyes darkening, his accent becoming more pronounced and far too sexy.

'It's still there, isn't it? That sizzle of attraction that kept us here, in this very room, in this very bed, night after night.'

Serena looked at him, her mind racing back to the time they'd spent here, to their first night together. That night he'd kissed her softly, his lips teasing and gentle. She'd known then for certain that this was the man she wanted to give herself to completely. She'd wanted him with such abandon she'd have done anything to show him how much she loved him.

She'd instinctively known that what they'd had was special, that the attraction was one she might never find again. Now, as she stood looking at him, her heart was heavy— because it hadn't been like that for him. It had been nothing more than a passing affair. One he'd hoped he could turn his back on.

She stepped away and looked out of the open window to the sea moving restlessly in the darkness, its salty tang lingering on the warm breeze. This would be her child's heritage—one it might never see if she walked away now. But how could she stay when he didn't want her? Let alone the child she carried?

'Serena…'

His voice was husky and he stood right behind her, the

heat of his body almost too much. She shut her heart against thoughts of what might have been as he placed his hands on her shoulders. Mesmerised by his spell, she turned, looking up into his face. His blue eyes were heavy with desire as they looked into hers, urging her towards him.

She closed her eyes, but that didn't help, and when his lips brushed hers she jumped back and glared at him. 'Don't you *dare* think you can seduce me with kisses this time.'

'I don't need kisses to get what I want.'

He moved closer to her, forcing her against the wall, but she held her ground and maintained eye contact, even though inside she was quaking.

Those hard words had suffocated any lingering illusions of love she'd had. He didn't care about her. He didn't care about the baby. This was all about getting what he wanted.

'So what *is* it you want?' she asked haughtily, testing him. Would he openly admit to being that callous, that cold?

'I want you to come to Athens with me, Serena.'

Each word was full of determination, softened only by the accent that she found so sexy.

She shook her head. 'That's not going to happen, Nikos.'

'Then why are you here?'

She stepped up to him, lifting her chin and glaring angrily at him. 'I came here to tell a fisherman he was to be a father—to tell him that no matter what I'd never stop him from seeing his child. But that fisherman is not you.'

Memories came unbidden to her mind of that night on the beach—the night they'd made love without any thought of contraception. The night they'd created the new life she now held within her. The life whose future she could determine by her choices now.

'It's just as well that I am *not* that fisherman, because

now I can give you what you want—but only if you become my wife. No child of mine will be born illegitimate.'

'You think you have all the power, don't you, Nikos? But you can't *drag* me up the aisle.'

Unnerved by his certainty that he could get what he wanted, she moved away from him and to the door of her room, opening it wide in the hope that he'd leave.

That hope faded instantly.

Nikos remained resolutely still, biting down hard against the anger that coursed through him. How dared she think she could calmly dismiss him from his child's life? He hadn't wanted to be a father, but there was no way he would turn his back on his child—allow it to grow up wondering where he was.

As the challenge of her actions settled around them he knew exactly how he was going to handle this. Serena would be his wife—his *willing* wife—no matter what. His child was going to be born without the stigma of illegitimacy.

He ignored the waves of anxiety rushing through him at the thought of commitment. And he didn't even know if Serena would stay and go along with his plans or if she'd be just like his mother—too selfish to care—and walk away.

'You *will* be my wife. The child you carry is my heir and I will not allow you to keep me from it.'

Hostility poured off her as she stood, rigid and tall, by the open door of the hotel room. With each passing second she was challenging him further, pushing him to limits he'd never thought it possible to go to.

'What are you going to do? *Force* me to marry you?'

The curtness of her tone irritated him further, and he crossed his arms and glared coldly at her.

'I'm going to make you an offer you can't refuse.' Dominance in the boardroom was something he was used to, but overpowering a woman—one he still wanted and desired—was a totally new concept.

'You don't have anything I want, Nikos.'

The hint of confusion in her voice made him raise a brow in speculation. Surely she was curious to hear the terms of his deal?

'If the baby is mine—' he began, but halted as she gasped loudly, her delicate brows furrowed, her soft lips open and her hand against her stomach.

'How *dare* you suggest it isn't?'

'I have no evidence that it is.' He snapped the words at her, feeling her anger as she glared at him, her green eyes sparking.

She spun round so quickly to reach for her handbag that he thought she might fall. She pulled out a small black-and-white photograph.

'Here.' She thrust it at him. 'The evidence you want. That is what you mean, isn't it? Conclusive dates to match the date of that night on the beach?'

'This will do for now, but I would like you to see a doctor here in Greece.'

What kind of fool did she think he was, simply to take her word that she was carrying his child?

He'd seen men cheated into bringing up other men's children, and whilst he would stand by his child he had to *know* that it was his.

Even as the thought entered his mind he knew that it was. She'd been a virgin when she'd met him. He remembered vividly the moment he'd realised the truth. He had cursed aloud, the look of shock on her face forcing him to quell his reaction as he'd focused on giving her as much pleasure as he'd felt. Now all he felt was guilt about questioning her.

'That won't be necessary.' She pushed away from him roughly. 'I have seen doctors in England.'

He looked again at the image, his sharp gaze scanning the information. All the evidence he needed that the baby was his was there, but it was seeing the fuzzy image, knowing it was his baby, that pulled on his heart, creating a tight band across his chest as unfamiliar as if the sea around the island had frozen.

'Even so, you will see a doctor once we arrive in Athens.'

'I'm not going with you, Nikos. And I can't marry you.'

Her voice was filled with emotion, and if he'd been a man with a heart he would have asked why. He would have taken her hand and told her they'd work it out. But he didn't have a heart.

'Once you agree to be my wife, to stay in Greece and to live as a family, I will give you what you want.' He delivered the words in a cool and dominant tone, ignoring the way she visibly flinched.

'I've told you—I don't want anything from you.'

'I'm sure your sister wouldn't like to know you'd turned down a chance of her continuing with her IVF treatment.'

'What?' She crossed the floor and came to stand directly in front of him. 'That is *blackmail*.'

'No, it's getting what I want at whatever price has to be paid.'

'It's blackmail—and totally ruthless.' She hissed the words at him and, despite the situation, he admired her staying power.

'Ruthless, maybe—but it is my only deal.' He laid his final card down and waited for her surrender. 'Take it or leave it.'

'How can you even think I would accept such terms?'

She snatched the scan photo back and looked down at

it, holding it tightly. When she looked up at him the glitter in her eyes bellied the anger he'd provoked.

'Don't go against me, Serena.'

The warning in his voice didn't go unnoticed.

'I'm not going against you. All I want is to do the best for us both—me and my baby.'

Anger shattered around the periphery of his vision and he inhaled deeply, locking his gaze to hers. He'd never expected such challenge, such dismissal of his deal.

'You forget. It is my child too.'

The bristling atmosphere pressed down on Serena as Nikos stood watching—waiting for her answer. She looked again at the scan photo in her hands. The knowledge that she had the power to give the same experience to her sister, or deny her, sickened her. She closed her eyes against the nausea—and against Nikos's merciless scrutiny.

Secretly she'd dreamed of marriage and happy-ever-after, but those dreams had finally died the moment she'd heard Nikos condemn the idea of love. How could she marry a man who not only admitted he hadn't ever wanted to be a father, but one who firmly believed love had nothing to do with marriage?

'But marriage…?' Still stunned by his proposed deal, delivered without a hint of compassion, she could hardly form a sentence. Exasperation and fury raged through her, quelling the nausea of moments ago. 'That's a drastic step, Nikos. What if you meet someone you actually *want* to marry?'

'Marriage has never been on my agenda.'

The icy tone left her in no doubt that he meant it.

'So why marry me?'

Deep down she knew the answer—knew it was because he was opposed to his child being illegitimate. But that went against everything she'd ever wanted for her future. It meant their being forced together because of a baby—a copy of her childhood exactly.

He closed the distance between them, coming so close her heart raced—whether due to the attraction she couldn't completely dismiss or the seriousness of their discussion, she couldn't tell.

'Call me old-fashioned, but my child—my heir—will not be born out of wedlock.' His voice dripped with disdain as he towered over her. 'You must decide, Serena— and right now. My plane is waiting.'

All sorts of scenarios rushed through her mind as he watched her, and she wondered if he could see them playing out. She saw her sister happy and content, with a baby in her arms. Saw her own child looking into its father's eyes and smiling for the first time. These were things she could control just by accepting this bizarre proposal.

An image of herself in Nikos's arms, being kissed with fiery passion, followed swiftly. The passion had existed once, but could it ever turn to love? Could he ever fall in love with her the way she'd fallen in love with him? If they could find that passion again, surely they could find love one day.

'Serena?' he said sternly, pushing her for a decision.

She wanted to rally against him, tell him she needed more time to think—but hadn't she already done plenty of that? And yet if she said yes she'd be doing exactly what he'd suggested when he'd repeated what she'd said— anything to help her sister have a baby of her own.

She saw him draw in a breath of exasperation. Time was running out. If she said yes, went with him now, she would be buying more time to think.

'Very well. We'll do it your way.'

CHAPTER FOUR

As THEY ARRIVED in Athens Serena was still in a state of shock, unable to believe the man she'd fallen in love with could be so cruel.

After the private plane had whisked them from Santorini she'd fully expected a chauffeur-driven car to meet them at the airport, but one of the city's many yellow taxis seemed to be what Nikos wanted.

During the flight she'd played Nikos's words over and over in her mind, each time coming to the same conclusion. She had to accept his so-called deal—for her child and for her sister. She refused to admit that she hoped he might revert to being the man she'd first met and tell her what she most wanted to hear.

She looked across at him as they sat in the taxi. His profile was stern and unyielding. Could this man ever be the Nikos she loved? He looked at her, and even in the semi-darkness as they were driven through Athens at night she felt his icy cold glare.

Instantly she averted her gaze and looked out of the window, amazed by the sights and desperately wishing she wasn't so tired, so confused.

'It's stunning—and so beautiful,' she said as she caught sight of the Acropolis, lit up and standing proud on its rocky vantage point above the city, thankful for its distraction from thinking about the conversation they'd had in her hotel room.

It still hurt, and it proved he didn't have any kind of feelings for her. As far as he was concerned she and his child were nothing more than a commodity to be bargained for.

'It never ceases to please me.' Nikos spoke softly, leaning closer to her as he looked out of the window like a tourist too, seemingly happy to put aside all that had unfolded that evening. 'We should go there one day.'

Serena shrank back in her seat; his words bringing it all back and making her presence on the mainland of Greece sound permanent. It was. She didn't have any other choice.

She pushed those thoughts from her mind, too tired to deal with them any more tonight, but she was still curious as to why Nikos was here when he'd grown up on the island of Santorini. Was that fabrication too?

'How long have you lived in Athens?'

'I came here as a teenager, after I finished school and found myself a job with Xanthippe Shipping. The rest I'm sure you know.' Bitterness edged his words and he too sat back, the beauty of Athens now spoilt for him as much as her. 'My apartment is not far now.'

'I should stay in a hotel,' she volunteered quickly. She'd been too tired to give any thought to where she was going to stay once she was in Athens, but she'd already questioned the sanity of staying with Nikos.

Now she did so again—because of what had been said this evening and the way her body had reacted to him, the way she still wanted and loved him. Staying with him would be a temptation to believe things would work out, when the way he'd reacted earlier told her that was never going to happen.

'No,' he said quickly, then started speaking in Greek to the taxi driver. Within moments they had stopped. He got out and walked around to open her door, his gaze locking with hers.

She stepped out and looked up at the smart modern apartment building blending tastefully with the older buildings around. The street lamps glowed like gold, giving it a magical appearance as well as an affluent one. It was so different from the small whitewashed house nestled on a hillside of Santorini overlooking the sea, which Nikos had pointed out during those blissful two weeks. He'd told her it was his home, igniting all sorts of romantic notions in her head, but after tonight's revelations nothing he said could be trusted.

'You are tired and you will stay with me.'

A hint of compassion lingered in the heavily accented words, and if she closed her eyes, pretended the previous hours hadn't existed, she might almost believe he cared.

'I'm not sure that's such a good idea.'

She scrabbled to think of a reason, but couldn't come up with one. They'd already slept together, seen each other naked, so even those excuses didn't fit. The reality was that she did want to be with him. That was why she'd made the journey to Greece instead of calling him. She'd hoped those two weeks together had meant something.

'I'm not going to argue with you any more, Serena. You will stay with me tonight, and after my meeting tomorrow morning we can talk further.'

Inwardly she sighed as the taxi driver pulled away. She was tired—of travelling and of talking. Sleep was what she needed now and the thought of insisting on going to a hotel, then checking in, filled her with dread. She'd stay—tonight, at least—but not in his bed. In the morning she'd be able to think more clearly.

Shouts in Greek caught her attention as a car pulled up alongside them. She turned to look just as Nikos put a protective arm around her, responding in the same language. Just seconds before a camera flash penetrated the night Serena realised they were journalists. Uncomfortable doubt crept over her. Was Nikos such a high-profile figure that they followed him around?

'What do they want?' She glanced quickly at them as they still lingered close by, watching them with suspicion.

She couldn't keep the sceptical edge from her voice as he held the main door to the apartment building open for her and she walked into a bright lobby, the white walls a stark contrast to the darkness outside.

'They wanted to know who you are.' He took his keys from his pocket then pressed the button to call the lift.

'Why am *I* of any importance?' She frowned as she watched the numbers above the lift counting down the floors, trying to appear unfazed by the event.

He sighed and she felt his gaze on her face.

'It has been an obsession with them for the past year or so. The more successful my business becomes, and the more unattached I remain, the more determined they are to dig something up.'

'So what did you tell them?'

Her heart began to thump harder as he looked into her eyes. The depths of his were darkening to a sultry blue, which made her stomach flutter wildly. She cursed her body—and her emotions—for falling under the spell of his charm.

'The truth.'

The lift doors swished open. He walked inside and then stood looking at her, the spark of mischief in his eyes and the quirk of a smile on his lips almost her undoing.

Determined not to let him see just how easily he could crash through her defences, she marched in after him.

'What *is* the truth?'

'That we are engaged.'

Serena wasn't sure if it was the movement of the lift or the words he'd just spoken that made her stomach lurch and her head spin. She clutched at the handrail inside the lift and closed her eyes against a wave of nausea.

Nikos moved quickly as Serena's face paled. Her knuckles whitened as she gripped the handrail and he wrapped an arm around her, pulling her close against him. He could feel her sliding down, so scooped her up into his arms just as the lift doors opened.

Furious that she'd allowed herself to become so exhausted by travelling all the way to Greece alone, risking his child, he marched towards his door. With each step he took he could feel her body against his, and an unknown emotion of protectiveness swept over him, but he pushed aside the unfamiliar sensation, not wanting to know why or how.

Swiftly, and with ease, he unlocked the front door and angled himself so he could negotiate the doorway without letting her go. Full of concern, he looked down at her just as her eyelashes fluttered open. Relief filled him as green eyes, full of questions and shock, met his.

'You are supposed to do this *after* we are married...' Her voice was weak, more like a throaty whisper, and her pale face looked anxious.

'I always do things *my* way, Serena.'

The words came out harder than he'd intended, and he felt her sharp intake of breath as he held her.

She wriggled in his arms as he made his way into the open-plan apartment. The view of the city lights twinkling beneath the floodlit Acropolis didn't move him this evening. Concern for Serena and his baby took precedence, as did his guilt at flying her back here tonight.

He could have made the flight alone, attended his meeting, then gone back for her—but instinct had warned him against that. Everything she'd said had made him sure she wouldn't meekly be waiting for him to return. He knew she was only here because of the deal he'd offered and nothing more.

Satisfied that the child she carried was his, he was not going to let her go easily. He was prepared to do anything to create a family for his child. The kind of family he'd craved as a boy and thought he'd never have. It didn't matter what excuses or what reasons she gave him, he was going to give his child what he'd never had.

'You can put me down now.'

She pushed her hands against his chest and he heard the strength in her voice returning. As did the spark in her eyes, making them resemble the bright green leaves of spring.

'It was the lift that made me dizzy. It's been a long day.'

'I will order in something to eat, then you can rest.'

He let her slide from him, feeling every delectable curve of her against his body, arousing all the passion he'd been suppressing since he'd got the message from her this morning. He couldn't allow lust to complicate things—certainly not his inability to control it. Lust-filled desire had already caused enough problems.

She nodded and walked towards the balcony doors. Glad of her acceptance of the situation, he slid open the large glass doors, letting the buzz from the city streets flow in.

'Enjoy the view.'

She turned, her gaze meeting his, and another pang of guilt rushed over him. She looked so tired—but there was still a hint of the feisty woman who'd met him just a few hours ago. Their differences were far from settled. But this wasn't something which could be settled overnight. This was much more, and the full implications of what Serena's presence in Greece meant finally hit him.

What he did now would affect not only his life but his child's—and Serena's. Despite that, he didn't regret the deal he'd put to her. It had presented itself so innocuously that at first he hadn't seen it as important, but he knew that without it Serena would have walked away from him for ever, taking his child too.

It was far too close to the pain of his own childhood, and thoughts of his father's blatant denial of his existence rushed forward like the tide with gale force winds behind it. He'd watched him withdraw until he could no longer look at his only son. There was no way he was going to deny *his* child existed, ignoring it like an inconvenience.

For the first time ever he knew he wanted to be different. Better. He wanted to be a father in every way—to be there each day and each night for his son. But to do that he needed Serena to stay with him…something his mother had been unable to do.

Those thoughts jarred inside him as he made a call to organise an evening meal to be brought in, trying not to think beyond that moment. He joined her on the balcony, where the warm evening air was finally cooling as he stood next to her.

It had been the same kind of warm weather the night he and Serena had walked along the beach for the last time. That night should have been for them to say goodbye, but one kiss had turned it into so much more.

His pulse began to pound like a drum and the hum of desire warmed his blood as he remembered the night that had changed his life for good.

He'd taken Serena in his arms, knowing it was time to say goodbye, to push her away, to deny himself the love which shone in her eyes each time they met. She deserved more than a cold-hearted man such as him: a man who could not and would not allow love into his life—and never into his heart.

She'd whispered his name as she'd kissed him, and he'd held her so tight, deepening the kiss, his hands caressing her body, committing to memory each and every curve. As passion had swept them away the champagne supper he'd organised as a farewell meal had lain abandoned beside them on the blanket. With the moon and the stars shining above them he'd made her his one last time, without thought of anything else.

'Nikos, I love you,' she'd whispered as his pulse rate had returned to normal.

Every drop of blood within him had frozen, crystallising in his veins, choking him. It wasn't possible. He was unlovable. Hadn't his mother said as much? Then, as the ice had splintered around them, he'd realised what had happened. He hadn't used any form of contraception. He had broken the one rule he'd always followed and in doing so had exposed himself to the possibility of fathering a child.

Before he'd known how he'd been standing on the sand, looking down at her, with the blanket rumpled beneath her and the glasses of champagne spilt. Fury had boiled inside him at how easily he had been distracted. What if this moment of mad lust resulted in a child? He didn't want to be a father. He *couldn't* be a father.

As memories of that night rushed through him he knew that whatever he'd previously thought he could not turn his back on his child—ever. But that night he'd spoken starkly, each word more forceful than the last. 'If there are consequences of what has just happened you *will* tell me.'

Anger had blinded him to anything else, and the evening he'd planned had dissolved around them. She'd got up, dusted the sand from her clothes and looked at him, her beautiful face paling. Before he'd been able to say anything else she'd fled, running from him as if he was the devil.

The damning words of love she'd said had replayed in his mind like a haunting melody, and with a cowardice he'd never before known he had remained where he was, watching her run from him.

Now she stood resolute and courageous on his balcony, with her gaze meeting his and the gold glow from the city casting shadows around her. For the first time he'd recalled what she'd said that night. *That she loved him.* Fear gripped him—not because of what she'd said, but because briefly he'd believed he could love her. If only his childhood experience of that powerful emotion had been different.

'Excuse me. I will get the food,' he said quickly, grateful of the distraction.

He didn't want to think about what those words had meant, much less acknowledge them.

Exhaustion swept over Serena and she knew she couldn't eat another bite of the delicious meal or engage in any more small talk. She had to sleep. She couldn't put it off any longer and wished she'd insisted on a hotel. At least that would have given her some much needed time alone.

'I'll show you to your room,' Nikos said, and he stood up, uncannily reading her thoughts.

He dominated the room, looking so handsome her heart hammered, but she couldn't let that sway her. She had to remember what he was capable of.

She should feel relieved that she was to have her own room—that he wasn't assuming they were going to continue where they'd left off. But she didn't. It was like a rejection of her as a woman.

'Thank you,' she said, reassured by the patience in his tone. It still hurt, but she kept up a facade of defiance, not wanting him to know how disappointed she was and how much she wished things could be different.

Isolation crammed in on her. If only she'd been able to talk to her sister—confide in someone sensible and rational. Sally, eight years older, had always been her place to go for advice, which made the secret she now kept even harder to endure. Especially as it was the very thing Sally desired most in the world. Marrying Nikos was the only way to give that hope back to Sally.

'I will be leaving early in the morning. I have an important meeting tomorrow. Relax, enjoy the apartment and I will be back at lunchtime.'

His blue eyes were full of concern, and for a moment she thought she saw genuine warmth in them. He stood holding the door open as she walked past him and she caught a hint of his aftershave. Citrus aromas mingled with crisp pine, reminding her of what it was like to be close to him.

'Sleep well.'

He was leaving her alone—tonight and tomorrow. All sorts of scenarios, from boarding the first UK-bound plane to luxuriating here in his apartment, filled her mind. 'Aren't you worried I will leave?'

'You may do whatever you wish, Serena, but I'm sure you want your sister's happiness as much as I want to be a part of my child's life.'

'You're hateful,' she whispered harshly, the reminder of his terms knocking out any misplaced hope she might have been nurturing.

'Just remember this: no matter where you go, I will find you.'

A hard edge of warning crept into his voice and she swallowed back her retort. Her heart thumped at the implication of his words.

'Goodnight, Nikos.' She stood behind the door of her

room, using it as a shield against the darkness of his glittering eyes.

'Goodnight, Serena.' He turned and walked away, his footsteps on the marble floor as insistent as his voice.

She closed the door and took her phone from her handbag. Two missed calls from Sally. Her heart plummeted with dread. Could she say anything to her without blurting out the sorry tale of her and Nikos? She pressed the button to dial and waited as the call was connected, relieved when Sally answered almost immediately.

'Serena, where are you? Not in Greece, by any chance, with your handsome fisherman?'

The teasing tones of Sally's words made her smile, despite the weight of what she wanted to confide in her sister.

'As a matter of fact, yes.'

'That's *such* good news. I've been worried about you.'

Guilt washed over Serena. The last thing Sally needed was more worry than she already had, but she'd always been mothered by her elder sister. She had stepped in when their parents had been too busy avoiding each other instead of being around for their daughters.

'I'm fine—but what about you?'

'It's not good news, I'm afraid.'

The wobble in her sister's voice nearly broke Serena's heart. She sat down on the bed, her dizziness making the room slowly turn.

'I'm sorry, Sally.' She closed her eyes, feeling the cage Nikos had used to trap her shrinking. There wasn't any escape now. She had to accept his barbaric terms.

'It was the last time. I'm never going to be a mother now.'

She could hear Sally's pain searing at her from across the miles and wished she was there to hug away her hurt. Instead she placed her hand over her still flat stomach and a tear slid down her cheek. Guilt mixed with grief was threatening to overpower her. She couldn't confide in her now. Not tonight, anyway.

'We'll find another way. I promise.'

Serena's body had turned cold. There was only one other way.

'Now, you get back to your Greek,' her sister said, and she could hear her effort to remain bright. 'And, Serena…?'

Serena's breath caught in her throat as she registered the pause in the conversation. 'Yes?'

'Stop using Mum and Dad's marriage as an example. Create something better for yourself. If you find love, grab it and hang on to it. Be brave, Serena. Be *brave*.'

Serena nodded, not able to form any kind of reply, knowing her sister's advice was well meant. But what if the man you loved didn't want to love *you*?

More tears prickled in her eyes and she knew she had to end the call. 'I will. See you soon.'

With Sally's goodbye ringing in her head, she cut the connection and lay on the bed, desperately needing to sleep. But her sister's advice played over and over again in her head. Were her parents and their unhappy marriage the reason why she'd never had a long-term relationship? Had that been why she'd pushed everyone away?

With shock, she realised the truth of her sister's words and knew it was time to stop hiding from life—and love. The father of her child might not love her, but she loved him. Was that enough—for her and her child?

Other people's happiness now rested on it. It would have to be.

CHAPTER FIVE

NIKOS'S MOOD WAS dark as he called a halt to his meeting. It had been intense, and there had been moments when his usual ruthless and determined manner had been nudged sideways by thoughts of the redhead he'd left sleeping peacefully in his apartment.

Yesterday his life had been normal. Uninvolved and normal. Now, with Serena's return, it had been turned completely inside out.

Impatience to end the meeting and return home had made him even more aggressive in his approach to the final stages of the takeover than he would usually be. Abruptly he'd put his deal on the table, insisting further negotiations were off the agenda. He wanted the company badly, but right now he had far more pressing things to worry about.

The most important deal he had to strike was keeping his child in his life—and to do that he had to ensure Serena became his wife. The cruise company could wait.

As he arrived at his apartment several photographers rushed forward and he cursed what he'd told that one opportune photographer last night, when he'd been asked who Serena was. Not for the first time when he was around her, he hadn't thought of the consequences of his actions. He had known his playboy reputation and current business dealings would make him tabloid fodder.

'Where is your fiancée?'

They hassled him, their Greek words fast and furious, their cameras clicking.

'Did you get the deal as well as the girl?' Another asked as he reached the front doors of his apartment block, with the traffic rushing by almost drowning out the bombardment of questions.

'I do not have answers to your questions yet, gentlemen, but soon.'

He used the charm he was renowned for, keeping a cool exterior. Inside, emotions he was unfamiliar with mixed with irritation.

He pushed open the door, making sure it was firmly shut behind him as he walked into the cool quietness of the lobby. Several flashes bounced off the white walls as he waited for the lift, his back to the doors and reporters, so as not to give them the photo they wanted.

Since Serena's text had come through nothing had gone to plan. The business deal he had previously been sure of clinching now hung in the balance, due to his earlier hardened dealings, and he had no idea if Serena would still be there. He'd left her alone purposely, to think through the offer he'd put to her and also give her ample opportunity to leave and get a flight home. Had that been what the reporters meant when they'd asked where she was? Had they witnessed her leave? Seen her get a taxi to the airport?

The thought of being denied his child sent a storm-surge of anger charging through him. Even if she chose to run she was never going to be able to keep him from his child.

The lift swiftly moved upwards. A small part of him wished it would stop, and along with it the whole world, so that he didn't have to witness and acknowledge that the only woman who'd made him want more had walked away from him. Just as his mother had.

Outside the door of his apartment he paused. Why did this feel so raw? Why was it like standing on the beach as a six-year-old boy waiting, hoping, for his mother to return? For a long time he hadn't believed his mother had meant it when she'd told him she didn't love him and that he'd be better off without her, but her continued absence had backed up her cold claim.

Enough. The word snapped in his head like an arrow from a bow. Now was not the time to dwell on the past. He couldn't influence that any more, but he could control the present.

With renewed determination he unlocked the door and walked in.

The balcony doors were open and sounds from the street drifted up and into the apartment. He strode towards the balcony, feeling as if his heart was in his throat. He wasn't quick enough to smother a sigh of relief at the sight of Serena, sitting in the shade, typing away on her laptop.

So she was preparing her story, was she? What headline would she use?

'Working?' He threw the word at her gruffly, accusation bound tightly up within it.

She physically jumped, her head turning towards him so fast her silky red hair splayed out like a fan around her before falling neatly to her shoulders in a way that snared his attention, reminding him of the times he'd seen it spread across a pillow.

She smiled at him, her green eyes sparkling and alert after a night's sleep. 'I wasn't expecting you back for hours yet—a busy man like you. What with your shipping company to run and the glamorous social life you lead.'

The sarcasm in her voice was not lost on him and he moved closer, lured by something he didn't yet understand—something he didn't want to understand.

She returned her attention to her laptop, saving her work before closing it down, and then stood up. His eyes were drawn to her figure and the way her pale green dress hugged her breasts and skimmed her waist. He would never have known she carried his child if she hadn't told him.

'It sounds like you've been doing some research.' He should feel irritated that she'd been here in his home, researching him on the internet, but instead he was shocked to find the thought amused him. 'You could just *ask* me about my life. After all, you can't believe everything the papers say.'

'You weren't honest with me when we first met, so why should I believe anything else you tell me?'

The light tone of her voice was in complete contrast to the stern look on her face and he fought the urge to pull her to him, feel her body against his and kiss her. He shouldn't desire her, but he did.

'You probably know all there is to know now.'

He glanced out at the Acropolis, busy with people visiting in the sunshine. The thought that they should go there wandered idly through his mind.

'Hmm,' she said, and walked towards him, testing his restraint too much. 'It's a shame I prefer the fisherman I first met to the businessman I now see. But he wasn't real—was he, Nikos?'

He moved closer, clenching his hands against the urge to take her in his arms and kiss her. Inside, the need to show her he was the same man grew stronger by the second. His guard slipped like a sail unfurled just before the wind filled it. He wanted to tell her he was the same man inside, that he desired her as much as he had when they'd first met, but that would be showing his hand—something he couldn't ever do.

Then, as if the sail had been filled with the ocean wind, his guard was back, rising higher than ever.

'Right now I'm not just a businessman. I'm also a fiancé who needs to take his intended bride shopping for a ring.' He growled the words as his control was tested far more than he'd ever thought possible. What *was* it about her that made him like this?

'Out of necessity!' She tossed the words lightly at him as she walked back into the apartment.

Of course she was right. She was carrying his child, his heir, and he had every intention of doing the right thing. No matter the cost, emotionally or financially, his child would be born within marriage.

Marriage.

The word bounced around inside his head like a shout echoing in a cave, taunting him. Marriage was something he'd never aspired to. There had been no need. He'd never wanted to be a father. But one spontaneous and out of control night had changed all that.

'We cannot be married without first being engaged.' His voice was rough and hard as he pushed back emotions from the past that he couldn't deal with now. He'd always looked forward—looking back only caused pain.

'Perhaps you'd better look at the headlines today.' She smiled sweetly and made her way to the kitchen.

He watched her as she poured iced water into two glasses and handed him one.

'The reporters last night have taken you at your word, judging by their photos.'

His comment last night might have been made without the thought he usually gave dealing with the press, but it had certainly sparked a furore of media interest. He just wished he'd seen it first.

'Is that a problem?'

'Of course it is. You've made certain I have no option but to accept your absurd deal. But I hate you for it Nikos—with all my heart.'

Serena saw the colour drain from Nikos's face. Last night she hadn't realised there had been calculated planning behind making such an admission to the press, but now she did. It had been made to remove that tiny window of escape, to force her to accept his deal.

She hadn't arrived looking for marriage—just the opportunity to do the right thing and tell him face-to-face. After her talk with Sally last night she knew deep down she wanted to be with Nikos, to raise his child. But he must never know that—not when he could use her so cruelly after all they'd shared.

It was perfectly clear he didn't want commitment, and if their last night together hadn't resulted in pregnancy she would never have seen him again. Somewhere deep inside she'd known that all along, but now he was forcing her into a marriage neither wanted. A marriage just the same as her parents had had, until their divorce a few years ago. One for the sake of their child—and *she'd* been the one who'd paid the price.

She inhaled deeply. Her child might not have been planned, but she'd never let her child think he or she was a mistake, never make it feel guilty for forcing its parents to be together. The idea of marriage to Nikos had been a far-fetched dream, but now it was a harsh reality that would enable her sister's dreams to come true. A high price, but one she would willingly pay if it meant Sally becoming a mother.

'I have a charity party to attend this evening. I need to talk with some business acquaintances. You will come too.'

He'd recovered his composure quickly. The ruthless

businessman was well and truly back in control and today he looked even more so than he'd ever done. The fisherman she'd met wasn't evident at all. The tailored suit that hugged his body with agonising perfection and the crisp white of his shirt shouted professionalism, but the expensive watch on his wrist and gold signet ring screamed success.

Before seeing him this morning she'd already decided she had no choice but to stay, to give marriage to him a chance not just for her child but for Sally. It was Sally's advice that had taken the sting out of Nikos's deal, warning her she mustn't base her life on her parents' marriage. She had to find her own happiness and she owed it to her child at least to try.

Despite that, she couldn't keep a cutting remark from leaving her lips. 'In what capacity? Your fiancée—as you told those reporters last night?

His blue eyes darkened. Glittering sparks shot from them and he set his lips in that all too familiar line that she was fast becoming accustomed to. It was something she'd never seen the fisherman she'd fallen in love with do.

'Of course. We are to be married—that is why you are still here, is it not?'

'I'm still here because it helps my sister.' She threw her retort back at him, infuriated by his arrogance.

'I will buy you a ring so big there will not be any questions as to my intentions towards you.'

His acerbic tone cut deep, but she didn't let it show. Instead she took a sip of water. The ice clinking in the glass as her hands shook almost gave away how much his words had hurt.

'After those newspaper headlines that will save a lot of awkward questions.'

Buying an engagement ring with a man in such a harsh

mood wasn't at all what she'd hoped for. Even though theirs wasn't going to be a marriage made out of love, she'd hoped the desire and passion they'd once shared would count for something.

'I had no idea the story would get out. It won't help my current negotiations if I'm seen to be going back on my word to the woman I've proposed to. Are you ready to go right now?'

'I'm ready,' she said—though she wondered if she was ever going to be ready to enter into a loveless marriage. It was her parents all over again. Their unhappiness had been her fault, and now she was going to lay that guilt on her own child—but with Sally's happiness at stake she had little choice…for now at least.

Half an hour later, having been driven through the rush of Athens traffic, she was in an exclusive and very expensive jewellers with an attentive Nikos at her side. His acting skills were incredible, and he lovingly laid his arm around her shoulders as she tried the biggest diamond ring she'd ever seen on her finger.

The assistant gushed, but her Greek words were totally lost on Serena. It was an amazing ring—a big show of wealth—but it wasn't at all what she wanted.

'No,' she said decisively, and the assistant's smile slipped. 'This is too big…too expensive.'

'Expense doesn't come into it.'

His sexy voice was deep, almost a whisper, sending shivers of awareness down her spine. She reminded herself that it was all for show. She mustn't for one moment think he cared. He didn't.

'Very well—it's too big.' She looked at him, unable to keep the confrontation from her eyes. 'This is much more to my taste.'

She picked up a small but beautiful emerald ring, and

was about to try it on when Nikos took it from her, held her hand and slid it on to her finger.

She looked at him and her breath caught in her throat. The intensity in his eyes warmed her from the inside out. Her heartbeat raced and her stomach fluttered. His gaze, darkening to resemble the sea at night, held hers, and she might have been back on the beach, just before they'd made love. His eyes had swirled with the same ardent passion then too.

'This is the ring.'

His voice was husky, his accent heavy, making her heart pound harder.

'Serena, will you marry me?'

She swallowed hard, aware that her breathing had deepened and each breath was harder to come by. Would he think she was acting the part too? She certainly hoped so, because he must never find out how much she loved him.

'Yes.'

She responded with the answer she knew he wanted for the sake of acting the part. Would she have given the same answer if he'd asked her last night, instead of blackmailing her with something as cruel as her sister's happiness?

His lips brushed hers so briefly she wondered if it had happened. Her sigh of pleasure couldn't break the connection that arced between her and Nikos at that moment. Serena couldn't breathe as he continued to hold her hand, his fingers warm against hers. It felt so real, so passionate, so loving.

It's just pretence, she reminded herself sternly.

Nikos's heart beat faster than he'd ever known. What was the matter with him? He was getting carried away with the moment. He looked into her eyes again and lifted her fingers to his lips. The green of her eyes was flashing brighter than the emerald on her finger and he wanted her with a force that stunned him.

'The gemstone of the goddess Venus. A symbol of hope,' the assistant said in stilted English, her words breaking the spell.

Serena pulled away from him, her eyes downcast and her long lashes sweeping down, locking him out.

'Then it is a perfect choice,' he said softly, and lifted her chin, forcing her to look into his eyes once more.

'It brings lovers closer if the giver's motive is pure love.' The assistant continued with her sales talk.

What did it mean if his motive was convenience coupled with lust? He looked into Serena's face. Her porcelain-like skin was faintly flushed, but her gaze held his boldly. Was she wondering the same?

Before he had time to think, to rationalise his actions, he lowered his head and brushed his lips over hers. A startled gasp of shock broke against his lips, lighting the fire that only she had ever truly ignited. He wanted to pull her close, to kiss her harder. He wanted so much more but propriety surfaced. Now was not the time or the place.

'Nikos...' she whispered quickly, and pressed her palms against his chest, pushing him away, her thoughts obviously echoing his.

He smiled down at her, took her hand in his and then turned to the assistant to pay for the ring. All the time he held her hand, keeping her at his side. He could feel the warmth of her body invading his and wished they were anywhere else but here. The passion that had exploded between them when they had first met was still burning—and it was becoming stronger and harder to resist.

The deal they'd struck had just become very interesting.

'We have more shopping to do yet,' he said as they emerged into the sunshine of the afternoon.

She pulled him to a stop, but he didn't let go of her hand. Instead he pulled her closer as the desire he'd suppressed in the shop simmered through him.

'We don't need to buy anything else. A ring is enough for anyone to believe we're getting married. Nobody has to believe it's because we're in love.'

His brows rose in question and the word *love* all but doused the fire that burned for her. He didn't worry about people questioning if they were in love—it was his business reputation, his ability to keep his word, that mattered most.

'We agreed that marriage was best in the circumstances.'

'Agreed?' She glared up at him, her eyes flashing with challenge.

'You came to Athens with me. You obviously agreed with my terms. And as I told the press last night we were engaged you now need to be seen wearing my ring. Do you think my business associates will take me seriously otherwise? Having people believe we are "in love" has nothing to do with it. I want people to see that I honour my word, my promise and most importantly my obligations to the child you carry.'

Irritation surged forward, overriding all his previous emotions. It was for the best, he thought as he looked down into her face, at her eyes shrouded in confusion. If he had to keep playing the role of lover it would lead to temptation and desire, which would only complicate the situation.

'Do you *really* think we agreed on marriage? It was more of a case of you deciding it would happen and instigating it with little regard for anyone else.'

Her words were sharp and she stood her ground, and he became aware that they were attracting the attention of passers-by.

'Come,' he said, in a growly voice that did little to hide his jumbled emotions. 'You must get something to wear at the party tonight.'

'I don't need anything new.'

Her voice rose a little and her shoulders straightened, warning him of her intention to go against him.

'As my bride-to-be you will be expected to look amazing. Anything less just isn't acceptable.'

He looked at her, seeing her confusion become quickly masked by spirit.

'I can't compete with the models you've dated. Even the most fabulous dress won't do that.'

'I do not expect you to compete with anyone,' he said calmly, and moved closer to her, dominating her with his height. But again she held her ground and looked up at him, her lips set in a pout of annoyance, just begging to be kissed.

It was an offer he couldn't refuse. Before she had time to move he pulled her close with his free arm, pressing her against him while still holding her hand. His lips burned as they met hers. Their initial resistance melted almost immediately and he felt her body relax and mould against his.

He broke the kiss and pulled back from her. He had to stop kissing her in public. He promised himself that next time it would be in the privacy of his apartment, where he could give in to the carnal hunger she provoked.

He glanced up and down the crowded street and found what he was looking for—an exclusive boutique. 'This way. Unless you want me to kiss you again.'

To his relief the threat worked, and she fell into step beside him as they made their way up the busy street. As soon as they entered the shop assistants came forward, as keen to help as the one in the jeweller's. He informed them in Greek of what Serena needed and turned to her, amused by the stunned look on her face.

'I have calls to make, but they know what I want.'

'What *you* want?' Incredulity rang out from each word and those lovely green eyes widened with shock.

'Yes, what *I* want. I will see you in an hour.'

He turned and left the shop…before he kissed the look of astonishment from her beautiful face.

Serena fumed as he turned and walked away. Just who did he think he was? And how had she ever fallen for his gentle fisherman act? Had she been so blinded by her love for him she hadn't seen even a *hint* of his lies? She'd lived her life watching her father lie, hiding his love affairs behind his work. Was she now going to be forced to live with a man who lied to achieve his goals?

Further thoughts were brushed aside as the assistants all but whisked her away. Dress after dress was held up to her, and the rapid exchange of Greek almost made her head spin, but when they finally agreed on a dress she couldn't help but smile with pleasure.

She tried it on and looked at her reflection. The pale green silk skimmed over her curves and the small swell of her stomach would never be noticed—not even by the most observant. Her eyes looked vibrant and alive, and her hair contrasted beautifully with the dress, lying on bare shoulders. It was perfect. Maybe she *could* be as glamorous as the women she'd seen Nikos spread all over the internet with that morning.

Apprehension rushed in, knocking the confidence from her. Would Nikos notice her—desire her as he'd once done—like this? The thought ambled around her mind only to be forced out. The ruthless businessman that Nikos truly was wouldn't notice her, but she hoped the man she'd met—the loving fisherman—would.

Reluctantly she removed the dress and put her sundress on again. The glamorous and bright-looking woman she'd seen reflected in the mirror disappeared. In her place stood a normal and very plain woman—one who would never have turned the head of a Greek billionaire. He'd been amusing himself at her expense, letting her fall in love with him whilst she was researching her article, safe in the knowledge that she would go home and never return.

But she *had* returned.

She'd returned carrying his child and he'd been forced to admit who he really was. He'd dragged her into his world of luxury and wealth and tonight she would play him at his own game. She would be someone she wasn't. She would make him want her. And then, like in a fairy tale, she would revert to her usual self by dawn.

CHAPTER SIX

NIKOS WAS STUNNED into silence as Serena came out of the guest room, ready for the party. He knew he was staring at her like an unpractised youth. But what man wouldn't? He'd never seen her dressed like this, and wondered how she'd ever thought she couldn't compete with other women. She'd outshine them completely—and not just in *his* eyes.

She was utterly gorgeous and he wished he hadn't accepted the party invitation. Right now all he wanted was to be alone with her, to taste the desire they'd shared and experience the passion once more.

The uncertainty in the green depths of her eyes tugged at his heart. A heart he had thought to be frozen since the moment his mother had walked out of his life, showing him the cruel side of love. But his heart would have to remain icy-cold, devoid of emotion. It would be better that way—for both of them.

His attention was caught by her heels daintily tapping out a beat as she walked towards him—a beat that matched the throb of desire within him, which was increasing with each second.

'I had no idea what was needed for this evening, but the shop assistants assured me, as best they could in Greek, that this was it. I trust it meets with your approval?'

He let his gaze blatantly slide down her, marvelling at her resolute composure. 'It is more than everything I anticipated,' he said forcefully. The words *You look so beautiful* were suppressed, along with the weak-willed wish that things were different.

'I don't want to stand out too much,' she said, and she lowered her gaze to fiddle with her clutch bag.

A surge of unfamiliar protectiveness flared within him. 'You will stand out—but it will be for the right reasons.'

'It will be bad enough not understanding what's being said all night, without wearing the wrong thing.'

'Bad enough?'

Most women he knew would be desperate for the chance to be bought a pretty dress and taken out for the evening— but Serena wasn't most women. He was fast realising she was different. Too different.

'The headlines,' she said quickly, then looked at him, a hint of disappointment in her eyes. 'Have you forgotten that all of Greece now believes we are engaged?'

'No, I have not—and I will be with you at your side all night.'

His swift reply banished any further discussion.

He *did* have business connections to make, and originally his intention had been simply to halt any rumours that might be growing about her arrival. But as he looked down at Serena he knew having her at his side would make a nice change from the frivolous models he usually chose as company for such occasions. Not one of the women he'd dated had ever affected him the way Serena had—and still did.

If he was honest with himself it went back to their time in Santorini—to a time when his guard had been lowered... a time when he'd tasted what might have been if only his life had been different.

'We will leave now, if you are ready?'

She nodded, briefly looking nervous before smiling. 'I'm ready.'

The party had been underway for some time when they arrived, and he felt Serena tense as they entered the large room. The hum of chatter continued, but he was aware of speculative glances being cast their way, and whispers that were far from discreet.

With his arm around her, and his hand resting at her waist, he guided her through the throng of the elite of Athens society. It seemed the fundraiser had pulled people in from far and wide.

'Nikos!'

He paused at the mention of his name and saw Christos Korosidis, the head of a rival shipping company. In the boardroom they would be enemies, but in the buzz of a party—especially a fundraising event—they would assume the air of friendship.

'So the rumour is true?' Christos said, his admiring gaze sweeping over Serena, sending a zip of totally alien jealousy hurtling through Nikos. 'I would never have thought you were the marrying kind, Nikos.'

He could hear the conjecture in the other man's voice and knew Serena's sudden appearance in his life was causing as much controversy as his bid to take over Adonia Cruise Liners. A company Christos also had his sights on.

Nikos wondered if Christos would use the current news of his engagement to slip in under the radar and make another bid. He should have been angry at the idea, but he wasn't. If the deal failed—it failed.

This was a completely new way for him to look at things. He didn't *care* if Christos put a new offer in and won. Right now all that mattered was his child, his heir, and in order to be a part of its life he had to keep Serena at his side. As far as he was concerned his marriage was the most important deal right now. It would legitimise his son and heir. Not that he'd ever hint at that to Christos.

'Appearances can be deceptive,' he said with a smile as he took a glass of champagne and handed it to Serena.

She frowned, making it clear she wasn't drinking alcohol, but took it from him, holding it with elegantly manicured hands. In that second he cursed his stupidity. She might not have chosen to disclose the reason for her return to Christos, but he was an astute man. Her reaction to the champagne hadn't gone unnoticed.

'Nikos and I met several months ago in Santorini.'

Serena's soft voice broke through his turmoil and his body heated as she moved closer against him, her smile distracting Christos instantly.

'Serena has thankfully just returned to Greece,' Nikos said, and looked down at her when she glanced up at him. He brushed his lips over her forehead lightly, then turned his attention back to his sparring partner in business, trying to ignore the warmth that flooded through him. 'And not a moment too soon.'

Beside him he felt Serena stiffen and try to pull away, but he kept her close. Her light floral scent was invading his senses, stirring them evocatively and unbalancing him further. But it was as she remained stiffly at his side that the implications of his words sank in. All he'd meant was that he hadn't been able to stop thinking about her— which in itself had been truthful—but what he'd just said could be taken another way. Or was that his guilty conscience at work…?

'Nice to have met you.' Christos bestowed another charming smile on Serena and moved on in his mission to circulate.

Nikos inhaled slowly. He had to regain control of his emotions. He was more distracted than he'd ever been by Serena, and wondered how long he'd be able to keep up the pretence of being a caring fiancé when all he wanted was to claim her as his in every sense.

'That went well.'

Serena's feisty remark cut off all thought and he turned his attention back to her, taking the glass of untouched champagne from her and placing it on a nearby table.

'Was that your way of covering up the truth?'

'If I wanted to cover up the truth, as you put it, I would adopt a very different tactic—one that would leave nobody in any doubt about the irresistible passion that has brought you back to Greece.'

'And that would be what?'

'I'd kiss you deeply and passionately, right here, for all to see.'

His blood heated as she glared up at him, her lips parted, almost daring him to carry out his threat. It was all he could do *not* to pull her into his arms and kiss her— deeply and passionately.

Her brows rose and a teasing smile lit up her eyes. 'You wouldn't dare…'

'You're playing a dangerous game, Serena.' The thud of desire quickened, and without thinking of where they were he stepped closer to her. 'Is that what you want me to do? Kiss you?'

'No, I don't.'

Her firm words pulled him back, then he laughed softly.

Did she think playing such games in public would force him to show there was more to their marriage than an accidental pregnancy?

'I know you don't really want me. You just want your child—but without any scandal. I can see that now. And for the record,' she said flippantly, her eyes flashing with provocation, 'you wouldn't *dare* kiss me here. At least not in the way you're threatening.'

'Don't challenge me, Serena,' he whispered, and he lowered his head closer to hers.

He heard her sharp intake of breath. Satisfaction rushed through him. It didn't matter what she led him to believe—she was far from indifferent to him. For whatever reason she'd put up a barrier, and was intent on keeping him on the outside, but he wasn't going to allow that.

She placed her hand on his arm, the heat of her touch scorching him through his jacket and shirt. And as she pushed him gently back away from her she lifted her chin, bringing her lips tantalisingly close to his…

A sudden burst of applause crashed into his stirred-up senses so spectacularly he stepped back, momentarily unsure of what was happening.

Serena took in a deep breath when he drew back, as if she was surfacing from the sea. Her pulse raced wildly and the lingering scent of his spicy aftershave was doing untold things to her already unbalanced body. She'd never been so bold or so daring before. *Ever.*

She glanced up at Nikos, who seemed completely unruffled and totally composed as he turned his attention to the announcements being made. They were all in Greek, and she amused herself by observing the world Nikos inhabited. It was so far from the world she'd thought he lived in it was surreal.

Women so glamorous they might have stepped off the front of any celebrity magazine glittered with jewels. Serena found herself wondering, who, if any of these women, had been at such an event before on Nikos's arm. The array of images she'd seen on the internet that morning proved he was anything but the ordinary fisherman she'd thought he was. He was powerful, wealthy and if the array of beautiful women he'd dated was anything to go by very much a playboy.

As the speeches and applause went on Serena's mind slipped back to the first time she'd seen him. Nothing about that tanned, handsome fisherman had suggested he was anything else. But he'd been a cunning liar.

He'd smiled at her as she'd sat on the beach, enjoying the early evening sunshine, then a short time later she'd walked past the local fishing boats and had seen him again. He'd talked to her, telling her things about fishing and the local restaurants he supplied that would be useful for her article.

The attraction between them had sparked and from then on they had spent every moment they could together. Soon hot, passionate nights had followed. He'd been the man she'd been waiting for—the man she'd wanted to lose her virginity to and the man she'd thought she would be able to go on loving. She'd believed they had a future—until that last night on the beach, when his harsh words had shattered that illusion.

'Daydreaming?'

Nikos's gentle accented voice broke through her thoughts, rushing her back to the fundraising event and the glamorous reality of his life.

When she looked into his handsome face she could almost see the Nikos she'd first met and it tugged at her heartstrings. Which was the real Nikos?

'I was just wondering how you came from a small island fishing village to this.' She gestured around her at the no-expense-spared glamour of the party, at the guests moving to the sides of the room as the lights dimmed and music began.

'It's a long story,' he said, his face sombre, his eyes strangely hollow and lacking emotion.

Deep inside her she recognised pain, but before she could say anything he took her in his arms, moving them onto the dance floor as other couples began dancing around them.

She wanted to ask him more—to find out about the man she was now engaged to—but the sensation of being held close against his body as music filled the room was too much. Every move he made sent shockwaves through her and she lowered her face, keeping her eyes firmly fixed on his shoulder, not wanting him to see the flush of desire that must be evident on her cheeks.

She closed her eyes against the urge to reach up and kiss him, to indulge her fantasy of being loved by him. She couldn't let him know that was all she needed, all she wanted—not when he'd lied to her, believing she was looking only to further her career and her position in life.

The music changed, the tempo becoming faster, and she pulled back from him, thankful of the excuse to do so. The darkness of his eyes as they met hers was so consuming she drew in a sharp and ragged breath.

He took her hand in his and led her away from the bustle of dancing. Doors opened out onto a balcony, lit with an array of coloured lights that reminded her of Christmas. She glanced around to see they were alone. The music floated out on the warm evening air, and laughter could be heard, but it was just the two of them here and her heart-beat joined in with the sway of the music.

'Nikos…' she whispered, aware he was holding back from her. 'Your story—it's one I need to hear if we are going to make any kind of future together.'

A smile of satisfaction spread across his lips, drawing

her gaze briefly away from the blue of his eyes. 'So you *are* considering a future with me?'

His brittle words reminded her that they were not in love—that this was a deal, one brokered in the interest of their child. The mood changed, killing any romantic notions the dance had allowed to slip into her head.

'We are having a child, Nikos, and as much as I can't bear the idea of a marriage for that reason, or the hideous terms you've attached to it like a business deal, I don't want my child not to know his or her parents.'

She pushed thoughts of her sister aside as her mind flew back to the arguments her parents had always had. The hateful accusations they'd hurled at each other. She knew she didn't want to live like that. Worse were memories of the realisation that *she'd* forced them to stay together just by being born. She didn't ever want her child to feel that guilt. The secret love she had for the Nikos she'd first met would have to be enough—for both of them.

'Why is that a bad reason? Surely marrying for the sake of a child is best?'

'Not always, Nikos.' She smiled up at him, aware of his diverting tactics and employing some of her own. 'How did you end up here?'

What would he think if she told him about *her* childhood? Would he think that what they were doing was a mistake if she told him about how guilty she felt? She couldn't risk him turning his back on her—not when the chance to give Sally all she wanted was so tantalisingly close.

The warm wind ruffled his hair as he leant on the balcony, looking out across Athens as if it would give him answers. She moved closer to him, and the sweet fragrance of flowers around them did not quite mask the scent of his aftershave.

Without looking at her, he spoke. 'I was brought up by my grandparents and I inherited a small fleet of fishing boats when my grandfather died. I owe them a lot. They took me in when my mother left and after my father fell apart, when the truth about my mother was exposed. They gave me a start in life—which was more than either of my parents did.'

Serena remembered his insistence that he'd never wanted to be a father and her heart softened a little. The hardness of his own heart must have been caused by what he'd experienced as a child. They had both suffered due to their parents. For different reasons neither of them had seen the joy and love marriage could bring, and while she believed it might one day be possible he did not.

'But that doesn't explain how you came to be in Athens,' she said softly as she turned her back on the view and looked up at him. The soft lights highlighted his features, making his cheekbones prominent, as if they'd been chiselled from stone, hardening his expression.

'I couldn't stay on the island. It was suffocating me. So I followed an example I'd seen as a boy and left. I came here with virtually nothing but my name and began working for Dimitris, the owner of Xanthippe Shipping. He became the father I should have had.'

She frowned as she took in what he'd told her, knowing there was more buried deep inside him and knowing it was hard for him to have told her this much.

'He taught me all he knew and, without his own heir, left me his legacy. One I have built up to the global business it is today.' He turned to look down at her, his blue eyes holding her attention. 'When I first met you it was a refreshing change not to be known for my success and wealth first.'

A tang of bitterness filled her mouth. 'Did you think I

was with you for that? Or did you believe I was looking for a big break—a story that would launch me from travel writer to being the journalist I'd trained to be?'

'Both.' Suspicion and anger were woven inextricably in that one word.

His honesty stung more than lies would have done, and she pushed herself away from the balcony and moved towards the door and the sounds of the party. Behind her she heard his footsteps, felt his presence.

She didn't want to turn and see the contempt in his face—the truth of what he really thought of her. His questions about whether the baby was his now made so much more sense. As did his sudden change of mood after they'd made love that last night on the beach. Did he think she'd tricked him all along? Seduced him so brazenly she'd ensured he hadn't given contraception a thought?

She couldn't stay here any longer. She felt stifled by his pain and her love. She had to get out of here right now.

'Serena!'

Her name chased after her as she made her way into the throng of partygoers, completely oblivious to the curious stares coming her way. With her chin held high and her eyes firmly fixed on the door they'd entered earlier she walked quickly. The air was hot, the noise was too much and she needed to get out—*now*.

How had she ever thought what she felt for Nikos would be enough?

She pushed the door open and went out to the hotel lobby and on to the street. *Now* what should she do? She had no idea where she was or where she needed to go to.

Tears of frustration threatened but she took in a deep breath, forcing her shoulders to relax. As they did so large, warm hands covered them. She knew it was Nikos. Every nerve in her body tingled wildly. Nobody else did that to her.

'You can't keep running for ever, Serena,' he whispered against her hair as he pulled her back against his body, holding her close.

He obviously intended anyone watching to think their lovers' tiff was over, that passion and love had won. He wanted the scandal she threatened to be quelled and subdued.

'I didn't feel well. I needed to get out,' she said, knowing it was only half the truth.

Slowly he turned her round in his arms, giving her no alternative but to look at the firm wall of his chest or up at his face. When she did look up, what she saw made her knees weak with longing. His blue eyes were full of concern, and if she didn't know any better she'd believe it was real and not for the benefit of anyone who'd witnessed her hasty departure.

'Maybe we shouldn't discuss the past—not tonight, at least.'

His accent was heavier than ever, and his eyes reminded her of the night sky as passion swirled in them. Her heart thumped in her chest as his breathing deepened, coming faster. *This* was the man she'd fallen in love with. Handsome and passionate.

'Nikos…' she breathed as her body swayed against him. The temptation was too much in her state of heightened emotion.

His hold on her tightened as his lips met hers, tenderly stroking, forcing the fire that burned within her higher. She wound her arms around his neck, heedless of her gauzy wrap falling from her shoulders. All she cared about was being kissed by Nikos. The man she loved. The father of her child.

His lips left hers fractionally. 'We should go home,' he whispered against her lips, and she closed her eyes at the erotic sensation.

'Yes, take me home, Nikos.'

Her husky whisper ended as his lips claimed hers once more, demanding and hot. She was lost. Completely and utterly lost. Despite everything, *this* was what she wanted.

CHAPTER SEVEN

NIKOS SAT IN the back of the car, Serena's sensational body against him, and had to force himself not to touch her. Not because of the presence of the driver, but because if he did he knew he wouldn't want to stop. All he could think of right now was the privacy of his bedroom.

He watched the lights of Athens rush by, focusing on the illuminations of the Acropolis as they headed towards his apartment—anything to distract himself.

Even though his head and most definitely his heart had refused to admit it, his body had wanted Serena every night since she'd left. He'd craved her touch like a lovesick teenager, needing to feel her against him, wanting her in a way he'd never wanted any woman before.

Now she was back—and tonight he would make her his. This time, for the sake of his child, he wouldn't allow her to leave.

The car pulled up outside the apartment building and she moved away from him, across the seat and out into the night, as the doors opened. He followed her, glad to see that the reporters had moved on—probably all at the charity ball. It would be their perfect chance to get pictures of the rich and famous, and he was thankful he and Serena hadn't been noticed leaving so early.

Quickly he keyed in the number for the outside door

and, with his arm protectively around her, walked towards the lift. She hadn't spoken since they'd left the party, but he guessed the same desire that raged inside him was keeping her silent.

Ever since they'd first met that desire had been a powerful force to resist. It had drawn him in, making him lose all sense of reason—and tonight was no different. He wanted her, but he had to retain control—had to remember this was a deal she'd agreed to. And it hadn't been because of their baby, but because of the money to help her sister.

The lift doors opened and they walked in. The bright lights were almost too much. Serena leant against the wall of the lift and lowered her gaze, looking intently at the floor. Was she trying to prevent him from seeing those beautiful green eyes of hers? Afraid to show the burning passion he'd felt in her as they'd danced?

'You look beautiful.'

The husky tone of his voice surprised him, and his breath caught momentarily in his chest as she looked up at him. The green of her eyes, almost drowned by her enlarged pupils, made her look far sexier than he'd ever seen her. He wanted her—more than he'd ever done.

Lust hurtled round his body as her lips parted, and he noticed the rise and fall of her breasts, her breathing deepening.

'Thank you.'

The words were barely audible, but his body had heard them, felt their seductive vibration caress and taunt him.

The lift doors opened but he couldn't move, his gaze remaining locked to hers, his own breathing becoming heavier by the second. Slowly she stood taller, straightening her spine, her eyes holding his as she took one step towards him.

'This is what it was like that last night on the beach,' she

whispered, so softly he wondered if she'd actually meant
him to hear. 'I couldn't fight it then either.'

'You drove me mad with desire that night,' he said,
moving close enough that he could take her in his arms.
But he didn't, not trusting his power of control.

His pulse throbbed with building desire, the beat thump-
ing in his ears, and he flexed his fingers then curled them
tight into his palms. He couldn't take much more of this.

Her neat brows furrowed slightly and questions raced
across her face. 'It was our last night. It should have been
goodbye.'

The lift doors closed, breaking the spell that had woven
inextricably around them. Serena looked away, almost
flustered by what had just happened, and frustration gave
way to irritation as he pressed the button to open the doors
again.

Whatever had been started that night on the beach in
Santorini was far from over. He didn't appreciate the hold
she had over him, the way she could make him want her
just with a glance or a whispered word, but he couldn't
ignore it any longer.

He stepped out of the lift and turned to see her watching him. 'I want you, Serena.'

He couldn't explain why he'd said it, why he'd exposed
his emotions. He pressed his lips firmly together to avoid
saying anything else he might regret—something she
might later use against him. He *did* want her—of that
there wasn't any doubt—but that didn't mean he had to
bring emotions into it. That was something he could never
do…especially when she was here for her own reasons.

She stepped towards him, her long legs outlined through
the pale silk of the dress, causing the blood to pound harder
around his heated body and his thoughts to spiral away
to nothing.

'I want you too.'

The tremulous whisper, so timid and quiet, made him grit his teeth together. She deserved better than him. She deserved a man who would love her—one who would be what she needed him to be. But fate had intervened and, as much as he desired her, he didn't know if he could be that man. His past had shaped him to an emotionally cold man who would never be able to love a woman with real sincerity, but inside he still burned with desire for her.

Serena saw his jaw clench and knew she shouldn't have said anything. She shouldn't have told him she wanted him, giving him power over her once more. Such thoughts made everything impossible.

She couldn't take a single step towards him, and stayed inside the lift as he stepped out.

Nikos had proposed to her, bought her the most gorgeous engagement ring—not only out of duty, but because of the deal they'd made. It was pure blackmail, but it would enable her sister to become a mother. Her spirits dropped at the thought that none of it would have happened if their night together hadn't resulted in consequences.

As the assistant in the jeweller's had spoken of lovers being brought closer by emeralds her heart had flickered with a little flame of hope. He'd taken the ring and purposefully put it on her finger, but she knew he hadn't given it because of love. Deep down, she knew he didn't love her and never would. He only wanted his child and he was prepared to offer anything.

She looked at Nikos, resplendent in his evening suit, so handsome he took her breath away. As his gaze met hers, full of desire, she saw the man she'd fallen in love with— the one she'd thought she knew so well. His gaze lingered on her, and despite the trappings of wealth and power the fisherman who'd stolen her heart was still there. Deep beneath the surface, but still there.

The flicker of hope that something could be salvaged grew.

The doors of the lift began to close again, startling her, and with lightning-quick reaction Nikos moved forward, stopping the doors. He held out his hand to her, his face serious and intent. If she took his hand now it would mean so much more than this moment. She would be accepting everything.

Her heart beat a loud rhythm as she looked into his eyes, searching for answers to questions she dared not ask. He didn't move, didn't break eye contact as a myriad of thoughts crashed over her. Finally she did what she knew she had to, what she knew was inevitable, and placed her hand in his.

He braced his body against the lift doors as they threatened to close again and closed his hand around hers. His blue eyes continued to lure her as she walked towards him, and with her hand tightly in his, her body sizzling from his touch, they walked out of the lift and towards his apartment.

The key turning in the lock made a loud click, highlighting the laden silence. With purpose he opened the door, leading her through and then pushing it swiftly shut behind him. Before she could say anything his body pressed her against the wall of the hallway, his hands against the wall on either side of her head. His lips claimed hers in a deep and demanding kiss and she arched herself against him, winding her arms about his neck.

This was what she'd wanted for the past three months. As the magnitude of her pregnancy had registered, shocking her with its implications, she'd still wanted him. Even the shocking deal he'd put to her hadn't dampened the passion in any way, and right now all she wanted was to love him—enough for both of them.

'Serena…' he whispered as he pulled back from her, his fingers tangling in her hair. 'With passion such as this burning between us it doesn't matter why we are together. The marriage *will* work.'

Her heart broke a little. But what had she expected? Words of love? In reality she knew she'd never hear such words from Nikos. He didn't want to love or be loved, but he was right about the passion. It sparked between them like fireworks on New Year's Eve. It was wild and reckless and totally consuming.

'Yes—yes, it will.' She stumbled over the words, her breath coming in short gasps. She couldn't completely take in what he'd said. Her body trembled too much with need for his touch.

He lowered his head, pressing his lips so gently against hers she almost cried. Then he traced a line of soft kisses down her neck, lingering on her shoulder as she tilted her head to one side, allowing him greater access and sighing with pleasure. The fingers entwined in her hair pulled free and stroked her cheek tenderly.

She reached up, placing her hand over his, stilling the movement. It was too much. It made her dare to believe he loved her. But she knew he didn't. She knew it was nothing more than lust.

He looked into her eyes and smiled, the lips that had just kissed her neck so persuasively drawing her gaze.

'I will make you mine, Serena, and the only place for that is in my bed.'

She couldn't fight him any longer. Being in his arms, his bed—it was all she wanted, all her body craved.

'Then take me there,' she teased, shocking herself, but enjoying the sexy look Nikos gave her. Would it be so bad to give in to what raged between them when they were to be married?

He stood back from her, his heavy gaze sweeping down her body, lingering on her breasts for just long enough to send heat hurtling through her. Again he took her hand and led her through the apartment to the only room she hadn't yet seen. His bedroom.

He opened the door, revealing a masculine space dominated by a large bed, bathed in the glow of golden light coming through the balcony windows.

He drew her into the room and looked down at her. Slowly he pulled his tie undone, tossing it to the floor, where it was soon joined by his jacket. She looked at the shirt, so white against his dark skin, and willed her eyes to stay open instead of closing in pleasure.

She remembered how his chest felt. How the hair there enabled her fingers to glide across his muscles. But most of all she remembered the firmness, and she ached to touch him again. She reached out and spread her fingers over his chest, relishing the feel of his arms pulling her to him, holding her there.

'I need you,' she said softly, not daring to look into his face in case her love shone out.

Instead she concentrated on opening one button of his shirt, then, when she didn't meet any resistance, another and another, until she could slide her hand inside. The groan of pleasure escaping him encouraged her further.

His fingers struggled briefly with the zip on her dress and she stifled a nervous laugh.

'I want to see you,' he said hoarsely. 'I want to see all of you.'

Seconds later the bodice of her dress loosened as he unzipped it, and then the pale green silk slithered down, leaving her naked apart from her panties and dainty sandals.

She resisted the urge to cover herself with her arms. She'd never stood so blatantly naked before him, always shielding herself from his gaze, anxious because of her innocence. It took great effort to remain under the scrutiny of those sexy blue eyes without covering herself as they devoured her hungrily.

A guttural growl of Greek words rushed from him as his gaze lingered on her. Before she could ask what he'd said his fingers caressed a blazing trail down her arms, stroking all the way to her hands, then her fingertips. He lightly lifted her fingers and brought each in turn to his lips and kissed them, and all the while his gaze, heady and deep blue, held her face, making her blush with desire.

'You are a goddess,' he said, kissing along one arm until he came to her shoulder.

Her whole body was on fire, her breasts tender and full, yearning for his touch. But still he kissed her shoulder, teasing and tormenting her as she'd never known before. Then slowly the fiery trail of kisses moved downwards and she gasped in pleasure, hardly able to stand.

'A goddess who is all mine,' he said huskily, and each word was interspersed with kisses, pressed enticingly against her, moving down between her breasts until she ached for him to kiss them.

His head moved lower, his kisses now on the soft swell of her stomach, and she plunged her fingers into his hair, closing her eyes.

'Nikos…' His name rushed from her lips on a wave of pleasure and she pressed them tightly together in case she said more.

'Such a beautiful body.'

His kisses moved down over her stomach, lingering as his hands skimmed her bottom, the sensation almost unbalancing her. She felt his warm breath against the silky panties that left little to the imagination and fought hard to remain standing.

Just when she thought she might collapse onto the bed behind her his fingers trailed down her thighs and towards her ankles.

'I intend to savour every part of it.'

Nikos looked up at Serena, her face so flushed with desire. The blood pounded harder around his body. He took a deep breath, fighting to regain some kind of control. He wanted to push her onto the white covers of the bed and lose himself inside her until the madness she evoked stopped—but he couldn't. This time he had to take it slow, had to keep a tight rein on the desire that burned inside him, because this was different from any other time.

He didn't known how or why. All he knew was that this was the woman he was going to marry, the mother of his child, a woman who'd unlocked something deep inside him that he couldn't yet acknowledge. From the moment he'd met her she'd changed him somehow, but he couldn't analyse it now.

Whatever it was it had the potential to be painful, the capability to be render him helpless, just like the hurt that had crushed him as a boy, and he never wanted to put himself in the firing line of that kind of pain again.

He stood up and looked down into her face, saw the nervousness in her eyes and felt as if his chest was being squeezed. 'This is what you want?'

Her big green eyes blinked rapidly, then she smiled up at him and his heart seemed to stop.

'Yes,' she whispered softly, tilting her chin and pressing her lips against his in a tormenting and lingering kiss. 'Yes, it is. I want you, Nikos.'

He pulled her against him, wishing he wasn't still

clothed so that he could feel her soft skin against his. A groan of desire escaped him as her feather-light kisses teased his senses, pushing him to the edge of his control.

He took her face between his hands, holding her at just the right angle, and kissed her until she murmured against his lips. Then he slid his tongue between them, deepening the kiss.

He closed his eyes against the exquisite pain of having her all but naked in his arms and having to exert control, trying to consider her condition. It was torture. He could feel her hardened nipples pressing against his chest, with only his partially open shirt between them, and as she wound her arms around his neck, pulling her body closer still, he had to hold back the urge to allow his desire to get the better of him.

He let go of her face, kissing her harder and deeper. His hands skimmed down the curve of her back, making her arch even closer, then he held her, pressing her against him. It wasn't enough. He wanted more—much more.

He grasped her thighs, lifting her off the floor until she wrapped her legs about him. Her fingers tangled in his hair as she kissed him deeply, her sighs of pleasure rushing into him, entwining with his. Slowly he walked the few paces to the bed and, with a steadiness that tested all his strength, lowered her onto the white covers. Then he hooked his fingers inside her panties and pulled them down, not taking his gaze from her face as she smiled seductively at him, passion making her uninhibited.

The golden glow from outside was the only light in the room. Every curve of her delicious body was bathed in soft amber and he inhaled deeply, trying to keep his rush of lust under control.

She slithered up the bed, away from him, but he caught

her ankle in a firm grip that made the breath rush from her lips.

'Now these,' he said, and unfastened the tiny straps of her sandals, inwardly cursing as his fingers fumbled with the delicate buckles.

She propped herself up on her arms and watched him. As he dropped the second glittering sandal to the floor she reached for him. He knelt on the bed, his body over hers, and kissed her, wishing he could touch her, but his arms had locked, supporting his weight. He didn't want to hurt her.

Her heated kisses became frantic, her breath fast, as her fingers continued what they'd started earlier and she opened his shirt, pushing it over his shoulders. He shook with the effort of restraining his control.

She kissed down his neck, over his shoulder, her hands tugging at his shirt until it was tight around his arms. He pushed back so that he straddled her legs, almost ripping the shirt off, and was rewarded with the darkening of her eyes until they were like the heart of a forest on a moon-lit night.

'How did I ever think I wanted to let you go?'

As he said the words her fingers traced the line of hair down over his abs, making breathing almost impossible. She lingered at the fastening of his trousers, the smile on her lips telling him she knew exactly the effect she was having on him.

'Do you really feel that?' she whispered, her fingers teasing as they travelled up and down the line of dark hair. But she refused to meet his eyes, shielding her face from him with a curtain of glorious amber hair.

'Yes,' he growled harshly, his lips claiming hers as he pushed her back against the bed.

If he said any more now he would be going into emotions he didn't want to explore—feelings he didn't want to admit to, let alone experience.

Her hands moved to rest on his thighs, inflicting yet more torture.

Serena's heart raced. He hadn't wanted to let her go. Did that mean he felt something for her? Even if it wasn't love?

She kissed him hard, demanding more from him as his body forced her to lie back against the bed. Her fingers tightened on his strong thighs and his groan of pleasure exploded into her mouth.

He wanted her—*really* wanted her. All her naivety and innocence had been left behind as she'd entered the apartment. She was his and his alone.

'Nikos...' It was all she could say, her breathing deep and ragged. But she wanted to tell him she was back and that she would never go. They were bound together by their baby, and maybe with passion such as this burning between them he would one day love her.

'This is too much. You tease and taunt me, pushing me beyond my control.'

He caught her hands in his, holding them against his thighs, preventing her teasing. His face was stern, his eyes so dark that only blue flecks remained.

With a swift suddenness he moved off her, springing to stand by the bed, removing the last of his clothes, tossing them carelessly away. Her heart pumped ever harder and she couldn't drag her gaze from his magnificent body. Her fingers itched to touch him, to caress every part of him, but most of all to feel him against her, then inside her, making her completely his.

The need she had for him was like nothing she'd ever known. Feeling brazen and emboldened, she looked at his naked and aroused body. 'No more teasing,' she said in a broken whisper as heat gathered low in her stomach. If he didn't make love to her soon she'd go insane.

'No,' he said huskily as he lay on the bed next to her, and the command in his voice was palpable. 'Not from you at least.'

Her eyes closed and a sigh of pleasure escaped her as he bent his head, kissing her nipple and sending shockwaves of pure pleasure through her. She arched her back, lifting herself higher as he nipped gently at it, but when his hand rested on her stomach she almost didn't dare breathe. After a moment's pause he slowly moved it lower, exploring the part of her that wanted him with a fiery heat that refused to be put out.

'It's my turn,' he said as he raised his head, her nipple tingling from his kisses.

He turned his attention to the other one as his fingers caressed her, stoking the fire of passion almost to breaking point. She gripped his arm, wanting him to stop, wanting her moment of ecstasy to be shared with his.

'No, Nikos!'

'Yes,' he said against her breast, exerting more of his power over her, and she dug her fingers harder into his arm.

Just when she thought he'd gone too far he stopped the torment and moved over her, his knees nudging her legs apart as he kissed her deeply, bruising her lips with the intensity of his kiss. She felt the heat of him against her and lifted her hips, begging him with her body for release.

Gently he slid into her, bringing tears to her eyes, and she wondered if he was restraining himself, holding back because of the baby. Instinctively she wrapped her legs around him, pulling him deeper into her. His arms, braced tightly to keep his weight off her, began to shake with the effort and she kissed his chest, his neck, his chin until they both lost control.

Nikos kissed her back, interspersing his kisses with Greek words she had no hope of understanding, but it didn't matter. Her mind was floating too much even to even form the question and ask what he'd said. Maybe it was better if she didn't. Maybe she should pretend they were words of love…feed her fantasy of a happy-ever-after.

As she moved beneath him she realised it had never been like this before. The wild passion they shared had never tipped her so far over the edge. She clung to him, not wanting the moment to end.

Finally her breathing slowed and he lowered himself over her, propped on his elbows, but his heated skin was still touching hers, sending a tingle of pleasure all over her.

He dropped his head against her shoulder, his thick dark hair tickling her cheek. 'You will not leave again.'

The words were muffled, his voice hoarse and uneven, but she couldn't miss the aggressive harshness in it. There was no mistaking its dominance and power. The fairy tale was over.

She closed her eyes and cried inside. He was still angry. Did he even now resent having her in his life? Resent the baby they'd created in the summer? Was she right to have come back? Was she right to have accepted his offer to help Sally, tying herself and her baby to him for ever?

CHAPTER EIGHT

THE SUN WAS streaming in through the windows when Nikos woke the next morning, shocking him. He *never* slept late. He moved and a sigh of contentment from Serena stirred his senses—along with memories from last night. He'd made love to her until exhaustion had claimed them both. No wonder he hadn't woken at his usual early hour.

'Morning.'

Serena's husky voice caught his attention and he looked down at her as she moved against him, unwittingly enticing him once more.

Never before had he woken with a woman in his bed. He'd always slipped from *their* beds, early in the morning, preferring not to get into those *what happens next?* discussions. Leaving them sleeping had always given a clear message. Just as never taking a woman to his own bed served as a constant reminder why he shouldn't get involved in long-term affairs.

So why had he felt the need to bring Serena here when she'd offered to check into a hotel? Was it just because he was going to marry her? Or was it more than the need to keep her in his life now that she was carrying his child?

He pushed the suggestion firmly from his mind and inwardly cursed his train of thought. What was the matter

with him? He'd never agonised over spending the night
with a woman before.

'Are you rested enough to go out today?' He asked the
question as he moved away from the temptation of her
lush curves, throwing back the covers and walking naked
to the bathroom.

He splashed cold water over his face in an attempt to
cool his returning ardour, as well as shock the heavy combination of sleep and passion from his body. An icy shower
was what he needed most. And as the cold jets of water
pounded his skin he thought back to every minute of last
night, to the way Serena had made him feel.

His desire had not been for her alone, but for things he
shouldn't want. From the very first night they'd spent together she'd made him want more, and each time that need
filtered through his mind just a little more clearly. But he
couldn't allow it. He would not let himself feel anything
other than passion for any woman—especially not Serena.
If he did it was sure to spell disaster. Hadn't his past proved
he was incapable of loving or being loved?

With an unsettled feeling he switched off the shower,
towelled his hair dry and then slung a white towel around
his hips and returned to the bedroom. Serena was still
in bed, half asleep and looking as lovely as ever, her red
hair not in its usual sleek style, but ruffled from a night
of making love.

'I thought you would be going to the office,' she said
softly, pushing her tumbled hair from her eyes and sitting
up, pulling the white sheet against her, looking suddenly
vulnerable.

As he watched her it was as if someone had notched
something tight around his chest, but he smiled at her
modesty, tempted to remind her that last night she hadn't
cared if he saw her body.

'Not today.'

'What about your deal? I thought it was getting close to completion?'

She curled her legs underneath her and knelt on the bed, moving the sheet, giving him a glimpse of her thighs.

'It's Saturday, and we need to be seen out together.'

He knew what she'd meant, and it had nothing to do with their deal. After each night they'd stayed together in her hotel room in Santorini he'd slipped away as dawn had broken, his job—which she'd believed was fishing—being the perfect reason and therefore not requiring any justification.

'There is nothing more to be done with that deal until Monday.'

Unlike the deal he'd struck with Serena.

She smiled and something tugged hard on his guilt. She really did deserve a man who could love her—but he could never be that man. He didn't want the experience of watching someone leave again, her cruel words haunting him ever since.

'If we must go out, I'd like to go to the Acropolis.'

Her excitement cast a glow over her face and he realised she looked the happiest he'd seen her since she'd returned to Greece. For the first time since her text had come through the thought came that things could work out between them. Providing she didn't ask for that one thing he couldn't give—emotional commitment.

'Then I suggest you get dressed.'

He turned and selected clothes from his wardrobe, dropping the towel with scant regard for his nakedness. Behind him, he heard her intake of breath and smiled. The passion of last night still simmered within her, just as it did for him, and if he didn't get out of the bedroom now he was in danger of spending all day in bed—and that was something for lovers to do.

Serena felt as if her whole body glowed as she and Nikos walked along the path towards the Acropolis. The sun was hot, but her memories of last night were hotter, and now, with her hand in his, she felt the fizz of passion brewing again, along with the warm glow of hope. Last night had been just like when they'd first met. It had proved the heated passion that they had always shared was still there—but was it enough?

Around them crowds of tourists posed for photos and admired the view over the rooftops of Athens. Children squealed in delight as they clambered over the many rocks and Serena watched them, the reality of her situation coming to her clearly. This was her child's history, and by staying and marrying Nikos she would give her sister the same chance of motherhood she now had.

A pang of guilt slid over her.

'Are we doing the right thing?' She looked out at the view, not daring to look at him. His hand around hers tightened, but he continued to walk.

'How can we *not* be doing the right thing, Serena?'

His words were firm and quiet as he guided her towards some meagre shade, out of the way of a large tour party noisily heading towards them.

She looked up at him, glad of the shade, and waited until the tourists had passed, with their enthusiasm and animated exclamations of delight.

'I find it hard to believe a man like you hasn't married.'

His dark brows arched, and she wasn't sure if it was the shade of the trees or what she'd said that had given his face those stern and sharp lines.

'A man like me?' He let her hand go and thrust it into the pocket of his casual beige chinos, his stance suddenly annoyed, his expression confrontational.

'You have it all, Nikos. Surely women have been throwing themselves at you, looking for marriage? So why me? Why now?' She pushed on, determined to clear the doubts that had begun to surface since she'd arrived, only to be pushed aside last night by passion. But as that passion had cooled those doubts had slipped back into her mind—like snakes slithering undetected through the long grass.

'Why?' His deep voice was harsh, causing a passing tourist to glance their way, and Nikos took her arm and walked her further away from the path and the crowds. He stopped and turned to look at her. 'Do you really need to ask that?'

She drew in a deep breath, lifted her chin and met his glittering blue gaze. 'Yes.'

She *did* need to ask. She needed to know if there was even an inkling of love there for her. Sally's advice was fading fast as the reality of the deal he'd offered sank in. She didn't think she could go headlong into marriage without knowing he felt *some* kind of affection for her. What if he later resented her, when he couldn't attend parties like last night's as a single man? What if he fell in love with another woman?

'You are carrying my child. My heir.'

Fury spiked every word but she stood her ground. She had to know.

'Nothing else?' She pressed him further, ignoring the glitter of anger in his eyes.

'Is that not reason enough?'

He turned away from her, looking out over Athens towards Mount Lycabettus and St George's chapel reaching into the blue sky. His anger was in complete contrast to the sublime weather.

She moved to stand by him, her flat shoes crunching on the path, the sound so loud it was almost too much in the heavy and expectant silence which had settled around them.

'Is it right for us to marry just because of the baby? What about the baby's feelings? Should it grow up thinking it's the mistake that forced us together?'

The pain and guilt of her own childhood poured from her heart, seeping into every word she said, but still he remained ramrod-straight, looking anywhere but at her. A small part of her wanted to tell him she knew what that was like, but lifelong guilt kept her silent. She couldn't admit her part in her parents' unhappy marriage—not out loud.

'What do you want me to do? Declare my undying love for you?' His voice was low, vibrating with anger. 'You accepted my terms. You need this marriage and all it offers as much as I do.'

She balked at his mention of the deal he'd offered—the one she was prepared to take if it meant helping Sally get what she wanted. She still hadn't told her sister yet. The thought of ringing her and telling her she could continue with IVF treatment was exciting, but explaining how it was going to be achieved was daunting. As was telling Sally of her own pregnancy. It was a conversation to be had face-to-face.

'We can't build a marriage on a child and a foundation of lust. What happens when that lust dies?'

She forced her voice to be strong and wished they weren't surrounded by people of all nationalities, that this discussion was taking place in private—but maybe the restraint of being here was better.

He turned to look at her, his hands taking hold of her

arms, forcing her to give him all her attention. Her skin burned where he touched her and a sizzle of undeniable attraction skittered down her spine. How could she find such a ruthless man so attractive?

'Love dies too, Serena.'

His deep, accented words, said with such earnestness, forced her to search his eyes. They looked so black and solemn that a tingle of fear chased after the sizzle of attraction she'd tried so hard to ignore. The sombre tones of his voice left her in no doubt that he was talking from experience.

'What happened?' She wanted to reach for him, to soothe the pain which lingered in his eyes like dark shadows in the night.

He didn't say anything, and nor did he break eye contact. Even when a particularly noisy party of tourists started posing for photos with Mount Lycabettus as a backdrop, intruding on their private moment, he remained rigidly silent.

He waited, and she hardly dared to breathe, sensing that the impenetrable barrier around him had opened just enough for her to slip through—if she dared.

'You'll find it on the internet, I'm sure.'

The spiked and curt words reminded her of the expression of regret she'd seen on his face yesterday, when he'd arrived from the office to find her working on her laptop. She hadn't been searching for stories of him then, but knew that was what it must have looked like. What was in his past that was so bad? What was he avoiding?

Something akin to fear gripped her heart and she had to hear it from him. 'I want *you* to tell me.' Her voice was a whisper, but a firm and decisive one. He'd said this much and she couldn't let him shut down on her now.

He let go of her and turned to stand looking out at the

view. His profile was set in stern lines, but she moved towards him, her body so close to his they were almost touching. Almost.

'I'd been here in Athens for two years and had put my every waking hour into Xanthippe Shipping. I'd made the money I wanted and more. Everything finally seemed to be going right—until my mother wrote to me.'

'I don't understand,' she said softly, placing her hand on his arm.

He looked at her, his fierce blue eyes a total contrast to the way he'd just spoken. '*Don't* you?'

The question hurt. It was prodding, as if to try and revive a dying flame. Memories of a childhood that had made her push men away as a young woman, wary of being hurt, rushed towards her in a stampede.

She shook her head.

'No, of course you don't. *You* had the happy home every child deserves.' His brow furrowed.

He was too close now to her upsetting childhood, and her heart thumped so hard it blocked out the hum of tourists talking and laughing. There was no way she could tell him the truth. How could she say she'd loved him from the moment they met when he thought she'd only returned for financial gain? Hadn't she confirmed his suspicions by accepting his offer to fund more IVF for Sally—accepting his marriage deal?

'You don't know anything about me,' she whispered in a half-truth, desperate to look away from the accusation in his eyes but not daring to. 'And that's changing the subject. What happened, Nikos?'

She saw his jaw clench, the hard lines highlighting his cheekbones, his eyes hard and suspicious. 'My mother's "*love*" died when she found someone with more wealth, more able to give her all she wanted. She left me with my

father. He didn't care about my pain—just drank himself
into oblivion.'

The harsh way he'd all but snarled the word *love* was
not lost on her and she drew in a ragged breath, moving
away from him, away from his contempt of the emotion
she felt so strongly for him.

Nikos stood looking at the view of St George's chapel. The
sun was bouncing off its white walls as it sat perched on
top of the tree-lined mountain opposite. This was supposed
to be a day out. A time for Serena to see a place she'd expressed an interest in—a place that was part of his child's
legacy. Instead it had turned to deep and unwelcome ex-
ploration of his past.

He sensed Serena by his side, the heat of her body reminding him of the passion they'd shared last night. That
passion would be the foundation for their marriage. Serena had shown her true self in accepting his deal. She
would do whatever it took to get what she wanted. Love
hadn't been a part of what they'd shared those few weeks
on Santorini, and it certainly wouldn't be a part of their
marriage. Lust was all he could offer—because he couldn't
give more. Not ever.

'My mother walked away without a backward glance.'
He said the words aloud, not realising he had done so until
he felt Serena move at his side. He looked down at her. 'We
are better off marrying for our convenience—and for the
baby, Serena. Emotions are messy and complicated things.'

He'd wondered initially at Serena's motives when
she'd returned—had been sure that she'd discovered his
true identity, that she was looking for whatever it was
his mother had found in the man she'd left his father for.
That fear hadn't dissipated. Still doubts niggled. But one
thing was certain. He could not and would not be a victim

of love again. He'd care for Serena in every way possible, but never again did he want to expose himself to such rejection, such heartache.

Nothing else in his life compared to the pain he'd carried since the day his mother had left. Her words still haunted him, killing any of the attempts to make amends she'd made over the years.

Serena moved away from him, walking among the scattered stones as they lay in the parched earth and for a moment he couldn't move. Then she turned and smiled so bright he wondered if he had imagined all they'd just spoken about.

She held out her hand to him. 'There is more to see?'

He was grateful for the change in subject and, slamming the door of his past shut, he walked over and took her hand.

The wonder on her face as she walked towards the Parthenon a short time later held his vulnerable emotions captive. He watched as she reached out and touched the cream stone that had been there for thousands of years, and despite their earlier conversation he was glad he'd chosen to spend the day with her.

The two weeks they'd spent together on Santorini came back to him. Nothing else had mattered. He'd lived those two weeks only for each moment, for each smile from her adorable lips, each kiss which had set light to him, and each gentle and alluringly innocent touch.

It had been like looking in on the life he could have had—but they would never find that again. No, those two weeks now meant he was to be a father.

The thought filled him with wonder and dread.

As the sun grew higher in the sky Serena looked weary. She still smiled, still wanted to know all he could tell her about the ancient temple, but she was looking hot and tired. Concern for her and for the baby filled him.

'We should go now.' He looked at his watch, surprised that they had been out so long. The appointment he'd arranged with a doctor before leaving Santorini was in just an hour. 'The doctor is calling later.'

'Doctor?' She blinked in confusion and fixed him with those green eyes. 'On a Saturday? I don't need to see a doctor that urgently.'

'Maybe not, but you will. It has all been arranged.'

He took her hand, but sensed her hesitation as they began to walk back through the mass of tourists. At least they would have some time alone at the apartment. His body heated at the memory of their last hours alone together.

'Do you still doubt you are the father?'

He turned to her instantly, to see that she was looking at the ground, as if concentrating on every step instead of meeting his gaze.

'In the past two days you have flown across Europe alone and then travelled here to Athens. You admitted you were ill for the first months of your pregnancy. You *will* see a doctor. I do not want my child being put at risk.'

She stopped and looked at him. Hostility and disbelief were burning in her eyes, but she didn't say anything. Before he could rein in his frustration at knowing she'd spent those months alone and ill, unable to tell anyone, she began walking again—but this time with purposeful strides which clearly displayed her annoyance.

Serena answered all the questions the Greek doctor put to her, aware of Nikos's brooding presence behind her. He didn't trust her. That much was evident. But was it because he didn't believe the child was his or because he genuinely cared about it?

As the doctor spoke in Greek over her, ignoring her, her temper simmered. Nikos didn't care—not about her. All he cared about was making sure the baby was his. How had she been so stupid as to think that the hours they'd spent making love last night would make him see her differently?

She couldn't sit here and allow them to talk about her like this. It was, after all, *her* baby they were talking about.

'What is he saying?' she asked a little too firmly, her irritation directed at Nikos, not the older man.

'That you need to rest and must take things easy.' He looked at her, his eyes glittering like the sea had done on that day they'd first met, as if sprinkled with diamonds.

'Yes—rest,' added the doctor in heavily accented English as he made his way towards the door. 'The nausea will subside and you will feel well again soon.'

She smiled her thanks at him, wondering how she could ever 'feel well again', knowing the man she loved would never love her.

'Thank you. Sorry to have troubled you.'

'Nothing is too much trouble for Nikos. He was like a son to my cousin and he made him very happy.'

She frowned at his words as Nikos shut the door after the doctor and returned to the living room. 'Who is his cousin?'

'His cousin was the man I worked for when I first came to Athens—the man I looked up to and the man who was more of a father to me than my own.'

'Do you ever see your father and mother?'

As he looked at her she saw his eyes dim, as if a shutter had been drawn down over them.

'My father died when I was a teenager, but I hadn't really known him since my mother left. It destroyed him, changed him. I went to live with my grandparents.'

Serena's heart went out to him as she imagined what he must have felt. Her parents had constantly squabbled, and her home had sometimes felt unsettled as divorce threats were bandied about like a ball on the tennis court, but they had always been in her life.

'What about your grandmother? Do you see her?' she asked, remembering the woman he'd said lived in the small white house, perched on the hillside overlooking the sea.

'She took me in and raised me—gave me everything she could,' he said gruffly. 'I returned that care when my grandfather died and at her insistence I kept his small fleet of fishing boats.'

'That is why you were helping with the fishing when we met? When you couldn't tell me the truth?'

Things were starting to fit together now, but it still didn't explain his need to strike such a deal with her.

He nodded and walked to the balcony, but she wasn't going to be knocked off course so easily.

'Will your grandmother approve?'

Serena wondered about what the old lady would think of him taking an English bride—and a pregnant one at that. What would she think of the terms of their marriage?

'She is a very wise lady.' He looked down at her where she sat. 'She would also tell you to rest, to look after yourself and the baby.'

Serena placed her hand over her stomach and looked into Nikos's eyes, her heart somersaulting at the swirling desire she saw in them once more, and found herself longing for this evening. Would he take her to his bed again? Make love to her gently and yet so passionately? She knew she shouldn't want that, but she did. She couldn't just switch her love off—or her hope that one day he might love her.

'Does she know about the baby?'

He shook his head and she couldn't help voicing her concern.

'Because you doubt the baby is yours?'

There—she'd said the words aloud, cast them out like a fisherman's net, giving him the chance to agree, to call a halt to everything.

He didn't. He merely looked at her. A long, cold stare that made her want to shiver, as if winter winds were suddenly being blown in off the sea.

'I have never doubted the baby is mine, Serena,' he said as he sat down next to her. 'But I do doubt that you are looking after yourself. You should not have flown all the way here alone. You should have called me from London—as soon as you knew. As I asked you to.'

'What could you have done—or what could the man I *thought* you were have done? *He* wouldn't have been able to arrange for a private plane to fly him to England.' Hurt smarted inside her as she remembered his deceit, but maybe after their brief talk today the reason was a little clearer.

He stepped closer, leaned down and kissed her softly on the lips, his dark mood thawing as passion took over the blue of his eyes. 'It doesn't matter who you thought I was when we were together. I've told you—I didn't want to spoil our time with each other, a time that was special. Different.'

She searched his face and placed her palm against his cheek, feeling a fresh growth of stubble, but she knew that the special time they'd shared during the summer was over. Reality had impinged on it.

'You could have told me the truth.'

His answer was to pull her into his arms and kiss her, engulfing them both in a desire that would have only one outcome. She kissed him back, hoping the love she had for him, a love he would never want, would be enough— for her *and* their marriage.

CHAPTER NINE

NIKOS WAS SURPRISED by the ease with which he had slipped into sharing his life with Serena. Each morning for the past week he'd kissed her goodbye, tearing himself from her warm body to go to the office. He'd been pleased that she'd taken the doctor's advice and was resting, and each day she looked more radiant and more vibrant, which was having an uncontrollable effect on him.

He thought it was what a real relationship might be like, and that was something he'd become an expert at avoiding. But two weeks with Serena in the summer and one intensely passionate night had changed his life, forcing him to look his worst fears in the eye. Fear of failure and an even bigger fear of love.

This morning the deal he'd been working on had finally gone through. He was now the owner of the largest shipping company in Greece, with both cargo ships *and* cruise liners that would sail the seas under his name. He'd achieved his ambition. Now it was time to seal a different deal—one that would bind Serena to him for ever.

But before he could do that he had to visit his grandmother on Santorini. He couldn't put it off any longer, and hoped the news of their engagement and the baby didn't reach her before he did. His conscience unsettled by such thoughts, he'd ordered his plane and was now flying across a glittering sea littered with islands.

A soft sigh from Serena drew his attention back from the view and he looked across at her. Even though the afternoon flight was short, she'd fallen asleep almost immediately. A little spike of guilt caught him unawares. Had their passion-filled nights tired her too much?

She opened her eyes, sat up and looked at him, the smile on her lips making him want to lean across and kiss her. But the crew who manned his private plane were now preparing for landing. He would have to wait until they were alone at his villa this evening.

'We will be there soon,' he said, and put the papers he had hardly looked at away, having preferred instead to watch Serena while she was sleeping.

He still couldn't comprehend that he'd spent a week enjoying coming home to her each day, savouring the nights with her sleeping in his arms. He'd been stunned when he'd realised that he now lingered in the mornings, not wanting to leave her. He hadn't ever done that with any other woman. Even when he and Serena had shared nights of passionate sex whilst she was staying in the hotel when they'd first met he'd slipped from her bed as the sun rose.

So what had changed?

She now wore his ring, making his intention to marry her clear to everyone. But why, after locking his heart away, was he even considering marriage? Deep down he knew it was more than just the fact that she was carrying his child, his heir, but he didn't want to look beyond that right now—was worried that if he searched too hard for answers it would all be destroyed, that history would repeat itself and he'd be declared unworthy of love or affection.

He narrowed his eyes as a new thought slipped insidiously through his mind, pushing aside the need to question his motives. She'd come back because of the baby, declaring she had no intention of staying. Would she have come back, contacted him again, if it hadn't been for his warning that night on the beach? She'd walked away from him then. Had she meant it to be for good?

He relaxed as the answer came to him like a bolt of lightning. She had come back because she had known all along who he was—had known of his wealth and had come to get what she wanted. Money for her sister.

'Nikos…?'

His name, softly spoken, with a question in it, dragged him from his black thoughts.

'Is something wrong?'

'No.' He forced a smile to his lips and pushed away the shadows of doubt, returning to his first thoughts. 'I just hope my grandmother hasn't heard our news second hand.'

'Is that likely?'

A worried frown creased her brow and her eyes looked so soft they reminded him of the deep green of the sea on calm days, when he stopped his boat to cast the nets.

He thought of the headlines their engagement had made, coupled with the deal he'd successfully completed. It would be a miracle if his grandmother *didn't* know. What would she think of him taking an English bride after everything his mother had put the family through?

'I think it is. She may live in a small village, but others will have told her.'

It was far better that Serena was prepared. His grandmother was a wise and canny lady, who wouldn't appreciate being outsmarted.

He thought of the basic house she lived in—more of a tourist attraction than a home—and wished his grandmother had been less stubborn and moved into the villa he'd built for her on the island. She'd refused completely, and after several years of it being empty he'd decided to use it as his base when he was back on the island. Whenever he returned there his grandmother always knew, so why should knowledge of his engagement be any different?

Nikos didn't want to tell Serena that news travelled fast the other way too—that he'd known of her arrival on the island before she'd sent him that text. She'd been asking for him, and his friends had told her he'd gone away for a while, but let him know she was there. It still hadn't prepared him for seeing those words boldly glaring up at him from his phone, for knowing that the consequences he'd least wanted had happened.

She looked dismayed, and he pushed aside his unease to allay hers. 'It will be fine. If anyone is to blame it is me. I should have told her.'

Serena took Nikos's hand as they climbed the twists and turns of the steps to the little white house almost at the top of the hill. She was totally charmed by all the houses, which appeared to be clinging to the hillside. Most were white, reflecting the heat of the sun and making sunglasses necessary, but others were pale pink or cream, and some had the blue-painted domed roofs typical of the region.

'How do people *live* here?' She laughed as she paused to rest on a flat area that seemed suspended above the houses below, their roofs like steps back down to the sea.

'You get used to it.' He looked at her with genuine concern, despite his light-hearted response. 'Are you feeling okay?'

'I'm fine.' She laughed again. 'I just wanted to stop and take in the view.'

She turned and looked out to the sparkling sea and felt Nikos stand close behind her. A fizz of desire shimmered through her and she turned to him, the view suddenly losing its appeal.

'You won't see much that way.'

His roguish smile melted her heart and she leaned towards him, wrapping her arms around him, almost sighing with pleasure as he lowered his head and kissed her gently. Her love for him was growing, and moments like these gave her hope that the man she'd fallen in love with would find his way back to her and one day love her too.

'If you keep kissing me like that I won't want to see anything,' she said impishly as he pulled her tighter to him. 'Where are we staying? The hotel?'

'I've made other arrangements,' he said, and a wicked glint entered his eyes, making her pulse leap with anticipation.

All week he'd treated her like a princess, showered her with gifts and made love to her in a way that had made her heart melt. But he hadn't said how he felt, or even hinted at it, and she'd kept her love for him tightly locked away, sensing he wouldn't want to hear those words even in the height of passion.

'And what would *they* be?' she teased, and stood on tiptoe to brush her lips over his.

'Patience,' he said, his accent suddenly pronounced, and she knew she was tormenting him as much as he was to her.

He smiled. A lazy, desire-laden smile. And her heart flipped as she smiled back at him, relishing the moment as he kissed her tenderly once more. It was a gentle kiss, but loaded with the promise of so much.

'Nikos!'

His name, called from above, and a flurry of Greek drew her attention. He let her go as she sprang back from him and he laughed—a deep, sexy sound that heated the very core of her, making her wish they were going to wherever he'd made his 'arrangements'. Anywhere they could be alone.

'My grandmother,' Nikos explained, and he called up to the elderly woman standing by a bright blue-painted door that was surrounded by a flush of gorgeous red flowers. He took her hand and climbed the remaining steps towards his grandmother.

Serena held back as he embraced the tiny woman dressed almost completely in black, her grey hair covered by a black scarf tied under her chin. Rapid Greek rushed between them and then the old lady turned to look at Serena.

'Welcome,' she said, in very stilted English, and her lined face was full of kindness and warmth.

Serena stepped forward, about to put out her hand to take the old lady's, but she was pulled into a hug and had no choice but to reciprocate.

As Nikos's grandmother finally let her go the old lady turned to Nikos and spoke in Greek.

'She says you are very beautiful and she wishes she could say more than the few English words she knows.'

Serena blushed and looked from the smiling face of his grandmother to Nikos. His handsome face was relaxed and he was looking much more like the man she'd first met. He looked as if he'd left the worries of the world in Athens—as if here he could be the real Nikos. Hope grew in her heart.

'I hadn't expected her to be able to say anything to me. Tell her I love her home.'

Nikos relayed the message. The old lady nodded her head knowingly and walked through the tall blue door into a courtyard. He turned to Serena as she looked about her, taking in the array of pots filled with flowers in full bloom.

'My grandmother learnt a little English when my mother was here, but hasn't had any use for it since she left.'

Serena knew her eyes must have widened, but couldn't keep the shock from showing or sounding in her voice. 'Your mother was *English*?'

His mouth suddenly set into a hard line, his features becoming chiselled, his eyes glacial blue. 'Half-English. The only thing I have to thank my mother for is her blue eyes.'

Each word he spoke was brittle, but she kept her gaze focused on him. He hardly talked of his mother and had never mentioned that she was half-English. Questions rushed forward, but as she glanced at the wary expression of his grandmother she knew now was not the time.

It had been Nikos's blue eyes, so sexy and passionate, that had snared her heart from the first glance, making her fall in love so fast. She'd wondered whom he'd got them from, but hadn't for one moment thought his mother might be from an English family.

'I didn't know,' she said softly, and turned her attention to the flowers, reaching out to touch the delicate petals of those which climbed up the white courtyard walls— anything other than look at him.

His grandmother spoke and she turned to look at her, wishing she could understand at least *something*. The old lady smiled and gestured them inside.

'Thank you,' she said as she moved from the bright sunlight to the cool shade of her house.

Nikos followed her in and she felt every step he took, the spark of sexual attraction mixing with sympathy for the little boy he'd once been. He placed his hand against her back as they stood in the small but very comfortable little house. Having him next to her, overpowering her so that she could think of nothing else but him, was almost too much, and she glanced about the house in an attempt to distract herself from the heat of his touch.

One end of the house was used as a living room, with an old fireplace that filled one corner. It looked as though it would be bliss to enjoy on cooler evenings. At the other end was a kitchen, basic and very dated, but obviously much loved. The tiny windows in the thick walls let in only a small amount of light, but Serena was thankful to be out of the sun.

'Relax,' Nikos said, his voice deep and sexy as he showed her to the only comfortable-looking chair in the room. 'Lunch is a bit of a tradition when I visit my grandmother.'

He looked down at her as she sat, and again she saw much more of the man she'd fallen in love with. Leaving Athens and his business behind must allow him to relax, to be who he really was. But whoever he was the spark of attraction hadn't diminished.

She sat back, then realised she must be in his grandmother's chair. She was about to get up to offer it to her when the old lady smiled, a twinkle making her eyes sparkle just as Nikos's sometimes did.

'Please—have your chair,' Serena said, frustrated by the language barrier.

'No.' The old lady shook her head and sat on one of the four chairs around the small table, speaking to Nikos, who was now busy in the kitchen.

Serena looked at his broad shoulders as he set about preparing their lunch, his back to both her and his grandmother. Seeing him in this environment, almost without a trace of the ruthless streak he used as his barrier against the world and especially against her, made her heart soften and love flow.

'She says you are the guest and also that you must rest.'

Nikos glanced over his shoulder at her, his eyes sparkling with hidden meaning. 'She *knows*.'

Serena blushed, and the old lady laughed as Nikos returned his attention to preparing their meal. Then she looked earnestly at Serena and spoke, the tone of her voice quite different from the happy way she'd greeted them.

'I'm sorry...' Serena was flustered, not sure how to interpret what was being said.

'She says you hold the key,' Nikos said over his shoulder, without looking round.

Serena frowned. The key to what?

In answer to her thought his grandmother leant towards her in her seat, as if to be sure she had Serena's full attention. She pointed at Nikos, then to her heart, and finally she pointed at Serena.

Serena frowned, unable to decide if what she was being told was good or bad. The old lady spoke the same words again and made the same actions. *You hold the key.* That had been the translation. Serena looked at Nikos. Without thinking she touched her hand to her heart and then slid it down to the small swell of her baby.

Realisation dawned. His grandmother thought the baby was the key to Nikos's heart—but he didn't have one.

She looked at his grandmother, her hand still on her stomach, and the woman smiled a wise and knowing smile, nodding her approval. Serena was relieved that Nikos had been occupied during this exchange. The poor old lady must be longing for a great-grandchild.

'Lunch,' said Nikos as he placed a large bowl of salad with olives and feta cheese in the middle of the table, breaking the moment between Serena and his grandmother, but seemingly oblivious to their silent exchange. 'I hope you are hungry, Serena?'

His grandmother looked at Nikos as he sat at the table

and he spoke to her again, then looked at Serena as she got up from her chair and joined them. The tone he used when he spoke to his grandmother was a complete contrast to the voice of man she'd spent the past week with. Their nights might have been passionate, but by day they sparred with one another as she struggled to hide her true feelings.

'My grandmother is happy for us and she knows you understand.'

He looked at her, his brows raised in question, leaving Serena feeling bemused by the whole exchange.

At least his grandmother was happy about the baby.

The baby she'd been told was the key to Nikos's heart…

The afternoon's visit had been a success, and Nikos had re-assured himself that his grandmother was well and happy. He employed local people to look after her, but it still helped to see her himself. She was the only person in his life who'd showed him unconditional love, the only person never to have let him down, and the only person it would ever feel safe for him to love in return.

'We will go now,' he said, aware that Serena was looking tired, and he said the same to his grandmother, sensing Serena watching as they spoke in Greek to say their goodbyes.

'So where are we going?' Serena asked as they made their way back down the steps while the sun began to slide towards the horizon.

'Somewhere we can be alone.'

He put his arm around her, pulling her close. All afternoon he'd watched her, his body aware of every move she made, desire burning inside him. Now he fully intended to take her to his villa and spend a weekend relaxing and losing himself in the pleasure of her body.

'It's just a short drive along the coast.'

His car was waiting, as requested, and soon he was driving away from the village he'd grown up in and towards the open countryside. Its ruggedness always appealed to him and made him feel at home, which was why he'd decided that this was where his child would grow up and he and Serena would live—if she stayed long enough. Once she had the money for her sister there was nothing stopping her from leaving…walking away just as his mother had done.

The villa had always been his private retreat, a place to hide from the world, and it felt as if he was opening himself up to Serena by taking her there, let alone announcing it as her new home. He nudged the nervous vulnerability of that thought to one side and focused instead on the pleasure of a night in his bed with the woman who ignited such an intense passion inside him, unlocking feelings he didn't recognise.

'This is it,' he said, and drove off the road, tyres scrunching on the gravel driveway.

A stifled gasp slipped from her lips as she looked at the villa and he was glad she was seeing it for the first time at dusk. The light illuminated the clean modern lines of the villa, which had been built in keeping with the traditional buildings he'd grown up in. The housekeeper would be long gone and he could finally be alone with her.

'It's beautiful,' she said as she slipped down from the vehicle.

He took her hand and led her towards the door. 'This is where our child will grow up.'

The reality of those words hit him as if he'd been punched in the stomach. The villa he'd built would finally become a home.

A home for *his* family.

His child.

He would never have thought it possible. He had always

been careful to ensure it wouldn't be—except for that one passionate night on the beach with Serena, when common sense and thoughts of contraception had eluded him.

'Not in Athens?' she questioned as she walked into the villa, the sound of her heels echoing from the walls.

'No,' he said firmly.

There was no way his child would grow up anywhere else than on the island of Santorini—he was more certain of that with each passing second. He wanted his child to know all the good things he'd known and so much more—because his child would be wanted, his child would have a father who took the time to be there, to be interested.

'But your business…?' The question lingered in the air as she walked into the spacious living room.

'That is not for you to worry about.' He opened the sliding patio doors to reveal the pool, lit with soft amber lights. 'I have an office here, linked to my Athens office with every technical device possible.'

He intended to spend more time on the island. His grandmother was getting older, and most importantly he wanted to be there for his child. He also wanted to be with Serena—something which had shocked him when he'd first realised it.

Whilst he didn't want to tango with love for a woman, he knew he wanted to try and give his son all he'd never had. He hadn't known the love of a mother but by marrying Serena, offering her that deal, he could ensure history didn't repeat itself. He also hoped that by being there for his baby from the day it was born he could love it as his father should have loved him.

'You and my child will have everything I can give you.'

He saw Serena's expression become doubtful and unease slipped over him. Did she doubt his ability to love his child as much as he did?

CHAPTER TEN

THE REALITY OF her situation began to slide over Serena. Nikos intended her to stay here and bring up their child while he returned to Athens and continued with his life as normal. Was this her payment for the IVF funds? Disappointment crashed over her, destroying the small glimmer of hope she'd glimpsed this afternoon.

The villa was amazing—a gorgeous home—but she didn't want it. Not if the man she loved wouldn't be part of it. She didn't want the ruthless Nikos who'd met her on her return to Santorini. She wanted the man she'd fallen in love with three months ago—the man she'd seen again briefly this afternoon.

He'd shown a gentle side as he'd ensured his grandmother was well, but in such a subtle way that only someone who looked beyond the calculating businessman would see it. As he'd looked at his grandmother Serena had seen real affection. So how could he now be someone different, trying to push her to one side?

'It *is* something for me to worry about,' she said as she sat at the table beside the pool, her strength having ebbed faster than an outgoing tide.

All along she'd fought against the worry of their being forced together, as her parents had been, but after the week she'd spent in Athens she'd hoped her fears were unfounded. Despite his hard deal, all she wanted was for them to be happy together and maybe one day for him to come to love her. Now it appeared he had every intention of sending her to live here while he stayed in Athens. That wasn't going to happen. She might as well be in England, bringing up the baby alone, just as she'd originally planned. At least she'd be close to her sister.

'This is the perfect place to bring up a family.'

His voice startled her and she turned to see him looking out beyond the gardens into the darkness of the night.

'A family?' The question slid from her before she could stop it. He hadn't said a child, but a *family*.

'Yes—a family.'

His expression was set. He'd obviously made up his mind. But that didn't mean she could stay. Not now. His callous insistence that she become his wife in return for funds for Sally rushed back to her. How could she have pushed such emotional blackmail aside? *Because you've fallen deeper in love with him.*

The thought unnerved her and she stood up, restless and on edge.

She glanced at him and for a brief moment their eyes locked. His gaze was fierce with determination, but she knew hers would be soft and gentle, full of concern for her future and love for the man whose child she carried. She wanted to tell him she couldn't stay here alone, a banished wife, while he returned to Athens and continued with his life as if they didn't belong together. But as he walked towards her, his blue eyes darkening with hungry desire, each word dissolved from conscious thought, never making it into spoken words.

'You and the baby are my family now, and you will live here, with every luxury possible yours for the asking.'

He moved towards her, his long legs needing only two

or three strides to cover the distance, but the passionate intent in his eyes left her in no doubt that talking of such matters right now was not on his agenda.

'But what about your grandmother?' She sidestepped the issue as his arms wrapped around her, pulling her close, but what he'd just said had caused an uneasy feeling to settle over her. How could he expect her to live here, in such a beautiful place, when his grandmother had only her small and dated house?

She tried to resist the need to press herself against him, to feel the hardness of his body, determined he wouldn't sway her from her questions with kisses and heady glances. She couldn't let him seduce her again.

He smiled at her, almost hypnotising her with his blue eyes so full of desire and so incredibly sexy. 'My grandmother will be happy that you are living here.'

'But *she* should be living here—in this luxury.'

She couldn't help raising her voice a little. The injustice of the old lady living in such an old-fashioned house while he offered her this fabulous villa was too much. What kind of cold-hearted man was he? How could he build and move into this villa, leaving his grandmother in her little white house overlooking the sea?

'Do you always worry about everyone else?' His voice had deepened to a rough growl, but a trace of humour lingered there too.

Before she could answer his lips were on hers, insistent and powerful. Unable to resist, she gave in to what had been building between them all afternoon and met his kiss head-on with all her desire and love. What she felt for him was becoming too powerful to control, too intense to mask, but she was wary of letting him know. That solid wall, so impenetrable, was still firmly around him, and he showed no intention of letting her in.

She pushed those doubts to the back of her mind and gave herself up to his kisses. With a sigh of contentment she wrapped her arms about his neck, pulling herself ever closer, feeling the rising heat of his desire.

He broke the kiss, his face close to hers, and whispered, 'I love that about you.'

Serena blinked in disbelief. Those first two words had shocked her, and then the final words had slammed into her and what he'd *really* meant had finally registered. He wasn't telling her he loved *her*.

A weak smile played at her lips and an arrow of sorrow penetrated her heart. Would she ever hear real words of love from his lips? Words of love for her?

'It's not right,' she said, and looked about her, searching for anything to change the subject. She came back to his grandmother. 'Your grandmother's house is so *old*.'

He stepped back from her, but kept her hands in his. 'Do you really think I haven't tried to tell her that?'

Softness had entered his eyes, but still her doubts remained. A man who was capable of blackmail as a prelude to marriage was capable of anything.

'Her house is adorable, but so old, and all those steps...' Was he that heartless?

His hands let go of hers, and before she could register what he was doing he'd cupped the back of her head and moved against her, his lips lingering over hers.

'She wouldn't leave her "adorable" little house, as you put it. I built this as a surprise for her, but she is stubborn and she has lived in that house for many years. When she wouldn't leave it I employed young villagers to help her discreetly.'

Serena's heart skipped a little beat. The uneasy suspicion that this was to have been a home for a past lover was quashed. She smiled, looking deep into his blue eyes.

'Maybe you are not as ruthless as you like people to think.'

He frowned at her. 'Don't be fooled, Serena. I am nothing else.' A hard edge had crept into his voice. Was he aware that he'd just dropped his guard, even if only briefly?

The arrow of sorrow slipped deeper into her heart. That was a warning. He'd never love her.

'Have you *ever* loved?' The question inadvertently slipped out, and instantly she wished she could snatch it back.

His brows dropped into an irritated frown, almost hiding his eyes, now an icy blue, from her. 'No.'

His admission hurt. To hear it said aloud, when he kept whatever it was he felt for *her* tightly locked away, forced her eyes shut. She couldn't look at him but she was trapped by his hold, unable to step away physically or emotionally.

His free hand lifted her chin, his fingers warm against her skin, and her eyes snapped open to see his darkened and swirling with passion.

'Don't waste your time looking for love, Serena. Our marriage is only a deal—for the sake of the baby. My heir must be legitimate. Nothing else is important.'

She tried to keep herself focused. She'd gone along with his plans, pushed aside the bitter taste of accepting his offer of money for Sally. She'd believed her love would be enough for both of them. Now she knew for certain it would have to be.

She nodded.

His smile held a hint of relief, as if he'd expected her to demand more from him than he was prepared to give. His thumb caressed her lips and she closed her eyes against the pleasure just that simple touch evoked.

Be brave, Serena. Be brave.

The advice Sally had given her filtered through her

mind like water through limestone and she knew that was all she had left. Her love, her bravery and her sister's happiness.

'Let's just focus on us—on the moment right now.' She whispered the words, desperate not to think too much about the reality of what was happening and unaware that she'd voiced what was in her mind.

He pulled her roughly against him, pressing his lips to hers in a passionate and demanding kiss that she answered with every bit of love she felt for him. If she couldn't say the words she would show her love in other ways. Tonight, at least, she would be brave.

A flourish of husky Greek rushed from him as he broke the kiss. She had no idea what he was saying, but she imagined they were words of love and kissed him deeply, forcing him back a step. His hands skimmed down her body, over her hips to her thighs, making her sigh with pleasure. She pushed her fingers into his thick hair, gripping it tightly as urgency overtook her. Tonight she wanted to lead this erotic dance, to show him how it could be if only he'd let her in.

More Greek words were breathed out against her lips as one hand moved up her body to cup her breast, releasing a jolt of heady desire. She let her head fall back, sighing in pleasure as he kissed her throat. She arched towards him, supported by the strength of his arm, as his thumb and finger teased her nipple. Shockwaves of desire rushed through her.

'I think we should take this inside.'

His husky voice sounded far away as desire rushed around her, more consuming than she'd ever known it.

She lifted her head, bringing her face so close to his that she felt his breath warm on her face and the beat of his heart as it thumped in unison with hers. She couldn't speak, couldn't say a word. She was choked with emotion, so full of the most powerful need of him.

As if sensing this, he swept her from her feet, his strong arms holding her in a firm grasp. Every step he took as he marched purposefully back into the villa shuddered through her, increasing the desire which threatened to consume her completely.

'This is becoming a bit of a habit,' she said, keeping her voice light as they entered the villa and he made his way up the wide staircase into what could only be the master bedroom.

She slid from his hold and stood before him, the urgency of her need for him almost too much. Judging by the hard set of his face and his passion-darkened eyes, he was struggling with the same desire.

The need to show him that she too could be ruthless, could take what she wanted, was rushing over her so strongly she couldn't fight it any longer. She placed her palms on his chest, forcing him back until he had no option but to sit on the end of the bed. His eyebrows shot up as she continued her dominance, her legs astride his as she moved over him, her lips meeting his, demanding, fierce and brave.

His hands gripped her thighs, his fingers digging erotically into her flesh, and she moved against his erection, making him groan. The sound was snatched away by her kiss. She pushed her body forward, forcing him back against the white duvet, teasing him as she held herself above him.

The deep growl of words which rushed out between kisses sounded so passionate, so erotic, and all she wanted was for them to be loving words.

'This is what we have,' she whispered, surprised at how husky her voice had become. 'Passion and pleasure.'

His hands slipped under her dress and up her bare legs. She stilled in anticipation of his touch, and when it came she gasped with shocked pleasure. He stoked the fire of urgency ever higher, despite the barrier of her panties, and she almost fell apart just from that touch.

Quickly she moved away from him, tugging at the fastening of his jeans. His large hands covered hers, stilling their desperate fumbling, and his gaze locked with hers.

'Allow me,' he said sexily, his words so deep and accented they were barely discernible as English.

She slid away as he practically ripped the denim from his legs, throwing his jeans aside without a care. She glanced at the black hipsters that stretched tightly across him and raised her brows.

He laughed—a throaty sound that made a coil of lust unfurl at the very core of her.

'This is a new side to you. I like it.'

Before she could think of a response he pulled them off, lying back against the bed, his eyes daring her to take control again. She didn't need any more invitation. She loved him and she wanted to show him exactly how much—just once, at least.

Without a thought for anything other than this, she sat on him once more, pressing herself intimately against him, feeling his scorching heat against her. But still it wasn't enough. She wanted more—much more.

He reached up to her shoulders and dragged down the straps of her dress and bra in one move, exposing her breasts, her nipples hardened by desire. She arched towards him, sighing in pleasure as he lifted himself up, taking one nipple in his mouth. The sensation was so wild it was all she could do to support herself over him. As his tongue tortured first one nipple, then the other, he moved his hands quickly to her panties, tugging at them until the flimsy material ripped and she could feel his heated flesh against her.

His hands held her hips, keeping her over him. She'd never been in control of the moment. He'd just let her think that and now he was taking charge.

'Nikos…' she gasped as he lifted himself against her, sending a shudder of desire through her.

He dropped down against the bed, watching her intently. Her nipples were hard and damp, after he'd kissed them so passionately, and she moved over him, believing she was back in control. He guided her hips to exactly where he wanted them and thrust hard into her as wild urgency suddenly took them both.

She stifled a cry, causing him to stop for a moment, but she didn't dare open her eyes and look at him. She wanted to believe he loved her so much that he was consumed by the same fierce need that engulfed her.

'Don't stop,' she gasped as she moved against him, feeling his fingers grip her hips as a groan of pleasure left him.

The wildness which exploded within her was so powerful that she moved quickly against him, setting the pace and regaining the control she wanted.

'Serena…' he growled as he rained kisses over every part of her body he could.

She moved frantically, a need so wild pushing her to a dizzying height she'd never been to before. So high she was scared to let go. Each thrust he made into her pushed her higher still.

'Nikos!' she gasped, sitting up on him and throwing her head back. The sensation was so acute she could hardly think as he filled her, moving with her in this new and exciting erotic dance.

The whole world shattered around her and she heard

him shout out. But she had no idea what he said, and nor did she want to know. The sensation of falling to pieces didn't stop and her body shuddered with an ecstasy that overwhelmed her completely.

'Nikos, I love you…'

Nikos wrapped his arms around Serena as she fell against his chest. He couldn't believe he'd been so forceful with her. Each time they'd made love he'd been gentle—cautious, even. But her teasing had pushed him over the edge, driven him wild.

He'd let her think she was in control, that she was leading him, because he'd enjoyed it. But then it had all become too much, and now her heart was pounding so hard he could feel it.

As cooling air slipped over him he wondered if his heart had stopped beating all together. Then the words she'd gasped aloud, full of pleasure, finally registered.

I love you.

He could scarcely breathe, and as if she sensed the change in him she moved to sit on the edge of the bed, her green eyes wide and, if he wasn't mistaken, misting with tears. She didn't say anything else. Instead she waited for him.

A still calmness settled in him, pouring over the passion that had rushed through him moments ago. She couldn't love him. She *mustn't* love him. He didn't want her love. It would only end in disaster.

'I love you, Nikos,' she said again, in a tremulous whisper that pushed him further away than ever.

'*Love?*'

He was out of bed faster than he'd ever tumbled a woman into it and pulling on his jeans. Her horrified expression should hurt him, or at least make him feel guilty, but it didn't. He had to keep her at a distance—and not just for her sake.

That fact that he didn't feel any guilt proved he was incapable of loving anyone and completely unworthy of love. It backed up everything he'd felt—all the pain and anguish—from the day his mother had left. As a young boy he'd thought he was unlovable, and now, as a man, he certainly was.

'Yes, Nikos, *love.*'

Her voice was firmer now and her chin tilted defiantly as she straightened her dress, pulling the straps up to cover the body which had just given him such pleasure.

'You don't know what love is. You have no idea of its power to destroy, its ability to render a person helpless.'

He crossed the room and turned on the main light, hoping to instil some sense into their conversation—one that he really didn't want to be having.

'That's unfair.' She jumped up from the bed, her anger coming off her in waves.

'Serena, you've grown up in a safe family, experienced the lighter side of love.' That was something he had been denied the day his mother had walked away. His half-English mother. And now he was about to take an English wife. Would she too walk away? Deny her child love as he had been denied? Was that the reason for his doubts and reservations?

'You know *nothing* of my childhood, Nikos.'

She virtually hissed the words at him and he paused for a moment, frowning in concentration, trying to recall just what she had said about her family. The only thing he really knew was that her sister was desperate for a baby. That was the only reason she was here now. To help her sister.

'You're close enough to your sister to know how badly she wants a child, to have accepted my offer of help.'

Anger mixed with confused emotions was making his voice sharp, but she didn't flinch.

'I only said yes to marrying you because I was over-wrought with guilt. I had been accidentally given what Sally most wanted—the baby she'd been trying to conceive for years. How could I live with *that*?'

Those final words knocked the breath from his lungs, making them sting as he tried to take a breath in. Suspicious thoughts hammered into him and he fought the urge to walk away from the hurt and the pain.

'So the only reason you agreed to be my wife was to help your sister?'

'Yes,' she replied, in a tone that sounded as if she had no idea of the implications of what she was saying.

She'd never wanted to marry him, for them to bring their child up together. So why had she come to Greece? Why tell him the news personally?

'That was your plan all along, wasn't it?'

It was obvious he was second-best. Damn it, he didn't *want* to be second-best. Not ever again.

'I have no idea what you're talking about, Nikos. I didn't have a plan—except to tell the fisherman I thought you were that he was going to be a father. I didn't expect anything from him—not financially, anyway. But he'd lied.'

'So as soon as you discovered who I was you agreed to my proposal?'

He stood and watched her as she looked at him, her brow furrowing as she saw her future with him and all he could provide possibly slipping away.

'Are you serious?'

'Damn it, Serena, you've made a fool out of me. You've been working out how to get the best from this since we parted the night our child was conceived.'

'I have *not*. How can I have been so stupid? I believed things could work out between us. *You*, Nikos—you black-mailed me into staying, leaving me no option. I couldn't go back and flaunt my pregnancy in front of my sister, knowing I'd given up what is probably her last chance at being a mother. You have forced me into the worst pos-sible situation. But I can't do it any more.'

Before he could form a reply she'd marched from the room. She wouldn't be going anywhere now. It was nearly midnight and she didn't have a clue where she was. Maybe some cooling off time was best—for both of them.

Tomorrow they would draw up a plan for how to con-tinue. They would marry to legitimise the child and he would spend his time between London and Athens if it meant seeing his child grow up. And right now his child was all he cared about.

Serena sat in the darkened living room, the pale glow from the outside lights shining in through the windows the only light. If it had been daytime she would have gone—walked away without a backward glance. She was totally aware that her declaration of love had poured cold water over the desire that had been in every look Nikos had given her, every touch and definitely every kiss.

She had watched him get dressed and known that cold water had turned to icicles.

Now she sat alone and shuddered, despite the warm night air, thinking of that moment again. His ruthless streak was back in play—and it looked permanent.

Behind her she heard movement, but refused to turn and look. Finally Nikos's brooding silence snapped her willpower and she turned, bracing herself for his stormy mood.

'What do you want, Nikos?' She sighed as she spoke,

too weary for an argument, but she had to remain strong—just for a little while longer. Once she was home she could let the tears fall.

It hurt that he thought she had used the baby as a bargaining tool to get what she wanted from him when all along it was he who'd done that. First it had been his lies, and then his heartless demands for marriage and the terms attached. He'd known she had no alternative but to accept—he was that cruel. What had happened to him to make him like that?

He moved to stand in front of her, his tall and broad frame blocking the small amount of light and darkening everything. She looked up at him, saw the hardness he preferred everyone to see well and truly back on display.

'I want my child, Serena. You should not have come here expecting to strike a bargain with me. I will not make a deal for the right to be a father.'

Each word dripped with icy-cold disdain and her heart sank. All her dreams, every little bit of hope she'd had that her love would be enough for them both, slipped into oblivion. There wasn't hope any more…and there certainly had never been love.

'I found out too late that you were a powerful businessman—one with a ruthless heart—and I wish so hard I'd known sooner. If I had I would not have come. You lied from the moment we first met. I thought you were a different person. But he doesn't exist, does he, Nikos? He was just what you wanted me to see. He was just a way to seduce me.'

She looked up at him, her gaze meeting the frozen core of his eyes. She shivered, despite the humid heat of the night. He'd seduced her, lied to her, and now wanted to put terms on the life they'd created.

'You are a journalist. What was I supposed to do? Hand

you my life story and stand back and wait for it to be splurged around the globe?'

Arrogance poured from his voice and she looked harder at him, trying to see the man she'd thought she'd fallen in love with. But he was gone.

'A travel writer hardly constitutes a journalist. What are you so afraid of? Why are you hiding away?' She couldn't understand why he was so anxious about the press. Although they had been interested in them in Athens…true. 'A high-powered businessman like you must understand their interest—especially when you've just secured a big deal.'

His eyes narrowed and he inhaled deeply, his furious gaze never leaving hers. 'I am not afraid of anything. I simply prefer to keep my private life private.'

'You mean your mother?' Curiosity piqued, she pushed further than she would have done before. What did she have to lose? Nothing. She was leaving.

'By acknowledging my past I would be bringing my mother back into my life and I have no wish to do that— no matter how hard she tries.'

'Why do you want to shut her out of your life? She is your *mother*.'

'She gave up that right when she walked out.'

The fierceness of his words weren't lost on her, but she had no intention of engaging further in this discussion. All she wanted to do was leave. She'd tried to love him, tried to be what he needed, but she couldn't do it any more.

'I cannot stay here—not like this.' She gestured around her at the luxury of the villa, which must be staffed for him to have had it all lit up and ready for their arrival.

Indignation began to bubble up, bringing all her childhood insecurities with it. She looked at his brooding expression, her gaze locking with his, and wondered how she'd ever thought he was a gentle, loving fisherman.

His blue eyes almost froze, they were so glacial, and his jaw clenched, hardening the contours of his face until he looked as if he'd been chiselled from stone.

'There is one thing we need to get clear. You will not challenge my decisions.'

Each icy word hung in the air, freezing around them, reminding her of the kind of winter morning in England when her breath would linger in a white mist, suspended in the cold air.

Serena blinked hard a few times, trying to focus her gaze and see the real Nikos where he stood now, shrouded in the amber light from his villa's garden. The man she'd fallen in love with three months ago, given her heart and her virginity to, had never existed. Just as the man who'd filled her nights with such passion this past week didn't exist. This cold, ruthless man was the real Nikos.

She couldn't stay here—not just in the villa, or on the island, but in Greece. She would rather go home to England and face her family's disapproval and disappointment at her pregnancy than commit not only herself but her child to a life dominated by him. She hoped Sally would be behind her...that they could find another way to fund more IVF. Nikos couldn't be the only option. He just couldn't be.

She wanted to tell him she was leaving, but the words wouldn't come as he stepped towards her. His handsome face had softened slightly, giving her a tiny glimpse of the man she wanted him to be, and she had to remind herself it was just her imagination.

'You can live in London, if that pleases you, and still have the money you require for your sister. But you *will* become my wife.'

His hand reached out, his fingers stroking her cheek,

and she closed her eyes against the throb of desire which burst to life deep inside her.

'I can't, Nikos.' She opened her eyes as her voice whispered her inner turmoil. 'I can't live like that and I can't marry you.'

To accept those terms wouldn't be brave—it would be foolish. She'd be bringing her child up with the same insecurities and guilt that she'd had. Far better for one parent to raise their baby and love it completely than for it to realise one day that it was responsible for two unhappy lives.

'I don't want my child to be illegitimate. This is my heir.' His hand snapped back and he straightened, towering above her, dominating the very air she breathed.

'Our baby is not something to strike a deal over. I will not marry you, Nikos. I have made a big mistake and I am leaving—right now.'

CHAPTER ELEVEN

A SCORCH OF rage so intense it froze him to the spot hurtled through Nikos. She was leaving. Memories of the disappointment he'd felt as a young boy combined like thick syrup with the anger for his mother that he'd carried for most of his life. He'd loved his mother, just as any boy would, but the total devastation of being abandoned by the one woman who should never have turned her back on him had scarred him deeply. So deeply he'd never intended to commit himself emotionally to anyone.

But Serena had changed things.

The pain that gripped him now as he looked down at Serena was new and far more intense. He fought hard not to feel anything for her. But he couldn't stop whatever change she'd brought about. Already he knew there was a gap in his life just from thinking of her walking away. And it wasn't because she'd take with her his child, deprive him of being a proper father. There was something else too—something he just couldn't accept. Not now she was leaving.

'That is not what you agreed.'

The words were squeezed out between gritted teeth as he stood, rigid with anger, watching as she got up and walked towards him, her face imploring.

'I didn't agree to anything other than going to Athens with you.'

She stopped a little way from him, as if sensing that his anger would burn her as much as it consumed him.

'You wear my ring.'

He still couldn't move. Serena had walked away from him once because of his cold words, and now she was intent on doing it again.

'That doesn't mean anything, Nikos—not when it was given to me as part of the show you were putting on for your business acquaintances at the party. And let's not forget the press. All you wanted to do was avoid gossip and press speculation because of your takeover bid.'

She looked at the ring on her finger. Her hair, which glowed with fire beneath the golden lights, fell like a curtain on either side of her face, cutting him out. Despite the bitter anger which bubbled inside him he wanted to reach out, to push it back and tuck it behind her ear as he'd so often seen her do.

She shook her head and her hair shimmered, then she looked up at him, her expression open and pained. 'You can't even defend that, can you?'

'Why should I have to defend it?'

Something snapped and he finally moved—but not towards her. He marched away, into the open-plan kitchen, before turning to face her.

'Do whatever you have to do, Serena, but remember this. You will *never* keep me from my child.'

Her head shot up, her green eyes so wide and so dark. She flung her hands out in exasperation, palms up. 'You never wanted a child—you admitted that much. If you hadn't lied to me about who you were I would never have come back.'

'What do you mean, you would never have come back?'

'An astute businessman can hold his own, but a fisher-

man eking out a living is different.' Her eyes were fiercely
hot as she glared indignantly at him.

'Is it? A father is a father, no matter what he does.'

'Damn it, Nikos, I came back because I thought you
had a right to know—that even if you couldn't or didn't
want to be a proper father to my baby you would know
you had a child.'

She paused and he waited for the inevitable.

'It's not going to work. I can't live like this, Nikos. I
can't do it to my child—not when I know how it feels to
be the mistake that forced your parents together.'

The passion in her voice struck a chord in his heart,
touching something lying deep and dormant within him.
But it also angered him. She'd grown up with *two* parents.
How could she stand there and lay the blame on them because she wanted to leave now?

'The mistake?' He heard his voice rise and saw her
shoulders stiffen, as if to deflect the word. He wasn't the
only one hiding things.

'Yes, the mistake. My sister is eight years older than me,
and by the time she started school my parents' marriage
was already falling apart. They had even separated—not
that they ever told me. Sally and I talked about it as we
grew up. *She* became more like a mother to me.'

A pang of guilt plucked at him as he stood taking in
this information. 'But your mother didn't leave. She didn't
just turn and walk away.'

He couldn't help but make the comparison. At least
she'd had a family—the one thing he'd hungered after all
his life. His inability to love or be loved had always managed to destroy his chances of getting what he'd wanted.
He'd done it again this evening, when he'd brushed aside
those dreaded words of love.

'No, she didn't leave. But she made it abundantly clear

that she had only stayed with my father because of me. They had separated, and I was the result—or, as you would say, the *consequence* of an attempt at reconciliation. Because they stayed together, bound in an unhappy marriage, she blamed me for everything that was wrong in her life.'

'Wouldn't she have stayed for your sister too?' He tried to pour rational thought onto Serena's raw words—something he could never do for himself.

'Not when she was old enough to be sent away to school—which she wished they'd do. Instead my parents moved us and tried to make a new start. But it didn't work. It didn't change a thing. My father still saw other women, covering his tracks with ever more elaborate lies, and my mother still resented me—her mistake.'

The comparison didn't go unnoticed. 'And is my baby *your* mistake?'

She glared at him, waves of anger coming from her, and he knew the answer before she even said it. It was exactly as he felt. The baby they'd created that night hadn't been planned, but neither was it a mistake. He was prepared to do anything for it.

He didn't ever want his child to think it was a mistake. His lack of family as a boy made him want to give his child all he'd never had. Which was exactly what he'd intended to do as he'd stood there, anger simmering, the day he'd got that text from Serena.

'Coming back here has been my mistake.'

Who *was* this cold woman? Every last trace of warmth had left her and she stood like an ice queen, strong and determined before him.

'I don't want my child to grow up wearing the label of a mistake. I want it to be happy. But that will never happen because its parents will be constantly arguing. I've seen it all before, Nikos, and I won't do it to our child.'

He saw her hands gripping each other tightly, felt the heated anger of her explanation in every word.

She was right. They couldn't live together—not happily. He'd have to accept that being the part-time father of a happy child was the only and best solution.

'Very well. I shall make arrangements for you to return to England today.'

If she was planning to walk away from him then he'd make the arrangements for her. It would give him back control—make the decision his as much as hers.

She looked momentarily dazed. What had she expected him to do? Beg her to stay? He'd done that with his mother but she hadn't listened. Why should Serena be any different?

He hadn't even been able to call her name after their passionate night on the beach. He'd watched her walk away and despite the way she'd made him feel, the things she'd made him want, had remained steadfastly silent.

'Thank you.'

She pulled the engagement ring from her finger and walked towards the table, which had now been set for breakfast. She placed the ring on the polished wood.

'I have all my belongings with me. I don't need to go back to Athens for anything. If you'll excuse me? I want to shower and change.'

Her big green eyes held his and he saw her lips press together, hinting that she wasn't as strong as she wanted him to think. Then he looked at her dress, rumpled from their passionate tumble on the bed. Had that really happened? It seemed like days—weeks, even—since they'd been at his grandmother's and she'd laughed and smiled. It didn't seem possible that it had only been a short time ago that she was seducing him, tormenting him so wildly with her body.

Those three words, seemingly harmless, had done nothing more than suffocate what they'd shared since returning to Athens. It had all been an act of convenience—one to secure her sister's future along with her child's. She had gone too far when she'd said she loved him. And if that wasn't harsh enough she'd tried to back it up later—as if he would fall for such nonsense. It had been the last straw.

He watched her walk into the bedroom and clenched his hands into tight fists. He would not beg—not even to make arrangements for his child's future. He'd never beg for anything from a woman.

Serena closed the bedroom door, shutting out the black mood that had Nikos in its grip, and sat on the bed, totally shocked that just a short time ago they had been there, making love. Everything had been fine until she'd told him she loved him. She'd tried to be brave, tried to grasp love and hold it, hoping he would be infused by her love for him and help her to create a happy home for the baby. She had been wrong. So very wrong.

With a sigh she got up and slipped out of her dress and headed for the shower. It might be just superficial, but she had to wash Nikos away—scrub him from her skin as well as her mind. She had a baby to think about now, and whatever else happened she was determined her baby would grow up and never for one moment question if it had been a mistake that had altered her life.

Refreshed from the water, and dressed in loose-fitting trousers and a top for travelling, she emerged from the bedroom. Daylight caressed the horizon and Nikos was standing outside by the edge of the pool. Her heart constricted as she looked at him. The rigid set of his shoulders warned her there wouldn't be any last-minute admissions of need, let alone love. Nothing had changed. Nikos didn't need anyone and he certainly didn't want to love anyone.

He turned as if he'd sensed her. 'I have arranged for you to be on the first flight available to London.'

So this was it. It was really goodbye.

He didn't even seem concerned about what would happen once the baby was born, proving she'd been wrong to try and make things work. This past week had been all about control and power. *His* control and power.

'When?' The word was firm and sharp as she held on to her emotions, and if it made her sound cold and heartless then so much the better.

He looked at his watch, the movement snagging her attention. 'A taxi will be here any minute.'

She nodded her acceptance. The sooner they were apart the better.

'Serena…?'

He said her name as a question and turned to look at her just as the engine of the taxi could be heard on the other side of the garden wall.

Her heart pounded so hard she could hardly breathe. She willed him to speak, willed him to tell her to stay, to say that he'd realised he couldn't live without her, that he loved her. She wanted to go to him, to place her hand on his arm, to look into his eyes and whisper, *Yes, Nikos, what is it?*

'Your taxi.' The words cracked from him like shots from a gun. 'My solicitor will write to you about the baby.'

His solicitor? Had they moved to that level already? Well, two could play that game. She pulled her notepad from her bag and scribbled her address down, tore out the page and handed it to him.

For a moment he didn't move, just glared at her. Even the morning chorus of the birds quietened, as if they sensed the seriousness of the moment. Then he took the piece of paper and without looking at it folded it and put it in his pocket.

'Goodbye, Serena.'

She could hardly speak, the lump in her throat was so large, but somehow she managed to push two words out. Two strong words.

'Goodbye, Nikos.'

Every day for two weeks Nikos had sat at his desk trying to work, but that morning it hadn't been figures for his new company that had glared accusingly back at him but tabloid headlines—and they had opened up just about every door he'd hidden his past behind.

He'd kept a low profile since Serena had left. Their engagement had been so public, and he hadn't wanted the humiliation of seeing her absence commented on in the papers. He'd thought back to the brief conversation they'd had about his mother, just as he and Serena had arrived at his grandmother's house, recalling her surprise that she was half-English. Had that really been enough for her to dig a story up? To expose his humiliating past and of course their broken engagement?

As the sun had streamed in through his office windows he'd looked again at the words, and at the photo of a woman he barely remembered—his mother. Intermittently she'd tried to contact him, but he'd always ignored her, preferring to keep her in the past—something he could no longer do.

According to what he'd read, his mother blamed not only herself but his father for his unhappy childhood and she wanted to make amends. And he had a good idea just who'd given her the opportunity to put her words into the hands of the press.

Now, with the sky over London heavy and grey, he sat

in the back of one of the city's black cabs as it negotiated the early-evening traffic. The newspaper he'd looked at this morning in his office was rolled tightly in his hand and anger was making adrenalin flow through him.

Could Serena be responsible?

He recalled the moment she'd left, a vividly played out scene in his mind. She'd been distant and cold to the point of icy, making him wonder if the hot passion they'd shared only a short time before had been nothing more than an act—a smokescreen to hide her true motives behind.

He could still feel the edges of the emerald digging into his palm as he'd crushed her engagement ring in his hand after she'd calmly taken it off, leaving it on the table. It had all been a mistake—that was what she'd said. But he'd been deafened by the thud of his heart as fury had forced it to pump harder.

The taxi stopped and he looked up at the white town-house nestled in a quiet and affluent street. He'd never given a thought to where she lived, knowing only that he wanted it to be with him in Santorini, but this grand house was not what he'd expected and it only added to the notion that she'd sold his story.

He inhaled burning disappointment. He would have given her all he could. Hadn't he honoured his side of their deal, sending her sister ample funds for further IVF treatment?

'This is it?' he queried of the taxi driver, hoping that it wasn't.

'Yes. This is it.'

Nikos paid the fare and stepped out onto the pavement, still damp from earlier rain. He looked up at the building as the taxi pulled away. He clutched the newspaper tightly in one hand and climbed the steps towards the imposing black door of what must have once been a very majestic home but was now several flats.

Would she let him in? He stood debating what to do. Indecisiveness was a new experience. One he didn't like. He took in a deep breath and let it go, then pressed the buzzer for her flat.

'Hello?'

He hadn't prepared himself for his reaction when he heard her voice, and he certainly hadn't expected her to sound so tired and weary. Concern flooded him, overtaking the rage that had bubbled continuously on the flight from Greece. Surely the woman who'd whispered those words of love wouldn't want to ruin him?

But the doubts that had plagued him constantly, the erosion of his instinct to trust her and his initial reaction to the headlines surfaced once more. They blended with the taste of what might have been, if only she hadn't admitted her feelings to him. But could he believe those words of love she'd murmured at him? He wanted to.

'Serena, we need to talk.'

He had thought they needed to talk about the article, about the way she'd sold his past to the highest bidder. But all that got pushed aside just at hearing her voice as emotions he'd refused to acknowledge tumbled over him. Right at this moment he just needed to see her, to reassure himself she was well.

The door hummed, then clicked, and he pushed it open, disappointed that she hadn't said anything else. Not even an acknowledgement that it was him. Was he so easily dismissed from her life?

He took the stairs two at a time, following the signs for her flat's number. At the top of the stairs he saw her front door ajar, knocked, then walked in, closing it behind him and finding himself in a long hallway. As he walked down it, his shoes tapping on varnished wooden floorboards, she came from a door at the end of the hallway, light haloed around her, forcing him to stop.

The cream jumper and black skirt she wore couldn't disguise the bump of his baby. He hardly registered her frosty reception, unable to take his gaze from her—until he looked into her face. Her green eyes were unfriendly, and glittering like the emerald ring she had given him back.

'I expected correspondence from your solicitor,' she said, her voice firm and decisive. 'I didn't expect you.'

He walked towards her, trying to ignore the dark circles under her eyes and the powerful burst of lust that hurtled through him faster than the plane he had just been on. He had to remember the article—how she'd sold him for her own gains. It was what had prompted him to come here. Or was it?

'I am the father of your child—you can't just write me out of your existence.'

She glanced at the rolled paper he had firmly in his hand, then looked back at him before walking into the room she'd come from without saying a word.

He followed quickly, taking in a spacious room, half given over to a kitchen and dining area and half to a comfortable living space. Large sash windows let in the grey light of the afternoon. Shopping bags littered the floor and partially unpacked baby garments were laid out on the sofa. He looked at them. His child would wear those. Would he ever see it in them? Not if Serena had her way.

He looked back at Serena. She remained resolutely silent, but a blush was creeping over her pale face as she realised what he'd been looking at.

Serena's heart was pounding so hard she almost couldn't breathe, and she certainly couldn't say anything. Nikos looked again at the baby clothes she'd just begun to unpack after a day of shopping with her sister. Sally had been trying to lift her spirits, the whole sorry tale of her last visit to Greece having been splurged out amidst tears as soon as she'd returned from Santorini.

She had been unable to hide the truth of Nikos's deal from Sally, but still reeled at the shock of being told that Nikos had already sent money to her sister, with strict instructions not to tell her. She couldn't believe he'd done that—not after she'd backed out of their deal.

Was he here now to ask for it back? She'd never be able to pay it all—not now Sally had already used a considerable amount.

'I have come about this.' He unrolled the paper and handed it to her.

She took it from him, her fingers brushing his, sending a short-circuit of hot need rushing through her. She ignored it. She couldn't act on that any more. It was too painful.

'It's all in Greek. I have no idea what this is.'

She handed it back to him, still unsure what this was all about, but certain it had nothing to do with visiting or custody rights.

She watched as he walked to the table and smoothed the paper out, his large hands pressing it flat. The signet ring she'd only seen him wear as Nikos the businessman caught the light. She pushed away just how those hands had felt caressing her body and how much pleasure and passion they had evoked. It was too late to think back to those times now.

He straightened and looked at her. 'I told you my mother was half-English and you have come back here and dragged her out into the open and well and truly back into my life.'

'What?'

Of all the things she'd expected or hoped he might say

this was not it. She looked at the image of a woman who could only be Nikos's mother, judging by the blue eyes she'd passed on to her son. She remembered that moment outside his grandmother's house, when he'd told her his mother was half-English. The dismissive way he'd spoken of her suggested that there wasn't an ounce of love between them.

'You calmly walked away from me because you had found something better—my story to sell to the highest bidder.' He stood resolutely with his back to the window, his arms folded and the crumpled newspaper spread out between them on the table. 'You came to Greece looking for whatever you could so that you could return to England and raise my child.'

'That's not true!' She gasped the words at him, shaking her head in denial.

'You said you wanted to tell me face-to-face, that you didn't want anything else from me—but you did.' His accent had deepened and his voice had become gruff with pent-up anger.

She rubbed the pads of her fingers across her eyes, forgetting the make-up she'd applied that morning, for the first time since she'd returned from Greece. She let her hand fall to her stomach. The movement snagged his attention and his expression changed to a glower.

'I'm sorry, Nikos, but you are going to have to explain this. I have no idea what you are referring to.'

She needed to sit. Her legs felt weak and the temptation to pull out a chair was great. But with his dominating presence filling her flat she had to remain standing.

'You were looking for an alternative to marrying me ever since you arrived back on the island. You made up a story about your sister, goading me into making a deal, then accepted my offer of marriage not because you wanted to bring up the child with me but because you didn't have a better option. But as soon as a hint of scandal presented itself as something that would give you a big payout, you left.'

'That's not how it happened at all. How can you *think* such a thing?' She stood and blinked against the anger of his outburst, even knowing that some of it was true.

He pointed to the paper. 'These are *your* words, Serena. *"Nikos and I met several months ago, in Santorini."*'

Involuntarily she moved towards him, sensing the pain behind his anger. He moved to pace across the room like a caged animal and she dragged out a chair, not able to stand any longer.

'I shouldn't have said anything about my sister, but that wasn't the reason I said yes to you.'

'Why *did* you say yes, Serena?' He folded his arms across his chest, looking more territorial by the minute.

What should she say? Should she tell him it was because she'd loved him? No, she couldn't do that—not after his reaction to those words two weeks ago.

'I hoped we could make it work—for the baby's sake. I didn't want to be a single parent, Nikos. And I felt guilty for having what Sally most wanted. All I knew was that I couldn't let my child grow up with the same guilt I had known as a girl.' She heard the passion in her voice, saw his questioning expression, but continued. 'I am obviously not your first choice for mother of your baby, because I'm English, but whatever has happened between you and your mother I have not breathed a word of it to anyone. Why *would* I?'

'Why would you?' He repeated her question and moved towards the table, pulling out the other chair and sitting down.

His knee touched hers and fire leapt within her. 'What could I gain—even if I knew what the story was?'

'A big payment, to start with.'

She gasped in surprise. How could he think that of her? 'You think I've used my contacts to dig this up?' She pushed the paper away from her, hurt at his accusation.

'I told you'd I'd support you—this wasn't needed.'

He placed his hand on the newspaper, the movement bringing him closer to her, and she fought hard not to inhale the heady masculine scent that was Nikos.

'I haven't written this, and I haven't had anything to do with it—but I will use my contacts to prove that if you can't take my word. The only piece I've written that is remotely connected with you is about holidaying in Santorini… about the restaurants and the sights.'

She pointed to the printed copy of her article on her small desk, awaiting a final reading before being submitted. He looked at it, then straight back at her, and she saw his guard slip, saw the pain in his eyes. Pain carried through childhood—the kind she too knew about.

He glared at the newspaper, a deep and heavy scowl on his face. Then realisation hit her hard. She *had* spoken to one person—and said those exact words.

'I *did* say that to someone…' she whispered softly.

He looked at her slowly, disappointment washing over his face. 'Who?'

'At the party—I said that to Christos.'

Suspicion filled her mind. Could *he* be the source of this story?

She put her hand over his as it lay on the paper and, emboldened when he didn't withdraw it, asked quietly, 'What happened, Nikos? Please tell me?'

'As far I am concerned it's in the past—and that's where it should stay.'

He pulled his hand back and she felt the moment being lost—especially when he got up and walked to the window and stood looking out at the street.

She moved quietly and walked over to him, leaning against the other side of the window. His profile was set in firm lines and everything about his stance was defensive.

'I need to know, Nikos. Whoever sold this story, and whatever the outcome for us, that woman is your mother— your child's grandmother.'

He looked at her, and she inhaled deeply as she saw the naked emotions in his eyes.

'When I was six she told me she was going away, that she didn't love my father—or me. She told me I was unlovable.'

Serena's heart filled with pity for the little boy she imagined him as. How could any woman leave her young son? No wonder he'd been so angry, so against fatherhood. She looked deep into his eyes, offering comfort with hers but not saying anything.

Nikos was numb. He didn't see the tall white houses on the opposite side of the street. That image was replaced by the sea and the empty horizon on Santorini as he'd stood and waited each day in the hope that the next boat in to the island would have his mother on it—that she would return saying she'd made a mistake and of course she loved him.

'If my father had loved her more she would never have left.'

He felt Serena touch his arm, her hand warm through his suit jacket, but it wasn't enough to pull him from the past. Even the question of who had exposed the story wasn't important now. All he could see was his mother walking away. All he could feel was the agony of knowing he wasn't loved.

'Sometimes it's better if parents *don't* stay together. Maybe that's what happened with your parents.'

He looked at her, remembering all she'd told him about her childhood. How she felt she was the mistake that had forced her parents to stay together. Was *he* the mistake that had forced his apart?

'I have never seen her since.' The admission made him press his jaw firmly together. It was the first time he'd wanted to talk about her for a very long time. 'I gave up wishing she'd come back for me. Accepted she didn't love me.'

'Nikos…'

She breathed his name and he finally looked at her. Those big green eyes were filling with undisguised tears and he wanted to kiss her, to feel her lips on his, bringing him to life once more with her love. A love he'd rejected. A love he didn't deserve.

He moved away from her—away from temptation— and as he did so saw again the baby clothes neatly laid out on the sofa. Not only did he not deserve Serena's love, he didn't deserve his child's love either.

'I wanted to be a better father to my child.'

He spoke harshly, glad of the anger that filled him as he thought of how cold and distant his own father had been and how Serena's walking away had deprived him of that chance to right the past.

'And you will be—once we sort things out between us. I may not be able to pay you back the money you gave my sister, but I will never stop you seeing your baby grow up, Nikos. It will be difficult, given that I'm here in London and you are in Greece, but we have to make it work.'

He turned and looked at her. The firm tone of her voice brooked no argument. He knew there and then that his being there wasn't serving any purpose. If anything it was making things worse.

She hadn't written that article, or instigated it in any way. Christos had betrayed him, exploiting his weakness for all to see. Deep down he'd known Serena wasn't behind it, but he had used the excuse of confronting her to fly to London. He'd needed to see her, to hear her voice.

He didn't understand this burning need. Lust and passion were involved—and, yes, she was having his baby—but it was more than that. It was so much more than he deserved.

'I want the baby to have my name.'

When she'd left the bedroom after their last night of passion he'd decided that they would have to marry, no matter where they lived, and that still stood. His child must legitimately have his name.

'That can be arranged,' she said with a hint of suspicion in her voice. 'You can be named on the birth certificate as the father.'

'That's not enough,' he said, and found himself moving towards her.

He wanted to touch her, to place his hand over his baby. Then he paused, remembering what his grandmother had said to Serena. He'd been distracted with lunch preparations that day, but he could still hear himself translating what she'd said.

You hold the key.

At the time he'd put it down to the ramblings of an elderly lady, but now he wasn't so sure. *Was* the baby they'd created the key? And, if so, to what? Had she meant the key to being able to lay his ghosts to rest, to being the kind of father he'd wanted to have?

It was then that he knew. His grandmother believed the baby was the key to burying his past—but he could only do that if he married Serena and if they lived as a family. The happy, loving family he'd never had.

'There isn't any other way to do it.'

She looked imploringly at him and her words dragged him back to the present. She was wrong. There was one thing they could do.

'There is if you marry me and return to Greece.'

CHAPTER TWELVE

IT WAS AS if the floor had opened up and swallowed her. To have Nikos in her home was unexpected, but for him to accuse her first of selling his story, then all but demand she go back and marry him, was beyond comprehension. Was this his way of collecting her debt?

For a moment, when he'd spoken of his childhood, she'd almost gone to him, almost put her arms around him and given in to the need to hold him close. But those last words had cooled the burning need.

She'd tried to love him, but he had pushed her away, locked her out. She had wanted them to be a couple, but it hadn't worked. Neither would getting married because of the baby. She was convinced they would be exactly the same as her parents had been. Unhappy.

'No, Nikos. We have already proved that's a bad idea.'

She shook her head in denial as he moved closer to her, looming over her, his height making her feel intimidated, as it had the night she'd first returned to Santorini. He would make a formidable adversary in the boardroom, of that she was sure, but here in her home she wouldn't be dominated.

'Is that so?'

'You know it is.' The answer came out in a strangled whisper as she tried to hold on to her senses, even as the fresh scent of his aftershave invaded every nerve cell in her body.

How had they come so far from that week of romance they'd spent in Athens? The emerald ring he'd given her hadn't changed anything—probably because he hadn't given it out of love, as the assistant had thought. She lowered her gaze, not wanting to look into his, not wanting to see those blue eyes darken and warm with passion. The husky note in his voice was one she'd come to know, one she loved, and one that would spell disaster if she responded now.

He reached for her face, his fingers briefly touching her chin. He wanted her to look up at him. She ducked out of his way and moved into the living room, quickly collecting up the baby clothes she'd bought that afternoon. Those few hours of shopping with Sally seemed as if they had happened weeks ago, but Sally's admission over her secret IVF funds still felt painfully raw.

'Please, Nikos, you should go. There is nothing we can say to one another that hasn't already been said.'

Her heart ached as if it was breaking in two. This was the man she loved completely and utterly, the man whose baby she carried, and yet they couldn't be together. His ideals and expectations meant they'd be a carbon copy of her parents. She couldn't do it—not to herself or the baby. She wanted to be happy and loved.

'I haven't said all I need to,' he said as he walked towards her, his eyes penetrating hers.

She swallowed hard as he towered over her, determined she wasn't going to move away again. It was time to face up to him—and to the fact that he didn't love her.

'You made it clear as I left the villa that you had nothing more to say to me. Now you turn up here and accuse me of selling your story. One I know nothing about.'

'I'm sorry,' he said and her gaze flew to his at this uncharacteristic admission.

'Have you ever had any contact with your mother since?'

Suddenly she had to know the whole story. She had to know *his* story—not the one in the paper that Christos had told. She thought of the words his grandmother had said about her having the key. Had the old lady meant that their baby would be the key to healing his past? Surely *she* hadn't known his mother's story would hit the headlines.

'She tried to contact me when my father died, and several times since, but…' He paused and looked at her, the expression in his eyes far away, wrapped in past hurt.

'But what, Nikos?' she asked, gently touching his face with her hand, feeling the sharpness of stubble that was also out of character.

It tore her apart to see him like this. She'd do anything she could to make it right for him, but agreeing to marry him wouldn't work. Whatever was haunting him needed to be brought out into the open, and it was something she needed to do before she moved on to being a mother.

'I couldn't let her back into my life. She walked out on me when I was a child—a young boy.'

She heard the pain in his words, felt it transferred to her through the fingers that touched his face. A touch he seemed oblivious to.

'She didn't come to your father's funeral?'

The movement was hardly visible, but he shook his head.

'They should never have got married. They didn't belong together. I remember soon after she'd gone my father caught a butterfly, held it tight in his cupped hands, and told me my mother was like a butterfly.'

Serena frowned, not knowing what he was saying, but an image of the brightly coloured creature contained in large manly hands sprang to her mind. 'What did he mean?' she whispered, unsure of the relevance this had.

'He said we had to let it go or it would die.' The stark and matter-of-fact words sounded numb, devoid of any emotion.

Inside her she wept tears for the boy who had been forced to grow up without his mother, but she wondered if that had been what his mother had really wanted. Could a mother *really* walk away from her child so coldly?

Before she could say anything else Nikos continued as if he had never expected her to respond.

'That's the last time I remember my father being a man I looked up to. He began to drink heavily, became someone to avoid at all costs. That's when I went to live with my grandparents. I was eight years old.'

Suddenly he looked down at her, his eyes searching hers, and then his gaze dropped further, to the small white baby vest she held. Tension filled the air and she held her breath as he took it from her, his hands so big and tanned against the little garment. He pressed it against the palm of one hand and she bit hard into her lip and looked at his bent head, at the thick, dark, almost tamed curls she'd plunged her fingers into in the throes of passion. He was making everything so much harder.

'Nikos.' He looked up at her and as his eyes met hers again she took the vest from him. 'Don't do this.'

'Do what?' he said hoarsely.

'Make it harder.' She heard the catch in her voice and moved away from him, dropping the vest onto the pile, unable to deal with the flood of love and despair that ravaged her heart.

'I will not walk away from my son, Serena.' His eyes

glittered with determination and his voice reverberated with outrage. 'I can't.'

'You don't know it will be a boy.' She frowned at his insistence that the baby was a boy.

'No,' he said curtly, the firmness she'd come to expect in his voice back, and then he looked at her.

His defensive wall was in place once more. If only it had stayed down long enough for her to cross—long enough for her to slip through and show him what love could be like.

But that was impossible. He didn't let anyone close. She knew that now.

Nikos fought hard to push down the rampage of emotions holding that tiny scrap of material had unleashed. It weakened him—weakened his resolve.

As he'd left Athens he'd kept telling himself he was only coming to see her about the newspaper article. Now he knew that had never been true. If he was honest, he'd wanted to see Serena, to ask her to reconsider, even as the plane had soared above the blue waters of the sea heading for London.

He hadn't acknowledged it then, but he was now prepared to do and say whatever was needed to win her back. She was the mother of his child and he wanted her in his life.

'I *will* be a father to my child—a full-time father.' He couldn't let his son—or daughter—grow up without him. He wanted to give his child what he'd never had: a family home.

Images of that butterfly all those years ago, as it fluttered its wings and flew away, became vividly clear. Was it the same for Serena? He'd bullied her into agreeing to marriage, exactly as his father had his mother—something he hadn't known of until he'd read the article. He should let her go—but he couldn't.

She shook her head. 'I can't do that, Nikos. I can't risk our baby growing up thinking it is the mistake that keeps us together. I want our child to be happy and loved. *I* want to be happy and loved too.'

He heard the pain in her words and suddenly the puzzle of what his grandmother had meant hit him. The baby *was* the key—but not to his past. It was the key to happiness, and more importantly to love, because he would love his baby unconditionally. His grandmother had known that— but she'd also known, in her wise and old-fashioned way, something he hadn't admitted.

He loved Serena.

Everything slid into place, as if a key was being turned in a rusty old lock, opening a door that had been closed for many years. Finally he could admit what had been there since the day he'd met Serena. It had been there since the first moment he'd looked into her beautiful green eyes.

Love.

'Sometimes you have to take risks in life,' he said softly as he took her hand, his fingers caressing where the emerald ring should be. He wished he'd brought it with him. He wanted to give it back to her, this time with love.

He was taking a risk—a risk he'd never taken since he was six years old. He was going to hold on to what he wanted—fight for it if he had to. He wasn't going to lose her now. Serena was his. They belonged together.

The fury that sprang from her took him by surprise.

'You have done nothing but deceive me since we first met, and now you come here and accuse me of selling stories about you. So give me one good reason why I should believe anything you say.'

He wanted to tell her how he felt, that he loved her, but the words froze on his tongue. The urge to reach for her and take her in his arms was overpowering. He wanted to kiss her and hold her tight, but he deserved her anger, deserved the pain that struck through him at the thought of life without her.

He had lied, concealing his identity not for malicious reasons but because for the first time since he was a teenager he was being liked simply for who he was—not what he had or could give.

'When we first met you were like a breath of fresh air—a woman who was interested in me for me alone. You didn't see the wealth of my business, my success or the way I lived, you just saw *me*.'

Finally he could speak, but he still couldn't tell her what he needed to—the very thing that could change her mind about marrying him. He couldn't believe it was so hard to say the words, but he'd never used them, and the thought of doing so left him emotionally exposed and vulnerable. Love had only ever caused him pain.

'I didn't see any of that because you didn't *let* me—you covered it up. You lied, and that hurts, Nikos.'

Her sharp words felt like an attack, and before he could respond she continued.

'Did I *look* like a journalist—one who would sell your story to the highest bidder? It wasn't as if I introduced myself as such when we first spoke.'

'Damn it, Serena.' He crossed the room and took the paper from her, tossing it savagely onto the table. 'I didn't tell you who I was because there was no need.'

'No. A few weeks of seduction was all you'd ever planned. But then what you'd most dreaded happened. *Consequences*. Something neither of us wanted. A mistake—one that hurts so much.'

Her voice was a mixture of anger and frustration, and he heard the wobble beneath its firmness and guilt slashed at him.

He recalled what she'd said about her childhood, about the guilt she'd carried, and finally understood her reluctance to marry him purely for convenience. He cursed himself for not seeing it sooner. But *would* he have seen it? He'd stubbornly refused to accept what he felt for Serena. He hadn't been able to admit that the aching emptiness inside him when she'd left after the passionate night on the beach was love.

The first moment their eyes had met, as he'd been maintaining his nets, something had happened. Now he knew what it was.

He stood and faced her, vulnerability prickling all over his skin, as if a chill wind had entered the flat. There wasn't the adrenalin rush he experienced in board meetings, or the ecstatic thrill of landing a good catch, there was only complete emotional exposure. Everything he felt was there for her to see in his eyes—if only she looked.

'Serena, our baby will *never* be a mistake. He or she will *not* grow up laden with guilt as you did, watching your parents quarrel with each other. It will grow up with two loving parents.'

She closed her eyes as she stood before him, as if trying to banish the image of the memories his words provoked. Slowly and with tentative fingers he brushed her hair back from her face. He heard her breath catch and knew she was far from immune to him. It lit the torch of hope and he pushed on.

'You know what that's like—I understand now.' He lifted her chin with his thumb and finger, willing her to open her eyes. 'Serena…?'

'That's why marriage just wouldn't work,' she said, in

a firm whisper that echoed with a strength he was far from feeling.

'I know your pain, Serena. I know what it's like to be a child who constantly waits for its parents to realise it exists, to want to be a family. You don't trust me, and for that I'm sorry, but I don't want my child to wonder where I am, why I am never there.'

Her green eyes widened, frantically searching his face, then she shook her head, her shoulders dropping in defeat. 'I'm sorry, Nikos, I can't pass on that guilt to my baby. Surely we can love our child even if we are apart?'

'But we can't love each other if we are apart.'

He let the words fall between them, staggered by the heavy thump of his heart as the silence grew more intense. He saw her swallow hard, saw the movement of the creamy softness of her throat where he'd kissed her so often.

'I've been a fool, Serena, a stubborn fool—and I've hurt you so much. *You* are my butterfly, but I can't let you go.' Inwardly he cursed. Why couldn't he just tell her he loved her instead of dancing around the issue?

'It's too late, Nikos. I tried to love you, hoping it would be enough, but it never will be. You threw my love back at me. Now it's gone.'

Her fingers closed around his, pulling his hand away from her face, and he looked down at his hand, partly covered by her small one. It couldn't be too late—it just couldn't. He wouldn't accept that. Not now he'd finally opened his heart to love—*her* love.

As the panic of losing her raced through him she let go of his hand and walked away towards the front door of her flat. She wanted him to go. He followed her to the door, but knew he couldn't do that until he'd told her. If he didn't say it now he would have no alternative but to walk away and remain silent for ever.

Her fingers reached for the lock, but he took her hand, holding it tightly in both of his, then took a deep breath as confusion raced across her face. Finally he managed to form the words that could change his life, chase the demons of the past away and bring him happiness.

'I love you, Serena.'

Serena heard her breath dragged in as the words she'd longed to hear rushed from his lips. She looked at his face. His blue eyes, usually so vibrant and alive, were subdued, veiled with what looked like pain.

'No...' she whispered, and tried to pull her hand free, but he held it firmly.

How could he expect her to believe him now, when he'd proved he would do anything he had to to get what he wanted? She had to remember the deal he'd so coldly laid before her.

'It's too late.'

'Too late?'

His deep voice rumbled around the narrow hallway, his proximity making her light-headed. Why couldn't he just leave? Then she could crawl into her bed and cry her heart out all night. Tomorrow would be a fresh start, the beginning of her life without Nikos.

'Too late for what?'

'Why have you waited until now to tell me?' She surprised herself with the forthright and businesslike tone of her words and lifted her chin, determined to show a fighting spirit she was far from feeling.

He frowned, and before he could answer she did it for him. 'Because you will do anything to get what you want. You lied to me once, Nikos, I won't fall for it again. I don't love you. I can't love a man with such a ruthless and closed heart.'

'You have changed that, Serena. My grandmother saw it even when I hadn't.' He kept her hand firmly in his and moved towards her, forcing her back against the wall of the hallway. 'She saw what I had been trying to ignore—that I was in love with you.'

She lowered her gaze, refusing to look into his eyes, refusing to be drawn in yet again. 'That doesn't matter—it's still too late. I don't love you.'

Each word was a painful lie. She *did* love him, but she didn't dare admit it now. She couldn't have it tossed back at her again.

'I don't believe you.'

She looked up at him, the firmness of his voice forcing her to look into those gorgeous eyes once more. As she did so he lowered his head and kissed her, the light touch of his lips so teasing and tantalising that despite all her efforts a sigh of pleasure escaped her.

This was what she'd wanted all along. Declarations of love and sweet kisses. But were they for real?

'I love you,' he whispered, and his hands let hers go, holding her face as he kissed her again, so tenderly, so gently, she closed her eyes to the pleasure of it. 'I won't accept that it's too late. I can't. Not when I love you so much. I can't let you go, Serena.'

She pulled away from him, her breath ragged with desire and threatening tears. She leant against the wall, her heart beating rapidly with a confused mix of elation and disbelief. *Did* he love her? Or was he just saying what he thought she needed to hear? Could she take one last risk? Could she be brave just once more?

'Don't you understand?'

He smoothed his thumb over her cheek, releasing a rush of need she had to close her eyes against. As tears threatened she inwardly cursed her emotions, all awry—and not just because of the baby.

'No, I don't, Nikos,' she said, and she looked up at him.

She'd known she loved him before she'd left Santorini the first time. She'd known it as she'd arrived to tell him he was going to be a father. But she didn't know if she could risk her heart once more.

'I couldn't let myself love you. I was afraid.' His voice was a harsh whisper, the effort of saying it aloud all too clear.

She blinked in shock. Nikos? Afraid? How could a man as powerful and in control as him be afraid—of *love*?

Before she could voice her question he answered it for her. 'I watched my mother walk away. It tore me apart. As a young boy I resolved never to put myself in that position again. I chose never to love anyone.'

'You have never loved *anyone*?' Had he been alone all his adult life? Was that why he had an almost endless string of women he dated, never settling with any of them for long?

'Each time I met a woman I would remind myself of how it had felt to watch the one person I loved walk away. I wasn't going to make the same mistake again.'

'And if I'm a mistake...?' She let the question linger even as her hopes rose higher.

'You could never be a mistake,' he said softly, and he reached out and caressed her cheek, smashing down the last of her doubts.

'I don't want to get it wrong, Nikos.'

'Then marry me. Let me spend the rest of my life showing you we belong together.'

His blue eyes were dark and demanding as he looked into hers and she felt her resistance slipping away to nothing.

He loved her. He wanted to marry her. And that would banish not only her childhood pain but his too, because she had never stopped loving him.

Still doubt lingered. 'But what if…?'

She didn't finish the sentence—didn't manage to ask him what would happen if things went wrong between them as they'd already proved they could. He kissed her deeply, setting free the desire for him which still slumbered within her so that she couldn't help but wrap her arms around him, pulling herself close, inhaling his heady scent.

'Don't fight me,' he said, and pulled back from her, his warm breath caressing her lips as his stayed unbearably close. 'I love you, Serena. Please say it's not too late.'

'It's not,' she whispered, unaware she was trembling in his arms. 'I love you, Nikos, and always have.'

His sigh of relief made her smile, lightening the mood. 'You have the key—that's what my grandmother said. Do you remember?'

'Yes,' she said softly, smiling shyly at him. That afternoon was etched in her mind, and she'd been wondering ever since what the old lady had meant.

'You don't have the key, Serena,' he said as he kissed her gently on the lips, making her tremble even more.

'I don't?'

'No. You *are* the key. The key to my heart and to my love.'

EPILOGUE

'I CAN'T BELIEVE Sally is finally coming here to Santorini.' Serena couldn't keep the excitement from her voice as she looked up at Nikos.

He put down the paper he'd been reading whilst sitting in the shade, keeping a watchful eye on his sleeping young son. After satisfying himself that Yannis was still asleep he walked over to her, his sexy laugh sending a spark of pleasure all through her. It intensified when he put his arm around her, pressing his lips gently against her hair.

'It will be our first family occasion here at the villa. A chance for Yannis to meet his cousins.'

Nikos glanced across at their son and Serena's heart filled with love and happiness.

'I just hope her flight was okay…' She couldn't quite keep the anxiety from her voice.

'Sally has twins—and, knowing what it's like to travel with *one* baby, I would imagine flying with two is difficult. I did ensure extra staff were on board to help with the babies.'

'I can never thank you enough for giving her the chance of motherhood, despite the fact that I left.'

'I did it for *you*, Serena, to make you happy—and because I'm a man who honours his promises,' he said gently, looking down at her, his expression filled with love.

She loved how understanding Nikos could be. As soon as Sally had told them she was expecting twins he'd done everything possible to enable them to marry in England, so that Sally didn't have to fly to Greece. His grandmother had been disappointed, but a lavish blessing on the island on their return had soon made amends.

Serena couldn't possibly love him more for everything he'd done—not just for making Sally's wish come true, but her own. She loved everything about him, and often silently thanked Christos for contacting the newspapers when he had, even if it had been with malicious intent. If he had not Nikos might never have confronted his past, nor even come to London.

She wondered again if the headlines created by his mother to tell her own story, bringing Nikos's past so harshly into the open, had been her way of trying to make amends. She'd counteracted the attack Christos had launched and put her life under the microscope of the press, admitting that what she'd told Nikos had been an attempt to stop him looking for her, or waiting and pining.

'You should have invited your mother to the christening.'

She looked at him reproachfully but he shook his head, still not yet able to come to terms with all he'd found out about his parents' marriage.

'It's early days, and we both agreed that a big family celebration wouldn't be the best time for her to meet everyone.'

'I think it *would* be the best time. If christening a baby isn't a day for letting go of the past and moving forward, I don't know what is.'

She smiled at him as he stroked her face, his love for her shining from the blue depths of his eyes.

'I understand that she wants the past forgotten, especially now it's come out just how cruel my father was to her.'

A shadow of regret chased across his face and she knew he was thinking of the revelations about his parents' short marriage.

'You can't punish yourself for ever, Nikos. You were a young boy. How were you to know the truth? Besides, your grandmother wants her back in the family.'

'You and my grandmother are conspiring against me, I see.' A hint of amusement lingered in his voice.

Serena laughed. 'Would I do such a thing?'

'Yes, you would.'

He made a show of annoyance, but Serena was too excited about the arrival of her family for the christening—including her parents, who were, amazingly, travelling together—to let anything spoil it.

'Okay, you get your way. She didn't see our wedding or the blessing, so I *will* ask her to come to the christening.'

'You could both fly back from Athens together after your meeting tomorrow.' She dropped the suggestion lightly as she took a sip of her iced water, pretending not to notice the suspicion narrowing his eyes.

'We could...yes.'

Nikos looked reproachfully at his wife, but she just laughed, and he fought the urge to silence her with a kiss. He thought of the long, painful talks he'd had with his mother, which had revealed that whilst she hadn't wanted to remain married to his father she'd never wanted to leave her son. At first he hadn't been able to understand why she hadn't tried to mend the marriage, but then all the sorry truth had come out and bit by bit he had learned to forgive her.

Now he just needed to let go of the past once and for all. He was married to a woman he adored, and loved with all his heart, and he had the most beautiful son. He had everything he'd thought impossible.

'It would make us complete—the family, I mean,' she said wistfully. 'Grandparents on each side for Yannis, and even a wonderful great-grandmother.'

'I love you, Serena.' He kissed her passionately as she looked up at him. 'And if it makes you happy I will insist she comes.'

'Being with the man I love makes me happy.'

He held her against him, his life complete, and knew he wouldn't change a thing.

* * * * *

LARENZO'S
CHRISTMAS BABY

KATE HEWITT

CHAPTER ONE

THE SOUND OF the car door slamming echoed through the still night. Emma Leighton looked up from the book she'd been reading in surprise; as housekeeper of Larenzo Cavelli's isolated retreat in the mountains of Sicily, she hadn't been expecting anyone. Larenzo was in Rome on business, and no one came to the villa perched high above Sicily's dusty hill towns and villages. Her employer liked his privacy.

She heard brisk footsteps on the stone path that led to the villa's front door, an enormous thing of solid oak banded with iron. She tensed, waiting for a knock; the villa had an elaborate security system with a numbered code that was only known by her and Larenzo, and the door was locked, as Larenzo always insisted.

She held her breath as she heard the creak of the door opening and then the beep of buttons being pressed, followed by a longer beeping indicating the security system had been deactivated. As her heart did a queasy little flip, Emma tossed her book aside and rose from her chair. Larenzo never came back early or unexpectedly. He always texted her, to make sure she had everything ready for his arrival: his bed made with freshly ironed sheets, the fridge stocked, the pool heated. But if it *wasn't* him…who was it?

She heard footsteps coming closer, a heavy, deliberate tread, and then a figure, tall and rangy, appeared in the doorway.

'*Larenzo—*' Emma pressed one hand to her chest as she let out a shaky laugh of relief. 'You scared me. I wasn't expecting you.'

'I wasn't expecting to come here.' He stepped into the spacious sitting room of the villa, and as the lamplight washed over his face Emma sucked in a shocked breath. Larenzo's skin looked grey, and there were deep shadows under his eyes. His hair was rumpled, as if he'd driven his hand through the ink-dark strands.

'Are you—are you all right?'

His mouth twisted in a grim smile. 'Why, do I not look all right?'

'No, not really.' She tried to lighten her words with a smile, but she really was alarmed. In the nine months she'd been Larenzo's housekeeper, she'd never seen him look like this, not just tired or haggard, but as if the life force that was so much a part of who he was, that restless, rangy energy and charisma, had drained away.

'Are you ill?' she asked. 'I can get you something…'

'No. Not ill.' He let out a hollow laugh. 'But clearly I must look terrible.'

'Well, as a matter of fact, yes, you do.'

'Thank you for your honesty.'

'Sorry—'

'Don't be. I can't bear lies.' A sudden, savage note had entered his voice, making Emma blink. Larenzo crossed the room to the liquor cabinet in the corner. 'I need a drink.'

She watched as he poured himself a large measure of whisky and then tossed it back in one burning swallow. His back was to her, the silk of his suit jacket straining against his shoulders and sinewy back. He was an attractive man, a beautiful man even, with his blue-black hair and piercing grey eyes, his tall, powerful body always encased in three-thousand-euro suits.

Emma had admired his form the way you admired Michelangelo's *David*, as a work of art. She had decided when she'd taken this job that she wasn't going to make the mistake of developing some schoolgirl crush on her boss. Larenzo Cavelli was out of her league. Way, way out of her league. And, if the tabloids were true, he had a different woman on his arm and in his bed every week.

'I wasn't expecting you until the end of the month,' she said.

'I had a change of plans.' He took out the stopper in the crystal decanter of whisky and poured himself another healthy measure. 'Obviously.'

She didn't press the point, because, while they'd developed a fairly amicable working relationship over the last nine months, he was still her boss. She couldn't actually say she *knew* Larenzo Cavelli. Since she'd taken the job as housekeeper he'd come to the villa only three times, never more than for a couple of days. He mostly lived in Rome, where he kept an apartment, or travelled for work as CEO of Cavelli Enterprises.

'Very well,' she finally said. 'Will you be staying long?'

He drained his glass for a second time. 'Probably not.'

'Well, the night at least,' she answered briskly. She didn't know what was going on with Larenzo, whether it was a business deal gone bust or a love affair gone bad, or something else entirely, but she could still do her job. 'The sheets on your bed are clean. I'll go switch the heating on for the pool.'

'Don't bother,' Larenzo answered. He put his empty glass on the table with a clink. 'There's no need.'

'It's no trouble,' Emma protested, and Larenzo shrugged, his back to her.

'Fine. Maybe I'll have one last swim.'

His words replayed through her mind as she left him and walked through the spacious, silent rooms of the villa to the back door that led to a brick terrace overlooking the mountains, a teardrop-shaped pool as its impressive centrepiece. *One last swim.* Was he planning on leaving, on selling the villa?

Emma gazed out at the Nebrodi mountains and shivered slightly, for the air still held a pine-scented chill.

All was quiet save for the rustling of the wind high up in the trees. Larenzo's villa was remote, miles from the nearest market town, Troina; in the daylight Emma could see its terracotta-tiled houses and shops nestled in the valley below. She went there several times a week to shop and socialise; she had a couple of friends amidst the Sicilian shopkeepers and matrons.

If Larenzo was planning on selling the villa, she'd miss living here. She never stayed anywhere long, and she would have probably started feeling restless in a few months anyway, but... She glanced once more at the night-cloaked hills and valleys, the mellow stone of the villa perched on its hill gleaming in the moonlight. She liked living here. It was peaceful, with plenty of subjects to photograph. She'd be sad to leave, if it came to that.

But maybe Larenzo just meant a swim before he left for Rome again. She switched on the heating and then turned to go inside; as she turned a shadowy form loomed up in front of her and her breath came out in a short gasp. She must have swayed or stumbled a little, for Larenzo put his hands on her shoulders to steady her.

They stood like that for a moment in the doorway, his strong hands curling around her shoulders so she could feel the warmth of his palms through the thin cotton of her T-shirt, and how her heart pounded beneath it. She didn't think he'd ever actually touched her before.

She moved one way, and he moved another, so it was almost as if they were engaged in a struggle or an awkward dance. Then Larenzo dropped his hands from her shoulders and stepped back.

'Scusi.'

'My fault,' she murmured, her heart still thudding, and moved quickly through the kitchen to flick on the lights. Bathed in a bright electric glow, things felt more normal, even if she could still feel the imprint of his hands on her shoulders, so warm and strong. 'So.' She turned to him with a quick smile, a brisk look. 'Have you eaten? I can make you something.'

He looked as if he was about to refuse, and then he shrugged. 'Why not? I'll go change while you cook.'

'What would you like to eat?'

Another shrug as he turned away. 'Whatever you make will be fine.'

She watched him disappear down the hallway, her lips pursed in an uncertain frown. She'd never seen Larenzo like this. Not that they'd actually had that much conversation, beyond discussing pool maintenance and house repairs. But even when talking about such mundane matters, Larenzo Cavelli had exuded a compelling charisma and energy, a life force. He was a man who, when entering a room, made everyone turn and take notice. Men tried to suppress their envy, and women undressed him with their eyes. Emma counted herself as wilfully immune to the man's magnetic vitality, but its absence now made her uneasy.

Her frown deepening, Emma opened the fridge and stared at the few items inside. She always did a big shop right before Larenzo arrived; she bought all the ingredients for gourmet meals for one and made them for him to eat alone, usually out on the terrace overlooking the mountains.

Now she glanced askance at the half-dozen eggs, a few slices of pancetta and the end of a wedge of cheese that comprised the entire contents of the fridge. With a sigh she took it all out. A bacon and cheese omelette it was.

She was just sliding it onto a plate when Larenzo came downstairs, dressed now in faded jeans and a grey T-shirt, his hair damp and spiky from a shower. She'd seen him casually dressed before, many times, but for some reason now, perhaps because of how different Larenzo seemed, her heart gave a weird little flip and she felt awareness shiver over her skin. Clearly he still possessed some of that charisma and vitality, for she felt the force of it now.

'Sorry it's just an omelette,' she said. 'I'll do a big shop tomorrow.'

'That won't be necessary.'

'But—'

"Aren't you going to join me?' He arched an eyebrow, nodding towards the single plate she'd laid out, a challenge simmering in his eyes.

In the handful of times he'd been at the villa, Larenzo had never asked her to eat with him. The two of them alone on the terrace would have been awkward, intimate, and Emma happily ate leftovers in the kitchen, one of her photography books propped against the salt and pepper shakers.

'Um…I've already eaten,' she said after a second's pause. It had to be past ten o'clock at night.

'Come have a glass of wine. I don't feel like being alone.'

Was that a command? Emma shrugged her assent; she wouldn't mind a glass of wine, and perhaps Larenzo would tell her what was going on.

'Okay,' she said, and she fetched two glasses while Larenzo selected a bottle of red wine from the rack above the sink.

While Larenzo took his plate of eggs out to the terrace, Emma retrieved her sweater from the sitting room, slipping her arms through the sleeves as she stepped outside. The moon was high and full above the pine-blanketed hills, the Nebrodi range's highest peak, Mount Soro, piercing the night sky. Larenzo was already seated at a table over-looking the pool, the water glimmering in the moonlight, but he rose as Emma came forward with the two glasses and proffered the bottle of wine. She nodded her assent and sat down while he poured.

'This is very civilised,' she said as she accepted the glass.

'Yes, isn't it?' Larenzo answered. 'Well, let's enjoy it while we can.' He raised his glass in a toast and Emma lifted hers as well before taking a sip. The wine was rich and velvety-smooth, clearly expensive, but she put her glass down after one sip and gave her boss as direct a look as she could.

'You're sure everything is all right?'

'As right as it can be,' Larenzo answered, taking a sip of wine.

'What does that mean?'

He set his glass down and stretched his legs out in front of him. 'Exactly that. But I don't want to talk about my-self, not tonight. For a few hours I'd just like to forget.'

Forget what? Emma wondered, but clearly Larenzo didn't want her to ask.

'You've been my housekeeper for nearly a year and I don't really know the first thing about you,' he continued, and Emma stared at him in surprise.

'You want to talk about *me*?'

'Why not?'

'Because…well, because you've never expressed an in-terest in knowing anything about me before. And actually, I'm quite a boring person.'

He smiled, his teeth gleaming in the darkness. 'Let me be the judge of that.'

Emma shook her head slowly. This evening was becoming almost surreal. 'What do you want to know?'

'Where did you grow up?'

An innocuous enough question, she supposed. 'Everywhere, really. I was a diplomat's kid.'

'I think I remember you mentioning that in your interview.' He'd interviewed her in Rome, where she'd been working as a chambermaid in a hotel, just one in a string of jobs she'd had as she moved from city to city, exploring the world and taking photographs.

'And you haven't minded being stuck up here in the hills of Sicily?' he asked, his wine glass raised to his lips. 'All by yourself?'

She shrugged. 'I'm used to being on my own.' And she preferred it that way. No ties, no obligations, no disappointments. The occasional bout of loneliness was not too high a price to pay for that kind of freedom.

'Even so.'

'You obviously like it,' she pointed out. 'Since you own this place.'

'Yes, but I travel and spend time in cities. I'm not up here all the time.'

'Well, as I said, I like it.' For now, anyway. She never remained anywhere for too long, always preferring to move on, to find new experiences, and from the sceptical look on Larenzo's face he seemed to guess a bit of her natural wanderlust.

'Have you met anyone up here?' he asked. 'Made friends?'

'A few people down in Troina.'

'That's something, I suppose. What do you do for fun up here?'

Emma shrugged. 'Walk. Swim. Read. I'm easily entertained, fortunately.'

'Yes.' He gazed out at the mountains and Emma had

the sense he was thinking about something else, something painful.

'But it's not the kind of job you'd stay in for ever,' he said at last.

'Are you trying to get rid of me?' she asked lightly. She'd meant it as a joke but Larenzo took the question seriously.

'No, definitely not. But if something were to happen…' He trailed off, his gaze still on the hills, and Emma set down her wine glass.

'Larenzo, are you thinking of selling this place?'

'Not selling it, no.'

'But something,' she pressed. 'What's going on, really? Do I need to start looking for another job?'

He let out a long, low breath and raked his hands through his hair. 'Whatever happens, I'll make sure to give you a good reference.'

'What are you talking about, whatever happens?' Emma shook her head. 'I don't understand you.'

'I know, and I don't want to explain it now. It will all become clear soon enough.' He nodded towards the pool. 'How about a swim?'

'A *swim*?' Emma glanced at the pool, the water glimmering in the moonlight. 'It's a bit cold for me.'

'Not for me,' he said, and she watched in amazement as he stripped off his shirt and jeans and, clad only in his boxer shorts, dived into the pool.

The splash echoed through the still air and Emma watched, shivering slightly, as Larenzo swam the length of the pool before surfacing and slicking back the wet hair from his face.

'Come in,' he called. 'The water's lovely.'

Emma shook her head. 'I only just turned the heating on. It's got to be freezing.'

'Even so.' He arched an eyebrow, his mouth curling in a smile that was pure temptation. Emma's gaze was inexorably drawn to his bare chest, all lean, rippling muscle, his bronzed skin beaded with water. 'Dare you.'

Emma hadn't thought this evening could get any more surreal. But swimming with her boss in a freezing pool?

'Come on, Emma.' He held out his hand. 'Just jump in.' Heat simmered in his eyes and she felt an answering stab of lust through her middle.

This was so foolish, so dangerous, and yet…the sight of Larenzo in the pool, nearly naked with moonlight streaming over his body and droplets of water twinkling like diamonds on his bronzed skin, was hard to resist. And already this evening felt separate from reality, a time apart.

'Chicken?' he taunted, his eyes and teeth glinting in the darkness, and Emma laughed.

'You really want to get me in that pool.'

'I want someone to swim with.'

Excitement licked through her veins. She didn't think Larenzo was coming on to her; he never had before. And yet…

'Fine,' she said, and, shrugging off her sweater, she dived fully clothed into the deep end.

She surfaced, sucking in a hard breath, because the water really was cold. 'And now I'm getting out,' she told him as she trod water. 'It's as freezing as I thought it would be.'

'I didn't think you'd do it,' he said, laughter threading his voice, and Emma was glad that she'd managed to distract him from whatever had been bothering him, even if she got hypothermia in the process.

'You thought wrong,' she said, and swam towards the edge of the pool. With her wet clothes weighing her down it was hard to haul herself up on the pool's edge.

And then she felt Larenzo behind her, his hands on her shoulders, the strength and heat of him just inches from her back. She sucked in a shocked breath as he slid his hands to her waist and helped her up.

She flopped inelegantly on the side of the pool and then scrambled to her knees, amazed at how much that one little touch had affected her. She shivered, for with her soaked clothes the night air now felt icy.

'Here.' Larenzo hauled himself up and went to the heated cupboard for several towels. 'Wrap yourself up.'

'I should really change,' she said. She glanced down at herself and saw that her T-shirt was sticking to her skin, revealing even the floral pattern on her bra, her nipples peaked from the cold. 'Thanks,' she muttered, and clutched the towel to her chest.

Larenzo's gaze hadn't dropped to her chest, but his mouth curved all the same and again Emma felt another kick of excitement. She retreated back to the table, the towel still clutched to her chest.

'I should go to bed.'

'Don't go quite yet,' Larenzo answered. He slung the towel over his shoulders and sat down across from her, pouring them both more wine. Emma eyed the full glass and Larenzo's bare chest, his perfectly formed pecs flexing as he moved, and felt as if she'd just jumped into the deep end of an entirely different kind of pool.

'I'm freezing—' she began and he nodded towards the cupboard.

'There are towelling robes in there. Change out of your wet things. I don't want you catching cold.'

'Larenzo…' Emma began, although she didn't know what she was going to say. Why was she protesting so much, anyway? Chatting in the moonlight with a devastatingly attractive man was no hardship. And it wasn't as if Larenzo was going to make a move. He might have dared her to jump in the pool, but she was pretty sure her boss didn't mix business with pleasure.

Even if she wanted him to…

'Fine,' she said, and retreated to the towelling cupboard.

With the door serving as a screen between her and Larenzo, she tugged off her wet clothes and wrapped herself in the heated dressing gown. The sleeves hung past her hands and the sash trailed the ground, but at least she was warm again. She doubted she'd provide any sort of temptation to Larenzo now.

'Tell me your favourite place you lived in as a child,' Larenzo commanded as she sat down across from him and picked up her wine glass—he'd filled it again, while she'd been changing.

Emma considered for a moment. Answering questions, at least, kept her from gawping at Larenzo's chest. Why on earth she was feeling this unwelcome attraction for him now, she had no idea. Perhaps it was simply the strangeness of the evening, his unexpected arrival, his demand for her company. 'Krakow, I suppose,' she said finally. 'I spent two years there when I was ten. It's a beautiful city.' And those years had been the last ones where she'd felt part of a family, before her mother had announced her decision to leave. But she didn't want to think, much less talk, about that. 'Where did you grow up?' she asked, and Larenzo swirled the wine in his glass, his expression hardening slightly as he gazed down into its ruby depths.

'Palermo.'

'Hence the villa in Sicily, I suppose.'

'It is my home.'

'But you live most of the time in Rome.'

'Cavelli Enterprises is headquartered there.' He paused, his shuttered gaze on the darkened mountains, the moon casting a lambent glow over the wooded hills. 'In any case, I never much liked Palermo.'

'Why not?'

He pressed his lips together. 'Too many hard memories.'

He didn't seem inclined to say anything more, and Emma eyed him curiously, wondering at this enigmatic man who clearly had secrets she'd never even guessed at before.

Larenzo gazed round the terrace, the patio furniture now no more than shadowy shapes in the darkness, and then turned to look once more at the mountains. 'I'll miss it here,' he said, so quietly Emma almost didn't hear him.

'So you are thinking of leaving,' she said, and Larenzo didn't answer for a long moment.

'Not thinking of it, no,' he said, and then seemed to shake off his weary mood, his gaze snapping back to her. 'Thank you, Emma, for the food and also for your company. You've done more for me than you could possibly know.'

Emma stared at him helplessly. 'If there's anything else I can do…'

To her shock he touched her cheek with his hand, his fingers cool against her flushed face. *'Bellissima,'* he whispered, and the endearment stole right through her. 'No,' he said, and dropped his hand from her face. 'You've done enough. Thank you.' And then, taking his plate and his glass, he rose from his chair and left her sitting on the terrace alone.

Emma sat there for a few moments, shivering a little in the chilly air despite the dressing gown. She wished she could have comforted Larenzo somehow, but she had no idea what was going on, and she wasn't sure he'd welcome her sympathy anyway. He was a proud, hard man, caught in a moment of weakness. He'd probably regret their whole conversation tomorrow.

Sighing, she took the wine bottle and glasses from the table and headed inside. Larenzo had already gone upstairs; the lights were off, the house locked up. After rinsing out the dishes and switching on the dishwasher Emma went upstairs as well.

She paused for a moment on the landing; Larenzo's

master bedroom was to the right, her own smaller room the last on the left. She heard nothing but the wind high up in the trees, and she couldn't see any light underneath Larenzo's doorway. Even so she had a mad urge to knock on his door, to say something. But what? They didn't have that kind of relationship, not remotely, and knocking on Larenzo's bedroom door, seeing him answer it with his hair rumpled and damp, his chest still bare…

No. That was taking this strange evening a step too far.

Still she hesitated, glancing towards his doorway, and then with a sigh she turned and went to her own bedroom, closing the door behind her.

CHAPTER TWO

HE COULDN'T SLEEP. Hardly a surprise, considering all that had happened in the last few days. Larenzo stared gritty-eyed at the ceiling before, with a sigh, he sat up and swung his legs over the side of his bed.

All around him the house was still and silent. It was nearly two in the morning, and he wondered how long he had left. Would they come for him at dawn, or would they wait for the more civilised hour of eight or nine o'clock in the morning? Either way, it wouldn't be long. Bertrano had made sure of that.

Letting out another sigh at the thought of the man he'd considered as good as a father, Larenzo slipped from the bedroom and walked downstairs. The rooms of the villa were silent, dark, and empty, and he was loath to turn on a light and disturb the peacefulness. He could have stayed in Rome, but he'd hated the thought of simply waiting for the end, and he'd wanted to have a final farewell for the only place he could call a home. Bertrano would tell them where to find him; the police in Palermo had most likely already been alerted. He had a few hours at most.

And for those few hours he wanted simply to savour what he had. What Bertrano Raguso had given him, although Larenzo had worked hard for it. Ironic, really, that the man who had saved him would also destroy him. Fitting, perhaps.

He ran his hand along the silky-smooth ebony of the

grand piano in the music room; he'd bought it because he loved music, but he'd never found the time to learn to play. Now he never would. He played a few discordant notes, the sound echoing through the silent villa, before he moved onto the sitting room, stopping in front of the chessboard on a table by the window, its marble pieces set up for a game he would never play.

He picked up the king, fingering the smooth marble before he laid it down again. Bertrano had taught him how to play chess, and Larenzo had savoured the evenings they'd spent together, heads bent over a chessboard. Why had the man who had treated him like a son turned on him so suddenly? Betrayed him? Had it been a moment's panicked weakness? But no, it had gone on longer than that, perhaps even months, for Bertrano to lay the paper trail. How had Larenzo not known? Not even guessed?

He glanced at the pawns neatly lined up. In the end he'd served no more purpose than they did. With a sudden burst of helpless rage he struck the pawns, scattering them across the board with a clatter.

The realisation of all he was about to lose hit him then, with sickening force, and he dropped his face in his hands, driving his fingers through his hair, as a single sob racked his body.

Bertrano, how could you do this to me? I loved you. I thought of you as my father.

'Larenzo?'

He stiffened at the sound of Emma's uncertain voice, and then he lifted his face from his hands, turning to see her standing in the doorway of the sitting room. She was in her pyjamas, nothing more than boy shorts and a very thin T-shirt; Larenzo could see the outline of her small breasts and he felt an entirely inappropriate stab of lust, just as he had when he'd seen her soaked and dripping in the pool.

He hadn't spared much thought for his housekeeper before tonight, but now he envied her freedom, her ease.

'Couldn't you sleep?' she asked as she came into the room. She glanced at the scattered chess pieces, a silent question in her eyes.

'No, I couldn't.' He turned to the fireplace, where the kindling and logs were already laid for a fire. 'It's cold in here,' he said, and reached for a match to start the blaze. From behind him he could hear Emma righting the chess pieces.

When the fire was cheerily crackling in the hearth he turned to face her; she was touching the pawns he'd knocked over, her head bent, her hair swinging down to hide her face.

'Fancy a game?'

She looked up in surprise. 'What?'

He nodded towards the chessboard. 'Do you play?'

'I know the rules.'

'Well, then. It appears neither of us can sleep. Shall we play?'

'All right,' she said after a pause, and she sat down in one of the chairs as Larenzo sat in the other.

'White goes first,' he told her and she bit her lip, studying the board with a concentration so intense he found it endearing. Again he felt the powerful thrust of attraction. These few hours of enjoyment would be the last pleasure he had for a long while.

Finally she moved her piece, her slender fingers curling around the figure. She glanced up at him, a smile lurking in her eyes, playing with her lips. 'Why do I have a feeling you're going to crush me?'

'You can always live in hope,' he answered lightly, and moved his pawn.

She laughed, shaking her head. 'That would be foolish in the extreme.'

'Perhaps.' He liked watching her, seeing the way the

firelight played over her golden skin, how humour lit her golden-green eyes. He stretched out his legs and his foot brushed her ankle, sending another throb of desire through him.

He thought she felt something too, for her eyes widened and her body tensed briefly before she moved another piece on the board.

They played in silence for a few minutes, the tension spooling out between them. Larenzo brushed her foot again with his own, enjoying the silky slide of her skin. She sucked in a quick breath, her fingers trembling as she moved her rook.

'I'm four moves away from checkmate,' he told her, and she let out a shaky laugh.

'I knew this was going to happen.' She glanced up at him wryly and he held her gaze, felt the force of the attraction between them. He'd never considered his housekeeper as an object of desire before; employees had always been off limits, and he'd seen her so rarely. But tonight he craved that human connection, the last one that might ever be offered to him. To touch a woman, to give and receive pleasure…

Setting his jaw, Larenzo turned back towards the board. Making love with Emma tonight would be an entirely selfish act. He couldn't drag her down with him. It was bad enough that he was here at all.

He moved his bishop, and then stilled as he felt Emma's hand on his own, her skin cool and soft.

'Larenzo, I wish you'd tell me what's wrong.' He didn't answer, simply stared at her fingers on his. He stroked her palm with his thumb and she shivered in response but did not remove her hand.

'It doesn't matter,' he said in a low voice, and stroked her palm again. 'There's nothing you can do about it, and it's my own fault anyway.' For trusting someone he'd loved.

For believing someone could have pure motives. For being so bloody naive. So damn *stupid*.

'Are you sure I can't help?' Emma asked softly. She squeezed his fingers and Larenzo closed his eyes. Her touch was the sweetest torture he'd ever known. He thought of telling her the one way she could help, the one way she could make him forget what dawn would bring. He resisted. He could not be that selfish, not even on the threshold of his own destruction.

'No, I'm afraid not. No one can.'

Her gaze searched his face and then she rose from her chair. 'Perhaps I should leave you alone, then.'

'Wait.' The single word was wrenched from him. 'Don't go.'

He felt her surprise as the silence stretched on. She didn't move, either backwards or forwards. He bowed his head.

'I don't want to be alone tonight,' he confessed, his voice low, and then she took a step forward, laid her hand on his shoulder once more.

'You aren't,' she said simply.

Emma didn't know whether it was Larenzo's obvious pain or the attraction that had snapped through the air that had compelled her to stay. Perhaps both. She wanted to comfort him, but she couldn't deny the yearning she had felt uncoil through her body when Larenzo had looked at her with such blatant desire in his eyes. No man had ever looked at her like that before, and it had thrilled her to her core.

The moment stretched on between them as she stood there with her hand still on his shoulder, his head bowed. His skin was warm and smooth underneath her palm, and slowly Larenzo reached up and covered her hand with his own, his fingers twining with hers. The intimacy of the gesture rocked her, sent heat and need and something even deeper and more important spiralling through her. They were simply holding hands, and yet it felt like a pure form of communication, the most intimate thing she'd ever done.

Finally Larenzo broke the moment. He took his hand from hers and turned. Emma could feel the heat rolling off him, inhaled the tangy scent of his aftershave, and desire crashed through her once more. This man was more than a work of art. He was a living, breathing, virile male, and he was close enough for her to touch him. To kiss him. Which she wanted to do, very much.

'Do you have family, Emma?' he asked, startling her out of her haze of desire.

'Y-y-y-yes.'

'Are you close to them?' He gazed at her, his silvery eyes searching her, looking for answers. 'You must not see them very often, living here.'

'I...' How to answer that seemingly innocent question? 'I see my father sometimes. He's currently posted in Budapest, and we've met up occasionally.'

'And your mother?'

Why was he asking her all these questions? She didn't want to talk about her family, and certainly not her mother, yet in the darkened intimacy of the room, of the moment, she knew she would answer. 'No, I'm not close to my mother. My parents divorced when I was twelve, and I didn't see her much after that.'

'That must have been hard.'

A small shrug was all she'd allow on that subject, but Larenzo nodded as if she'd said something important and revealing. 'And siblings? Do you have any sisters or brothers?'

'One sister, Meghan. She lives in New Jersey, does the whole stay-at-home-mom thing.' The kind of life she'd deliberately chosen not to pursue or want. 'We're close. We Skype.' She shook her head in confusion. 'Why are you asking me all this, Larenzo?'

'Because I never had a real family of my own, and I wondered.' He turned, his back to her as he gazed at the fire. 'I wondered how families are. How they're meant to be.'

'What happened to your family?'

'I don't know. My mother left me to fend for myself when I was young, maybe two or three. An orphanage took me in, run by a convent. Not the nicest place. I ran away when I was eleven. Spent the next few years on the street.'

He recited these facts dispassionately, without any self-pity at all, and somehow that made it all the more terrible. 'That's awful. I'm sorry.' Emma would never have guessed such a past for this man, with his wealth and power and magnetism. 'Was this in Palermo?'

'Yes.'

'Those are hard memories.'

'Yes.' He let out a long, low sigh. 'But let's not talk about that tonight.'

'What do you want to talk about?'

'Anything.' He sat down on the sheepskin rug in front of the fire, and patted the floor next to him. Emma came to sit across from him, folding her legs underneath her, conscious of the strangeness of this situation: both of them in their pyjamas, the firelight casting pools of light over their skin, and yet of the ease of it too. It felt weirdly natural to sit there with Larenzo, in the dark, with the fire. Surreal and yet somehow right.

'What do you want to do with your life, Emma?' he asked as he tossed another log on the fire. 'I assume you don't want to be a housekeeper for ever.'

'Would there be something wrong with that?'

He gave a faint, bemused smile. 'No, there's nothing wrong with that. But you are a beautiful, capable young woman, and I imagine you want to see more of the world than a remote Sicilian hilltop.'

'I like to travel,' she admitted. 'I've moved around a lot already.'

'As a diplomat's kid.'

'Yes, and since I finished school. Itchy feet, I suppose.'

'What did you study at school?'

'I did a photography course just for a year, and then I got a backpack and a rail pass and went to see the world.' Determined to enjoy everything life had to offer, never to be tied down, never to be hurt.

'Sounds fun.' He turned to her, an eyebrow arched. 'I think I've seen you with a camera round the place. Have you taken photos here?'

'Yes…'

'May I see them?'

She hesitated, because no one had ever seen her photographs. No one had ever asked. And showing them now to Larenzo felt even more intimate than when they'd held hands. She'd be showing him a part of her soul. 'Okay,' she finally said. 'I'll go get them.' She hurried up to her bedroom, and then leafed through several folders of photos before selecting a few of her favourites. She brought them back to Larenzo, handing them to him silently.

He studied each one carefully, a slight frown puckering his forehead as Emma waited, nibbling her lip. She realised she wanted him to like them, to understand them, and she held her breath as she waited for his verdict.

'They're not holiday snaps,' he said finally and she let out a little laugh.

'No.' She preferred to take candid shots of people, strangers and sometimes friends caught in an unexpected moment, held in thrall by an emotion, whether it was happiness or sorrow or something else.

'This one.' He gestured to a portrait of Rosaria, one of the shopkeepers in Troina. She was sitting on a stool in the back of her bakery, her hands on her thighs, her head thrown back, her face a mass of wrinkles as she let out a deep, belly laugh. 'That's joy,' Larenzo said quietly, and Emma's heart swelled with the knowledge that he did understand, that he'd seen what she'd been trying to capture.

'Yes.'

'I don't think I've ever felt that.' He turned to give her a swift, dark glance. 'Have you?'

Shock rippled through her at the question, and the answer that slipped from her lips without her even realising she was going to say it. 'No,' Emma whispered. 'I don't think I have.' She'd travelled the world, climbed mountains, scuba-dived, done a million and one adventurous and amazing things, had always considered herself a happy person…and yet joy? That kind of deep, abiding, *real* joy?

It had remained beguilingly elusive. And she hadn't realised it until Larenzo had asked her the question.

'You have a skill,' Larenzo said as he turned back to the photographs. 'A true talent. You shouldn't squander it.'

'I'm not—'

'I mean you should exhibit these.' He glanced at her, his eyebrows raised. 'Have you shown them to anyone, to a professional?'

'You're the first person who has seen them.'

He held her gaze, his own darkening. 'Thank you,' he said quietly, and wordlessly Emma nodded.

The moment spun out, stretching and shifting into something else as their gazes remained locked and Emma's breath shortened. A log popped in the fireplace and embers scattered across the hearth, but neither of them so much as twitched.

The desire Emma had felt before now crashed over her in an overpowering wave, obliterating rational thought, obscuring everything but this moment. She wanted this man more than she'd ever wanted anything or anyone before, and as she saw the heat blaze in his eyes she realised with a thrill he felt the same.

Slowly, deliberately, Larenzo reached one hand out towards her, his fingers first skimming her cheek and then his palm cradling her face. The warmth of his palm against her cheek felt electric, every nerve ending she had tingling and quivering with awareness. Larenzo's thumb brushed her mouth, and her lips parted in expectation as a tiny gasp escaped. If he kissed her, she'd be lost. And she knew she wanted to be lost.

His hand tensed briefly against her cheek, and for a terrible second she thought he was going to drop it and move away. This glorious moment would be over. Then he brought his other hand up to frame her face, cradling her between his palms before pulling her inexorably towards him, his lips coming down on hers, soft and hard, cold and hot, everything all at once as a thousand new sensations blazed through her and her mouth opened to his kiss.

Larenzo hauled her towards him, her legs sliding across his as she straddled him, felt the hard press of his arousal against the juncture of her thighs and excitement pulsed hard inside her.

He was kissing her deeply now, with a hungry urgency that Emma felt in herself as she drove her fingers through his hair and pressed even more closely against him, her body arching instinctively as Larenzo pressed back.

After an endless moment that still didn't seem long enough, Larenzo broke off the kiss, his breath coming out in a rush.

'I wasn't going to do that.'

'I wanted you to do it,' she whispered. She couldn't bear it if he stopped now.

He leaned his forehead against hers, their bodies still pressed together, both of their hearts thudding. 'I want you, Emma. I think I want you more than I've ever wanted anyone before.'

A thrill ran through her at this simply stated fact. 'I want you too.'

'But I can't offer you anything other than this night.' He closed his eyes briefly. 'A few hours at most. That's all. That's all it could ever be.'

'I know,' she said softly. When he'd kissed her, she hadn't thought of anything but the moment, yet she acknowledged now that she'd never have expected some kind of commitment from a man like Larenzo. 'I don't want more than this night,' she told him. 'I'm not looking for some kind of relationship, Larenzo, trust me. I just want you, tonight.'

He leaned back a little so he could look into her face. 'If you're sure…?'

She nodded, amazed at just how sure she was. Everything about this night had been surreal, even magical. This felt, bizarrely and yet completely, like the logical and necessary conclusion. 'I'm sure.'

'Then come with me.' He untangled himself from her and rose from the rug in one fluid movement, holding his hand down to help her up. With their fingers linked he led her silently upstairs to his bedroom.

Emma gazed at the king-sized bed with its navy silk sheets she'd changed herself and felt a tremor of—what? Not fear. Anticipation. And a little nervousness, because, while she *was* sure, this was still a new experience. An entirely new experience, and she didn't want to admit to Larenzo just how new it was, how unlike her this decision had been.

He glanced back at her, his fingers still twined with hers. 'Having second thoughts?' he asked quietly, his gaze sweeping over her. 'Cold feet? I wouldn't mind.' He let out a ragged laugh. 'Well, I'd mind, but I'd understand.'

'I'm not having second thoughts.' She swallowed, lifted her chin. She wouldn't tell him about her inexperience. It didn't matter to her, and she didn't want it to matter to him, or put him off. 'Are you?' she challenged, and he let out a soft huff of laughter.

'Definitely not.' He tugged her towards him. 'Come here, Emma.'

And she came willingly, her breasts pressing against his bare chest as his mouth came down on hers once more and for a few blissful, buzzing seconds she forgot everything but the hunger and need for this, for him.

Larenzo reached down and with one swift tug he had her T-shirt up and over her head; the feel of her breasts brushing the crisp hair on his chest was so intense it almost hurt. She'd never felt so much, felt so alive, not when she'd been on top of a mountain or deep in the ocean. All her adventures paled in light of this.

She let out a gasp that he muffled with his mouth, his hands sliding down her back and then cupping her bottom as he settled her against his arousal.

He moved his mouth from her lips to the curve of her neck, the touch of his tongue against her sensitive skin making her shiver.

Then he drew her to the bed, laying her down on top of the silken sheets and covering her body with his own.

She twined her arms around his neck and arched up towards him, craving the connection of their bodies fused in every place. Of being that close to another person… even if it was just for a single night. A few hours. And she knew Larenzo needed it too, craved it as much as she did. She was giving him herself, the only comfort she could offer him now.

Larenzo slid a hand between her thighs, slipping her pyjama shorts down her legs and then tossing them on the floor. The feel of his fingers against her most sensitive flesh had Emma arching upwards again, her head thrown back as sensations fizzed and popped inside her.

And then they exploded and her breath rushed out on a ragged cry as Larenzo worked magic with his fingers and left her boneless in his arms.

'Oh...'

'That's just to start,' he promised with a soft laugh, and then he tossed his own pyjama bottoms aside before he slid seamlessly inside her—and then stopped. 'Emma...'

She saw the confusion on his face, the uncertainty, and knew he'd guessed her inexperience. 'You haven't...' he began slowly and she answered by tilting her hips up.

'It doesn't matter,' she said fiercely, and as her body found its instinctive rhythm Larenzo matched it, burying his head in the curve of her shoulder as his body surged into hers.

If she'd felt any pain or discomfort, it was long gone as the exquisite friction of Larenzo's body created a pleasure deeper and fiercer than what she'd already felt at his experienced hands.

She let out another long, ragged cry as the sensations exploded inside her again and with a shudder Larenzo emptied himself into her and then was still.

They lay like that for a few seconds before he wrapped his arms around her and rolled onto his back.

'Why didn't you tell me you were a virgin?' he asked quietly.

Emma could still feel him inside her, still feel the bone-melting ripples of pleasure that had utterly rocked her moments before. 'Because like I said, it didn't matter.'

'I might have done things differently...'

'I liked the way you did things.'

He laughed softly then, his arms tightening around her. 'Thank you, Emma,' he said quietly, and she wasn't quite sure what he was thanking her for. She propped herself on her elbows to gaze down at him, and saw the ravages of both grief and pleasure on his face. She had no regrets, and yet she still wished she could smooth the furrows of worry from his forehead. She brushed his hair from his eyes instead, savouring the feel of him.

'I should be thanking you,' she said, and Larenzo smiled faintly before glancing out at the night sky; the moon was on the wane, dawn only an hour or two away. 'You should sleep.'

Did he want her to leave? Uncertainly Emma started to roll off him, but Larenzo clasped her to him once more.

'Stay,' he said, his voice rough with emotion. 'Stay until morning.'

And so she did.

CHAPTER THREE

THEY CAME AT DAWN. Larenzo heard the first car drive up, the crunch of gravel, the sound of a car door shutting quietly, as if they were trying to hide their presence. As if they could.

He stilled, every muscle tensing, Emma still in his arms. *Emma.* He would spare her an ugly scene. She deserved so much more than that, but that was all he could give her now.

Slowly he slipped from the bed, doing his best not to disturb her. She sighed in her sleep and turned, her tousled hair falling across one cheek, a tendril lying across her breast.

He gazed at her for a moment, drinking her in: the golden, freckled skin, the wavy golden-brown hair, her lashes fanned out on her cheeks, although he knew if she opened her eyes, they would be golden-green. His golden girl for a night, gone in the morning.

At least he would be gone.

Quickly Larenzo turned, reaching for his jeans. He pulled on a rugby shirt and ran his hands through his hair, took a deep breath. And looked one last time at Emma, at freedom and happiness, pleasure and peace. He'd known them all with her last night, and now they were nothing but memories. Resolutely he turned from her and left the room.

Emma awoke to the thud of boots on the stairs, the sound of stomping down the hall. She was still blinking the sleep from her eyes, one hand reaching for the sheet to cover herself, her mind barely processing what she'd heard, when the door was thrown open and three men crowded there, all of them glaring at her. Her heart seemed to still in her chest, everything in her going numb with horror as she stared at these strange men.

'What—?'

They spoke in rapid Italian, too fast for her to understand, although during her two years in Sicily she'd become fairly conversant in the language. Still, she understood their tone. Their derision and contempt.

She clutched the sheet to her breasts, her whole body trembling with indignation and fear. *'Chi sei? Cosa stai facendo?'* Who are you, and what are you doing? They didn't answer.

One man, clearly the leader of the pack, ripped the sheet away from her naked body. Emma gasped in shock. *'Put-tana.'* He spat the single word. Whore.

Emma shook her head, her mouth dry, her body still trembling. She felt as if she'd awakened to an alternate reality, a horrible nightmare, and she had no idea how to make it stop. *Where was Larenzo?*

One of the men grabbed her by the arm and yanked her upwards. She came, stumbling, trying futilely to cover herself. He reached for her T-shirt and shorts discarded on the floor and threw them at her.

'You are English?' he asked, his voice clipped, and she nodded.

'American. And my consulate will hear—'

He cut her off with a hard laugh. 'Get dressed. You're coming with us.'

Quickly, clumsily, Emma yanked on her clothes. Dressed, even if only in flimsy pyjamas, she felt a little braver. 'Where is Signor Cavelli?' she asked in Italian.

The man eyed her scornfully. 'Downstairs, at the moment. But he'll spend the rest of his life in prison.'

Emma's mouth dropped open. *Prison?* What on earth was he talking about? Were these awful men police?

'Come on,' the man commanded her tersely, and with her mind spinning she followed the men downstairs.

Larenzo stood in the centre of the sitting room, his eyes blazing silver fire as he caught sight of her.

'You are all right? They didn't hurt you?'

'Shut up!' The words were like the crack of a gunshot as one of the men slapped Larenzo across the face. He didn't even blink, although Emma could see the red imprint of the man's hand on Larenzo's cheek.

'They didn't hurt me,' she said quietly and the man turned on her.

'Enough. Neither of you are to speak to one another. Who knows what you might try to communicate?'

'She has nothing to do with any of it,' Larenzo said, and he sounded scornful, as if he were actually in control of the situation. With an icy ripple of shock Emma saw that he was handcuffed. 'Do you actually think I'd tell a woman, my housekeeper no less, anything of value?'

The words, spoken so derisively, shouldn't have hurt. She knew, intellectually at least, that he was trying to protect her, although from what she had no idea. Even so they did hurt, just as the look Larenzo gave her, a look as derisive as those of the *carabinieri*, did.

'She's nothing to me.'

'Even so, she'll be taken in for questioning,' the man replied shortly and Larenzo's eyes blazed once more.

'She knows nothing. She's American. Do you want the consulate all over this?'

'This,' the man snapped, poking a finger into Larenzo's chest, 'is the biggest sting we've had in Sicily for twenty years. I don't give a damn about the consulate.'

They'd been speaking Italian, and, while Emma had caught the gist of it, she still didn't understand what was going on.

'Please, let me get dressed properly,' she said, her voice coming out croaky as she stumbled over the Italian. 'And then I'll go with you and answer any questions you might have.'

The man turned to glare at her with narrowed eyes. Then he gave a brief nod, and, with another policeman accompanying her, Emma went upstairs to her bedroom. The man waited outside the room while she pulled on underwear, jeans, a long-sleeved T-shirt, and a fleece. She brushed her teeth and hair, grabbed her purse and her passport, and then, just in case, she took her backpack and put a change of clothes, her camera, and her folder of photographs in it. Who knew when she'd be able to return? Just the realisation sent another icy wave of terror crashing through her.

Taking a deep, steadying breath, she left the room. The man accompanied her downstairs; the front door was open and she saw several cars outside. Larenzo was being shoved into one. She turned to the man.

'Where are we going?'

'Palermo.'

'Palermo? But that's nearly three hours away—'

The man smiled coldly. 'So it is. I'm afraid you'll have to be so inconvenienced.'

Three hours later Emma sat in an interrogation room at the anti-Mafia headquarters of Palermo's police department. She'd been given a paper cup of cold coffee and made to wait until finally the man who had made the arrest back at Larenzo's villa came and sat down across from her, putting his elbows on the chipped tabletop.

'You know your boyfriend is in a lot of trouble.'

Emma closed her eyes briefly. She was aching with exhaustion, numb with confusion and fear, and she missed Larenzo desperately even as she forced herself to remember she hadn't actually known him all that well. *Until last night. Until he held me in his arms and made me feel cherished and important.* 'He's not my boyfriend.'

'Whoever he is. He's going to prison, probably for the rest of his life.'

Emma licked her dry lips. 'What…what has he done?'

'You don't know?'

'I have no idea. All I know is he was—is—CEO of Cavelli Enterprises.' And that when he kissed her her mind emptied of thoughts. He made her body both buzz and sing. But then words began to ricochet through her, words Larenzo had spoken to her last night. *It's my own fault.* What had he done?

The man must have seen something of this in her face for he leaned forward. 'You know something.'

'No.'

'I've been doing this for a long time.' He sounded almost kind. 'I can tell, *signorina.* I can tell when someone is lying.'

'I'm not lying. I don't know anything. I don't even know what Cavelli Enterprises did.'

'And if I told you Larenzo Cavelli was involved with the Mafia? You wouldn't know anything about that?'

Bile rose in her throat and she swallowed hard. 'No, I certainly wouldn't.'

'It didn't concern you, the amount of security he had for that villa?'

She thought of his insistence on locking the doors, the elaborate security system. 'No.'

'Don't play dumb with me, *signorina.*'

'Look, maybe I was dumb, but I really didn't know.' Emma's voice rose in agitation. 'Plenty of people have detailed security systems.'

'Cavelli never said anything to you?'

Again his words raced through her mind. The grief on his face, the resignation she'd heard in his voice, the sense that everything was over, that this was his last night. He must have known they were coming to arrest him. He must have realised his activities had been discovered. Even so she couldn't reconcile the man she'd known, however briefly, with the Mafia. And yet as tender a lover as Larenzo had been, he was still virtually a stranger. She had no idea what he'd got up to when he'd been away from the villa. No idea at all.

'Signorina?'

'Please,' Emma said wearily. 'I was his housekeeper. I barely saw him. I don't know anything.'

Eight endless hours later she was finally released from the police. When she asked about returning to the villa, the man at the desk shook his head.

'The villa is being searched by the police. Everything there is potential evidence. You won't be able to go back for some time.'

And so Emma headed out into the busy streets of Palermo, mopeds and sports cars speeding by, her mind spinning as she tried to think what to do now. She had no real reason to go all the way back to the villa. She had nothing of value there but a few clothes and photography books.

But where could she go?

She ended up at a cheap hotel near the train station; she sat on the single bed, her backpack at her feet, her whole life in tatters.

She told herself she was used to moving on, and it would be easy enough to look for a new job. She could spend some time with her father in Budapest while she decided where she wanted to go, what she wanted to do.

And yet that prospect seemed bleak rather than hopeful; she might be used to moving on, but she hadn't been ready this time. She'd liked her life in Sicily. The villa had been the closest thing she'd ever known to a home.

And as for Larenzo...

She'd known, of course she'd known, that their one night together wasn't going anywhere. But it had still *meant* something. She'd felt a deep connection to him last night, an understanding and a tenderness... Had it all been false? According to the police, he was a Mafioso. The inspector had told her they had incontrovertible evidence, had said there were photos, witnesses, files. Everything to convict Larenzo Cavelli of too many horrible crimes. Extortion, the police had said. Theft. Assault. Organised delinquency, which was the legal term for involvement in the Mafia.

Faced with all of it, Emma knew she had no choice but to believe. Larenzo Cavelli was a criminal.

The next morning, after a sleepless night, Emma went to an Internet café to arrange her passage to Budapest. Yet as she clicked on a website for cheap airfares, she realised she didn't want to go there. She didn't want to traipse around Europe, taking odd jobs, at least not yet. She wanted to go somewhere safe, somewhere far away from all this, to recover and heal. She wanted to see her sister. Quickly Emma took out her mobile and scrolled through for Meghan's number.

'Emma?' Concern sharpened her sister's voice as she answered the call. 'You sound...'

'I'm tired. And a bit overwhelmed.' She didn't want to go into the details of what had happened on the phone; they were too recent, too raw, and she was afraid she might burst into tears right in the middle of the Internet café. 'My job in Sicily has ended suddenly, and I thought I'd come for a visit, if you don't mind having me.'

'Of course I don't mind having you,' Meghan exclaimed. 'Ryan will be delighted to see you.'

Emma pictured her tousle-haired three-year-old nephew with a tired smile. It had been too long since she'd seen him or her sister. 'Great. I'm going to book a flight for tomorrow if I can.'

'Let me know the time and we'll pick you up from the airport.'

Twenty-four hours later Emma touched down in New York and, after clearing immigration, she walked straight into her sister's arms.

'Is everything okay?' Meghan asked as she hugged her tightly. Emma nodded wordlessly. Nothing felt right at that moment, but she hoped it would soon. All she needed was a little time to get over this, and then she'd be back on the road, taking photographs, looking for adventure, as footloose as ever. The prospect didn't fill her with anything except a weary desolation.

She spent the next week mainly sleeping and spending time with Ryan and Meghan; she wanted to shut the world out, but she couldn't quite do it, and especially not when her sister looked up from *The New York Times* one morning, her eyes narrowed.

'I'm just reading an article about how business CEO Larenzo Cavelli was arrested for being involved in the Mafia.' Emma felt the colour drain from her face but said nothing. 'Wasn't that your boss, Emma?'

'Yes.'

'That's why your job ended?'

Emma nodded jerkily as she poured some orange juice. 'Yes.'

'You were working for someone in the *Mafia*?'

'I didn't know, Meghan!'

Meghan sat back in her chair, her eyes wide. 'Of course you didn't know. But good gracious, Emma. I'm so glad you're here, and you're safe.'

Emma closed her eyes briefly. She could picture Larenzo as he braced himself above her, his face suffused with tenderness as he gave her more pleasure than she'd ever known or thought possible. And then just hours later, when she'd heard the thud of the boots in the hall, the men glaring at her as they ripped the sheet away from her body…

'So am I,' she said quietly. 'So am I.'

After that she couldn't shut out the world any more. She read in the newspaper that Larenzo had confessed to everything, and there would be no trial. Within a month of her arrival he'd been sentenced to life in prison.

Two days after that, Emma realised she hadn't got her period that month. One three-minute test later, she discovered the truth. She was pregnant with Larenzo Cavelli's child.

CHAPTER FOUR

Eighteen months later

'LOOK AT ME, Aunt Emma!'

Emma waved to her nephew as he clambered to the top of the climbing frame at the playground near her sister's house. It was late October, and the leaves of the maple trees in the little park were scarlet, the sky above a cloudless blue. It was a beautiful, crisp day, and yet even so she couldn't keep herself from picturing the mountains of Sicily, and remembering how clear and pure the air was up there at this time of year.

Shivering slightly in the chill wind, Emma told herself to stop thinking about Sicily. She would never go back there. Never see the Nebrodi mountains again. *Never see Larenzo Cavelli again.*

Which was just as well, considering the man was a criminal.

Instinctively her gaze moved to the stroller a few feet away, where her daughter Ava was sleeping peacefully. She was ten months old, born on Christmas Eve, and Emma still marvelled at her. Still marvelled at the way her own life had changed so drastically.

When she'd discovered she was pregnant, she'd been shocked and numb for days, as well as embarrassed that she hadn't even *thought* about birth control when she'd been with Larenzo. That was how much he'd affected her. How much she'd wanted him in that moment.

Meghan, as eagle-eyed as ever, had guessed she was pregnant within a matter of days, and Emma had ended up telling her sister everything.

'What do you want to do?' Meghan had asked in her direct way as they'd sat at her kitchen table, Emma shredding tissues while Meghan got up to make tea. 'I love babies,' she continued as she switched on the kettle, 'and I think each one is a blessing, but I'll support you no matter what.'

'Thank you,' Emma had answered, sniffing. 'Truthfully, I don't know what to do. I never planned on marrying or having a family...not that marriage is a possibility in this case.'

'Why haven't you?' Meghan asked, one hip braced against the counter as she fixed Emma with a thoughtful stare. 'Most people think about being with someone, at least.'

'I don't know.' Emma shredded another tissue, avoiding her sister's perceptive gaze. 'You know me. I like to be on the move. See new things. I don't want to be held down.'

'And a baby is the ultimate in being held down,' Meghan answered with a sigh.

'Yes...' Which made it seem simple, but Emma felt as if nothing was.

'I know Mom leaving affected you badly, Em,' Meghan said quietly. 'More than it did me. I was at college. I was already out of the way.'

'She was your mother too,' Emma answered, still not looking at her sister. By silent agreement she and Meghan had never really talked about their mother. Emma hadn't even seen her in at least five years. Louise Leighton had moved to Arizona with her second husband when Emma was still in high school; Emma had spent a wretched few months out in Arizona with her, but it had been awkward and stilted and just generally awful, and she'd left pretty quickly, after one blazing argument. Her mother hadn't protested.

Since then, beyond a few pithy emails, her mother had never made any attempt to contact her. She didn't know if Meghan was in touch with her or not; she'd never asked, told herself she didn't care.

'Anyway,' Meghan resumed, 'what I'm trying to say is, I understand if motherhood scares you. You didn't have the best example.'

'I'm not scared,' Emma answered. She pressed a hand against her middle, almost as if she could feel the tiny life moving inside her. 'I just feel like my whole life has been upended. Everything that happened in Sicily…' She trailed off, fighting against the memories that continued to swamp her, and Meghan came over to give her a hug.

'It's hard,' she said. 'And you have some time.'

As the days slipped by Emma had come to accept this new life inside her, and realise that, to her amazement, she actually welcomed it. She watched her sister with Ryan and knew she wanted that same kind of bond, that closeness with another person. Already she felt a surprising and unshakeable love for this person who was a part of her.

Once she had pictured her life unspooling like a rainbow-coloured thread as she traipsed about the world, having adventure after adventure. But perhaps motherhood would be the greatest adventure of all.

It had been that, she thought now as she gazed at her sleeping daughter. From the moment she'd been born, dark-haired and grey-eyed, Ava had possessed the Cavelli charisma. Whether she was screaming to be fed or simply demanding to be heard, the force of her personality could not be denied. She was her father's daughter.

And her father was serving life in prison.

Emma had had a year and a half to become accustomed to the fact that Larenzo was a Mafioso, and yet the knowledge still had the power to stun her. She couldn't look back on their one night together without experiencing a shaft of bittersweet longing, as well as a sense of bewilderment that the man she'd thought she'd known, at least a little, was someone else entirely.

'Are you almost ready to go?' Meghan asked as she walked up to her in the park. Her cheeks were red with cold and she cradled a thermos of coffee. 'Ryan will want his lunch before playgroup, and, if I'm not mistaken, your little madam is going to wake up soon and want hers.'

'Undoubtedly.' With a wry look for her sleeping daughter, Emma reached for the handles of the pram.

'Emma…' Meghan began, and Emma tensed instinctively. She'd known a conversation was coming; she'd been living with Meghan and her husband, Pete, for over eighteen months now. They'd been happy to support her through her pregnancy and she'd taken a few odd cleaning jobs until she'd been too ungainly to manage it, in order to contribute to the household expenses.

Then Ava had been born, and her life had become a sleepless whirlwind; she'd stood in its centre, dazed and helpless to do much other than care for this baby that still managed to startle her with her existence.

But her daughter would be a year soon and Emma knew she needed to find her own way. Make her own life, for her own sake as well as her sister's.

'I know,' she said quietly, her gaze on Ava sleeping in the pram, the pink blanket pulled up to her chin, which had a cleft the same as Larenzo's. 'I need to get a move on.'

'No.' Meghan put a hand on Emma's arm. 'I wasn't going to say that. I'd never say that, Emma. You're welcome to stay with us as long as you like. Always.'

Emma shook her head. She knew her sister meant well,

but she also knew that she couldn't stay. She hadn't contributed anything to the household finances since Ava's birth, and she and Ava had taken up the spare bedroom for far too long. Meghan and Pete wanted more children, and they needed the space.

'I've been meaning to get my act together for months now,' she told her sister. 'I've just—' she let out a long, low breath '—felt frozen, I suppose. And keeping Ava fed and changed has taken more energy than I care to admit.' She let out a shaky laugh. 'I don't know how you do it.'

'Motherhood is never easy, and Ava is a demanding baby,' Meghan answered. 'But this isn't about me or Pete, Emma. It's about you. What's best for you. I want you to have your own life. Maybe meet someone…'

Emma shook her head. She couldn't even *think* about meeting someone. She might not have loved Larenzo Cavelli or had her heart broken, but even so something in her felt a little dented. A bit bruised. And she'd never been interested in a serious relationship anyway. She was even less so now, with a bad experience and a baby in tow.

'I know I need to get a job.'

'It's not about money—'

'But it is, Meghan, at least in part. As wonderful as you are, you can't support me for ever. I'm twenty-seven years old, and I chose to have a child. I need to step up.' She took a deep breath. 'I know I seem like a sleep-deprived zombie most of the time, but I have been thinking about possibilities. Maybe moving to New York and getting a job there, something to do with photography.'

As far as a plan went, it wasn't very sensible, and Emma could tell her sister thought so from the look on her face. 'New York? But it's so expensive. And I'm not sure there are too many jobs in photography going…'

'I know, but…' The other option was staying in New Jersey, finding some poky apartment she could afford on the salary she'd get as a waitress or cleaner, the only kind of job for which she was qualified. 'I like to dream,' she admitted with a wry sigh, and Meghan nodded in understanding.

'What about another job as a housekeeper? A live-in position, so you could have Ava with you?'

'I'm not sure there are many of those going around.'

'You only need one.'

'True.' Emma glanced down at her daughter, who was starting to stir, her little face turning red as she screwed her features up in preparation for one of her ear-splitting howls. 'We'd better get going,' she told Meghan. 'Princess Ava needs her lunch.'

Back at the house she and Meghan fed Ava and Ryan, and then ate their own lunch while the two children played nearby.

'All right, let's do this,' Meghan said, ever practical, and resolutely Emma nodded as her sister pulled her laptop towards her and brought up the webpage for an agency that supplied jobs in the cleaning and hospitality industries.

Emma suppressed a groan as some of the available jobs scrolled by: night-time cleaning at a business park in Newark, janitorial work in a local elementary school.

'I don't…' she began, but Meghan cut her off with a quick shake of her head.

'We'll find something. Something perfect. There's no rush.'

But there *was* a rush, Emma thought glumly, even if she didn't want to say as much to her sister. Meghan might be happy to have her stay indefinitely, but she wasn't always so sure about Pete; as the breadwinner he surely felt the strain on the family finances more than anyone.

And she also knew she wanted more for her life than living in a spare bedroom, changing diapers and dreaming of sleep.

Maybe a poky apartment and a job cleaning school toilets would be it, at least for the interim. If she was careful she could save enough money to go somewhere, maybe travel again, this time with Ava. She pictured herself working her way through Europe, her baby in a backpack, and, while it held a certain quirky charm, she was also realistic enough to acknowledge how difficult that would be.

She could, she supposed, go to stay with her father, but he had been decidedly nonplussed about his unmarried daughter having a baby by a man who was serving a life sentence in prison, and in any case her father was immersed in his work, as he had been since his wife had left him fifteen years ago. He hadn't even seen Ava yet.

No, she needed to do something on her own. Stand on her own two feet, however wobbly she was.

'Let me have a look,' she said, and pulled the laptop towards her. She browsed the jobs for a few more minutes, taking down details, until Ava started crying, ready for her afternoon nap.

'I'll take her upstairs,' Emma said, scooping her protesting daughter into her arms. Ava wrapped her chubby arms around Emma's neck and snuffled against her chest. Her daughter was demanding, even difficult, but she still managed to make Emma's heart melt with love. She'd never regret her decision, even if she ended up cleaning toilets for the rest of her life.

Life could still be an adventure, she told herself as she settled Ava in her crib. It was all about attitude. No matter where she was or what she did, she could still enjoy her daughter, maybe even try photography again. She hadn't picked up her camera since Ava's birth, except to take a few photos of her daughter. The spontaneous, candid moments she'd captured on film all over the world had been hard to find here, and Emma had been too exhausted and overwhelmed to look for them.

She was just coming downstairs, Ava asleep hopefully for at least an hour and Meghan at playgroup with Ryan, when the doorbell sounded. Hoping the noise wouldn't wake Ava, ever a light sleeper, Emma went to answer it.

And stared straight into the face of Larenzo Cavelli. Shock blazed through her as she looked at him; he was thinner, the angles of his cheekbones a little sharper, everything about him a bit harder. A faint scar ran down one cheek, starting by his eyebrow and ending at his jaw. She noticed these changes distantly, her mind dazed and spinning; she could not actually believe it was him. He was here. How? And *why*?

'Larenzo…' she finally managed, her voice a rasp, and his face didn't show so much as a flicker of emotion as he answered.

'Hello, Emma.'

Larenzo gazed at Emma dispassionately; she was clearly shocked to see him, but he felt nothing when he looked at her, except perhaps a twinge of remorse, a flicker of bittersweet memory. That night they'd shared so long ago felt as if it had happened to someone else. It *had* happened to someone else. Eighteen months in prison changed you. For ever.

'May I come in?' He took a step towards her and she drew her breath in sharply, one hand fluttering to her throat.

'Don't—' she began, and he stilled. She almost looked afraid. Afraid of him.

'Do you think I'm going to hurt you?' he asked, wondering why he was surprised. Everyone else had believed the worst of him. Why shouldn't she?

Emma's eyes widened, her hand still at her throat. 'I don't—I don't know. Why are you here, Larenzo?'

Her voice wavered; she really was afraid. She thought

he was *dangerous*. It should have occurred to him before, of course. He'd thought all of his naive delusions about humanity had been stripped away, but clearly he'd clung to this last one. The memory of his one night with Emma had sustained him through prison. He didn't like having it tarnished now.

'I'm here,' he finally said, his voice cool, 'because I felt I owed you something.'

'You don't.'

'Considering your employment with me ended so abruptly, I thought you deserved some recompense,' he continued as if she hadn't spoken.

'Recompense...'

He stepped past her and dropped the envelope with the bank draft onto the hall table. 'Six months' pay. I thought you should have it.'

She stared at the envelope with something like revulsion. 'I don't want your money,' she said in a low voice. 'I don't want anything from you.'

'This money was honestly earned,' Larenzo informed her coldly. 'I can promise you that.'

'Why should I believe anything you say?' she shot back. 'How are you even *here*? The judge gave you life in prison—'

'I was released last week. Clearly you don't read the papers.'

'No, I...' She licked her lips, her gaze still wide. 'I haven't had time.'

'Well, if you'd read them,' Larenzo said, his voice coming out in a cold drawl, 'you would have known that all the charges against me were dropped.'

'They were?' She looked bewildered, her gaze darting between him and the stairs. Was she thinking of making a run for it, barricading herself in a bedroom? Did she really think he was going to *hurt* her? He was caught between fury and despair at the thought, and then he blanked out both emotions. He might have held onto the memory of Emma through prison, and their night together might have compelled him to find her now, but he didn't actually feel anything for her. He couldn't feel anything at all.

'Yes, they were. Otherwise I wouldn't be here. Obviously. Unless you thought I'd escaped?' He arched an eyebrow, smiled as if this were all so very amusing. 'Stage-managed some sort of breakout?'

'I…I don't know what I think.' She walked slowly past him, to the small sitting room at the front of the house. Larenzo followed her, watched as she sank onto the sofa, her head in her hands.

'How did you find me here?' she asked after a long, silent moment, her head still bowed.

'This was the address you gave on your employment application.'

She glanced up at him, her eyes widening once more. 'And you came all the way to America to give me six months' pay? If you really possessed such a conscience to see me adequately *recompensed*, you could have just deposited it in my bank account. You should have my details from when I was in your employment.'

Larenzo's mouth tightened. 'I was in America anyway.' She shook her head slowly, still dazed. Larenzo let his gaze rove over her, remembering her golden skin, her laughing eyes that looked so serious and dark now. She looked different, he realised. More womanly. She must have gained a little weight, and yet it suited her. Her breasts were fuller under the soft pink sweater she wore, and her face was a bit rounder. Her skin was as golden as he'd remembered, her golden-brown hair wavy and tousled about her face. His golden girl. What a joke.

'Why are you in America?' she asked and Larenzo snapped his gaze away from her.

'I'm relocating to New York.'

'New York—'

'Is that a problem?' he enquired coolly. 'I only came here to give you your pay.'

'I know, but…' She glanced up towards the stairs once more, and Larenzo's gaze narrowed. That was the second time she'd done that. What was upstairs? Was Emma hiding something from him? God knew he'd learned to become suspicious of everyone and everything. Trust was a concept he no longer even remotely considered.

'It doesn't matter,' she said quickly, as if coming to a decision. She rose from the sofa. 'Thank you for the six months' pay. That was…kind of you, considering.'

'Considering?' he repeated, his gaze narrowing. 'Considering what?'

Colour washed Emma's cheeks. 'Just the situation…'

'You mean considering I'm a criminal? Is that what you mean, Emma?' He didn't know why he was pushing her, only that he was. That he wanted her to say it, admit what she thought of him. Perhaps it would be like lancing a wound.

Emma lifted her chin, her eyes flashing in challenge. 'And what if it was?'

'I thought you knew me better than that.'

'I didn't know you at all, Larenzo. You were my employer, and I saw you a few times. We never even had a proper conversation before—' She stopped abruptly, the colour deepening in her cheeks as she looked away.

'Before what?' he demanded, his voice low and insistent. He was punishing himself as much as her by raking this all up, bringing the memories he'd tormented himself with to the fore. 'Before I made love to you? Before you wrapped your legs around my waist and—'

'Don't.' The single word came out in a suffocated whisper. 'Don't remind me.'

Larenzo's lip curled. 'You don't want to remember?'

'Of course I don't.' She glared at him, her golden-green eyes full of misery. 'I don't know why you were released from prison, Larenzo, or why the charges against you were dropped, but I just want you out of my life.' She pressed her lips together as she held his stare. 'I trust that won't be an issue.'

'An issue?' he repeated. Fury beat through his veins, fired his blood. 'I came here as a matter of courtesy. Clearly the effort was wasted.'

'I think it's best if you go now.'

'Fine.' He nodded curtly and curled his hands into fists at his sides, not trusting himself not to grab her by the shoulders and demand to know what he'd ever done to make her think he was a mobster. A Mafioso. *Mio Dio*, how could everyone he'd ever known have judged him so harshly and completely?

Because the evidence had been there, thanks to Bertrano. Because he'd confessed, even if he'd felt he had no choice.

She held his gaze, her chin still lifted, her shoulders thrown back, standing proud and defiant even though he knew she was afraid. Of him.

He opened his mouth to say something of his innocence, but then he closed it. Why claim something she would never believe? 'Goodbye,' he said instead, and turned towards the hallway.

A child's cry suddenly echoed from upstairs. From the corner of his eye he saw Emma freeze, her face drain of colour. He wouldn't have thought anything of the cry, considering he knew Emma was living with her sister and her family. And yet...

The child cried again, the plaintive wail of a baby. Emma didn't move. Neither did Larenzo. Every sense he had was on alert, although for what he could not say.

'Aren't you going to go to the child?' he asked, his voice deliberately mild as the baby continued to cry, the sobs becoming louder and more urgent.

Emma swallowed, and he watched the workings of her slender throat. 'I will. When you leave.'

He gazed at her for a taut moment, saw how her eyes had become huge golden pools in a face drained of colour. 'Is it your sister's child? Why is she not going to fetch the *bambino*?'

'She's not here.' Emma licked her lips, and Larenzo thought he saw panic in that wide gaze. 'Please, Larenzo. Just go.'

'I will.' He cocked his head towards the stairs. 'But maybe you should get the *bambino* first.'

'No.' The word came out like a gunshot, fast and loud. Larenzo raised his eyebrows. Emma stared him down. 'I told you, I don't want you here. Now go.' Her voice rose in a raggedy edge of terror, and Larenzo took a step towards her.

'What are you hiding from me, Emma?'

'Nothing—' But it sounded feeble. He took another step towards her.

'Tell me the truth. You're hiding something. I don't know what it could be, but—'

'What do you think I'm hiding from you?' she cut him off scornfully. She nodded towards the stairs. 'A *baby*?'

The words hung there, seeming to echo through the sudden silence of the room. Larenzo stared at her, saw how bloodless her lips were as they parted soundlessly.

The thought hadn't fully formed in his mind until she'd said the words. He'd sensed she was hiding something, had felt her panic and fear, had heard the baby cry…

And yet it hadn't all come together for him. But it did now, crystallising with shocking clarity, and without a word for her he turned from the room and bounded up the stairs.

'Larenzo—' She hurried after him, one arm flung towards him in desperate supplication. 'Larenzo, please, don't—'

He could hear the child crying, the voice pitiful and plaintive. 'Mama. Mama.'

'Please,' she said again, choking on the word, and Larenzo ignored her.

Mama. Mama.

He threw open the door and came to a complete and stunned halt as he saw the baby standing in her crib, chubby fists gripping the rail, cherubic face screwed up and wet with tears.

Emma came into the room behind him, breathing hard, and the baby flung her arms out towards her. 'Mama.'

And Larenzo knew. He would have known just by looking at the child, with her ink-dark hair and large grey eyes, the cleft in her chin. He turned to Emma, who was gazing at him with undisguised panic.

'When,' he asked in a low, deadly voice, 'were you going to tell me about my child?'

CHAPTER FIVE

EMMA STARED AT Larenzo and saw the fury blazing in his gaze. Why, oh, why had she said that about hiding a baby? She'd meant to be bold, to pour scorn on the presumption, but she'd seen how she'd given him the idea instead. She'd told him about Ava.

Now she sagged against the doorway, completely at a loss as to what to do or say. Larenzo took a step towards her, his hands balled into fists.

'So this is why you were so desperate for me to leave—'

'Mama,' Ava called, her arms still outstretched, and Emma straightened and walked swiftly towards her daughter, scooping her up in her arms, and pressed her cheek against Ava's downy hair.

'Please,' she murmured to Larenzo. 'Let me settle her and then we'll talk.' Although what she could tell him, she had no idea. She'd never imagined this happening, ever. She'd never expected even to see Larenzo again.

Ava continued to snuffle against her chest and Emma soothed her mindlessly, her mind spinning in futile circles. She settled her back in the cot as Larenzo waited in the hall and hoped her daughter might drift off to sleep once more. She'd slept for only twenty minutes, which unfortunately wasn't that uncommon, but on a good day Emma could count on an hour.

Quietly she slipped out of the room and closed the door. Larenzo stood there, arms folded, eyebrows raised. He opened his mouth to speak but Emma shook her head and pressed a finger to her lips, cocking her head to indicate he should follow her downstairs.

In the kitchen she wiped the counters and tidied up the last of the lunch dishes, needing to keep busy, to keep from thinking how on earth she was going to handle this. Handle *him*. Larenzo watched her, one powerful shoulder propped against the doorway, everything about him arrogant, assured and definitely intimidating. She couldn't *handle* this man at all.

'You do not deny she's mine,' he said finally, and Emma shook her head.

'How can I? She looks just like you.'

'Yes.' He raked a hand through his hair, his gaze shuttered and distant as he shook his head slowly. 'We didn't use birth control.'

'No.'

'I never even thought…'

'Nor did I. Obviously.'

'She must have put a dent in your plans,' he said after a moment, his voice turning sharp, and Emma narrowed her eyes.

'What do you mean?'

'All your travel plans. You told me you liked to move around. Itchy feet, you said.'

She was surprised and weirdly gratified that he'd remembered what she'd said, but also piqued that he was throwing it back in her face now. 'That changed when I became pregnant.'

'You never considered a termination?'

Her mouth dropped open. 'Is that what you would have preferred? Because—'

'No.' He shook his head, one swift, violent movement. '*No.* But I could understand if—'

She let out a rush of breath. 'I thought of it at first, I

suppose, but never seriously. I never thought I wanted a husband or children, but I couldn't…she was a part of me.' A lump formed in her throat and resolutely she swallowed past it. 'I loved her even before she was born.'

'And you've been living here since her birth?' His gaze moved around the small kitchen, and Emma prickled.

'My sister has been very kind—'

'Yes, of course. But what about your father? Is he still in Budapest?'

So he remembered that too. 'Yes, he is, but I wanted to be here. And frankly he wasn't thrilled about me being pregnant, unmarried, and the father—'

'In prison,' he finished flatly, and Emma nodded.

'In any case, we're fine here.'

'But you can't stay here for ever.'

'Meghan is happy for us to stay,' Emma shot back. She wasn't about to admit to Larenzo that she might need to move out. 'Anyway, I don't see how this concerns you, Larenzo—'

'Are you serious?' He cut her off, his voice harsh. 'She's my daughter.' He paused, struggling to control his emotions while Emma watched in apprehension. 'What's her name?' he finally asked.

She hesitated, reluctant to part with even that much information. What if Larenzo wanted to be a part of Ava's life, of their lives? How on earth could she cope with that?

'Emma, I deserve to know her name!' His voice came out raggedly, and with a shaft of guilt Emma remembered how he'd told her about his childhood in Palermo, how he'd never had a real family. And with that came other memories of their night together, tender ones that she'd tried to keep herself from remembering. They tumbled through her mind in a bittersweet rush of poignant longing and she was helpless against it. No matter what Larenzo had done, she'd loved this man. For a night.

'Ava,' she said quietly.

'Ava,' he repeated, and she closed her eyes against the wonder she heard in his voice. 'How old is she?'

'Ten months. She was born on Christmas Eve.'

'Would you have ever told me about her?' he asked after a moment.

She opened her eyes and stared at him helplessly. 'Larenzo, you were in *prison*. You were convicted of about a thousand charges all related to being in the Mafia. How could I tell you?'

He gazed back steadily, unmoved by her argument. 'The charges were dropped.'

'I didn't know that. And I still don't know why they were dropped—'

'You still think I'm guilty?' he cut her off, his voice hard.

'I don't *know*,' she cried. 'Larenzo, you have to understand how it was for me. The day you were arrested… those men…'

Even now, a year and a half later, the memory of that night made shame and fear roil through her. 'It was horrible. And then I spent the whole day in the anti-Mafia headquarters in Palermo while they told me you were involved in the Mafia, how they had all this evidence…what was I supposed to believe?'

'Me. You could have believed me.'

'You confessed,' she shot back. 'I read it in the papers. So I did believe you.'

He pressed his lips together, his gaze narrowed and hard. 'Of course you did.'

'And yet you still seem to think I should have believed in your innocence.'

He didn't answer, and Emma bit her lip. She felt cold inside, so terribly cold. For a year and a half she'd been so certain of Larenzo's guilt, and yet now, having seen him only for a few minutes, she felt doubt creep in along with the bittersweet memories. Who was the real man—the Mafia monster or the one she'd made love to?

'But just now,' he finally said. 'You wanted me to leave. Even now, when you knew the charges had been dropped, that I was free, you were trying to keep me from my child.'

'Because as far as I know, you're still a dangerous man,' Emma retorted. Larenzo's eyes narrowed and she almost took a step back. Yet even now she realised she wasn't actually afraid of him. She didn't think he'd hurt her, but…

What was she afraid of, then? Because she certainly felt the cold claws of terror digging into her soul, icing over her mind. 'Even if you are innocent of the charges they laid against you,' she continued more calmly, 'you must have Mafia connections, something that made the police—'

'Not in the way you think,' he bit out, and Emma just shook her head, overwhelmed with too many terrible emotions to respond. 'I am a free man,' Larenzo said in a low voice. 'And you can't keep me from my daughter.'

Emma pressed her hand to her forehead. 'We can't talk about this now,' she said. 'My sister will be home in a few minutes, and Ava is going to wake up soon. I never even expected to see you again, Larenzo. Having you turn up out of the blue…' She shook her head. 'It's a lot to take in.'

'I understand,' he answered levelly. 'But know this. I *will* be back, and I will see Ava again. Don't think for a moment you can keep me from her.'

His mouth compressed and his eyes flashed silver and Emma's stomach did a sickening little flip. She had no idea what to think, to believe.

'We'll talk,' she managed. 'Soon.'

Larenzo held her gaze for an endless, agonising moment, and then with one swift nod he turned and left the room. Emma heard the click of the front door closing and she sagged against the kitchen counter, utterly emotionally spent.

'Emma?' A minute later her sister's voice, lilting with curiosity, floated down the hall. 'Who was that leaving the house?'

Emma straightened as her sister came into the kitchen with Ryan in tow, her eyebrows raised, a smile playing about her mouth. 'Do you have a secret admirer?'

'Hardly.' Emma took a deep breath. 'That was Larenzo Cavelli.'

'What?' The smile slid clear off Meghan's face and numbly Emma explained the events of the last hour. Ava woke up just as she was finishing and she hurried upstairs, grateful for a moment to collect her thoughts, few as she had.

'Mama.' Ava wound her arms around her neck as Emma closed her eyes and breathed in her daughter's scent, baby powder with a hint of the banana she'd eaten for lunch. Ava pressed her cheek against Emma's chest, letting out a snuggly sigh, and Emma's heart gave a painful squeeze. She would do anything for Ava. Anything to keep her safe... even if it meant keeping her from her father.

Yet how could she do that? And should she, if Larenzo were really innocent?

'Ava, sweetheart,' she whispered against the baby's silky hair. 'What are we going to do?'

She stayed upstairs for a few moments, cuddling Ava and then changing her diaper, wanting to put off the conversation she'd have to have with Meghan. Wanting to put off thinking about Larenzo Cavelli and what she was going to do.

Yet even in the dim quiet of her and Ava's bedroom, memories invaded. Memories not of Larenzo as he'd been only moments ago, coldly angry, clearly ruthless, but as he'd been the night their daughter had been conceived. The tenderness he'd shown, as well as the despair. That sorrow and resignation she'd felt in him, had yearned to take away, and the aching, reverent gentleness of his touch…

Remembering that man made all the certainties she'd cultivated over the last eighteen months scatter like ash.

What if he wasn't guilty?

But what if he is?

'Emma?' Meghan's voice was sharp with concern as she called up the stairs. 'Are you coming down?'

'Yes, I'll be there in a moment.' Taking a deep breath, Emma settled Ava on her hip and headed downstairs. Ryan was playing in the playroom adjoining the kitchen and she put Ava on the floor with him, scattering a few blocks and soft toys around. Knowing her daughter as she did, Ava would throw all the toys across the room and then try to grab the trains Ryan was playing with. Her daughter knew what she wanted…just like her father.

'I can't believe Larenzo Cavelli came here,' Meghan said, her voice hollow with shock. She filled up the kettle, shaking her head slowly. 'How did he even know…?'

'The address was on my employment application.'

'And he wants to see Ava?'

'I don't know what he wants exactly, but he told me I couldn't keep him from his daughter.'

Meghan was silent for a moment, her face pale with strain. 'So do you think he is innocent, if the charges were dropped?' she asked and Emma bit her lip.

'I don't know anything any more, Meghan. For a year and a half I thought I knew the truth. I didn't like it, of course, and at times I couldn't believe it, but I thought I *knew*.'

'And now you think you didn't?' Meghan sounded sceptical, and rightly so. How could Emma take anything Larenzo said at face value?

'I don't know. But I suppose I should find out why the

charges against him were dropped.' She reached for the laptop they'd left lying out on the kitchen counter, the browser still on the employment agency's listings. Had it only been a couple of hours ago she'd been worried about what sort of menial job she'd take? It almost seemed laughable.

Quickly Emma typed in the browser's search engine *Larenzo Cavelli charges dropped*. Hundreds of results came up within seconds. She clicked on the first one, and began to read the news article.

All charges have been dropped against convicted felon Larenzo Cavelli when new evidence came to light that business partner Bertrano Raguso was in fact behind the illegal activities...

Meghan peered at the article over her shoulder. 'Do you think it's true?' she asked in a low voice.

'I have no idea.' Emma scanned the rest of the article, skimming over the terrible list of Larenzo's alleged crimes that she'd read in the paper once already. Once had definitely been enough.

'If his business partner really was guilty, why would Larenzo confess?' Meghan asked as she nibbled her lip.

'I don't know.' Emma gazed at the photograph of Bertrano Raguso, a silver-haired man in his sixties, his face set into haggard lines. 'But if they let Larenzo go...'

'But they'd have to, if they have another confession.'

'I don't know if it's that simple.' Emma rubbed her forehead, felt the beginnings of a headache. From the playroom she heard the clatter of blocks being flung across the room, and then Ryan's yowl as one connected with his head. 'I need to see to Ava,' she said. 'I'll have to think about this later. About what I'm going to do.'

'You should consult a lawyer—'

Emma flinched at the thought. She didn't want to get involved in some messy, drawn-out custody battle that would no doubt be splashed across the newspapers, due to Larenzo's notoriety. But what if the alternative was granting him access to Ava? Exposing her to God only knew what kind of danger?

Unless he really was innocent…but how could he not have known about his partner's activities? And why would he have confessed?

Emma let out a tired sigh. Her mind was racing in circles and she knew she had no answers now. 'He might not actually want to be involved with Ava,' she said, trying to convince herself as much as her sister. 'He might just want to see her once…'

'You need to be prepared,' Meghan answered swiftly. 'Emma, the man is—'

'We don't know what he is.'

'Can you really doubt—?'

'I told you, I don't *know*.' And yet if there was any chance Larenzo was guilty, any chance of putting Ava in danger…

'I'll talk to a lawyer,' Emma said. 'I should do that much, at least. Just…just in case.'

Ava and Ryan had both started crying and so Emma scooped her daughter up and distracted her with a few board books before rejoining Meghan at the laptop. Her sister had typed custody lawyers into the search box, and, with her heart thudding sickly and her head still spinning from all that had happened in such a short span of time, Emma watched the results come up, and then she reached for her phone.

CHAPTER SIX

NERVOUSLY EMMA SMOOTHED her hair, straightened her skirt, and then opened the door to the restaurant where she was meeting Larenzo. It had been three endless days since he'd shown up at her sister's house, and Emma had almost started hoping that Larenzo had decided to leave them alone. Yet tangled up in that hope had been an absurd disappointment that he might have given up so easily.

She'd spoken to a lawyer two days ago, and he'd told her that since the charges against Larenzo had been dropped, he would most certainly have a legal right to see Ava. Access could be limited or denied if a court decided there was any danger to her daughter, but it was by no means clear cut or simple.

The next day Larenzo had called and Emma's heart had actually lifted at the sound of his voice. They'd set up a meeting over dinner at a local restaurant, and Emma knew she had no idea what she wanted from this meeting. Her emotions and thoughts were all over the place, and no matter how she tried to order them they raced off in all directions as soon as she thought of Larenzo, remembered how he'd once been with her.

The atmosphere, she saw as she came into the restaurant, was elegant and understated, candlelight flickering over snowy white tablecloths. It almost seemed romantic, which didn't help her disordered thoughts, her clamouring emotions. No matter what she and Larenzo decided about Ava, romance had no place in their lives any more.

She gave her name to the *maître d'* and he showed her to a table in the back, set in a private alcove. Larenzo was already seated, and he rose as she approached. He wore a white button-down shirt and plain grey trousers, and yet he still seemed bigger and darker and more magnetic than any other person in the room.

Once, only once, she'd allowed herself to be drawn by that magnetic force. Now she knew she needed to be immune. To stay strong.

Emma sat down across from him, busying herself with putting her napkin in her lap as Larenzo settled back into his seat, seeming to take up too much space, too much air. Why had it become hard to breathe?

'Thank you for coming,' he said.

Emma took a deep breath, letting the air fill her lungs. 'I didn't really have much choice, did I?'

He pressed his lips together and Emma could almost feel the tension crackle between them. 'This doesn't have to be unpleasant, Emma.'

'And how do you figure that?' she shot back. She'd wanted to stay calm for this meeting but already her composure was cracking, revealing the fear and uncertainty underneath. 'I'm here to discuss a man with Mafia connections being involved with my daughter—'

'*My* daughter,' Larenzo cut across her, his voice low and intense. 'She's my daughter too. Never forget that.'

'Unfortunately, I won't.'

He sat back in his chair, his fingers laced together as he gazed at her. 'Do you hate me?' he asked, as if it was a matter of academic interest, and Emma could only stare at him, flummoxed. *Where had that come from?* 'Because,' he continued, 'you seem as if you hate me.'

'I…' She searched for words, disconcerted by how

much his question had unsettled her. 'I don't hate you,' she said finally. 'I don't feel anything for you.' Which was a bold-faced lie. She didn't know what she felt for Larenzo Cavelli, but it was definitely something. 'But I love my daughter,' she continued shakily, 'and I want to protect her—'

'And you think I don't want that?'

'I don't know what to think about you, Larenzo. I have no idea what to believe.'

'How about the truth?'

'Which is?' she demanded, her voice rising. 'Eighteen months ago you confessed to a long, sordid list of crimes. A week ago, your business partner was convicted of those same crimes, thanks to new evidence, but what am I meant to believe? How on earth do you expect me to trust you?'

Larenzo expelled a long, low breath. 'I don't,' he said flatly. 'You can't trust anyone in this world. That's one thing I've come to realise.'

'Why did you confess if you weren't guilty?'

He pressed his lips together as he flicked his gaze away. 'Because there was overwhelming evidence to convict me.'

'How?'

'Look, I don't want to get into all that now. I left that life behind—'

'And I'm supposed to just *accept* that?'

Larenzo leaned forward, his gaze glittering. 'Emma, do you honestly think I'd put my own child in danger? Do you think I'd be here if I thought I'd be hurting Ava?'

Emma bit her lip. She didn't think that, but she was still afraid. Still reluctant to relinquish control, to let Larenzo into Ava's life. Into her life, in any way at all, and with a jolt she realised it wasn't just because of his possible criminal connections. It was because this man affected her. And she was afraid to let him do that again.

Larenzo leaned back in his chair. 'I left Italy for good

and severed all ties to Cavelli Enterprises. Bertrano Raguso is in prison for the crimes he committed. That is all you need to know.'

'Why New York?' Emma asked. The waiter came forward to take their order, and she gazed blindly at the menu. She had no appetite at all. Finally she picked a relatively plain chicken dish, and Larenzo ordered for himself, before they were left alone again and he answered her question.

'I wanted a new start. Cavelli Enterprises had no holdings in America.'

'What's happened to Cavelli Enterprises?'

'Its assets were seized by the government. Everything's frozen while the investigation continues.'

'So even though there was evidence…?'

Larenzo's mouth hardened into a flat line. 'Bertrano is claiming he is innocent, but the evidence is incontrovertible.' His mouth twisted. 'In the meantime the company will most likely be liquidated, and its remaining assets distributed to shareholders.' He spoke dispassionately, as if it was a matter of indifference to him. Emma searched his face, saw a hardness underneath his bland expression that she didn't think had been there before.

'Were you close to him? This Raguso?'

Larenzo hesitated, one hand resting flat on the tabletop. 'A bit,' he finally said.

'And do you think he did it?'

'I know he did.' He shifted in his chair, his gaze arrowing in on her. 'While I was in prison, my staff investigated and found proof of his guilt. But enough talk of what is past. It's the future that concerns me.'

'The past is important, Larenzo—'

'I've told you all you need to know,' he cut across her. 'I want to talk about Ava.'

She knew it was coming, and yet she still resisted. 'What about her?'

For a second his face softened, his mouth curving into something almost like a smile and just that little look made Emma start to melt. 'What is she like? From the little I saw of her already, it seems like she knows her own mind.'

'She does. She's a force to be reckoned with, that's for sure.'

'Her strength will serve her well later in life.'

'So I keep telling myself.' To her shock Emma realised she was smiling, and Larenzo was actually smiling back.

'I want to see her,' Larenzo said firmly, and Emma took a deep breath.

'There's a playground near the house—'

Larenzo's expression darkened, his eyes flashing silver fire. 'A playground? Do you think you can fob me off with an hour or two at a local park?'

'It's a start, Larenzo—'

'I've missed the first ten months of my daughter's life. I want to spend time with her, Emma. Real time. Not be introduced to her as if I'm some stranger in a park playground.'

Emma stared down at the table, conscious of how quickly Larenzo had torn apart her suggestion. She'd wanted to stage-manage his entrance into Ava's life, to exert some control over the proceedings, and hopefully to limit them. She should have known Larenzo wouldn't let her do that. He was a man who was in control. Always.

'Very well.' She took a deep, even breath and let it out slowly. 'What do you suggest?'

'I've taken an apartment in New York, and it has plenty of room. I suggest you and Ava move there with me.'

Emma gaped at him, stunned into silence for a few seconds. 'You want me to move in with you?' she finally managed, her voice ending in something close to a squeak.

'I'm not suggesting we have some sort of relationship,' Larenzo clarified coolly. 'I have no interest in that. But I want to see my daughter as much as possible, and be a real presence in her life. Your current living arrangements are neither sustainable nor suitable.' He lifted one powerful shoulder in a shrug. 'The answer seems obvious.'

'To you, maybe.' Emma nearly choked. She shook her head and reached for her glass of water. She'd never expected Larenzo to suggest something like this. To live with him…*to be that near to temptation*…

'I don't see an alternative,' Larenzo answered. 'I want unlimited access to my daughter—'

'Unlimited? Larenzo, be reasonable—' At the very most she'd thought she'd have to have some kind of joint custody arrangement with Larenzo. But this?

This was dangerous. Impossible. *Tempting*…

'I don't really see what the problem is,' Larenzo replied calmly. 'Surely you agree it's better for Ava to have two interested and loving parents in her life?'

Emma swallowed. 'Yes, but that doesn't mean we have to live together—'

'What, precisely, do you object to?' Larenzo asked. His voice had gone quiet, dangerously so. 'You'll have your own room, your own bathroom, and your quarters will be far more comfortable than they are currently.'

Emma stared at him helplessly. He made it all sound so simple, and yet it wasn't. It couldn't be. 'Everything's changed so quickly,' she finally said. 'I can't process it all—'

'Then take your time,' Larenzo answered. 'You have until tomorrow.'

'*Tomorrow*—'

'I want to see my daughter, Emma.'

'I know you do.' Except she hadn't expected Larenzo to feel this strongly, this *fiercely*, about his role as a father. That he did surprised her, but she realised she couldn't resent it. She knew what it was like to have a parent who chose a life without you. Who walked away from her child.

Despite all the obstacles, all the unknowns, she realised she was, amazingly, glad Larenzo wanted to be involved… even if she was scared about what it meant.

'I can't just *live* with you,' she finally burst out.

Larenzo arched an eyebrow, all arrogant assurance. 'Why not?'

'Because…because…' Because she was afraid of this man, and it had nothing to do with any criminal connections. She was afraid of his power over her, her need for him. 'I need to have my own life, Larenzo. I was planning on moving out of my sister's house for that reason. I'm twenty-seven years old and I'm not going to freeload off people for ever.'

'So this is a question of money?'

'Not just money,' she returned. 'It's about independence and autonomy. I need to be my own person—'

'And you can't do that living in my apartment?' He made her feel ridiculous, and yet she *couldn't* just fall in with his plans, fit into his life without having one of her own.

'I can't believe I'm even thinking of moving in with you,' she said, shaking her head slowly.

'It makes sense.'

Emma didn't answer. It *did* make a certain kind of bizarre sense, which both aggravated and alarmed her. Three days ago she'd thought Larenzo Cavelli would spend his life in prison. Two days ago she would have fought tooth and nail to keep him out of her daughter's life.

And now she was thinking of living with him? She pressed her fingers to her temples and closed her eyes. 'This is so crazy.'

'Maybe so,' Larenzo agreed with a shrug, 'but it's our reality. I won't take no for an answer, Emma.'

She opened her eyes and stared at him, saw that coldness in his eyes, the hint of how hard he could be. 'What would you do if I did say no, Larenzo?'

'It won't come to that.'

'But if it did?'

He hesitated, then stated flatly, 'I'd sue for custody.'

Emma jerked back, appalled. 'So this is basically blackmail.'

'No.'

'Then what would you call it? "Live with me or I'll take your child." That's what you're saying, Larenzo.'

'And what are you saying?' he answered, a hint of anger in his voice. '"You're my child's father and I don't want you involved in her life," even though you know I am innocent.'

'I didn't say that—'

'You've been saying that for ten months, Emma.'

She took a deep breath. Arguing would get them nowhere. 'Things have changed, Larenzo. I recognise that. But you can't expect me to fall in with your plans without a second's thought—'

'I haven't. I told you, you have until tomorrow.'

'Well, thanks for that,' she answered sarcastically. There was no reasoning with this man. No swaying him. So what was she going to do?

The waiter came with their meals, giving Emma a few minutes' respite from the intensity of their conversation.

She picked at her chicken, her gaze lowered; she didn't think she could swallow a single mouthful. Then, to her shock, she felt Larenzo's hand on her own, his palm warm and strong just as it had been a year and a half ago, when he'd covered her hand with his own and she'd felt, for a moment, closer to this man than anyone else on earth.

'Why are you fighting this, Emma?' he asked quietly, and his voice was as sorrowful as it had been back on that night. His touch and his words catapulted her to that time when she'd felt so much for this man, had longed to comfort him. Had seen tenderness and understanding in his eyes, had felt it in his arms.

A lump rose in her throat and she blinked rapidly, swallowed past it. 'I don't know,' she whispered, and it sounded like a confession.

'I want to be with Ava. I never had a family of my own, except...' He stopped, his voice choking, and shook his head. 'I don't want this to be acrimonious, God knows. I want to get to know my daughter and love her. Please let me do that.'

She gazed up at him, saw the sincerity and emotion in his eyes, and felt her last reservations melt away. She believed Larenzo. She believed he was innocent, but, more importantly, she believed he wanted what was best for Ava.

She only hoped it was best for her too.

CHAPTER SEVEN

'I can't believe you're doing this.'

Meghan stood behind Emma as she finished packing her suitcases—just one for her and one for Ava, really not much at all to bring to her new home. Her new life.

'It makes sense, Meghan,' she said, which was what Larenzo had said to her last night. Last night she'd lain in bed, staring at the ceiling, unable to sleep as she'd thought about her future, when she'd heard Meghan's and Pete's raised voices downstairs, and had known they were talking about her. She'd crept to the top of the stairs, everything in her stilling as Pete had declared,

'She can't stay here any longer, Meghan. I've been patient, God knows, but two more mouths to feed is expensive, and if this Cavelli character has connections to—'

'He was cleared of all charges,' Meghan had cut across her husband.

'Even so—'

'She doesn't have anywhere else to go, Pete.'

'Then she needs to find somewhere,' Pete had answered grimly, and Emma had crept back to her bed.

Pete was right. She couldn't stay here any longer, for too many reasons. And she no longer wanted to deny Larenzo access to his daughter, even if she was afraid of what that might mean. Not for Ava, but for her.

'You could stay here,' Meghan persisted, and Emma met her sister's eye in the mirror hanging over the bureau.

'You know I couldn't,' she said quietly, and Meghan flushed and looked away.

'I was afraid you might have heard that conversation—'

'Pete's right, Meghan.'

Meghan bit her lip. 'I like having you here, Emma. You've been away for so long—'

'New York City isn't that far. I'll visit lots, I promise.'

'I'll worry. I still don't trust Cavelli. Even if he was cleared of charges…'

'What happened to innocent until proven guilty?' Emma asked lightly. 'I trust him, Meghan, and I know he wouldn't hurt his daughter.' She paused, her gaze on the clothes she was folding. 'He was good to me when I worked for him.' She bit her lip as a pang of bittersweet longing assailed her. 'He was very good to me.'

'But can you really trust him?' Meghan persisted, and Emma thought of what he'd said last night at dinner. *You can't trust anyone in this world. That's one thing I've come to realise.* When had he realised that? When he was a child at the orphanage, or when he'd been sent to a prison for crimes he might not have committed? A lifetime of betrayal, perhaps, and yet there was still so much she didn't understand.

'Yes, I can,' she answered Meghan. 'At least when it comes to Ava.'

Twenty minutes later Larenzo pulled up in front of Meghan's house in a luxury sedan, a car seat already installed in the centre of the back seat. He loaded the two suitcases in the boot, glancing at Emma.

'That's all you have?'

'I travel light.'

'But Ava—'

'The crib and changing table and things belonged to Meghan. They're hoping for another baby someday, so…'

'You don't need to worry about any of that,' Larenzo said. 'I've taken care of it.'

'Okay,' she murmured, and Larenzo held out his arms for Ava.

'May I?'

Wordlessly she nodded and handed him their daughter. He held her awkwardly, clearly not used to the chubby bundle of arms and legs that was an almost toddler. 'Hello, sweetheart,' he murmured, smiling into Ava's inquisitive face. She gurgled and grabbed his chin in her chubby fists and Larenzo laughed, the sound rusty and surprising and also achingly wonderful. Emma realised she hadn't heard Larenzo laugh before. It reminded her of the photo she'd shown him, back in Sicily; it was a sound of joy. Suddenly she felt almost near tears. She swallowed hard and watched as Larenzo buckled Ava into her car seat; he fiddled with the straps and with a laugh that managed to clear the tears away Emma helped him.

'These things are impossible,' she said. 'Especially when Ava is resisting.' She buckled the straps over Ava's tummy, conscious of Larenzo standing so close to her, his head bent near hears. She closed her eyes, willed herself to develop a little strength. A lot of resistance. Otherwise she was going to have way too many difficult moments with Larenzo. 'There.' She patted the buckled straps and straightened, her breast brushing against Larenzo's arm as she did so. Desire shot through her veins and she quickly turned away and got in the car, deeply unsettled by her own reaction to this man who had catapulted so suddenly back into her life.

Larenzo started the car; Emma was in the passenger seat, her face turned towards the window. He had no idea what she was thinking, if she still resented his presence in Ava's life.

He'd told Emma he didn't trust anyone, and, while that

was true, he was conscious of how he was asking her to trust him with the most precious thing of all: their child. But he also knew he couldn't change who he was, who he'd become. Trust was now an alien concept, and always would be. Even so, he could appreciate what Emma was doing.

'Thank you,' he said abruptly, and she turned to him warily.

'For what?' she asked and he cleared his throat.

'For agreeing to live with me.'

'When the alternative is having you sue me for custody,' she answered after a moment, 'there wasn't really any question, was there?'

Guilt needled him at the realisation of how effectively he'd blackmailed her. Was he really any better than Bertrano, when he resorted to such tactics? And yet Emma would have denied him his own flesh and blood, the child he'd never expected to have, the family he'd longed for since he was a child himself.

'Well,' he said after a moment, 'I'm still grateful.' Emma did not reply.

They drove in silence for the entire hour's journey into the city; Ava babbled and gurgled in the back seat, and by the time they approached the Lincoln Tunnel she was tired of the car and began to protest, straining against the straps of her car seat.

Emma tried to distract her with a few toys and then a rice cake, all of which entertained Ava for about three seconds before she hurled each item to the floor.

'Sorry,' Emma said as she glanced down at the floor of the back seat. 'You have a sea of rice cake crumbs down there.'

'It doesn't matter.'

'Are you sure you're prepared for this?' she asked as Ava drummed her heels against the seat. 'Ava is a force to be reckoned with.'

'So I can see—and hear,' Larenzo answered dryly. 'I don't know if I'm prepared. But I'm willing to take it on.' She need never doubt him in that.

'Did you ever want children?' Emma asked. 'I mean, before…'

'Before I went to prison?' Larenzo filled in flatly. 'I don't know if I really thought of it. I didn't have time for a relationship.'

'Yet you've certainly had your share of women.'

His mouth tightened as he slid her a sideways glance. She'd spoken without expression, and he had no idea what she thought of that aspect of his past. Not that it actually mattered, since there would never be anything like that between them. He had nothing to offer Emma, or anyone. Not in that way. 'I don't deny it,' he said after a moment.

'Having a baby in your apartment, as well as her mother, might cramp your style a bit.'

Larenzo shook his head. 'I've no interest in anything like that any more.'

Emma raised her eyebrows, clearly sceptical. 'Larenzo, you're what? In your mid-thirties? Surely you're going to want a woman again.'

Want a woman. The last woman he'd been with had been Emma, and he'd wanted her almost unbearably. Just remembering the sweetness of her touch, the innocent and utter yielding of her body when he'd needed her so badly, made lust shaft through him with a sudden, painful intensity.

He shifted as discreetly as he could in his seat and kept his eyes on the road. He might have told Emma he wasn't interested in relationships or sex any more, and in truth his libido had disappeared while he'd been in prison, along with all of his other feelings and desires. But he could feel it returning in force now.

'What about you?' he asked. 'You might meet someone.' A thought that he disliked instinctively, although he knew he had no right to.

'I can't even imagine meeting someone,' Emma said with a small sigh. 'Ava takes up all my energy.'

'She won't be a baby for ever.'

'No,' Emma said slowly. 'But, Larenzo, this…situation can't last for ever.'

He turned to her sharply, his eyes narrowed. 'What do you mean?'

'I can't live with you for ever. I accept that it's expedient for now, and of course it gives you time to get to know her, but eventually…I need my own life. You'll need yours. When Ava is a little older, we can come to a custody arrangement we can both live with.'

Larenzo didn't answer for a moment. He knew she was talking sense but everything in him rebelled against it. Ava was the only family he'd ever had. He wasn't going to give her up, not even in part, as easily as that.

'We'll discuss the future when it is relevant,' he said, making his tone final. They'd driven through the Lincoln Tunnel and now came out into midtown Manhattan, all of them blinking in the bright sunlight. Even Ava had stopped protesting against the hated car seat as she gazed curiously at the gleaming skyscrapers and the streets teeming with people.

Emma turned to stare out of the window, and Larenzo saw she looked almost as wide-eyed as her daughter. 'Have you spent much time in New York before?'

'Not really. As a kid I always lived abroad. My apartment is on the Central Park West, right near the Natural History Museum. It's a good area for children.'

'You've only been in America for a week, haven't you?' Emma asked. 'How did you manage to secure an apartment so quickly?'

'Money talks.'

'And even though the assets of Cavelli Enterprises are frozen, you have money?'

'I had my own savings, which were released to me when the charges were cleared.'

She turned to give him a direct look. 'Are you ever going to tell me the whole story, Larenzo?'

His hands tensed on the steering wheel and he stared straight ahead as he navigated the roundabout at Columbus Circle. 'I've told you what you need to know, Emma.' Perhaps it was foolish to keep the truth from her about Bertrano; it was shaming that he still felt a loyalty to a man who, despite years of shared history, of happy memories, had completely and utterly betrayed him. And he knew that telling Emma his part of the story, how he'd been duped and deceived, wouldn't make much difference. Yet it would make a difference to him. He didn't want to admit how naive he'd been, how *hurt* he'd been. Not to Emma. Not to anyone.

And maybe Emma sensed some of what he felt, for to Larenzo's surprise she laid a hand on his arm, the touch of her fingers as light as a butterfly's. 'I hope you will be able to tell me someday, Larenzo. For your sake as much as mine.'

They didn't talk after that until Larenzo had pulled up to the elegant brick building that faced Central Park. A valet came out to deal with the car, and a doorman went for their bags.

Larenzo turned to get Ava out of her car seat; she practically flung herself into his arms and Larenzo held his daughter to him, breathing in her clean baby scent as her dark hair tickled his face. *His daughter.* Even now he nearly reeled from the shock and force of that knowledge. He had a family.

'Do you want me to take her?' Emma asked, reaching for Ava, and Larenzo shook his head.

'She's okay with me.' Although he wasn't so sure about that when Ava began to flail, scrambling to get down.

Emma laughed and reached for her, and reluctantly Larenzo gave Ava over to her. 'I guess she wants her mother.'

'Actually, I think she just wants to crawl all over this marble floor and get really dirty,' Emma answered lightly. She smiled at him, and he thought he saw sympathy in her eyes. 'She'll get used to you.'

He nodded, his throat too tight for words. He'd thought he had nothing left inside him; he'd been sure he was broken and empty inside. But knowing he had a daughter, knowing he could have someone to love and be loved by, filled him up to overflowing.

Emma followed Larenzo into the sumptuous foyer of the apartment building, all marble floors and glittering chandeliers. A doorman nodded respectfully to Larenzo as they passed, and then they stepped into a large wood-panelled lift, complete with a sofa and gilt mirror.

'Fancy,' Emma murmured as they soared upwards to the penthouse and then stepped into the huge foyer of Larenzo's apartment.

'This marble is a bit hard for a baby,' she said, tapping the black and white chequered marble with one foot. 'I wouldn't want Ava to fall and hurt herself.'

'I'll arrange to have it carpeted immediately,' Larenzo answered without missing a beat, and Emma wondered if she'd been challenging him. How far would Larenzo go to accommodate his daughter? Did she even want to answer that question?

She felt a churning mix of emotions as she stepped into the living room, its large windows overlooking Central Park, now ablaze in autumn colours. On one hand, she was grateful that Larenzo was interested in his daugh-

ter. How could she not be? And yet she was also afraid.
Afraid of the darkness of his past, the secrets he wasn't
telling her. But more than that: she was afraid of feeling
too much for him, of getting too used to this. To him. Of
caring for a man who had no intention of reciprocating her
feelings. Surely she wouldn't be so weak. She wouldn't let
herself.

'Would you like to come see the nursery?' Larenzo
asked, coming to stand behind her at the window, Ava in
his arms.

Emma turned. 'There's a nursery?'

'I had it all delivered yesterday.'

Wordlessly she nodded and followed Larenzo down the
luxuriously carpeted hall to the bedrooms.

'My bedroom is here,' he said, indicating a door on the
left. 'And your bedroom is here.' He pointed to a door directly across from his. 'The nursery is adjoining yours. I
thought you'd prefer that.'

'I do,' Emma said, although the thought of having her
own bedroom after ten months of sharing cramped quarters with her daughter was a luxury she intended to enjoy.
'Thank you,' she added belatedly, and Larenzo just nodded as he opened the door to the nursery.

She'd been expecting something basic and expedient,
ordered and set up in a hurry, but the room she stepped
into looked as if it had taken months of planning. The walls
were painted a pale lilac, and matching curtains framed
the deep window that overlooked the park. Deeper purple
accents were scattered around the room: a throw pillow on
the rocking chair, a silk-patterned lampshade, a close-up
photograph of a violet on the wall. It was a lovely, creative
room that was perfect for a baby without being cloyingly
sweet or infantile.

'I thought you might like something other than the stan-
dard pink,' Larenzo said, and Emma heard a surprising

note of uncertainty, even vulnerability, in his voice. 'But of course if you don't like it, you must change it. You can redecorate anything in the apartment as you like.'

'I don't want to redecorate,' Emma answered honestly. 'I love it. It's perfect, Larenzo. Thank you.'

'Good.'

Emma set Ava down on the plush carpet and she crawled towards a purple rocking horse—actually, Emma saw, a unicorn with a glittery horn—set in the corner, reaching up to grasp the handles as she pulled herself to standing.

'She's clever, isn't she?' Larenzo said with pride. 'She'll be walking soon.'

'And then there will really be no stopping her.' Emma gazed round the room again, noting all the unique touches. 'So did you hire an interior decorator?' she asked, and Larenzo shook his head.

'No, I did it myself. I enjoyed picking out all the things.'

'It must have taken an age—'

'No, just an afternoon. I hired painters to come and do the walls, and I put the furniture together myself.' He paused and then added, 'I told you I wanted to be involved, Emma.'

'I know, but…' She shook her head, overwhelmed by the thought and consideration Larenzo had clearly put into the nursery. She pictured him with an instruction leaflet and a set of tools, laboriously putting the crib and changing table together, and felt as if a fist had clenched around her heart. 'I suppose I didn't really think you'd be a hands-on dad,' she confessed, and Larenzo raised his eyebrows.

'Why not?'

'I don't know. You were so busy with work when I was your housekeeper. You hardly had time to come to the villa. And your lifestyle…'

'Things are different now.'

'Yes.' Emma swallowed, trying to banish the images

that had sprung into her mind, memories of the last night
Larenzo had come to the villa, had come to her. She had
to put that behind her. Heaven knew Larenzo had. 'Yes,'
she repeated more firmly. 'Things are different now.'

CHAPTER EIGHT

AFTER SETTLING AVA in her new crib for an afternoon nap, Emma went to her bedroom and began to unpack her few possessions. She could hear Larenzo moving around in his bedroom across the hall, and the closeness of the quarters made her feel…aware.

She was still overwhelmingly attracted to Larenzo. It was a fact she had to acknowledge, and perhaps acknowledging it would help her to deal with it. Larenzo had made it abundantly clear that he had no interest in her that way any more, and she didn't even want him to. At least, she *shouldn't* want him to. Emma let out a rueful sigh as she acknowledged the truth—and strength—of her feelings. But she also knew their relationship, if they even had one, was way too complicated already.

And yet the tenderness he'd shown with Ava, the consideration he'd shown her…they chipped away at her defences. Made her remember. Made her want things she had absolutely no business wanting.

She might believe in Larenzo's innocence, but that didn't mean he was *safe*.

Ava was still sleeping after she'd unpacked, and so Emma headed out to the living room. The room was spacious and luxuriously appointed, if a little bland. No personal photographs or mementoes, but then Larenzo had bought the place only a week ago. It had probably come furnished.

She prowled around the room, glancing at the antique vases, the gilt mirrors, feeling restless and not quite knowing why.

She gazed out of the window at the leafy enclave of Central Park and as she imagined taking Ava to one of the playgrounds there, exploring the city with her daughter, her spirits lifted a little. She could make this work. She had to make this work, at least for a little while.

'Was your room adequate?'

Emma spun around to see Larenzo standing in the doorway of the sitting room. He'd changed from his more casual clothes of this morning to a well-tailored suit in navy-blue silk, and he looked, as he always did, devastatingly attractive. Even from across the room Emma felt the force of his magnetism, and it nearly propelled her forward, towards him. She held onto the window sill for balance as she answered him.

'Yes, thank you. More than adequate. This is a beautiful apartment, Larenzo.'

'You must change anything you don't like.'

She thought of telling him she wouldn't be staying long enough to warrant such changes, but somehow she couldn't make herself say the words. She just nodded instead, and Larenzo turned towards the door.

'I have to go out now, for some business meetings, but I should be back this evening.'

'Okay.' Emma wasn't sure why this surprised her, but it did. What had she expected—she and Larenzo would spend the day together? Larenzo had made it clear they would be living separate lives, brought together only by Ava, which was how she wanted it. How she had to want it. 'Do you—do you want me to make something for dinner?' She saw surprise flash across Larenzo's face and she wondered if she'd pushed some undiscussed boundary, crossed some invisible line. Maybe Larenzo had no intention of eating with her or Ava. She had no idea how this was meant to work, how it was going to work.

'If it's no trouble, that would be fine,' he finally said.

'It's no trouble.'

With a nod of farewell, Larenzo left the apartment and Emma stood there for a moment, feeling the emptiness all around her, not able to decide if she was relieved he had gone...or disappointed.

She made her way to the kitchen, which was huge, a hymn to granite and stainless steel, with every possible kitchen gadget and appliance. There was, however, no food. She stared into the empty depths of the enormous sub-zero fridge and wondered what Larenzo had been eating for the last few days.

When Ava woke a little while later Emma buckled her daughter into the top-of-the-line stroller that she found in the foyer.

Outside on Central Park West, a brisk autumn breeze blowing and Ava thankfully distracted by all the sights and sounds around them, Emma headed towards Columbus Avenue and the local shops. She felt better with every step she took, the city's vibrant life seeming to infuse her with energy and purpose.

At a local grocery she bought all the ingredients for lasagne, a simple but warming meal on this cold autumn day. She paused in front of a wine shop and then recklessly bought a bottle of Chianti to go with it. She'd already pushed the boundaries of their arrangement by suggesting she cook for Larenzo. Why not own it?

This was her life, at least for now, and she wanted to enjoy it. Ava started getting restless in the stroller, so Emma headed back. Once she was up in the apartment she brought the groceries into the kitchen and settled Ava onto the floor with a few wooden spoons and copper pans. While her daughter made as much noise as she possibly could, Emma bustled around, assembling the lasagne and tossing a salad.

She started to relax as she worked; she'd always enjoyed cooking, and it actually felt good to be mistress of her own kitchen, instead of an interloper in Meghan's. As much as her sister had made her feel welcome, Emma had been conscious of how much of an imposition she really was. Here, at least, she had a job to do, a potential role. Perhaps she could act as Larenzo's housekeeper. It would be a way of earning her keep and making herself useful.

She was just sliding the lasagne out of the oven when Larenzo appeared in the doorway of the kitchen. He'd taken off his suit jacket and loosened his tie, and his jaw was darkened with five o'clock shadow, all of it making him look deliciously rumpled and sexy.

He paused, taking in the sight of the kitchen, and Emma realised what a mess it was, with pots and spoons all over the floor for Ava's entertainment, and the detritus from her cooking all over the counters.

'Sorry, I'm not very good at cleaning up as I cook,' she said.

'No, it's fine.' Larenzo glanced around the room again, and Emma couldn't tell anything from his expression. 'I like it,' he said at last. 'Shall I set the table?'

He was already getting the forks and knives from the drawer, and Emma watched him, a strange pressure building in her chest. This was all so…normal. So cosy.

Ava had noticed her father and abandoned her pots and spoons to crawl over to him and pull herself up, clutching his legs. Larenzo glanced down at her, his whole face softening into a smile that made that pressure in Emma's chest turn painful.

'I'm afraid she's dented a few of your pots and pans,' she said stiltedly, turning her gaze to the salad she was needlessly tossing. 'She doesn't know her own strength.'

'I don't mind.' Larenzo scooped Ava up with one hand, settling her on his hip as he took the cutlery to the table in the dining nook of the kitchen. 'This is a bit more manageable than the dining room,' he said as he laid the table. 'I think the table in there seats twenty.'

'Planning on having any dinner parties?'

'No. I don't think I know twenty people who would come to a dinner party I hosted, unless it was to gawp and gossip.' He spoke tonelessly, without self-pity, and Emma eyed him curiously as she brought the lasagne to the table.

'You don't have many friends in America?'

'I don't have many friends, full stop,' Larenzo answered. 'A stint in prison shows you who your true friends are, and mine turned out to be rather few.'

He tried to put Ava in the high chair he'd brought to the table, but the toddler shrieked and arched her back, sticking her legs straight out. Emma watched, amused, as Larenzo tried his best before looking up with a wry smile.

'She's really quite strong.'

'Yes, and she doesn't like being strapped in.' Emma plucked Ava from the chair and put her back down on the floor. 'She'll want to join us when we sit down.'

'I suppose I have a lot to learn.'

'Fortunately Ava provides a steep learning curve,' Emma answered with a smile.

Emma brought the meal to the table and they both sat down. Just as she'd predicted, Ava crawled over to them, wanting to be part of things.

Larenzo glanced down at his daughter, smiling when she lifted her arms for him to pick her up. He settled her in her high chair this time without Ava making any protest. 'Tell me about the last ten months,' he said to Emma when he'd sat down again. 'Or even before that. How was your pregnancy?'

'Mostly uneventful, thankfully,' Emma answered. 'I

was pretty nauseous for the first three months,' she continued. 'But then it settled down. She was quite the kicker, though. I couldn't sleep most nights because it felt like she was playing football inside of me.'

Larenzo smiled at that, his whole face lightening, and Emma quickly looked down at her plate. Larenzo's smile was dangerous.

'And the birth? It went well?'

'As well as these things go,' Emma answered frankly. 'It hurt. A lot.'

'Why didn't you get pain relief?'

'No time. She came a week early; she wasn't due until New Year's Eve. And I didn't think I could actually be in labour, because the contractions were irregular and they didn't hurt all that much.' She let out a sudden, embarrassed laugh. 'I can't believe I'm telling you all this.'

'Why not? I want to hear it.'

'Really?' She heard the scepticism in her voice, and Larenzo must have too, because he nodded firmly.

'Absolutely. I missed this, Emma. I want to know now.'

But would he have wanted to know then? If Larenzo hadn't gone to prison, would he have been an involved father? Would they be dating or even *married* now? Emma's cheeks heated at the thought. She was glad Larenzo had no idea the turn her thoughts had taken. She cleared her throat and continued. 'Well, Meghan had been telling me how first babies take for ever, and as it was Christmas Eve I was hoping the contractions might die down. I didn't want to be in the hospital over Christmas.'

'Understandable.'

'But they didn't, and by the time I realised we needed to go to the hospital, Ava was almost ready to make her arrival.' She smiled at the memory. 'Meghan was pushing me in a wheelchair into the delivery ward, and I was bellowing at the top of my lungs. I'm not so good with pain.'

'I wish I could have been there,' Larenzo said quietly, and Emma knew he meant it.

Before she could think better of it, she asked the question that had been dancing through her mind. 'What do you suppose would have happened, if you hadn't gone to prison?'

Larenzo frowned. 'What do you mean?'

'I would have stayed on as your housekeeper. I would have told you I was pregnant right away.' She held her breath, waiting for him to say something, although she didn't know what.

Larenzo sighed and leaned back in his chair. 'The truth is, Emma, if I hadn't gone to prison, if I hadn't known I was going to go to prison, there wouldn't have been a baby. That night happened because I knew I was going to be arrested in the morning.'

'Oh.' Emma blinked, stupidly feeling hurt by this, and not quite sure what to do with that emotion. 'I see.'

'You gave me something precious that night.'

'My virginity?' she filled in, trying to joke, but it came out flat.

'No, I didn't mean that, although that of course is precious too.'

She really didn't want to be having this conversation. She kept looking at her plate, focusing on the food she no longer felt like eating.

'I meant comfort,' Larenzo said quietly. 'Human connection. Pleasure, not just physical pleasure, although there certainly was that. But pleasure in talking to you, and being in your company. Playing chess, seeing your photographs… that night made a memory that sustained me through many dark days in prison.'

'Oh.' And now she didn't feel so hurt. She felt…*honoured* that she'd been that important to him, and deeply thankful that their one night together had meant something to him, as it had to her. 'Well, I'm glad about that, I suppose.'

'And look at the result.' He glanced at Ava, who now had tomato sauce in her hair, before turning back to Emma with a smile. 'I don't have any regrets, since she came out of it. But I think she needs a bath.'

'Do you want me to—?' Emma half rose from her chair as Larenzo unbuckled Ava from her high chair.

'I can do it,' he said.

'She can be pretty tricky in the tub—'

As if to prove her point, Ava started wriggling out of Larenzo's grasp, and soon his shirt was splattered with tomato sauce.

Larenzo looked rather endearingly amazed by his daughter's gymnastics and Emma rescued him. 'I've found this is the best way sometimes,' she said, and, tucking Ava under her arm as if she were a parcel, she took her to the bathroom.

Larenzo followed, standing in the doorway while Emma put Ava down and turned the taps on. 'Fortunately she likes her bath,' she said, and turned to look over her shoulder. Her breath dried in her throat as she saw he was unbuttoning his shirt. What, she wondered distantly, was so mesmerising about his long brown fingers sliding buttons out of their holes? Something was, because she couldn't tear her gaze away from the sight.

'I'd rather not get my shirt wet,' Larenzo explained. 'I have a feeling Ava is a splasher.' He shrugged out of his dress shirt, revealing a plain white T-shirt underneath that clung to the defined muscles of his chest and abdomen.

'She is,' Emma answered, and finally managed to drag her gaze to Larenzo's face. She couldn't read the emotion in his eyes, and she hoped that he hadn't noticed how she'd been staring. *Wanting.*

She knew she should go back to the kitchen and clean

up their dishes, but she felt as if her feet were rooted to the floor, and all she could do was watch as Larenzo battled Ava out of her clothes and then plopped her in the tub, one strong hand resting on her back to keep her steady.

'Is this right?' he asked, and the uncertainty in his voice made Emma's heart ache.

'Yes…yes, that's perfect.' She felt as if her feelings were a kaleidoscope that Larenzo twirled every time he spoke. In these unguarded moments of honesty everything in her swelled with feeling, ached with loss.

What if things could have been different? What if that night *had* still happened, without the arrest, and she and Larenzo had built a relationship? What if they'd become a proper family, rather than this awkwardly constructed temporary one?

Emma knew she shouldn't torment herself with such thoughts. She'd never been looking for that kind of relationship, and, in any case, there was no going back. And yet as she gazed helplessly at Larenzo bathing their daughter, she almost wished there were.

Half an hour later Emma had cleaned up the kitchen when Larenzo emerged from the nursery with Ava in her pyjamas.

'You've buttoned up her pyjamas wrong,' she remarked in amusement as Larenzo raked a hand through his hair.

'Those things are worse than a straitjacket. There are a million buttons.'

'It's a learned skill.'

'Clearly.' He pulled his damp T-shirt away from his chest, and Emma tried not to stare at his perfect musculature, or remember how warm and satiny his skin had felt, how she'd once put her lips to his taut abdomen…

'She's ready for bed, I think,' Emma said. 'I'll get her bottle ready.' She'd brought a can of infant formula from Meghan's, and now she poured cooled boiled water into a bottle and added a few scoops of the white powder. 'You were a little low on groceries, by the way,' she said. 'I don't think there's anything for breakfast.'

'I can arrange for food to be delivered, unless you'd prefer to do it yourself.'

'Actually, I was thinking about that,' Emma said. She'd finished making the bottle and Ava was reaching for it with both hands. 'I'm not comfortable just living off your generosity, and one thing I know how to do is be a housekeeper.'

Larenzo stilled. 'What are you suggesting?'

'I could be your housekeeper. You don't have to pay me, but at least it will make up for mine and Ava's room and board.'

Larenzo's face had darkened as she spoke. 'Ava is my daughter, Emma, and you are her mother. This isn't a question of *room and board.*'

Emma took a deep breath, knowing she needed to say this even if part of her didn't want to. 'It is for me, Larenzo.' He didn't answer and she continued, keeping her voice steady with effort, 'Look, you said yourself you aren't interested in a relationship. You want to get to know Ava, and I respect that. But the only reason I'm here is because Ava is. So it makes sense for me to have a role. A job.'

Still Larenzo didn't speak, and Emma could see the emotions battling on his face. She just didn't know what they were. Did he want there to be more between them? Or was that just her foolish, wishful thinking? Sighing, she hoisted Ava more firmly on her hip. 'I'm going to put her to bed. Think about it, at least.'

She was at the door when Larenzo finally bit out, 'Fine, you can act as housekeeper. But I don't want any responsibilities you needlessly put on yourself to take away from Ava's care.'

'Many women manage a home and a baby,' Emma answered, doing her best to keep her voice mild. 'I think I can too.' Larenzo said nothing and as she headed to the nursery with Ava, Emma wondered why this didn't feel more like a victory.

CHAPTER NINE

ANOTHER SLEEPLESS NIGHT. By now Larenzo was well used to insomnia. He'd slept badly in prison, on a thin mattress in a tiny cell with a thousand other prisoners shifting, coughing, and groaning around him. Ironic that he slept just as badly now that he was free, lying on a king-sized bed with the apartment quiet and still.

And Emma sleeping across the hall.

Although he knew he shouldn't, he imagined rising from his bed, opening his door, and going into Emma's room. Watching her sleep, her golden-brown hair spread across the pillow, her lithe body clad in those scanty pyjamas he remembered from their night in Sicily.

Then he imagined sliding into that bed with her, taking her in his arms, burying his face in her sweet-smelling hair, burying himself inside her body...

With a groan Larenzo rose from the bed and went to the en-suite bathroom to splash some cold water on his face. He had no business thinking of Emma that way. His libido might have leapt to life since he'd seen her again, but he had nothing left in his heart to give her. No ability to have a relationship, to trust or to love someone.

He loved Ava, because she was sweet and innocent, and she was his. His love for his daughter was rock solid, utterly unshakeable. But loving a woman? Trusting someone with the heart that had shattered into tiny fragments of nothingness?

Impossible.

And the alternative, some kind of fling or affair, would only further complicate what was already a tenuous arrangement. His face settled into a scowl as he thought of Emma's suggestion. *Housekeeper.* He didn't want her here as a housekeeper. She wasn't his damned employee. She was here because she was the mother of his child, because she *belonged*—

Larenzo let out his breath in a hiss as he bowed his head. Emma belonged with Ava, but not with him. Not like that. Never like that.

So perhaps, much as he had instinctively disliked the idea, it was better that she act as housekeeper. Perhaps having a clearly defined role would help them navigate this arrangement with a minimum of awkwardness.

A soft cry interrupted the wrangling of his own thoughts and Larenzo realised that Ava had woken up. Quickly he left his room and went to the nursery. His daughter was standing up in her crib, her face streaked with tears. Larenzo's heart twisted with a powerful mixture of love, protectiveness, and sorrow. Sleeping in a strange place had to be a frightening experience for the child.

He picked her up, and again his heart twisted as Ava settled against his bare chest, her cheek resting over his heart. Larenzo stroked her back and without even realising what he was doing, he began to croon a lullaby in Italian. *'E dormi, dormi, dormi, bambin de cuna. To mama no la gh'è la a-sé andà via.'*

The words came to him unbidden, from a deep well of memory. He stroked Ava's hair and watched as his daughter's eyelids eventually drooped.

After several minutes when he was sure she was deeply asleep, he laid her back in the crib and watched her for a moment, her thick, dark lashes fanning her plump baby cheeks.

'That's a beautiful lullaby.'

Larenzo stiffened, his gaze moving from his sleeping daughter to the woman standing in the doorway of the nursery. Emma's hair was tousled about her shoulders, her golden-green eyes wide and luminous. Larenzo dropped his gaze and saw with a hard kick of desire that she was wearing just what he'd imagined: a thin T-shirt that moulded to the shape of her breasts and a pair of boy shorts. He felt his body respond, and in only a pair of drawstring pyjama bottoms he knew Emma would be able to tell if she lowered her gaze just as he'd lowered his.

'She's asleep,' he whispered, and moved quietly out of the nursery, brushing past Emma as he did so. He sucked in a hard breath as her breasts nudged against his chest, and her hair whispered against his cheek. He inhaled the scent of her, sweetness and sleep, and he averted his face from the temptation of hers.

Emma closed the door behind him and they stood in the hallway, only a few inches separating them, the only light coming from a lamp Larenzo had left on in the living room, its warm glow spilling onto the floor.

It was so reminiscent of that night in the villa, the way things had shifted between them in the quiet and dark. Barriers had disappeared, defences had dropped. In that bubble of solitude and intimacy there had only been the two of them, seeking and finding both solace and pleasure.

And there were just the two of them now, standing so close together, the only sound the sigh and draw of their breathing.

'What did it mean?' Emma asked in a whisper, and Larenzo forced himself to meet her gaze, to hold himself still, when all he wanted to do was drag her into his arms, forget everything but this, *them*, for a little while.

'What did what mean?'

'The lullaby. I couldn't make out the Italian. I'm rusty, I suppose.'

'Oh… Sleep, sleep, sleep, cradle baby. Your mother is not here, she has gone away.' Belatedly he realised how it sounded. 'It's the only lullaby I know. I didn't even realise I knew it until I started singing.'

'Is it from your childhood?' Emma asked, and Larenzo blinked.

'I suppose it has to be. But I don't remember anyone singing me any lullabies.' He heard the note of bitterness that had crept into his voice and he tried to shrug it off. No point in dwelling on the past, just as he'd told Emma. 'Anyway, Ava seemed to like it.'

'Thank you,' Emma said softly, and she reached out and laid a hand on his arm. The touch of her fingers on his skin was electric, jolting his senses as if he'd stuck his finger into a socket. He held himself still, staring down at her hand, her slender fingers curled around his biceps.

She'd touched him like this back in Sicily. And he'd put his hand on hers, and for a moment he hadn't felt alone. He'd felt as if someone was on his side, someone actually cared…

But that was a lifetime ago, and it hadn't been true anyway. Their night together had been a moment out of time, out of reality. An aberration.

Larenzo forced himself to shake off her hand. 'It was nothing,' he said and without saying anything else he turned and went back to his bedroom.

Emma woke to sunlight pouring through the windows of her bedroom, and the sound of Ava gurgling with laughter from the adjoining nursery. She stretched, savouring the moment's relaxation before the day with all of its demands began.

Then she heard Larenzo's answering laughter and realised he was in the nursery with Ava. Just the rumbling sound of his voice as he talked to their daughter brought the memory of last night back with slamming force. Emma didn't think she'd seen or heard anything as beautiful, as *desirable*, as Larenzo cradling their baby to his bare chest as he sang her a lullaby in lilting Italian.

Watching him in the darkened nursery, she'd wanted him almost as much as she'd wanted him that night back at the villa. Wanted to feel his hot, hard skin against hers, his lips on hers as he treasured and cherished her with his body...

For a few seconds, when she'd touched his arm, simply because she had no longer been able to keep herself from it, she'd thought he was battling the same kind of temptation. Thought, and even hoped, that he might give in to it. In that moment she'd known if he'd kissed her she'd be lost, just as she had been before. Nothing would have kept her from him.

But he'd walked away instead, and Emma had spent a restless night trying to banish the ache of longing inside her. Now she got out of bed and hurriedly dressed in jeans and a sweater before going into the nursery.

Larenzo was dressed in an elegant and crisp suit, and he'd already changed Ava's diaper and was now wrestling her into a bodysuit. Ava was resisting him, her whole body rigid as she stared up at him in stubborn determination.

'I think she's winning,' Emma said, and Larenzo glanced up, his mouth curving wryly.

'There's no thinking about it. It's definite.'

'Do you want me to—?'

'Please.' He stepped aside and with a smile Emma finished dressing Ava, who saw that the jig was up and relaxed her body as she blew a raspberry.

'Clearly you have the touch,' Larenzo observed.

'Years, or rather, months of practice.' She turned to face

him, her heart bumping against her ribs as she realised how close he was. The woodsy scent of his aftershave tickled her nostrils and made heat lick low in her belly. 'You look smart. Are you going somewhere?'

'I have a few meetings at the office. But…' He hesitated, a note of uncertainty creeping into his voice. 'We can have breakfast first, if you'd like. I went out early this morning and bought some bagels and coffee.'

'Okay.' Emma followed him into the kitchen, Ava balanced on one hip. The smell of freshly brewed coffee and toasted bagels made her mouth water. 'So if you're not CEO of Cavelli Enterprises,' she asked, 'what are you doing exactly?'

'I'm starting a new company,' Larenzo answered as he poured them both coffees. Emma settled Ava into her high chair with a few torn-off pieces of bagel. 'LC Investments.'

'And what are you going to do?'

'I hope to invest in start-up businesses, the kind of places that might have trouble getting loans from one of the big banks.'

'That sounds rather noble.'

He shrugged and handed her a mug of steaming coffee. 'I have some sympathy for the underdog.'

Because he could relate? And yet Larenzo Cavelli was so powerful, so charismatic, so arrogant. He'd even seemed so back in Sicily when he'd been handcuffed and at the police's mercy. Standing there now, one hip braced against the counter, his large hands cradling a mug of coffee, he managed to look like the lord of all he surveyed, his confidence careless and yet utterly assured. And yet this man had come from the street.

'Did you feel like the underdog as a child?' she asked after a moment.

Larenzo pursed his lips as he considered. 'I suppose

I would have, if I'd thought about it. I was just trying to survive.'

'I'm amazed at how far you've come. You should be incredibly proud of yourself, Larenzo, going from street orphan to CEO.'

His mouth tightened and he shook his head. 'I had some help.'

Who from? she wanted to ask but decided not to. 'Even so.'

Larenzo put his empty coffee mug on the dish drainer. 'I should go,' he said shortly, and Emma felt his emotional withdrawal like a palpable thing. 'I don't know when I'll be home,' he added. 'Don't wait for me.'

Emma nodded, feeling the rejection even though she knew she shouldn't, and Larenzo left. He kissed the top of Ava's head before he went, and Emma sat down at the table to finish her coffee, caught between missing Larenzo and enjoying the prospect of a day spent in the city. She was looking forward to going out and exploring New York, and yet, even though he'd just gone, she already missed Larenzo. She was so curious about him—this man who was hardened and suspicious, who could be so ruthless and cold, and yet also showed such gentleness and kindness.

Her cell phone rang and Emma slipped it out of the pocket of her jeans, and saw that it was Meghan.

'Hey,' she said as she answered the call and Meghan drew her breath in sharply.

'Are you okay?'

'Am I okay? Yes.' Emma gazed out of the window at the view of Central Park, and then glanced at the remains of her perfectly toasted bagel. 'I'm fine. Just finishing breakfast.'

'Cavelli isn't…he's being decent to you?' Meghan asked cautiously.

'More than decent. He already has a bond with Ava. He

even got up with her in the night.' Emma pictured Larenzo wearing nothing but his pyjama bottoms, the lamplight washing over his bronzed skin, and she suppressed a shiver of desire.

'Really,' Meghan answered, the disbelief audible in her voice.

'Yes, really. I told you before, Meghan, Larenzo wants to be a part of his daughter's life.'

'I didn't realise you'd become his champion,' Meghan retorted, and Emma sucked in a breath.

'Meghan…'

'Seriously, Emma, you've changed your tune since yesterday.'

'I haven't—'

'How do you know Cavelli isn't just pretending he's interested in Ava—?'

Emma recoiled at the suggestion. 'He's not. Anyway, why would he?'

'I don't know, maybe he's trying to polish his image for the public? Whatever it is, I don't trust him, Emma, and you shouldn't either. I know the charges against him were dropped, but you know the saying, where there's smoke, there's fire.'

'And sometimes there's just smoke.' The fierceness of her response surprised them both. 'In any case,' Emma continued, 'you know as well as I do that I can't keep Larenzo from seeing his daughter.' And she didn't even want to any more. Not when she'd seen how tender he was with her.

'You still don't have to live with him. I talked to that lawyer again and mentioned that Cavelli had practically blackmailed you into living with him. It could provide evidence that he's unfit—'

'Meghan.' Shock as well as anger blazed through her. 'You have no right to talk about my business with a lawyer.'

'I'm looking out for you,' Meghan cried. 'Emma, obviously you still have some feelings for this man. That's understandable, considering your shared history. But I think you're in over your head. You don't know Cavelli, or what he's capable of. And someone has to be responsible and think about Ava—'

'I am thinking about Ava,' Emma shot back. Her voice shook with the force of her feelings. 'Trust me, I am. And Larenzo is very good with her. I don't want to keep him from Ava's life, no matter what happened in his past.'

'And what if it turns out he really is dangerous?'

'It won't. I trust Larenzo in that.'

'How can you trust—?'

'I just do, Meghan,' Emma cut her off, knowing she meant it. 'And I need to go now. Ava's starting to fuss.'

Ava, who was happily chewing on a bagel, looked at her curiously. Emma disconnected the call and flung the phone onto the kitchen counter. Her whole body was trembling.

She wanted to deny everything her sister had said; she wanted to scrub her brain and pretend she'd never heard it. And yet beneath Meghan's older-sister I-know-best attitude, Emma knew there was concern and perhaps even truth.

She still didn't know Larenzo at all. It just felt as if she did.

Ava threw the bagel onto the floor, and Emma decided it was time to go out for the day. All of New York was waiting for her to explore, and she could certainly use the distraction.

She fetched Ava's coat and hat and then buckled her into the stroller, armed with an arsenal of snacks and toys to keep her daughter entertained. Then she hit the streets.

Central Park on a crisp autumn day was one of the loveliest places on earth, Emma decided as she wheeled Ava along the twisting, tree-shaded pathways. She could hear the distant laughter of children on a playground, and some tourists were posing for photographs in front of the statue of Christopher Columbus. Every colour seemed sharp and bright, as if the whole world had been brought into crystalline focus.

As Emma strolled along Ava watched everything avidly; they made it all the way to the Central Park Zoo where they both watched the animal statues dance around the iconic clock. Emma bought a hot dog from a cart and shared it with Ava, enjoying people watching from a park bench, and then when her daughter fell asleep in her stroller she walked back uptown, stopping in front of the gorgeous esplanade with Bethesda Fountain as its magnificent centrepiece.

Every step she took felt as if she were breathing life back into her soul. She hadn't realised until then just how much of a rut she'd been in, living with her sister and staggering through her days. It had taken Larenzo's suggestion to get her out of it, and for that she was grateful.

Ava was starting to stir, and so Emma walked back towards the apartment on Central Park West. She stopped at the playground directly opposite the park's entrance and unbuckled Ava from her stroller before putting her into one of the baby swings. Ava chortled with glee as Emma pushed her, enjoying the autumn sunshine on her face.

She didn't know how long she spent in the playground with Ava, savouring the day, but it must have been more time than she'd thought for the sun was starting to sink behind the buildings on Central Park West when a hand suddenly clamped down hard on her shoulder.

Emma whirled around, her heart seeming to leap right into her throat, and saw Larenzo glaring at her ferociously.

'*Where* have you been?'

CHAPTER TEN

'YOU SCARED ME, LARENZO.' Emma shrugged off his hand and pressed her palm to her thudding heart. 'Good grief. Why did you sneak up on me like that?'

'Answer the question, Emma.'

She blinked up at him, amazed at how different he seemed now, scowling down at her, everything about him hard and fierce and utterly unyielding. Right now she could almost believe he really was a Mafioso.

'Where have I been?' she retorted, her voice rising in both anger and fear. 'Here, in the park, with Ava. It's a beautiful day and I wanted to get out and see the city.'

'You didn't tell me you were going to the park.'

'I wasn't aware I had to inform you of all of my movements.' She glared at him, conscious that the parents and caregivers around them were obviously pretending not to listen while eating up every word. 'What's with the third degree?' she demanded as she lifted Ava from the baby swing.

Larenzo was silent for a moment, the ravages of his anger still visible on his face. 'I don't like not knowing where you are.'

Emma stared at him, exasperated. 'So what are you going to do? Implant a chip in my shoulder, or how about an ankle tag? Seriously, Larenzo, I need my freedom.'

Larenzo didn't answer and with a sigh she buckled a

protesting Ava into her stroller. 'Let's go back to the apartment. We're causing a scene.'

Larenzo glanced around the playground, his scowl deepening as he saw several mothers whispering and shooting them speculative looks.

'Fine,' he said, and reached for the handles of the stroller. Emma walked beside him while he pushed Ava back towards the park entrance.

They had just reached the park gates when Larenzo stiffened, and then, shoving the stroller towards her, strode across the pathway.

Emma watched in stunned disbelief as Larenzo approached a man and without so much as a qualm took the expensive digital camera he was holding and began to push its buttons.

'Hey, you can't do that—' the man exclaimed.

'Do not,' Larenzo said, biting off each word and spitting it out, 'take pictures of my family.'

'So the rumours are true, you do have a child?'

Larenzo's face was thunderous as he handed the camera back to the man. 'I repeat, do not take photographs of my family.'

Without another word he turned back to Emma, standing there with her jaw hanging open slackly.

'Cavelli,' the man called, 'is it true that you planted the evidence on Raguso? People are saying—'

'Come on,' Larenzo said, and took the stroller from her. 'Let's go.' He began resolutely walking towards the park entrance, and mutely Emma followed.

She waited until they were back up in the penthouse apartment and Ava was settled with some toys on the floor of the living room before she started asking for answers.

'Larenzo, what on earth was that all about?'

'The photographer?' He shrugged out of his suit jacket,

not even looking at her as he answered. 'He was a member of the paparazzi. I should have known they would realise I was here. Until the press dies down, you shouldn't take Ava out in public.'

'So I'm a prisoner here?' she demanded, and Larenzo turned to look at her, his mouth twisting grimly.

'It doesn't look like a prison to me.'

She flushed, realising her poor choice of words. 'You know what I mean, Larenzo. I'll go crazy if I have to stay in here twenty-four seven.'

'For a few days only. These things never last long.'

Emma took a deep breath. 'Why does he think you planted the evidence on your business partner?'

Larenzo's nostrils flared and Emma could see how the skin around his mouth had turned white. He was angry, very angry, and yet when he spoke his voice was measured and controlled.

'Because he is trying to sell newspapers, and to do that he needs a story. Surely you know how these things work, Emma.'

She thought of her sister's phone call this morning. *Where there's smoke, there's fire.* 'Is there any truth to that claim, Larenzo?' she asked quietly.

He stared at her for a long, taut moment, and beneath the icy anger Emma thought she saw a flash of hurt in his eyes, quickly veiled.

'What exactly are you accusing me of, Emma?' he asked.

'I don't know.' Belatedly she realised what she'd been implying. She didn't really think Larenzo was guilty, but she still didn't understand him. 'I just wish I knew more, Larenzo. I feel like there are things you aren't telling me—'

'I told you, Raguso is guilty. There is no doubt. The evidence was there.'

'You said there was evidence against you—'

'Because it was planted!' Larenzo's voice rose in a sudden, anguished roar. 'It was planted, all right? I was framed, and I was too stupid and naive to realise it.' He let out a shuddering breath as he raked his hands through his hair. 'Satisfied?'

Emma didn't answer, and Ava looked up, her lip wobbling at the shouting and the tension she sensed crackling between the two adults. 'If you were framed,' Emma asked slowly, 'why didn't you tell me that from the beginning? There is no shame in it—'

'I feel shame,' Larenzo answered. He dropped his hands and looked away from her, his expression shuttered even as his voice thickened with emotion. 'I feel great shame.'

She blinked back tears at the raw pain she heard in his voice. 'Oh, Larenzo—'

'We will not discuss this any more.'

Emma could sense when a door was being slammed in her face. And yet she'd finally received some insight into Larenzo's experience, even if it left her with more questions than ever. 'All right, fine, we don't need to talk about that. But why were you so angry when you found me in the park? I don't need you to keep tabs on me—'

'I phoned the apartment several times and there was no answer. With Ava's nap schedule, I thought you would have been in the apartment at least for the afternoon. I was worried.'

'But you said there was no danger—'

'I was worried you'd left,' Larenzo said starkly. He stared at her, his face filled with bleak honesty. 'I thought you had taken Ava and left me.'

Emma gaped at him, amazed and humbled by the vulnerability she saw in Larenzo's eyes. 'If I was going to leave, Larenzo,' she said quietly, 'I'd have the decency to tell you first. And anyway, I just got here. I'm not going anywhere.'

He shrugged, his face hard and impassive once more. 'I know your sister doesn't want you here. You are close to her. She is probably like a mother figure to you since you are not close to your own mother. I was afraid she'd spoken to you, and you had changed your mind.'

Emma swallowed, stunned by his perception. 'She did speak to me. She called me this morning.'

Larenzo nodded. 'And did she tell you to go back?'

'No, but you're right, she's not happy I'm here.' She thought of mentioning the lawyer, and then decided against it. She didn't want to make Larenzo angry, or worse, to hurt him, with such information, and she had a feeling it would. This man who seemed so proud and arrogant and untouchable hid a surprising vulnerability.

'I can understand your sister's point of view,' he said, and Emma raised her eyebrows.

'Can you?'

'Of course. If I were your sister, I would be wary too. But I hope she will realise in time that you are in no danger. I hope you realise that too.'

'I do realise it, Larenzo.' Guilt lashed her that he would believe she still doubted him. 'I'm sorry I keep questioning you.'

'It's understandable,' Larenzo answered wearily. 'This is a difficult situation for all of us, but for you in particular.'

'Thank you for acknowledging that.'

He nodded, and Emma felt they'd come to a truce, and even an understanding. She took a deep breath and then bent to scoop up Ava, who had started to grizzle.

'I should start making dinner. I didn't realise how late it had become, when I was in the park.' Which was, she supposed, a sort of apology.

'I'll watch this one while you do it,' Larenzo said and, in a gesture that felt both bizarre and natural, Emma handed over Ava, who went willingly to her father.

* * *

Over the next few weeks Emma settled into a new routine that felt both comfortable and strange. Larenzo worked most days, and, after seeing to her housekeeping duties, Emma spent the days with Ava exploring the city. The autumn days continued crisp and clear and she enjoyed getting out and walking through the park, going to the Children's Museum, which Ava loved, and visiting the local shops. She'd even signed Ava up for a toddler gymnastics class, and she'd met a few other mothers at the local library's story hour. It might not have seemed much to most people, but she was more active and involved here than she'd been in her months at Meghan's.

She also developed a routine with Larenzo. An early riser, he usually got up with Ava while Emma had the unimagined luxury of a lie-in, and then they all had breakfast together in the sun-filled kitchen before Larenzo went to work. He came home no later than six or six-thirty each weekday night, and they had dinner together before bathing Ava and reading her stories, a precious hour spent as a family. Because they were a family, even if it was unexpected and unconventional. Sitting on the sofa, their daughter between them, trying to race through reading a board book before Ava tossed it to the floor, comprised some of the happiest moments Emma had ever known, and yet they also felt tenuous. Fragile. She wondered how long this 'sort of' family could really last.

At first, when Ava was asleep, they went their separate ways in the apartment. Larenzo would work in his study and Emma would read or watch TV in her room. Then one night, a week or so after she'd arrived, restlessness drove her out of her bedroom to the living room, where she scanned the shelves of expensive leather-bound books.

Larenzo came out of the kitchen, stopping when he saw her. 'Is everything all right?'

'Yes, basically.' Emma glanced over her shoulder, her mouth drying at the sight of Larenzo in faded jeans and a T-shirt, his feet bare, his hair rumpled. He looked jaw-droppingly gorgeous and just the sight of him made her belly swoop. She'd thought in the weeks since she'd been here she'd get used to seeing him, but nothing ever prepared her for the devastating sight of him, or her body's unstoppable reaction.

He cocked an eyebrow, waiting for more, and Emma let out a little laugh. 'I'm just kind of bored.'

'Why don't you go out, see a film?'

'By myself?'

'You once told me you liked your own company,' Larenzo reminded her.

'I know,' Emma admitted. 'I just don't feel like it tonight.' She was tired of being alone. Spending time with Larenzo had made her realise how wonderful and invigorating and fun company could be. *His* company.

'Well, then.' Larenzo shoved his hands in the pockets of his jeans and rocked on his heels. 'How about a game of chess?'

Remembrance rippled through her as she thought of the last game they'd played, that night in Sicily. The expectation and awareness that had tautened between them...

'Okay,' she said, and followed him into the sumptuous wood-panelled room. Two deep leather club chairs flanked a large window that overlooked Amsterdam Avenue, a low table with a chessboard between them.

Emma sat down and studied the board with its ornately carved pieces. 'I think I'm about to get my butt kicked,' she said wryly. 'Again.'

'Don't give up before you've even started,' Larenzo answered with a faint smile as he sat down opposite her. 'White moves first, remember.'

'I remember.' Those two words seemed to fall into the

stillness of the room like pebbles tossed into a well, creating ripples of awareness. Larenzo's gaze was heavy-lidded and intent as he looked at her, and Emma's heart started to thud.

'I remember too,' he said softly, and she knew he wasn't talking about chess.

She stared down at the board, the pieces blurring before her eyes as she swallowed hard. 'Do you think about it?' she asked softly. 'That night?'

Larenzo didn't answer for a long moment and she didn't dare look at him. 'All the time,' he finally said, and Emma jerked her gaze up towards his, startled and yet suddenly, blazingly hopeful. 'You should move,' he said gruffly, and, barely aware of what she was doing, she moved her knight.

They played in silence, expectation and memory uncoiling inside her, seeming to fill the room with a palpable force. It would be so easy for Larenzo to reach across the board, frame her face in his hands as he had on that night. Slide his lips across hers as she opened and yielded beneath him…

Her hand trembled and she knocked a few pieces over, scattering them across the board. 'Oh, I'm sorry,' she said, biting her lips, and Larenzo righted them easily.

'It's all right. I was going to checkmate you in three moves anyway.'

'Oh, dear.'

'Good game.' He held out his hand, his eyes glinting with both challenge and desire, and Emma took it, her fingers sliding along his as a tingle spread from her fingers all the way up her arm. His hand was so warm and dry and strong. She pulled away reluctantly.

'Another?' Larenzo suggested, and she nodded, not wanting this evening to end.

'Okay.' She moved a pawn and Larenzo countered by moving one of his. Just a few moves later Emma was down a bishop. 'I'm hopeless at this,' she said as she studied the board. Even though she was losing, she was savouring this time with Larenzo. His study was cosy and warm, the lamplight spilling across the board, the heavy damask drapes now drawn across the window.

And as for the man himself… She didn't think she'd been imagining the heat in his eyes. She certainly felt an answering desire in herself. Every so often she sneaked a glance at Larenzo's face; his eyes were narrowed as he studied the board, his mobile mouth pursed. He rested his chin in one hand and Emma longed to reach out and touch him. *Kiss him.*

She forced her gaze back to the board. 'So how did you learn chess, anyway?' she asked. 'I don't imagine they taught that at the orphanage.'

There was a slight pause and then Larenzo answered, 'My business partner taught me.'

Emma looked at him in surprise. 'Your business partner? You mean Bertrano Raguso?' Larenzo gave a short nod.

'So you really were close to him,' she said slowly.

'We were friends,' Larenzo allowed. 'Good friends.'

'Was he the one who planted the evidence against you?'

Larenzo nodded again, and realisation swooped through her. No wonder Larenzo didn't trust anyone. 'I'm sorry,' she said quietly. 'That must have been very hard, to be betrayed by someone you cared about.'

'I wondered how he could do it,' Larenzo said after a moment, his gaze on the board. 'If he was just desperate… I wish he'd told me how things were. I would have helped him.' And then, as if he felt he'd said too much, he moved his queen and put Emma into check.

The weeks slipped by and the leaves fell from the trees, creating a carpet of red and gold on the lawns and pathways of Central Park. Ava had begun to cruise, clinging to coffee tables and chair legs as she made her way around the apartment. Each Saturday Emma took her to New Jersey to visit Meghan and her family; her sister had thankfully stopped warning her about Larenzo. Meghan didn't mention him at all, which Emma supposed was better than her running him down, but she wished Meghan could see, as she now did, how different Larenzo was from what they'd both once thought.

The more time she spent with him, the more she liked him. He could be dryly amusing or gently intent, and his tenderness with Ava had brought the sting of tears to her eyes more than once. And she was having more and more trouble ignoring the chemistry between them. Just brushing past him in the elevator or touching his hand when he handed her something made Emma's insides go liquid with longing. And knowing that he remembered their night, that he might feel even just a little of what she felt…

It was the sweetest form of torture. Emma knew she had to resolve it one way or another. Either she had to stop dreaming about Larenzo, or she needed to ask him if he wanted their friendship—because she did believe they were now friends—to turn into something more. But *something* had to give, because the truth was, she acknowledged one night as she stared up at the ceiling, that she was falling in love with the father of her child.

CHAPTER ELEVEN

'WHAT'S WRONG?' LARENZO glanced up from his tablet where he'd been scanning news headlines, and Emma jumped guiltily.

'Nothing's wrong,' she said quickly, and swiped at a few crumbs on the kitchen table with a damp cloth. Ava banged her spoon on the table and then happily flung it to the floor.

Larenzo picked it up and handed it back to his daughter. 'I can tell something's bothering you,' he said mildly. 'Why don't you tell me what it is?' He tried to ignore the tightening of suspicion and fear in his gut. These last few weeks with Emma and Ava had been nearly perfect. Perhaps too perfect, because perfection wasn't real, couldn't last.

And yet he'd enjoyed this time with Emma and Ava so much…the mornings alone with Ava, and then breakfast, the three of them around the table, a *family*. He, a street rat from the slums of Palermo, finally had his own family. It felt like a miracle. It *was* a miracle. And just seeing Emma frown, sensing her disquiet, made him fear the worst now.

This family, after all, still was more façade than anything else. It wasn't as if they actually cared about each other.

Although he knew in his gut—and his heart—that that wasn't true. He cared about Ava…and he cared about Emma.

'It's nothing,' Emma said as she swiped some more

toast crumbs into her hand and deposited them into the bin. 'Really, it's nothing.'

Larenzo let it go, because he wanted to keep things the way they were, and he was worried, judging from Emma's frown, that they were already changing.

'What are you up to today?' he asked instead and she rose from the table, moving around the kitchen a bit too briskly, not meeting his eye.

'Tumbling class for Ava and then a few errands.' She gave him a brief, distracted smile. 'Nothing too exciting.'

Did he detect a note of restlessness in her voice? Was she unhappy with her life here? He knew she hadn't wanted to come here originally, but he thought in the last few weeks she'd come around. He'd believed they'd enjoyed each other's company.

But maybe he was wrong.

'Sounds fun to me,' he said lightly, and Emma just shrugged. The fear and suspicion inside him felt like acid corroding his gut. She was hiding something from him, he was sure. He knew the signs. He'd lived them.

He rose from the table and pressed a kiss to Ava's head. It took all his self-control to smile at Emma as if nothing were wrong before heading to the office.

He had rented an office in midtown to serve as the headquarters of his new operation, LC Investments. It was, Larenzo realised with every day he spent trying to set things up, going to be a long, hard slog. Even though the charges against him had been cleared, mud stuck. People assumed he had some connection to or knowledge of the criminal activity Bertrano had been neck-deep in, and he could hardly blame them. He'd been so blind. Wilfully, stupidly blind, and he would pay the price for that for the rest of his life.

All he could do now was conduct himself honourably and prove to everyone, eventually, that he was indeed an honest man.

Prove it to Emma.

Did she believe in his innocence? Sometimes, when they spent time together, when she'd gazed at him so hungrily from across the chessboard and he'd imagined hauling her into his arms…then he thought she did. But other times he remembered how she'd flung so many accusations at him, how she'd tried to hide Ava from him, and he doubted. He feared. And fear, he'd learned, was a cripplingly powerful force.

Now he pushed those churning emotions aside and focused on work. He had a meeting that afternoon with a brilliant scientist who needed funding for a new voice-recognition technology he'd patented. Larenzo was looking forward to it; it was exactly the kind of thing he'd wanted to support when he set up his new business. It was the kind of thing he'd tried to support as CEO of Cavelli Enterprises, and he'd left the running of the company's other interests to Bertrano. He wouldn't make that kind of mistake again. He knew better now than to trust anyone, not even the people you loved.

As soon as Larenzo left the apartment, Emma breathed out a discontented sigh. He was amazingly attuned to her moods, but the last thing she wanted to do was tell him what was bothering her.

Last Saturday she'd taken Ava to New Jersey to see Meghan, and the conversation she'd had with her sister had kept her up for most of the night. It had started innocuously enough, with Meghan asking her to come for Thanksgiving, which was next week.

'I'm sure we'd love to,' Emma had said. 'I'll ask Larenzo.'

'Do you need his permission to come here now?' Meghan had asked frostily, and Emma had stared at her in dismay. Over the last few weeks they'd mutually, silently agreed on a ceasefire when it came to Larenzo, but her sister had looked as if she was about to come out with guns blazing.

'No, I don't need permission,' she'd answered, although that wasn't quite true. She always asked Larenzo if she could visit her sister on the weekends, since she knew she was taking away precious time he had with Ava. Larenzo had always said yes. But she hadn't been asking for permission. Not exactly. 'I just want to make sure he's free,' she'd told Meghan, who had stared at her as if she'd sprouted a second head.

'Who cares if he's free?' Emma had stared at her in confusion and Meghan had shaken her head slowly. 'Emma, you don't actually think I'm inviting him, do you?'

'I…' She'd stopped, because of course she had thought that. It was Thanksgiving, the holiday that was meant, more than any other, to spend time with your family. And Larenzo was part of her family, whether Meghan liked it or not. 'I suppose I did,' she'd said slowly, and Meghan had shaken her head again, the movement definitive.

'Emma, let me make this clear. I will never invite that man to my house, to my family, or into my life. The fact that you even thought for a second that I would shows me just how much he has brainwashed you—'

'Give me some credit, Meghan,' Emma had snapped. 'I can judge a person for myself.'

Meghan had pressed her lips together. 'I don't think you're seeing this particular person clearly.'

'And I don't think you are,' Emma had countered. 'Meghan, everything you know about Larenzo has come from newspapers trying to sensationalise a story in order to sell more papers.'

'Do you really think he can be entirely innocent?' Meghan had asked disbelievingly. 'There was so much evidence—'

'He was framed,' Emma had answered. 'He told me so himself.'

Meghan had rolled her eyes. 'Of course he would say that.'

'I believe him.'

'Of course you do. Emma, this man could be manipulating you—'

'And if he isn't? If he's completely innocent, and you're judging him without even bothering to get to know him?' Meghan hadn't answered and Emma had pressed her point. 'Meghan, Larenzo is part of my life now. He's Ava's father, and he's a *good* father. If you continue to blackball him like this, it will only end up driving us apart.'

Meghan had paled. 'So it's him or me?' she had asked, her voice choking.

'*No.* I don't want it to be that at all.' Emma had felt near tears as she'd stared at her sister, horrified at how quickly things had escalated. 'Please, Meghan.'

'You have to make your choice,' Meghan had insisted, and Emma had stared at her helplessly.

Now, as Emma buckled Ava into her stroller to take her to her gymnastics class, she wondered just how she could make such a terrible choice. With her father in Budapest and her mother out of her life, Meghan was the only family she had, the person she'd been closest to for her entire life. The thought of losing her made everything in her cry out in despairing protest.

And yet what was Meghan really asking her? To walk away from Larenzo? Her sister knew she couldn't, not even if she wanted to, and she *didn't* want to.

Which led her to the sinking realisation that whatever she had with Larenzo was neither real nor lasting. He'd made it abundantly clear that he wasn't interested in a relationship, had no time for either trust or love. Never mind that this attraction snapped between them, or that they'd actually enjoyed each other's company. Fundamentally

Larenzo couldn't change. He'd acknowledged that himself. He'd never changed his position on looking for a relationship, and she didn't think he ever would.

If Emma was smart, she'd do what her sister suggested and keep at least an emotional distance from Larenzo. She'd even start thinking about moving out, finding her own place, her own life. She and Larenzo could come to a custody arrangement as she'd originally suggested. That was the sensible thing to do, the only thing to do, and yet everything in Emma resisted.

Which was incredibly stupid, because she knew what it was like to care about someone more than they cared about you. To have someone walk away. Better to walk away first, to be that strong.

'So are you going to tell me what's bothering you now?' Larenzo asked that evening at dinner. His voice was mild, but she felt the steel underneath his words. He didn't like her having secrets.

Emma pushed the pasta around on her plate. 'How do you know anything's bothering me?'

'Because you're a naturally cheerful person. You have this…' Larenzo gestured with his hand '…glow about you.'

Emma looked up, her heart lightening ridiculously at his words. 'Glow?'

'You light up a room.' As if realising he'd said too much, Larenzo turned back to his meal. 'So I can tell when you're not yourself.' He paused, taking a sip of wine. 'You weren't yourself when I first came to your sister's house, but I think in the weeks since then you've gained some of your glow back. For lack of a better word.' He looked up with a faint smile, although his eyes were still shadowed.

'Moving to New York was good for me,' Emma admitted.

'Despite your initial reserve,' Larenzo stated dryly.

'Don't rub it in.' She toyed with her pasta some more, choosing her words with care. 'I do want to thank you, Larenzo, for giving me this opportunity. I was stuck in a rut living at Meghan's, and I didn't even realise how deep it had become until I left.'

He nodded, and Emma knew now would be the perfect time to tell him she was ready to move on to the next phase of her life, and find her own place. A real job. The words didn't come.

'Emma?' he prompted, because he could clearly see there was more she wanted to say. *Needed* to say.

'I spoke with my sister when I visited her,' she finally said. 'She's...not pleased about me being here.'

'I knew that.'

'I mean, really not pleased. She feels I'm becoming...' She hesitated, not wanting to reveal what she was starting to feel for Larenzo yet needing to tell him something of what was going on both with Meghan and in her own heart. 'Too friendly with you,' she finally said.

'A certain amount of friendliness between us is surely beneficial to Ava,' Larenzo answered coolly. Emma could already see how he was shutting down, his silvery eyes turning to blank screens, his mouth compressing. Even the temperature in the room seemed to have dropped.

'I think so,' she answered, 'but my sister doesn't.'

'So what does she want you to do?'

'Maintain a little distance, I guess,' Emma answered after a pause. 'Keep things...businesslike.' Meghan hadn't said as much, but Emma knew her sister would be pleased if she kept her arrangement with Larenzo as simply that: an arrangement.

'If that's what you prefer,' he said in a clipped voice. 'I suppose it's reasonable.'

'You do?' She struggled to keep the hurt from her voice.

Just like that, he was going to abandon their evenings playing chess, their precious time together with Ava?

'The most important thing is that we both have a strong and loving relationship to Ava,' Larenzo answered with a shrug. 'I don't suppose it matters what we do or don't feel for each other.'

'Right,' Emma answered numbly. 'Of course.'

'I have some work to do,' Larenzo said as he rose from the table. 'I'll give Ava a bath and put her to bed, and then I'll go to my study.'

Emma nodded, accepting the rebuff, and watched as Larenzo took Ava from her high chair. She felt as if she'd just ruined whatever they'd been building together, which showed, she supposed, just how fragile it really was.

She didn't see Larenzo again that night, and the next morning he left for the office as soon as she'd come into the kitchen for breakfast. As soon as he'd gone Emma sank into a chair, Ava on her lap, and indulged in a few minutes of wretched self-pity. Larenzo had completely withdrawn from her, and she knew now she'd told him about Meghan's concerns because she'd wanted him to dispel them. She'd wanted him to tell her how glad he was that they were friendly with one another, and even more than that. That he was starting to care.

But her gamble hadn't worked, because obviously Larenzo didn't feel the way she did. At all.

She straightened, forcing the sadness back, and reached for her phone to call Meghan and tell her she'd be happy to come for Thanksgiving.

That night she told Larenzo, keeping her voice as cool as his had been, that she'd be going to see her sister for the holiday weekend, leaving Wednesday and coming back on Saturday. She didn't ask if it would be all right.

His eyes narrowed as he gazed at her. 'Four days? That seems excessive.'

'Thanksgiving is an important holiday,' she answered. 'For family,' she emphasised, wanting in that moment to hurt him, but Larenzo's face remained expressionless.

'I see,' he said as he took a sip of his after-dinner coffee. 'I wouldn't know. Very well,' he finally said. 'I suppose you can go.'

Stung, Emma flung back at him, 'I wasn't asking your permission.'

'Even so, I am giving it,' Larenzo answered evenly. 'We are equal in Ava's guardianship and care, Emma.'

'Not legally—'

His eyes flashed and he put one hand flat on the table in a gesture that was controlled and yet somehow communicated a sense of great anger, only barely leashed. 'Are you threatening me?'

'No, of course not,' she backtracked, colour rising into her face. 'I only meant that we don't actually have a formal arrangement—'

'Then I will put one in place immediately. We can consult my lawyer on Monday.'

'I already consulted a lawyer,' Emma retorted before she could think better of it, and Larenzo went even more still.

'Did you? How…interesting.'

She searched his face, empty of expression as it was, for some flicker of emotion, some sense that he cared at all, and found nothing. Had Meghan been right? Had he been manipulating her with those forays into friendliness? Considering how completely he'd cut her off now, it seemed all too possible.

'We leave tomorrow morning,' Emma said, and without waiting for a reply she left the room.

Thanksgiving was miserable. She tried to enter into the spirit of the holiday, making handprint turkeys with Ryan and helping Meghan with the pumpkin pie, but everything in her felt weighed down, as if she could barely put one foot in front of the other. Meghan, of course, noticed.

'You really do care about him,' she said quietly, when it was just the two of them on the night of Thanksgiving. The turkey had been eaten, the dishes washed and dried, the children put to bed. Pete was upstairs reading stories to Ryan as Emma and Meghan enjoyed a glass of wine in the playroom, curled up on opposite ends of the sofa.

'It doesn't matter,' Emma answered listlessly.

'Why not?'

'Because I told him what you'd said, more or less, and he withdrew completely. We used to spend the evenings together, eat meals as a—well, together.' She swallowed past the lump that was steadily forming in her throat. 'Now I barely see him.'

'Now, that's interesting.'

Emma looked up from her moody contemplation of her glass of wine. 'Oh? How so?'

Meghan sighed. 'It shows he has a sense of honour,' she said. 'Maybe.'

'What do you mean?'

'That he would see the importance of family to you. That he would respect someone else's wishes.' She sighed again, shaking her head. 'I don't know. Ever since I spoke to you I've been regretting what I said. Maybe I was too harsh, but I'm just so afraid for you, Emma.'

'I know.'

'But if he really was framed like you told me, and he is a good father like you said…' Meghan trailed off while Emma waited, impatience brimming.

'Then?' she finally demanded. 'Then what?'

'I don't know,' Meghan admitted. 'Only that maybe we're doing him a disservice. And if you actually think you could care for him, or have a relationship…'

'I think that isn't a possibility now,' Emma answered. 'He barely wants to talk to me.'

'Because you told him about my ultimatum, and then you basically chose me,' Meghan answered bluntly. 'I don't blame him, Emma.'

'I can't believe after all this you're taking his side!'

'I'm not. I'm just trying to see things as a rational adult rather than a panicked older sister.' Meghan smiled wryly. 'I'm still not sure of anything.'

'What am I supposed to do, then? Go and tell him I changed my mind?' *That* wouldn't go over well. 'I'm not sure he's a good bet as a relationship anyway, Meghan. He told me he wasn't interested in one when we first saw each other again, and that he doesn't trust anyone, ever. And I believe him.'

'And no wonder, if his business partner framed him.' Meghan sighed. 'I really don't know. If you guys did decide to get together, it would be a hard road ahead. And you aren't used to that.'

'What?' Emma nearly choked on her wine. 'What do you mean, I'm not used to that?'

'I mean, you haven't been in a serious relationship, with all of its ups and downs. You've never committed to anyone or anything for the long haul. I don't think you've ever stayed in the same place for more than a year or two.'

Emma couldn't deny the truth of her sister's words but she still felt stung. 'There's a reason for all that, you know.'

'I know, because of Mom and Dad's divorce.'

'Not just their divorce,' Emma half mumbled. 'Mom leaving the way she did…not having any interest in us…'

'You made it pretty clear you weren't interested in her, Emma,' Meghan answered gently.

'And why should I, when she rejected us?' Emma demanded.

'She asked you to live with her a year later, didn't she? Out in Arizona.'

'Yes, and that was a complete failure.' Emma shook her head, not wanting to dwell on a memory that still had the power to hurt her. 'Total disaster. I left after only two months.' Meghan was silent and Emma glanced at her suspiciously. 'What?'

'Nothing,' Meghan said as she uncurled herself from the sofa. 'But it's getting late and I want to kiss Ryan goodnight.' She hesitated and then said, 'If you really do think Larenzo is innocent, Emma, and you really do care for him, you're going to have to try. That's all I'm saying.'

'And just a few days ago you practically threatened to disinherit me if I was friendly with him,' Emma couldn't keep from reminding her sourly.

'I know, I'm sorry. I panicked. But he is Ava's father, and you do seem to care for him. So…'

'So,' Emma answered with a sigh. *So what?*

Meghan's words rattled around in her head for the rest of the visit. Did she want to try with a man who had already declared he had no interest in her, couldn't trust? And yet those evenings she'd spent with Larenzo, the way they'd been as a family, had been so incredibly sweet. And she knew he was still attracted to her, just as she was to him. But was that enough?

Emma knew he'd been hurt badly by his business partner, and was perhaps irrevocably damaged by his time in prison. Did she want to try?

She was no nearer an answer to that question when she headed back to New York on the train on Saturday evening, packed with people returning to the city after a long weekend away. Ava was fractious and the train was delayed, so by the time she stumbled into the apartment at nine o'clock at night she was completely exhausted. Ava had fallen asleep in the cab on the way back from the station, and so Emma put her right to bed.

The apartment was silent and dark, and after a second's hesitation Emma went into the hall, flicking on the lights as she looked for Larenzo.

She finally found him in the study, slouched in one of the club chairs, a tumbler of whisky in his hand. His shirt was unbuttoned so she could see the bronzed column of his throat, and his hair was rumpled, his jaw shadowed with stubble. He looked sexy and dangerous and yet also almost unbearably sad as he glanced up at her with pain-filled eyes.

'So,' he said, his voice slightly slurred from the whisky. 'You came back.'

CHAPTER TWELVE

LARENZO GAZED AT Emma standing in the doorway, her hair creating a golden nimbus about her lovely face, and thought he was seeing a vision. Perhaps he'd drunk more whisky than he'd realised.

'Larenzo…' she whispered and he straightened in his chair, flinging his glass onto the table where it clattered noisily.

'I didn't think you were going to return,' he said. She shook her head as she moved into the room.

'Why would you think that?'

'Why wouldn't I? You've made no secret of how you resent me forcing you to come here. And I know I did blackmail you, Emma. I know that wasn't honourable, but…' He raked a hand through his hair, realising his tongue was a little looser than he'd thought. He shrugged and reached for his whisky again. 'Even now I have no regrets. Does that make me a bad man?'

'No,' Emma said quietly. She came to sit in the chair opposite him, the chessboard they'd played so many enjoyable games on between them. 'It doesn't make you a bad man, Larenzo.'

'Are you sure about that?' he asked and took a final swallow of whisky. It burned all the way to his gut. 'Everyone in the world still seems to think I'm guilty.'

'I don't,' Emma whispered and Larenzo turned to look at her.

'Do you mean that?' he asked, and to his shame his voice choked slightly.

'Yes. I do.' She gazed at him with her lovely golden-green eyes, everything about her steady, trusting. And yet how could he possibly deserve her trust? How could he trust *her*?

'Emma…' he began, and then, because he couldn't keep himself from it, reached out and curled his hands around her shoulders, then up so his fingers curved around the back of her skull and he cradled her face in his hands just as he had that night so long ago. Her skin was as soft and warm as he remembered, her lips just as full as he brushed his thumb across them.

Memories rushed through him, painful in their intensity, as Emma waited, her lips parted, her eyes closed.

How could he *not* kiss her?

And yet even as he bent his head, he resisted. He didn't want a fling with Emma, didn't want to hurt her, and yet he knew he wasn't capable of anything else. Even now, with everything in him aching with desire and longing, he knew that. He had no trust, no love, to give. And so he pulled away.

Emma opened her eyes and gazed at him for a long moment. Larenzo gazed back, and in the silence of their locked gazes he thought she understood. She sat back in her chair, disappointment twisting her features for a moment before she composed herself.

'So how was your weekend?' she finally asked and he managed a rusty laugh.

'Pretty awful. Yours?'

'The same.'

He nodded, not wanting to go any deeper with this conversation, knowing he wouldn't be able to handle it. 'I was thinking, I haven't seen any photographs of Ava from when she was small. You must have some.'

'Yes, I do. Would you like to see them?'

'Yes. Please.'

Emma nodded and then slipped from the room to re-trieve them. Larenzo leaned back in his chair and let out a shuddering breath, forcing back the desire that was still rampaging through his system. Nothing was going to happen with Emma. He wouldn't let it.

She returned a few minutes later, a pink baby book in her hands. 'I don't have all that many,' she admitted, 'because I was so sleep-deprived.'

'I suppose that's understandable,' he said, and Emma handed him the book. She settled back into her chair as he opened it and gazed in wonder at a photograph of Ava when she was first born, red-faced and wrinkly.

'She looks like a little old man.'

'Meghan told me most newborns do.'

'She also looks like she had a set of lungs on her even then.'

'That she did. She came out screaming and waving her fists.'

Larenzo smiled and turned the page. He studied each photograph in turn, transfixed by these images of his daughter: first tiny and swaddled with tufts of dark hair, and then chubby-cheeked and bald when it had fallen out, and then sitting on a rug, showing two milk teeth as she grinned.

'These are wonderful,' he said and looked up at Emma. He was disconcerted to see affection suffusing her face, and now that the whisky had cleared from his brain he re-alised how much he had revealed a few moments ago. He cleared his throat and handed back the book. 'Are you still pursuing photography? Beyond pictures of Ava, I mean?'

The question jolted her out of her moment's reverie. Watching Larenzo's face as he studied the pictures of their daughter had made Emma's insides twist with longing. He'd looked so loving, so *tender*. Now he was waiting for her answer and she straightened, shaking her head.

'Not really. I just didn't have the time or emotional energy for it.'

'You should start again,' Larenzo said firmly. 'You had such a gift, Emma.'

'It's nice of you to say so.'

'You don't believe me?'

She let out an uncertain laugh. 'No, I do. I think. I just…' She shrugged. 'I've let it fall by the wayside, I suppose.'

'Why do you think you stopped?'

Emma rolled her eyes. 'Because of a certain eleven-month-old, perhaps?'

Larenzo surveyed her thoughtfully, his silvery gaze seeming to see so much. 'Do you think that's really it?'

'What do you mean?' Emma demanded, but uncomfortably she heard Meghan's voice in her head. *You've never committed to anyone or anything for the long haul.* She'd loved photography, but she'd let it slide, hadn't figured out a way to pursue it with the demands of a baby. Hadn't committed to it.

'Are you afraid to exhibit them?' Larenzo asked.

Emma stiffened. 'Afraid?'

'Of trying and failing. Most people are.'

'Then most people are smart,' Emma answered before she could help herself. Larenzo arched an eyebrow, and she flushed. 'I mean, no one wants to fail.'

'If at first you don't succeed…' Larenzo quipped. Emma managed a small smile.

'In any case,' she said, trying for a brisker tone, 'I've never really been ambitious, for photography or anything else.'

'Why not?'

She shrugged, trying to put him off. These questions were too perceptive, too revealing. 'I always wanted to travel, live life on the road. A career seemed so stuffy.'

Larenzo nodded, not saying anything, and Emma wondered what he was thinking. Did he believe her? Did she even believe herself?

'Yet you gave up travel to have Ava,' he said after a moment, and Emma tensed.

'A decision I've never regretted.'

'Yet a surprising one all the same, considering your lifestyle choices previously.'

'Maybe,' Emma allowed, 'but you never know how you're going to feel until a situation arises. When I realised I was pregnant with Ava, and that she was a part of me…' Her throat thickened as she remembered the wondrous sense that here was a person to love, who would love her.

'A family,' Larenzo said softly and, blinking rapidly, Emma nodded.

'Yes. A family. Our family.'

Larenzo's eyes gleamed and for a moment they just stared at one another, overwhelmed by this simple yet incredible truth.

'Thank you, Emma,' Larenzo finally said, and although she didn't know what he was thanking her for, she still felt how it was a withdrawal. They were a family, but not the kind she wanted to be now.

A week slipped by, a week where Emma couldn't tell what was going on with her and Larenzo. They'd seemed to have come to a silent and somewhat uncomfortable truce, eating meals together, spending time with Ava. Yet the ease and enjoyment they'd had before that wretched conversation was gone, replaced with a polite and careful civility.

It made Emma ache for what they'd had, what they could have if both of them were willing to try. But she didn't even know if she had it in her to try, and Larenzo had given no indication that he wanted to start something more.

She remembered with an ache of longing that moment in the study when he'd almost kissed her, but he *hadn't* kissed her, even though her body had been sending out rocket flares of desire. There was no way Larenzo could have missed those signals. But he'd chosen to ease back, to pretend as if they hadn't been about to start something wonderful. She had to accept that.

Didn't she?

She wrestled with the question for a few days, wondering if she dared ask Larenzo if he would consider making their relationship romantic. The thought of him rejecting such an idea made everything in her cringe. She knew what rejection felt like. She'd kept herself from it for a reason.

Needing a distraction from her endlessly circling thoughts, she got out her camera and, with Ava in the stroller, headed for Central Park.

It was early December and the leaves had fallen, leaving the trees in the park bare, their stark branches silhouetted against a bright blue sky. Emma took a few photographs: the Bethesda fountain with its basin covered in a thin, glassy film of ice; the Mall, its cobblestones glittering with frost, the park benches that lined either side all empty; a rowboat that had come loose from its moorings and now drifted, empty, in the middle of the lake, bumping against the chunks of ice.

When Ava started grizzling from the cold, Emma headed back to the apartment. To her surprise Larenzo was home even though it was only a little after five. The sun was already starting to set, sending long, golden rays across the living room floor.

Emma unbuckled Ava from her stroller and peeled off

her puffy snowsuit; her daughter immediately started toddling towards Larenzo, her arms outstretched.

'I didn't think you'd be back yet,' Emma said. 'I haven't started dinner.'

'It's fine.' Larenzo scooped Ava up into his arms and nuzzled his face against her hair. Emma watched, a tightness growing in her chest. Would she ever get used to these unguarded moments when she saw so clearly how Larenzo loved his daughter? When his tenderness made her melt inside, and long for something she didn't think Larenzo had it in him to give her?

'I came home early because I wanted to talk to you,' Larenzo said, and he sounded so serious that Emma's heart seemed to flip right over. She didn't know whether to be excited or afraid.

As Larenzo put Ava back down and swivelled to her with an intent, sombre gaze she decided to be afraid.

'Is…is everything okay?'

'What?' He looked surprised, and his expression cleared a bit. 'Yes. Fine. Everything is fine.'

'It's just you were looking so serious.'

'No, no.' He ran a hand through his hair, rumpling it as he always did, his gaze distracted now. 'No, nothing's wrong. It's only there is a party I have to go to tomorrow night, an opening gala for a research company that is pioneering a new technology. A lot of people will be there, people I need to meet.'

'Okay,' Emma said after a brief pause. 'I suppose I can manage on my own for a night.' She'd meant it as a joke but Larenzo didn't even crack a smile. He looked even more serious than before.

'The thing is,' he said, 'I wondered if you would be willing to go with me.'

Emma's jaw nearly dropped. 'Go with you?'

'I can hire a babysitter, someone who is more than competent, and we don't have to leave until Ava is asleep.'

'Why do you want me to go with you?' Emma asked, and then could have kicked herself. Was she *trying* to get him to rescind the invitation?

He hesitated and then answered, 'I think it would be better if I bring someone to events such as this one.'

'Better? How?'

He sighed and raked his hand through his hair again. 'After everything that has happened, people still wonder if I was involved in criminal activity. I'm trying to build people's confidence and trust, and I think attending an event with you, the mother of my child, would help with that.'

Emma blinked, stung more than she wanted to reveal to Larenzo, or even to admit to herself. 'Well, at least you're being honest,' she said tartly.

Larenzo stared at her, a frown furrowing his forehead. 'You're angry.'

'Why should I be angry?' Emma countered, even though she didn't actually want Larenzo to answer that question. She was angry because for a moment her hopes had sailed sky-high as she'd thought Larenzo was actually asking her out on a date. She'd believed he wanted to be with her. But no, he was just using her as a way to restore his image, just as Meghan had once suggested. The realisation was bitter.

'I don't know why you should be angry,' Larenzo answered in that toneless voice Emma knew he used to mask his annoyance. 'I'm asking you to go to a party, that's all.'

That's all. 'Thanks for clearing that up,' she retorted and Larenzo spread his hands, clearly bewildered.

'What is wrong, Emma?'

'Nothing,' she replied, and blew out a breath. She was being unreasonable, she knew, by acting offended by Larenzo's invitation. He didn't know how she felt, how she wanted him to feel. 'Nothing,' she repeated, and lifted her camera from where it had been hanging around her neck.

Larenzo noticed, his eyes narrowing. 'Were you taking photos today?'

'I thought I might as well.'

'May I see?'

She hesitated, then, shrugging, handed him the camera. He flicked it on and began to scroll through the most recent photos, frowning slightly as he studied the images. Emma rescued Ava, who had crawled under the coffee table and managed to get herself stuck. Her heart was beating a little harder; she wanted Larenzo to like the photos. She wanted him to like *her*.

'They're good,' he said at last, 'if a bit bleak.'

A bit stung by the criticism, she grabbed the camera from him, setting Ava down with her other hand. Looking at the photos again, she realised they were rather bleak. The park had been full of people, but she'd made it look deserted. Empty and unloved. 'I suppose I was in a bit of a bleak mood,' she answered, and went in the kitchen to start dinner.

CHAPTER THIRTEEN

EMMA GAZED IN the mirror in her dressing room and felt the flutters start again in her belly. She'd spent a long time deciding on a dress; Larenzo had suggested she hit the boutiques on Fifth Avenue, the sky the limit, for her gown for the gala tonight.

While he'd watched Ava, Emma had gone out with Meghan, who had taken the train into the city, to shop. It had felt surreal and wonderfully decadent to try on designer gowns, swilling champagne and parading in front of mirrors.

'So do you think something is happening between you and Larenzo?' Meghan had asked. To her credit, her sister had been civil with Larenzo when she'd come to the apartment, and he'd been just as civil back. Still, it was a tense relationship, and perhaps it always would be.

'I don't know.' Emma had sunk onto the velvet chaise in the dressing room, the ivory satin of her gown poufing out around her. 'He told me he only was asking me because it would look good for his image.'

Meghan's mouth had curved wryly. 'At least he was honest.'

'I suppose.'

She'd gestured to the gown. 'What do you think about this one?'

Emma had glanced down at the crystal-beaded ivory

satin. 'It's gorgeous, but it looks too much like a wedding dress.'

Meghan had given her a look so full of sympathy that Emma had almost felt annoyed. She hadn't wanted to be pitied. She'd wanted to find a beautiful dress and enjoy her evening with Larenzo, no matter what his reasons for inviting her out.

Now she smoothed her hands down the bodice of the emerald satin gown she'd chosen. It was deceptively simple, strapless with a ruched bodice that clung to her figure before flaring out from her knees to her ankles. She'd left her hair loose about her shoulders and used only a little eyeliner and lip gloss to emphasise her features.

She couldn't remember the last time she'd worn something so elegant or felt so beautiful. She hoped Larenzo thought she looked beautiful. She hoped he would tell her so.

He tapped on the door of her bedroom, Ava squealing happily in his arms. 'Emma? Are you almost ready? I was just about to put Ava to bed and then we should go.'

'All right.' With one last glance at her reflection, she turned and opened the door. Her breath felt sucked right out of her lungs as she stared at Larenzo. She'd never seen him in black tie before. The crisp white tuxedo shirt emphasised his perfect physique, his chiselled jaw and bronzed skin. He held Ava, dressed in her pyjamas, balanced on one hip, and Emma didn't think she would ever see a man look so sexy and yet so heart-warmingly wonderful at the same time. Tuxedo and baby. A devastating combination.

Then she saw the blaze of heat in Larenzo's eyes and it suddenly felt hard to breathe. Hard to think. She moistened her lips with the tip of her tongue.

'Do you…do you like it?'

'The dress?' Larenzo clarified huskily. 'Yes. Yes, you look…stunning, Emma. Truly beautiful.'

'Thank you.' Her heart was beating so hard she thought he might be able to see it pounding through the fabric of her dress. She reached out to take Ava. 'I can put her to bed.'

'I don't think we should risk having her slobber on you,' Larenzo answered with a small smile. 'I'll do it. I don't mind.'

While Larenzo disappeared into the nursery with Ava, Emma fetched her matching wrap and clutch and then waited nervously in the hall. A few minutes later the baby-sitter, a competent woman in her forties whom Larenzo had hired from a well-reputed service, arrived, and then Larenzo came out, a finger to his lips.

'I think she's settled.'

He shook hands with the sitter and then, with one hand on the small of her back, he led Emma out of the apartment and into the elevator.

The elevator was huge, and yet it felt tiny and airless as they stood there, shoulders brushing, Emma's stomach clenching hard with suppressed desire.

'You look good too,' she blurted, because how could she *not* say it?

Larenzo arched an eyebrow. 'Thank you.'

She felt like an idiot, but she didn't even care. Tonight she just wanted to enjoy this time with Larenzo. Pretend, even, that it really was a date. Tomorrow they could go back to the reality of being sort of friends. Tonight was for magic.

Larenzo gazed at Emma covertly, out of the corner of his eye. She looked so very lovely standing there, like a proud, emerald flame in her dress, standing tall and straight, her chin lifted. Her hair, usually caught in a practical ponytail, was loose about her shoulders and Larenzo's palms itched with the desire and even the need to touch it. To slide his hands along her skull as he'd done the other night, but this time he wouldn't stop. He wouldn't ease away with regret. No, instead, he'd kiss her as he'd longed to then, deeply, exploring every sensitive curve and contour of her mouth, bringing her body in exquisite contact with his…

Too late Larenzo realised what this little fantasy was doing to him. He shifted discreetly, trying to ease the persistent ache in his groin, and then the doors of the elevator thankfully pinged open. It was going to be a long, uncomfortable night.

And yet he knew, as he took Emma's arm and helped her into the waiting limo, that he was going to enjoy every moment of it, with Emma by his side.

That presumption was questioned just twenty minutes later when he entered the ballroom where the gala was being held and heard the murmurs of speculation ripple through the room. Heads turned, eyes narrowed, lips pursed. Whispers seemed to mock him from every corner of the room.

Larenzo tensed, and then glanced down at Emma, who was gazing around the ballroom, enraptured. Had she noticed? Was he being too sensitive, or even paranoid? God knew he'd learned to be suspicious about everything and everyone. *Even Emma.*

Which was why they would enjoy this one evening together, and no more.

He looked up, and met the gaze of a CEO he'd been on friendly terms with before everything had come falling down. The man nodded curtly and then looked away.

In the two months since he'd been in America, Larenzo had kept a low profile, meeting privately with investors and entrepreneurs, working hard to restore his reputation one individual at a time. He hadn't gone to any major events because he hadn't wanted a reaction like this one. Yet he'd also known he needed to get out, show his face, prove to the world he had nothing to hide.

Clearly that was going to be a harder task than he'd anticipated.

Straightening, he guided Emma towards the bar in the corner. 'Champagne?' he asked and she nodded happily.

'Definitely.'

He procured glasses for them both and handed one to Emma. Tension was tightening the muscles in his shoulder blades, and he could feel the start of a headache. No one approached them, but he saw and felt the sideways glances, and knew Emma did too. She glanced up at him, her flute of champagne held to her lips.

'I see what you mean about needing to restore your image,' she said quietly.

He shrugged as if it were no matter, keeping his face blankly indifferent. He was good at that. He'd been hiding his emotions since he was a child, when the nuns at the orphanage took delight in your fear and considered any smile smug, laughter punishable.

'Shall we go chat?' Emma suggested brightly. 'That's why you're here, isn't it?'

He nodded tersely, dread pooling like acid in his stomach, corroding even the pleasure he had in being with Emma. It had been such a mistake to bring her tonight. He'd thought it would help, but now he cringed to think of her seeing his shame, the condemnation or at least awful curiosity on everyone's faces. Everyone here was wondering if he was guilty.

'Who should we talk to?' Emma pressed. 'What about the science technology guy? Is he here?'

Larenzo almost smiled at her tenacity. 'He's over there,' he said, nodding towards the other side of the ballroom, and determinedly Emma stared forward. Larenzo did smile then, wryly, and he guided her to Stephen Blane, one man, at least, who didn't think he was guilty. Or at least was willing to do business with him, guilty or not.

'Hello.' Emma stuck out her hand, which Stephen shook bemusedly. Emma was a force to be reckoned with, Larenzo thought, gazing down at her with bemused affection. She'd intimated that all of Ava's forcefulness came from him, but he knew it came from her too. She was a strong person, even if she didn't seem to realise it.

They chatted with Stephen for a while, and eventually a few other guests joined them. The conversation came in starts and stops, and Larenzo did his best to navigate its choppy waters, and ignore the occasional innuendo or sly glance, but each one rubbed him painfully raw.

Would it never end? Would he never be free from Bertrano's treachery and his own terrible mistakes?

Emma, he saw, kept her chin up the whole evening, her voice bright as she chatted determinedly with every person in their circle. But he saw the way her eyes widened when someone made some oh-so-clever quip—*How's America, Cavelli? The food's better than what you're used to, eh?*—and her body tensed. Larenzo ignored the sly innuendoes and the way people didn't always meet his eyes. They were curious, perhaps even a little afraid. He could wait it out. The people who mattered believed him.

Like Emma.

Even so, he'd never wanted her to hear this. See this. After an hour of it he'd had enough. Taking her arm, he propelled her to the dance floor.

'Let's dance.'

Clearly startled, Emma deposited her half-full flute of champagne on a waiter's tray before following him onto the floor. 'I didn't take you for a dancer.'

He wasn't, not really. 'No, why not?' he asked as he pulled her into his arms, sliding his hands down to her hips, the satin of her dress slippery under his palms. He could feel the warmth of her skin through the fabric. She draped her arms about his shoulders, her breasts brushing his chest. It was sheer torture to sway to the music and not pull her more snugly to him.

'You've always seemed so focused on work. Even when you were at the villa, you usually had your laptop with you out on the terrace. You never really relaxed, as far as I could see, except maybe a swim, and that was for exercise.'

'I know. I regret that.'

'Do you?' She tilted her head up to gaze at him, her golden-green eyes luminous, her eyebrows raised. 'Why?'

'Because I worked so hard and for what? It was all taken away in the end.' He heard bitterness spike his voice and strove to moderate his tone. 'I wish I'd enjoyed life more.'

Her lips pursed. 'You seemed to enjoy it well enough, judging from the photos I saw of you in the tabloids with one blonde beauty or another.' She glanced at him from under her lashes, waiting for his response.

His mouth tugged upwards in a smile. 'Jealous?'

'Hardly,' she scoffed.

He wished she were jealous. He wished she felt as much for him as he felt for her, even though he knew he couldn't act on it. 'That was just a form of exercise too,' he murmured, his breath fanning her cheek. He felt her shiver in response.

'Then you're obviously very fit,' she returned tartly, and he actually laughed. Emma was the only person who had ever made him laugh.

'Actually, I'm terribly out of shape. Do you know the last time I've…exercised, Emma?'

Colour washed her cheeks and he saw how her pupils dilated. This was such a dangerous conversation to have. He was flirting with fire, and yet he couldn't stop. He felt intoxicated, giddy with desire, even though he'd only had a few sips of champagne.

'I'm not sure I want to know.'

'You,' he said huskily. 'The last time was with you.'

The colour in her cheeks deepened and she looked away. Larenzo touched the tip of his finger to her chin, turned her back to face him. 'What about you?' he asked. Suddenly it was important to know.

'Me?' She let out a shaky, little laugh. 'I think the answer to that is obvious. In the nineteen months since—well, you *know*, I've been pregnant, had a baby, and been living with my sister. What do you think?'

A mixture of joy, pride, and overwhelming desire, the emotions primal and fierce, burst within him. 'Good.'

'Good?' Emma searched his face. 'Why exactly is that good, Larenzo?' she asked quietly. 'What…what are we doing here?'

He didn't answer, couldn't answer, because he knew the only thing he could say was nothing and he didn't want to say it. And Emma must have read all of that in his face for she stopped swaying to the music and broke out of his embrace.

'Excuse me,' she said, and walked quickly off the dance floor towards the ladies' room.

What was he doing? What was *she* doing? Emma stared in the mirror, saw how flushed her face was, how dark and dilated her eyes. She looked like a woman in the throes of desire. She *was* a woman in the throes of desire, and for a few exquisite moments on the dance floor she'd thought Larenzo felt something back. He'd practically been flirting with her, for heaven's sake, and then…

Then he'd pulled back. Again. Letting out a shuddering breath, Emma turned on the tap and ran cold water onto her wrists. Anything to douse this treacherous heat inside her. Every time she thought something was going to happen with Larenzo, he backed off. She didn't need to be a rocket scientist to figure out why; he'd told her himself, after all. He didn't trust people, didn't want that kind of relationship. And neither had she, for most of her life. But being with Larenzo, seeing him with Ava, had changed her.

Too bad it hadn't changed him in the same way.

Sighing, she dried her hands and turned to go back to the ballroom. Maybe she'd tell Larenzo they should call it a night. This evening had been emotionally exhausting in too many ways.

Two women brushed past Emma as they went into the ladies', their heads bent together as they gossiped. They didn't even notice her, but Emma stilled as their hushed voices penetrated the welter of her own miserable thoughts.

'He has some nerve, showing up here,' one woman said. 'I mean, *prison*.'

'It was all a bit suspect, wasn't it, his release? He confessed, after all.'

'It stinks to high heaven,' the first woman stated firmly. 'The investigation is still going on. Who knows which evidence was planted? Raguso was his mentor, you know. Like a father to him, apparently, raised him from when he was a boy. The whole thing is appalling, really.'

The women disappeared into the stalls and Emma walked out to the ballroom on stiff, wooden legs. She hadn't realised Larenzo had been *that* close to Raguso. She'd known he was his business partner, yes, but mentor? *Father figure*, raised him from when he was a boy?

And this was the man that had betrayed him?

Now his trust issues made even more terrible sense. Her steps slowed as she considered how badly Larenzo had been hurt. Could he, *would* he ever recover from that? Did she want to help him try?

You've never committed to anyone or anything for the long haul.

Could she, for Larenzo's sake? She was already falling in love with him. If she was honest, there was no falling about it. She was already there. Could she, loving him as she did, help him to heal? To trust and love again? Love *her*?

Her heart flip-flopped inside her chest like a landed fish and she pressed one hand to it as excitement and fear raced through her. She wanted to do this. She needed to try.

'You were gone a long time.'

Emma nearly jumped as Larenzo seemed to materialise next to her. She hadn't seen him approach, thanks to her whirling thoughts. Now she blinked back all the questions and offered him a smile. 'Not a very gentlemanly comment to make,' she teased, and Larenzo looked startled for a moment by her levity before he smiled faintly.

'I apologise.'

Belatedly Emma remembered how she'd left him on the dance floor. She linked her arm with his. 'Shall we dance again?'

Larenzo gazed down at her, studying her face, trying to gauge her mood.

'Please, Larenzo,' Emma said softly, and wordlessly he took her back out onto the floor.

This time when he took her in his arms Emma didn't hold anything back. She pressed her body against his, felt him tense as she wound her arms around his neck, trying to communicate in every way that she was his, that he could trust her. She knew she could hardly convince him with one dance, but it was a beginning.

It was the beginning, she hoped, of everything.

CHAPTER FOURTEEN

THEY STAYED ON the dance floor for nearly an hour, swaying to the music, needing no words. After the first dance Larenzo's body relaxed into hers, and he bowed his head so his lips brushed her hair. Emma closed her eyes and felt almost perfectly content, even as she ached for so much more. For the first time she hoped she and Larenzo might actually move on from this, to something far sweeter and deeper.

It was after eleven o'clock before they finally broke apart. Larenzo's expression was both dazed and intent as he looked down at her.

Then without any words he took her by the hand and led her off the dance floor, and away from the hotel. The December night air was a cold slap of reality but before Emma could consider what was happening between them their limo sidled to the kerb and the driver jumped out to open the door. Emma slid inside, followed by Larenzo. Their thighs touched and their hands were still linked. Neither of them spoke.

Expectation coiled more tightly inside her with every passing moment; the air felt electric, snapping with tension. Larenzo was staring straight ahead; in the darkness Emma could not see his expression, and she doubted she'd be able to read it anyway. But she *felt* his desire. She certainly felt her own.

Ten minutes passed in exquisite tension. The limo pulled up to their building and the driver opened the door.

'Good evening, Mr Cavelli,' the doorman called, but Larenzo brushed past him with no more than a nod, his hand still holding Emma's.

The elevator felt even smaller and more airless than before as they rode in silence to the penthouse. Emma could feel the heavy thuds of her heart, and each desperate breath she took sounded loud and laboured in the confines of the elevator. Larenzo's jaw was bunched, his gaze on the floor numbers as they slid past and the elevator rose higher, higher. Another breath. Her hands clenched into fists at her sides, and her wrap slithered off her shoulders, trailing to the floor.

Only a few more seconds and they would be in the apartment, they would be alone…

The doors swooshed open and Larenzo stepped out into the hallway, swiping his key card before the door creaked open. Emma followed behind him, the blood beginning to roar in her ears. She closed the door behind her as Larenzo turned to her, and even in the dim lighting of the hall she could see the hunger on his face, and it thrilled her.

He pressed her back against the door, his breathing ragged as he curled one hand around the nape of her neck and brought his lips down hard on hers.

'Mr Cavelli?'

The sound of the babysitter's voice, and her light footsteps coming down the hall, was like a bucket of ice water thrown over them. Larenzo jerked back and then turned to face the babysitter. Emma sagged against the door, disappointment swamping her along with the still-potent desire. Her lips burned.

Distantly she heard Larenzo speak to the woman, and numbly, with a murmured thanks, Emma moved aside so she could leave. The click of the door and the distant ping of the elevator seemed to echo through the foyer; Larenzo switched on the lights, bathing them both in an electric glow. Emma blinked under the bright glare, painfully conscious now at how completely the mood had been broken.

'Well.' Larenzo hesitated, his hands in the pockets of his trousers, his face partially averted from hers. 'It's late.'

Emma swallowed. 'Yes.'

The silence stretched on, but it didn't feel expectant. It felt like disappointment. Failure.

Larenzo let out a sigh so small and sad Emma almost didn't hear it. Almost didn't see the way his shoulders slumped for a single second before he straightened and turned away from her.

'Goodnight, Emma,' he said, and she watched him walk away. The click of his bedroom door shutting was as final a sound as she'd ever heard.

She stood in the hallway for a moment, then switched off the lights and breathed in the darkness. Once again Larenzo had backed off. Once again she was alone, aching with emptiness and unfulfilled desire.

But it didn't have to be this way.

The thought alone sent anticipation as well as fear racing through her, tingling every nerve ending. Quietly Emma moved through the apartment, switching on the dishwasher, tidying up the kitchen, checking on Ava. And all the while she was thinking about what she could do. What she wanted to do.

She could go in Larenzo's room, not even knock. Slip inside quietly and...

And what? Seduce him, when her only experience was that one night with him, and he had thousands of conquests notched on his proverbial bedpost?

Holding her hands up to her face, Emma let out a shaky laugh. The truth was, she had no idea what she was doing. No experience.

But she could try. Even when it was risky. Especially when it was risky. She knew bone-deep that Larenzo would keep backing off, because of his history. She was the one who needed to make the first move, take the first step. Risk her heart.

Alone in her bedroom, she gazed out at Central Park now shrouded in darkness. Her heart was starting to beat hard again, just as it had been when they'd been waiting in the elevator. When she'd been so sure something was going to happen.

But something could happen now.

Emma closed her eyes. What was the worst that Larenzo could do? Refuse her, send her back to her bedroom? It would hurt, yes, and it would be terribly awkward tomorrow, but the alternative, of doing nothing, was far worse.

Wasn't it?

Quickly she stripped off her gown and slipped on a white silk nightie that was the sexiest thing she owned. Not exactly the outfit of a great seductress, she acknowledged wryly as she glanced in the mirror. The nightie was simple but hopefully it would make her intentions clear.

Taking a deep breath, and before she could think better of it, she slipped out of her bedroom, tiptoed across the hallway, and knocked softly on Larenzo's door.

She didn't wait for him to answer, just opened the door and slipped inside, her heart beating so hard and fast she could feel it in her throat. Larenzo's bedroom was lost in shadow, the bed no more than a dark expanse in the middle, and for a moment she couldn't see Larenzo.

Then she heard his rapidly indrawn breath and she saw him standing by the window, the studs of his tuxedo shirt unfastened so it hung open, revealing the beautiful, bronzed expanse of his chest.

Emma stared at him dumbly, amazed she'd got this far and yet not knowing how to take that last step. *I've come to seduce you* sounded laughable. She moistened her lips and then croaked a beginning.

'Larenzo…'

She didn't get a chance to say anything more. As if propelled by a greater force, Larenzo strode towards her, then pulled her into his arms as his mouth came down hard and hot on hers. Excitement exploded inside her as she returned the kiss, hungry, desperate, overwhelming. Larenzo was already skimming his hands under her nightgown, tossing it the floor.

Emma pulled back his shirt; the sleeves snagged on his arms and she let out a ragged laugh as she tugged it off, the studs scattering onto the floor. She smoothed her hands along the hot, satiny skin of his chest and shoulders and let out a deep sigh of satisfaction.

She'd wanted this so, so much. And Larenzo must have too, because he barely gave her a moment to revel in the feel of him before he was carrying her to the bed, depositing her on top of the slippery satin duvet before joining her there, stretching his long, hard body out on top of hers.

She reached for the button of his trousers and with a few tugs and kicks the trousers were off, followed by his boxer shorts. Now they were both naked.

Emma drew her breath in sharply as her hand closed around the thick shaft of his arousal. Larenzo sucked in a breath too, his eyes closed, and then he leaned down and kissed her again. And again. Their limbs tangled as they drank deeply of one another, bodies pressed hot and close together, and even so Emma felt as if she couldn't get close enough.

She arched upwards as Larenzo skimmed his hand down her body before finding the juncture of her thighs and when he touched her so tenderly and yet so knowingly, she nearly wept. She'd missed this. Missed *him*, so much.

'Do you…do you have a condom?' she whispered, not wanting to break the moment but knowing she had to.

Larenzo let out a soft huff of laughter as he rolled off her. 'Actually, yes.'

Emma propped herself on her elbows. 'So you *were* hoping to get lucky,' she dared to tease.

'I guess I was. I just didn't want to admit it, even to myself.'

Her face softened and her heart ached with love for this man. This man who was such an astounding combination of pride and humility, hard and soft, need and arrogance.

'Come here,' she whispered, and held out her arms.

And Larenzo came, folding his body around her as he slid gently inside. Emma drew a quick, sharp breath at the intensity of it and he gazed down at her in concern.

'I'm not hurting you, am I?'

'No. No.' She wrapped her legs around his hips as she brought him deeper into her body. 'No,' she told him. 'Never.' It felt like a promise.

Larenzo lay with his arms around Emma, his heart still thudding and his body tingling with the aftershocks of their lovemaking. She curled her body around his, one leg across his hip, and his heart swelled with emotion, with love for her. Love he hadn't expected to feel, hadn't thought he had it in him to feel. He'd been so empty, and yet Emma had made him full again.

Yet even now he wondered. Doubted. Could this really work? He wasn't even sure what this was.

Shifting so she was resting more comfortably against him, he decided to go for light. 'So did you come in here for a reason?'

She laughed softly as she smoothed one hand down his chest. '*This* reason.'

'Ah.'

'Yes. Ah.'

They lay there in silence for a moment, and then Emma

raised herself up one elbow so she could gaze down at him. Her face was flushed, her hair like a golden-brown cloud, but her eyes were serious.

'Larenzo, at the party tonight, I overheard something.'

The sleepy relaxation that had been stealing through him vanished in an instant. 'Oh?'

'Some women in the ladies'. They said...' She nibbled her lip, and, despite the tension that was now keeping his body rigid, Larenzo felt another wave of lust crash through him. He almost reached for her again, to satisfy his desire as well as to keep her from talking. He didn't know what she was going to say, but he felt sure he didn't want to hear it. He didn't want to talk about how people had gossiped, speculated, *doubted*.

'They said Bertrano Raguso was your mentor,' she said quietly. 'Like a father to you.'

He blinked, shocked, because he'd been expecting her to talk about crime and guilt, not about Bertrano. Not about *feelings*.

'Was he?' she asked, her voice wavering slightly, and Larenzo shrugged.

'I told you we were close.'

'I suppose I didn't realise you were that close.' She hesitated, and then pressed her hand to his cheek, the simple movement nearly his undoing. 'I'm so sorry,' she whispered, and the realisation that she was sorry on his account, that she was *sad* on his account, made a lump form in Larenzo's throat and for a moment he couldn't speak.

'There's nothing you need to be sorry for,' he said gruffly as he gathered her back into his arms. 'It had nothing to do with you.'

'I'm sorry someone you cared about so much betrayed you so terribly. I thought it was bad enough that he was your business partner. But a man like a father—'

'Yes.' Larenzo stared up at the ceiling, as close to weep-ing as he'd ever been. Eventually he forced the feeling back. 'Yes, he was that.'

'How did you meet him?'

No one knew the story, and yet now, to his amazement, Larenzo realised he wanted to tell Emma. He wanted her to know.

'I was attempting to pick his pocket,' he said, and she let out a little startled laugh.

'Seriously?'

'Seriously. I was twelve. I'd been living on the streets for about a year. Surviving mainly by my wits, stealing, pickpocketing, occasionally making honest money by doing odd jobs. Sleeping rough, or sometimes in a shelter. For a few months, in winter, a couple of us clubbed together in an abandoned apartment building.'

She shivered a little in his arms. 'I can't imagine how hard that must have been.'

'It was better than the orphanage,' Larenzo answered. 'At least on the street I had control of my own destiny. In the orphanage…some of the nuns were kind. Others were needlessly cruel. They enjoyed meting out punishment, seeing our pain. I hated it.' Emma didn't answer, just put her arms more tightly around him, and absently Larenzo stroked her hand as the memories assailed him and then spilled from his lips.

'Anyway, when I was twelve, I saw Bertrano. He was in his forties then, a successful businessman. I remember his coat was the softest thing I'd ever touched. Cashmere.'

'And what happened? Did he catch you?'

'Yes, even though I must say I was a very good pickpocket. He caught me by the scruff of my neck and shook me hard. Told me he'd take me to the police, and that I'd end up in prison if…' Larenzo broke off. He *had* ended up in prison, thanks to Bertrano. Even now it hurt.

Gently Emma stroked his cheek, brought him back from

the darkness. 'If you didn't stop?' she guessed, and he nodded.

'Yes. I ran off, didn't really think anything of it. But he found me the next day, and bought me a meal. It went on like that for a few months. I was suspicious of him, but Bertrano, I think, was lonely. He'd lost his wife and son in a car accident. He had no family.'

'And you had no family.'

'No.'

'So what happened then?' Emma asked and Larenzo forced himself to continue. The memories were harder now, tainted as they were by Bertrano's betrayal, and yet he still wanted, or at least needed, to say them.

'He offered to send me to boarding school. He wanted me to do something with myself. I didn't want to at first. I knew what institutional life was like. But then one of my friends, a boy who was only ten, died. Knifed in an alleyway, and I realised I had to get out. So I accepted, and went to a school near Rome. At first I wasn't accepted, people could tell where I came from. But I didn't care. I had warm clothes and a bed and so much food. And I actually liked the learning.'

'It must have seemed like a whole new world.'

'It did. And then I won a scholarship to university, and when I graduated Bertrano asked me to work for him.' His throat had thickened again and he stared up at the ceiling, determinedly dry-eyed. 'I joined the business, and when I was twenty-five he changed it to Raguso and Cavelli Enterprises. When I was thirty, he changed it just to Cavelli. He said he wanted to bequeath the business to me, that I'd worked hard for it, for him, and I was as good as a son.'

'He loved you,' Emma said quietly. Larenzo swallowed.

'And I loved him. Which has made it all the harder to accept how he was willing to betray me.'

They were both silent, their bodies still wrapped around

one another's, the only sound their breathing. Eventually Emma stirred a bit.

'Do you think he's regretted what he did to you?' she asked quietly.

'I don't know,' Larenzo admitted. 'Even now I want to give him the benefit of the doubt. I want to believe he was just weak and afraid. I don't think he had criminal connections the whole time. I'd left a lot of areas of the company to him, and I think he got in over his head.'

'And that's why you confessed.'

'I confessed because the proof was there. I was CEO of the company, and Bertrano had put my name all over his shady dealings. I'd put my name all over it, by giving him that leeway.'

'You still could have fought it, Larenzo,' Emma insisted. 'But you didn't because you loved him. Because you were protecting him.'

He closed his eyes against the memory, and her flawless, painful understanding. 'Yes.'

She placed one hand on his cheek, forcing him to look down at her. 'That is nothing to be ashamed of.'

'Isn't it?' he demanded rawly. 'He might have loved me as his son once, but he still treated me as his stooge. And I let him.'

'He was an old, weak, frightened man.'

'You're pardoning him?' Larenzo demanded and Emma shook her head, certainty blazing from her eyes.

'No. I'm pardoning you.'

He took her hand in his then, and pressed it to his lips. Their gazes held, the communication between them silent and pure. *You are understood. Forgiven. Loved.*

'Thank you,' he whispered and she smiled even as her eyes filled with tears.

'Do you know that's what you said after the last time we made love? You don't need to thank me, Larenzo.'

'I've never told anyone all of that before,' he said. 'I'm grateful that you listened. That you understood.'

'I'm grateful you told me,' she answered, and they didn't speak after that. They didn't need to.

CHAPTER FIFTEEN

THE NEXT MORNING Emma got up with Ava while Larenzo slept. The sleep of the just, she thought with a wry smile as she gazed down at him. He looked glorious stretched out in bed, the sheet tangled around his hips, one arm thrown over his head, the morning sunlight touching his body with gold.

Ava let out another yowl and reluctantly Emma turned away from Larenzo. Her heart was light as she changed and fed Ava; last night things had finally shifted. Larenzo's story of his childhood made her heart ache with sorrow and grief for the lonely boy he'd been, but she was also thankful, so thankful, that he'd told her. They could go on from here, Emma thought. They could build something strong and true. Last night they had laid its foundation.

She was standing by the stove, scrambling eggs, Ava sitting in her high chair banging a spoon on the tray, when Larenzo came into the kitchen. He'd changed into jeans and a T-shirt but his hair was still rumpled, his jaw dark with stubble, and he looked so sexy that Emma's insides clenched hard on a spasm of longing.

'Hey,' he said, and she just about managed to keep her voice sounding normal as she answered.

'Hey.'

'Dada!' They both looked in surprise at Ava and then at each other as she proudly said it again. 'Dada.'

'That's right, sweetheart,' Emma said, her voice a little choked, and Larenzo scooped his daughter up into his arms.

'Aren't you the clever one?'

Ava grinned and patted his cheeks and then squirmed to get down. Larenzo let her down, watching in bemusement as she cruised from chair to table leg. 'She really will be walking soon.'

'Yes, maybe by Christmas.' Which was only a few weeks away. Emma turned back to the eggs and a silence stretched between them, one that was not precisely uncomfortable, but not comfortable either. She didn't know what it was…or what was happening between them.

'Emma,' Larenzo said finally, and she braced herself against that tone.

'Don't,' she said softly, her back to him as she stared down at the mess of eggs. 'Don't try to let me down easily, Larenzo. Not after last night. Not after everything.'

She heard him sigh, a long, weary sound. 'I'm grateful for last night,' he said. 'For…for everything.'

'But?' she prompted, and heard how her voice wavered. She didn't wait for him to tell her. 'Let me guess. But you don't have anything to give because you've been too hurt. You can't trust anyone. You're not looking for a relationship. Yada-yada-yada.'

Larenzo didn't answer and Emma forced herself to turn around. She could feel the tears start in her eyes and she blinked them back, determined to be angry instead of afraid. Strong instead of weak. 'Am I right?'

'A few weeks ago,' Larenzo said slowly. 'A few days ago, even, you were right.'

The first frail thread of hope began to unspool inside her soul. 'But?' she prompted again, and this time she waited.

'But I don't want to live my life in an emotional void. Perhaps I needed that for a while, after everything. It was a way of protecting myself, I suppose. Of…healing.'

'You're a regular armadillo,' she managed to tease, and he offered the most wonderful, crooked smile.

'That's me.' He didn't say anything more and Emma drew in a deep breath.

'Larenzo, are you telling me, in your awkward, emotionally stunted way, that you actually want to try something? With me? A relationship?'

He rubbed a hand over his face. 'Yes, in my—what was it? Awkward, emotionally stunted way, I am.'

With a laugh Emma rushed into his arms. Ava, clinging to a kitchen cupboard, regarded them both curiously as Emma buried her face in Larenzo's shirt and tried not to weep. 'I'm just happy,' she said with a trembling laugh and a sniff, and Larenzo stroked her hair.

'I am too,' he said, and he sounded wondering. 'But, Emma, the other stuff still applies. I don't…I don't know how much I have in me. I still don't feel…' He paused, searching for words, and Emma waited. 'Like a whole man. As if I've truly put the past behind me.'

'You've taken steps,' Emma answered firmly. 'That's the important thing, Larenzo. You can't expect everything to fall into place all at once. But it will.' She believed that absolutely. 'It will.'

He nodded, still looking doubtful, and she continued, 'And the past will always be there. You can't forget it. You can only learn to live with it.'

'With your help,' Larenzo said, and put his arms around her. Emma couldn't remember when she'd felt so happy, so *joyful*.

'Now I know what the woman in the photo feels like,' she said and Larenzo smiled faintly before kissing her lips.

'So do I.'

They had nearly three weeks of that joy. Things went on the same in many ways; Larenzo still worked, and Emma still stayed at home with Ava. But everything felt different. Everything *was* different, because they were a family now, in every sense.

Larenzo kissed her the moment he got home from work, and Ava squealed to be picked up. They spent the evenings together, watching a DVD or playing a game or just chatting; sometimes they would sit on the sofa, Emma's feet in Larenzo's lap while he worked and she studied the photographs she'd taken that day.

Her creativity had exploded along with her joy; suddenly she saw pictures everywhere, and she spent many crisp wintry days trawling the city streets with Ava in tow, snapping photos and capturing moments. So many wonderful moments.

'You really should try to exhibit these,' Larenzo said when she showed him her latest round of photos, candids of various people around the city who had been happy to have their picture taken.

'I wouldn't even know how to begin,' Emma answered. 'But I'll think about it. I'm just happy to be feeling creative again. I felt dormant for so long, just struggling through each day.'

'I know how that feels.'

'Was that…was that how you were in prison?' she asked hesitantly. They still hadn't talked about his time in prison, and after that one night of confession they hadn't spoken about the past at all. They were, as Larenzo had said, focused on the future. Their future.

'I suppose,' he answered now. 'I felt…not just dormant, but dead inside. As if there was nothing left to live for. As if I wasn't even alive, not in the way that counted.'

'And when you realised you could walk free?' she asked softly. 'That new evidence had been found?'

'It didn't sink in for a while. I didn't believe it, at first.

And then when I actually got out…' He shook his head. 'Feelings don't go away as quickly as that. I still felt empty.'

'And now?' she whispered.

'I'm filling up,' he told her, and she laughed to see the wicked gleam enter his eyes. 'You're filling me up,' he said, and reached for her.

If the days continued on as normal, the nights were wonderfully changed, long and pleasure-filled. Emma didn't think she'd ever tire of exploring Larenzo's amazing body, or having him revere hers. She wondered how she'd lived so long without knowing the pleasure of such intimacy with another person.

Larenzo clearly wondered the same thing, for one night after they'd made love he ran his hand along her hip and asked, 'So how come you were a virgin at age what? Twenty-six?'

She wriggled around to face him. 'Is it really so odd?'

'In this day and age, I'd say so.'

She shrugged. 'I just never met the right guy, I suppose.'

'But you must have had boyfriends.'

She hesitated, uncomfortably aware at how this conversation was leading them both into the uncharted and unknown territory of her past. 'A few, but no one serious. Obviously.'

'So?'

'I didn't want to get that close to somebody,' Emma said after a moment. 'I liked being on my own.'

'Why?' Larenzo asked, frowning.

'I suppose my parents' divorce affected me badly,' Emma admitted. Larenzo had been honest with her about so much; the least she could do was be honest in return. And it was hardly as if she had some great tragedy or injustice in her past, not as he had. 'My mother left,' she continued. 'When I was twelve. She'd had enough of moving every two or three years. She wanted to return to the States, live in one place.'

'And your father didn't want to?'

'I don't know if she gave him a choice. I wasn't aware of any tension or fights, at least. Just one morning at breakfast she told us all she was leaving. Going back to America. I thought she meant for a vacation.'

'And she didn't take you?'

'No.' Emma shook her head, the memory making her eyes sting even now. 'No, she didn't even suggest it. In fact…' She trailed off, and Larenzo slid his hand in hers, a small gesture of solidarity that strengthened her to continue. 'In fact, I asked her to take me. I was closer to her than to my father, mainly because he was so wrapped up in his work. And…she said no.'

'I'm sorry, Emma,' he said quietly.

'So am I.' She sighed and rolled onto her back. 'It is a terrible feeling, to be rejected like that by your own mother.'

'Yes,' Larenzo agreed. 'It is.'

Emma stiffened. 'I'm so stupid and callous,' she exclaimed. 'I'm sorry—'

'No, don't be.' He smiled and stroked his hand back up her hip, all the way to her shoulder. 'We were talking about you. Why do you think she said no?'

'I don't know. I didn't ask. I acted kind of bratty, to be honest, and made like I wanted to be with my dad anyway. And she went off to Arizona and met someone else.' Those were the facts, and yet Emma thought Larenzo could guess at the years of confusion and pain she'd felt at the way her mother had so easily left her.

'And then what happened?' he asked.

'We lost touch over the years. She did ask me to visit, to live with her for a year, when I was in high school. I went, and it was so awkward and just…awful. She was wrapped up in this new guy and he didn't want to have anything to do with me.' She paused, remembering the tension, the arguments, the misery. 'I told her I was leaving, and she didn't even seem to care.' She remembered telling her mother she was going, willing her to insist she wanted her to stay. She hadn't. 'I suppose it felt like another kind of rejection. After that we hardly spoke or saw each other at all.'

Larenzo gathered her up in his arms. 'And that made you stay away from real relationships?'

'I guess, although I didn't connect the dots that simply. But I've always moved around a lot, and I've spent a lot of time on my own. I never felt like I needed anything or anyone else.'

'So what changed you?'

'You did,' she said simply. 'You were the first person that made me want to be different.'

'I'm glad,' Larenzo said softly. 'Because you made me want to be different too.'

And during those few weeks, their happiness was not unalloyed; the past continued to mar the perfect landscape of their joy, as Emma had known it would, as she'd warned Larenzo it would, and yet...

It was hard. Harder than she'd expected.

More than once she woke up in the middle of the night to an empty bed, and when she went in search of Larenzo she'd find him in his study, working or sometimes just staring into space.

'I've had trouble sleeping since prison,' he told her, but Emma saw the way his gaze flicked away from hers, and she felt there was more he wasn't saying.

Several times she went out with Ava and returned late, to be faced with Larenzo's sudden and inexplicable wrath.

'You should have phoned,' he stormed one night when Emma had come back after dinner.

'I tried,' she answered as calmly as she could. Ava was squirming to get out of her snowsuit. 'But the reception was bad—'

'In Manhattan?' he scoffed. 'You can get reception anywhere. Or were you not in Manhattan?'

Emma sat back on her heels and looked up, meeting his gaze steadily. 'Are you accusing me of something, Larenzo?' she asked quietly and he sagged suddenly, looking older than his thirty-five years.

'No. No, of course not,' he said, and they both dropped it, but each of those tense interactions made Emma weary. Understanding someone had trust issues and living with it were two very different things.

But even worse than Larenzo's bouts of suspicion were the dark moods that overtook him so he retreated into himself and nothing Emma did could reach him. Eventually he'd come out of it again, whether it was hours or days, and he would shoot her a look of apology that Emma accepted with a silent nod. He had hard memories; she understood that. It didn't make it any easier to deal with.

The week before Christmas she went to New Jersey with Ava to visit Meghan. She'd already told her sister she would be spending Christmas in the city with Larenzo; Meghan had been disappointed but understanding.

'You look tired,' she said when she met Emma at the train station. 'Is Ava keeping you up at night?'

'No, she's actually sleeping through for once.' Emma opened the car door and began to buckle Ava into her car seat. 'I'm fine.' She avoided her sister's gaze as she said it; the truth was, she was tired because Larenzo had been up in the night, unable to sleep, and when Emma had confronted him about it he'd become angry and stalked off. In the morning they hadn't mentioned the argument, and now Emma wondered if it would always be like this.

'Are you happy?' Meghan asked bluntly. 'With Larenzo? Because I'll be honest, Em, you don't actually look that happy.'

'I am happy,' Emma protested. 'I love him.'

'Loving someone doesn't always equal happiness.'

'It should,' Emma answered as she stared out of the window. 'It should,' she said again, and she heard the defeat in her voice.

They drove in silence for a few minutes, the muted landscape of the suburbs in winter streaming by. 'So what's going on?' Meghan asked eventually. 'Because obviously something is.'

Emma sighed. 'Nothing, really, it's just…you were right. It's hard sometimes. Larenzo has a lot of…'

'Emotional baggage?'

'Yes. But I do too,' Emma said quickly, and to her surprise Meghan nodded.

'More than you think.'

'Now what's that supposed to mean?'

'Come on, Emma. Most people whose parents divorced when they were kids manage to get over it and have healthy relationships of their own.'

Emma stiffened. 'So what are you saying exactly? That I'm some kind of freak?'

'No, of course not,' Meghan answered. 'But Mom leaving was really hard on you. Maybe because of our lifestyle growing up, all the moves, all the different cities and schools. You never had a friend for long.'

'I know.' When she'd been about eight or so she'd stopped investing so much in friendships. In the circuit of international schools, people were always on the move. And she hadn't minded; you had a friend for a while, and then someone left, and you found someone else. It had been simple—until her mother had been the one to find someone else.

'So perhaps that's why Mom leaving you affected you so much,' Meghan finished gently. Emma stared out of the window.

'I asked her to take me with her,' she said after a moment. 'I don't think you knew that.'

'No,' Meghan said quietly. 'I didn't.'

'She said no. Obviously.' Emma took a deep breath. 'So that might be the reason why I'm a little gun-shy when it comes to relationships.'

'Maybe,' Meghan allowed, and Emma could tell she wanted to say something else.

'What is it? You might as well give it to me straight. It's not like you to hold back.'

'There was…stuff Mom didn't tell you,' Meghan said slowly. 'Because you were so young.'

'Stuff?' Emma stiffened. 'What kind of stuff?'

'She was depressed,' Meghan answered after a moment. 'Really depressed. She told me about it, when I was in college. She was trying to get help, but it was hard.'

'Depressed…?'

'Did you never notice anything? How tired she was, and how…I don't know…listless sometimes?'

Distantly Emma recalled how much her mother had slept. Often when she'd come home from school, her mother would be napping. She hadn't thought much of it, perhaps because she'd had no one to compare her mother to. 'I don't know,' she said finally. 'Maybe, a bit, but…'

'When she went back to America she went into a clinic,' Meghan said. 'For depression. She was there for six months. That's why you couldn't come.'

Emma swivelled to gape at her sister. 'And she never told me? Not once, in fifteen years?'

'I think she felt ashamed,' Meghan said quietly.

Emma sank back against the seat. Just as Larenzo had felt ashamed. And yet in both cases honesty, although harder, would have been so much better. So much more healing.

'I wish I'd known,' she muttered. 'She could have told me when I came to live with her.'

'I think she just wanted to forget that part of her past, of herself.'

'And that visit was a disaster,' Emma reminded her. 'It wasn't just about the depression, Meghan.'

'I'm not saying it was. I just wanted you to understand the whole picture. As for that time in Arizona…you left pretty quickly, Emma. Maybe that felt to Mom like you were rejecting her.'

'So you're blaming me?' Emma demanded, more hurt than she wanted to admit or reveal.

'No, I'm only asking you to look at it from both sides.'

Meghan fell silent, and Emma turned back to the window. Look at it from both sides? She realised she'd been clinging to her entitlement as the wronged party for so long. Her mother had rejected her. Her mother had failed her. It was a child's view, and one she wasn't actually all that proud of.

She wanted things to be different with Larenzo. *She* wanted to be different, to be patient and understanding of the man she loved, and to trust that he would put the past to rest, stay with her and love her for ever…even if he had trouble trusting her in the same way.

'Love is complicated,' she finally said to Meghan, and her sister laughed.

'You've got that right.'

Her conversation with Meghan was still rattling around in her head when she returned to New York that evening. Meghan had helped her to deal with her past issues, and maybe she needed to help Larenzo deal with his. Not just by being patient or loving, not just by waiting, but by dealing with them once and for all.

Ava had fallen asleep on the train, and Emma hefted her over one shoulder as she wriggled her way out of the cab and then up to the apartment.

Larenzo met her at the door, taking Ava from her aching arms. He put Ava to bed and then rejoined her in the living room, looking slightly wary, as he always did after she'd returned from her sister's. As if he were still afraid she might leave him.

'Larenzo, I've realised something,' she said, and now he looked even more suspicious.

'Oh?'

'We can't go on like this.'

He stilled, his face wiped of expression. 'I see.'

'No, you don't,' she said in exasperation. 'I'm not leaving you. I want you to leave me, for a little while.' He stared at her, nonplussed, and she took a deep breath. 'I want you to go back to Sicily.'

Larenzo's eyebrows snapped together. 'No. Never.'

'I want you to see Bertrano.'

'No,' he said again, his voice as hard as she'd ever heard it. 'I have no desire to see him again, Emma. Ever.'

'Don't you think you need closure?' Emma asked softly. 'For both our sakes? Meghan was talking to me and I realised how much of my past I'd avoided. I thought I could put all my bad memories in a box and pretend they didn't exist. But it doesn't work that way.'

'It can.'

'Please, Larenzo. Just to finally learn why he did what he did. To make peace with it, if you can.'

Larenzo flicked his gaze away from hers. 'And if I can't?'

'You can, Larenzo.' Emma laid her hand on his arm. 'I know you can.'

He said nothing for a long, long moment, and she could see the emotions battling in his eyes, on his face. Then slowly, painfully, he nodded.

CHAPTER SIXTEEN

LARENZO STOOD IN the small waiting room of the high-security prison near Terni, in central Italy. Sweat prickled his scalp and his stomach did a queasy flip. Just a little over two months ago he'd been behind those locked steel doors. He'd walked out a free man, but returning to the place where he'd felt so hopeless was not a comfortable feeling.

He took a deep breath and let it out slowly. He'd been waiting for fifteen minutes for the guard to tell Bertrano he had a visitor. Larenzo hadn't asked his former mentor if he could visit; he hadn't wanted to give Bertrano the opportunity to refuse. And he hoped, now that he was actually here, Bertrano wouldn't. He'd realised, in the few days since Emma had confronted him, that she'd been right. He needed to talk to Bertrano. He needed to understand.

'Come with me,' the guard told him in Italian, and with a terse nod Larenzo followed him through the heavy steel door, past the metal detector, and then to a holding cell where he was patted down before finally emerging in the visiting room, a dour place with half a dozen non-contact phone booths. Bertrano waited in one.

Just the sight of him caused shock and something worse, something like loss, to jolt through him. Bertrano was slouched in his chair, his face haggard and lined so he looked far older than his sixty-seven years. He lifted his bleary glance to Larenzo as he sat down, then looked away again, seemingly indifferent.

Larenzo took a deep, even breath and then picked up the phone. After a moment Bertrano picked up his.

'So you came,' he said flatly.

'Yes. I came. Which is more than I can say you did for me.' He hadn't wanted to start this conversation with bitterness, yet he couldn't seem to keep himself from it. Bertrano just shrugged. 'Did you think I wouldn't?' Larenzo asked, and the old man shrugged again.

'Frankly,' he answered, 'I didn't really care.'

Larenzo blinked. He realised he'd expected Bertrano's shame, his guilt, his anger, even his defensiveness…but this indifference shocked him.

'Why?' he asked eventually.

Bertrano glanced at him, shaggy eyebrows raised. 'Why what?'

'Why did you do it?' Larenzo asked, his voice low. 'I thought about it many times. I had many hours in prison to think about why you would betray me in such a fashion.'

To his amazement Bertrano let out a hoarse, rasping laugh. 'Betray you?' he repeated. 'Even now, you can think that?'

Larenzo stared at him. 'What do you mean?'

Slowly Bertrano shook his head. 'After all this time,' he said. 'After everything I've done, you still want an explanation? Isn't it obvious, Larenzo? Or are you just being blind? *Cazzaro*,' he spat, and Larenzo recoiled at the insult.

'I am not an idiot,' he said coolly. 'I am trying to understand—'

'Understand what? It's all pretty simple to me. I used you, Larenzo. I framed you. Which part don't you understand?' He shook his head before looking away.

'I know that. What I don't understand is how you could do such a thing, after all—' he broke off, feeling a pressure building in his chest, before he continued tightly '—after all our time together. You rescued me, Bertrano.

You *saved* me, you treated me with such kindness, and then to betray—'

'Oh, enough with the hurt feelings,' Bertrano said, flapping his hand. 'Enough, enough.' He leaned forward, his eyes glittering with a malice Larenzo had never seen before. 'Why do you think I saved you, Larenzo? You, a Palermo street rat, worthless, hopeless, rough and untaught? Why would I save *you*?'

Larenzo stared at him, the pressure in his chest painful now, taking over his whole body. He stared at the man he'd once thought of as his father and could not speak.

'No answer, eh?' Bertrano nodded. 'That's because the only answer is the one you've refused to accept, even when it was staring you in the face. You were my safety net, Larenzo. My backup plan. No more than that.'

Larenzo's hand was clenched so hard around the phone his fingers ached and his knuckles were white. 'Tell me what you mean,' he demanded.

'I wanted someone I could blame,' Bertrano said simply. 'That's all you ever were. What is the English expression?' He closed his eyes briefly, his mouth curving in a cold, cruel smile. 'A stooge.'

Larenzo didn't answer, couldn't speak. The question that burned in his throat was one he was too ashamed to say. And yet somehow he found himself saying it, needed to say it. To hear the answer. 'Didn't…didn't you ever care about me?'

Bertrano gazed at him pitilessly. 'No.'

And still he resisted that awful truth. 'But so many years…my schooling, the business…' But he wasn't thinking of that. He was remembering days at the beach, and evenings playing chess, and the way he'd felt loved and accepted by Bertrano. All of it false? All of it a *ploy*? He shook his head, unable to process it. Desperate to deny it.

'I was fond of you,' Bertrano allowed, 'in a way. You

were so eager to please, after all. But the reason I sought you out, Larenzo, was so I could put the blame on you if it all went bad.' He sagged against his seat. 'Which, of course, it did.' He shook his head. 'Your lawyers were tenacious, I'll grant you that. I thought I'd destroyed any evidence that could convict me. I suppose it's my own fault.' He shrugged wearily and looked away, a man who no longer had any hope. Just as Larenzo had been. Just as he felt now, for he was starting to see how it all made terrible sense.

The questions Bertrano had first asked, about whether he had family, or if anyone would come looking for him. Anyone who would care. And then how Bertrano had encouraged Larenzo to pursue his separate business interests while he tended to the rest. Putting the business into Larenzo's name. He'd thought Bertrano was being kind, but he'd actually just been constructing an elaborate web in which to ensnare him. All of it, everything, had been false. A lie. This was so much worse than what Larenzo had thought. Grief poured through him in an unrelenting river, a grief deeper and darker than any he had known before.

Bertrano let out a weary sigh. 'Poor Larenzo,' he mocked. 'Always wanting to be loved.'

Larenzo could take no more. He slammed the phone down so hard it cracked the cradle and then walked out of the visiting room without looking back.

Outside he braced his hands against the roof of his hired car and took several deep, even breaths to calm his racing heart.

All of it a lie. All of it a ploy.

Even now, he could scarcely believe it. This was what he'd come back for? This was to help him move on? Then, with a new, cold clarity stealing over him, Larenzo realised it would. Because now he knew that nothing was real. No one could be trusted.

* * *

Emma paced the living room restlessly, trying to suppress the anxiety that had settled like a stone in her stomach, weighing her down. Larenzo had been gone three days. He was due back tomorrow, on Christmas Eve, and yet he hadn't contacted her in over forty-eight hours. The last time she'd spoken to him had been when he'd arrived in Terni, intending to visit Bertrano in the morning. He'd sounded resolute and yet also upbeat, and Emma had felt so thankful for his willingness to do this, so admiring of his courage. Now she wondered sickly just what he had found.

She tweaked an ornament on the Christmas tree she'd had the doorman bring up to the apartment. She'd bought it outside the Natural History Museum, a mammoth tree whose top touched the ceiling. Ava was enchanted by it, but it meant Emma had had to decorate only the top half of the tree so her newly walking daughter couldn't pull all the decorations off.

Still, she thought the apartment looked beautiful, decorated for Christmas. Besides the tree she'd bought a nativity scene and set it up in the hall. Boughs of evergreen and holly garlanded every doorway, and filled the rooms with their fresh, spicy scent. She glanced under the tree to where she'd put several presents: a few toys for Ava, and a photograph for Larenzo. Her chest tightened as she thought of them all spending Christmas together, a family.

Why did she feel now as if it might not happen? *Why had he not called her?*

She heard the sound of the front door opening and everything in her stilled. Larenzo wasn't due back until tomorrow and yet he was the only one with a key card. Then she heard the slow, deliberate tread, and Larenzo appeared in the doorway. He looked…he looked as he had that night so long ago now when he'd come to the villa. Haggard. Resigned. As if he was missing an elemental part of himself.

Emma pressed one hand to her hard-beating heart. 'Larenzo. I wasn't expecting you until tomorrow.'

He tossed his key card on the table and walked past her, to the drinks cabinet, just as he had before.

'I decided to come home early.'

'Why didn't you call?' Not wanting to sound accusing, Emma strove to moderate her tone. 'I was worried about you. What…what happened with Bertrano?'

Larenzo poured himself a whisky, his back to her. 'He told me the truth.'

'What do you mean—?'

'It was very enlightening,' he cut across her. He turned around, the tumbler of whisky held to his lips as he leaned against the cabinet. 'Very enlightening,' he repeated, and took a long swallow.

Emma shook her head slowly. 'Why don't you enlighten me, then?' she asked, trying to smile. 'I was worried.'

'Were you?' He sounded disbelieving and Emma's insides lurched with fear.

'Yes, I was. Please, Larenzo. Tell me what is going on.'

'Perhaps you should tell me what's going on,' Larenzo returned coolly. 'Because it occurred to me, Emma, how easily you agreed to come live with me here. For a woman who was hell-bent on keeping me from her child, you changed your tune rather quickly. Rather conveniently.' He took another sip of whisky, watching her all the while through narrowed eyes.

'I don't understand what you're implying, Larenzo,' Emma answered. She tried to keep her voice calm, although she felt like screaming. Like flying at him and slapping some sense into him, because she could see he was in self-destruct mode and she didn't know how to get him to stop. 'Larenzo, please. Let's talk about this…'

'I am talking about this. I'm talking about the fact that you were desperate to have me out of your and Ava's lives, and then all of a sudden you changed. You'd called a lawyer, after all. You were serious, Emma. And then you just caved. Why?'

'Because I realised I wanted you involved in Ava's life,' she answered steadily. 'I know what it's like to have an absentee parent and I didn't want that for Ava. I didn't want that for you. You're a good father, Larenzo.' He didn't answer and Emma took a step towards him. 'Please tell me what happened in Italy.'

'What happened is I woke up and realised how deluded I've been about people. Everyone wants something, Emma. Everyone's looking out for the main chance. Even you. Especially you.'

She gasped, the sound one of pure pain. '*Especially* me?'

'You've got a pretty sweet deal here, haven't you? Luxury apartment in the city, every expense paid for.'

'I offered to pay my way—'

'Of course you would. You'd want to seem convincing.'

'Convincing? Convincing of what?'

'You wanted me to look out for you. To take care of you. Maybe you're even hoping for marriage.'

She shook her head slowly. 'What on earth has got into you, Larenzo? What did that evil man say to you?'

'Evil man? But you said he was just weak and afraid. You had quite a lot of sympathy for him, as I recall.'

'I had sympathy for you,' she corrected. 'Although it's disappearing fast.'

'Is it?' Larenzo's mouth curved in a cold smile. 'Good.'

'Good? *Good?*' Her voice rose in a scream as her hands clenched into fists. 'Are you going to throw away everything we've built together simply because of something Bertrano said to you?'

'Everything we've built?' Larenzo arched an eyebrow. 'It doesn't seem that much to me. A few weeks, Emma. That's all.'

Emma gaped at him, unable to believe that everything could fall apart so quickly. So utterly. 'What are you saying, Larenzo?' she demanded. 'How does Ava fit into any of this?'

'Ava is my daughter and I will have a place in her life,' Larenzo answered. 'Always. That won't change.'

'But us?' Emma forced herself to ask. 'What about us?'

For a second, no more, Larenzo looked conflicted. Tormented. Then his expression ironed out to pitiless blankness and he shook his head. 'There is no us.'

Emma couldn't keep herself from giving one small gasp of pain. 'I don't know what that man told you...' she began but Larenzo didn't say anything. She drew in a ragged breath. 'You know what? It doesn't even matter. I don't care what Bertrano Raguso told you, because nothing makes what you've said to me justifiable. You say you don't trust people,' she continued, her voice shaking. 'Well, I trusted you, Larenzo, and I shouldn't have.' A muscle flickered in his jaw, but that was all the response she got. She felt like hitting him, hurting him, and so she did the only way she knew how. 'I hate you!' she spat. 'I hate you for making me care about you, and then doing this.' And with tears spilling down her cheeks, she snatched up Ava and stormed down the hall.

Alone in her bedroom, she sagged against the door. Ava squirmed to get down and Emma let her before sinking slowly to the floor, her knees drawn up to her chest. Her head was spinning, tears still trickling down her cheeks. How had it come to this so quickly, so terribly?

She felt as she had when Larenzo had been dragged off by the police. *She felt as she had when she'd left her mother's.*

The realisation was like a lightning streak of pain. She was acting just as she had then, storming away, refusing to engage. She didn't even remember what the argument with her mother had been about, the one that had set them both off and made Emma leave. She just remembered feeling furious and hurt and unloved, and instead of staying and battling it out she'd booked a ticket back to Berlin, where her father had been living at the time.

This time, did she possess the strength and courage not to walk away, but to stay and fight? Fight for herself, fight for Larenzo, fight for their family.

Walking away had been a way to protect herself, to pretend she wasn't hurt when she'd spent years aching inside. She wasn't going to make the same mistake now. She'd learned that much, at least.

Taking a deep breath, Emma rose from the floor. She picked up Ava, settling her on her hip, and then flung open her bedroom door and marched out into the living room.

The sight of Larenzo slouched in a chair, his head in his hands, made her insides twist with sorrow.

'I'm not,' she announced, 'going to let you do this.'

Larenzo looked up, his hair ruffled, his skin nearly grey with exhaustion. 'Excuse me?'

'I'm not going to let you destroy us, Larenzo. Whatever Bertrano told you, it's not worth it. I'm not going to let you throw away the happiness we've found together simply because some selfish old man is trying to ruin it for you and for us.' She took a deep breath and then ploughed on. 'I love you, you know. I'm not giving up. Not that easily. I gave up on my mother, when I was a teenager. Meghan helped me to see my part in the failure of our relationship. I'm not giving up on you.'

He stared at her for a long moment and then looked away without speaking. So it wasn't going to be easy. She couldn't say she was surprised.

'I want to show you something,' she said, and, setting Ava down on the floor, she marched over to the Christmas tree and retrieved a present from underneath it. She thrust it towards Larenzo; he took it, resting it in his lap, making no move to open it.

'It's my Christmas present to you,' Emma stated. 'Open it.'

He glanced up at her, and then, with a tiny shrug, he opened the present. The frame was made of silver, an elaborate twisting of ivy that Emma had liked because it was a live and growing thing, just as their relationship was. Their family was.

And the picture the frame held—it was of their family. It had been taken a few weeks ago at the playground. Emma had put the camera on a tripod and timer and run over to pose with Larenzo and Ava; their faces were all smooshed together, filled with laughter. It wasn't a candid moment, but it was close, and it was a picture that was filled with love and happiness. With joy.

Larenzo stared down at it for an endless moment. Emma held her breath as he traced their three faces with his fingers. Then he closed his eyes briefly and her heart gave a painful squeeze. 'Emma.'

'Larenzo,' she said softly, waiting.

He didn't speak for a long moment. Finally he said, 'Bertrano told me that he…he never cared for me. The only reason he'd ever approached me was to use me.' He looked up then, his face so unbearably bleak. 'So if things went wrong, he could blame it all on me. It's diabolical, really, to use a child that way. But he did and it worked.'

'Oh, Larenzo.' She stared at him helplessly; she could not imagine what hearing that must have felt like. A whole new and worse kind of grief.

'The thing is, I never even guessed. I never doubted, growing up, that he cared about me. Oh, I was suspicious at first, of course I was. But the more time he spent with me, the safer I felt… I really did think he loved me, like a son.' He shook his head slowly. 'Even when he betrayed me, I thought how it must have hurt him. How it must have been a hard decision to make. What a fool I am,' he spat, his voice thick with disgust. 'What a blind fool.'

'You're a person who, despite everything, believes the best of people. That's not a bad thing, Larenzo.'

'I took the blame because I loved him,' he said starkly. 'I could have fought it. I might have even won. But I didn't because I wanted to spare him. Spare the man who felt only contempt for me.' He looked away from her. 'It makes me feel sick.'

'But Bertrano is the sick one, Larenzo. Sick and sad and cruel to treat anyone, much less a child, that way. Don't blame yourself for his evil.' She took a step towards him, longing to touch him, to hold him, but afraid even now he might pull away. 'Don't let his evil taint what we have.'

The silence stretched on as Larenzo kept his face averted. Emma had no idea what he was thinking, but she felt instinctively that their whole lives hung in the balance of this moment.

'I thought I loved you,' he said finally. 'But I'm not sure any more I know what love is.'

'I know what love is,' Emma answered. 'Love is waking up in the night with Ava. Love is the three of us laughing around the dinner table. Love is turning over in bed and seeing you sleeping with a smile on your face that I know I put there. And,' she finished, her heart starting to pound, 'love is trusting that we'll keep going no matter what happens. We'll stay together and we'll battle it out. I won't walk away and neither will you, and neither of us will let the other try to.' She felt her lips tremble and she blinked the tears back. 'Please, Larenzo.'

'Dada!' Ava squealed, jerking them out of the intensity of the moment. Emma watched, her breath held, as her daughter toddled towards Larenzo, stumbling as she reached him so he caught her in his arms and brought her up to his chest. He closed his eyes, his lips brushing Ava's hair.

'I'm sorry,' he whispered. Everything in Emma protested until Larenzo opened his eyes and gazed at her with so much hunger and need and love she nearly swayed where she stood. 'I'm sorry for putting you through so much. I'm sorry for being so…imperfect.'

'We're all imperfect.'

'I'm sorry for hurting you.' He stood up, Ava still in his arms, and walked towards her. 'I love you, Emma. And I'm so thankful you stayed and fought for me. For us.'

'Me too,' she whispered, and then he was folding her in his arms, and even better he was kissing her, as Ava patted both their cheeks.

'Dada,' she crowed. 'Mama.'

'Family,' Larenzo said, and kissed Emma again.

EPILOGUE

One year later

'CAREFUL NOW!' LARENZO called as Emma mounted the stepladder. She threw him a teasing glance over her shoulder and took another step up, the star in her hand.

It was Christmas Eve, and she was putting the star on top of their tree. Outside the city was blanketed in snow, and only that morning they'd had a birthday party for Ava, with Meghan and Ryan and his new baby sister Ella coming into the city to celebrate.

It had been a wonderful, crazy year, full of excitement and joy. So much joy. Emma had finally submitted her photographs and had had her first exhibition in SoHo. In May the investigation had finally concluded and Larenzo's innocence had been proclaimed in all the papers. The gossip had trickled away, and Larenzo's business had gone from strength to strength, as he'd built his client list and invested in innovative new technology.

They'd moved from the luxurious penthouse apartment to a Brownstone overlooking the park, with bedrooms for the children they hoped one day to have. Ava was already obsessed with babies, and Emma was looking forward to introducing her to a new brother or sister, whenever it happened.

Now she stood on her tiptoes and perched the star on top of the tree.

'Is it straight?' she asked.

'Perfectly,' Larenzo answered.

'Star!' Ava crowed and, smiling at them both, Emma came down from the ladder.

She glanced at the star and then burst out laughing. 'It's completely crooked.'

'I like it,' Larenzo answered as he pulled her towards him, Ava squirming as usual to get right between them. 'It reminds me of how you love me despite my many imperfections.'

Emma shook her head, smiling. 'You seem pretty perfect to me,' she said, and kissed him.

* * * * *

A VOW TO SECURE
HIS LEGACY

ANNIE WEST

Dedicated to those who work with the sick and frail: medical staff, technicians, administrative staff, care workers, paramedics and volunteers. Your skills and above all your kindness make such a difference!

Thanks too, to the lovely Fabiola Chenet for your advice. Any errors are all mine!

PROLOGUE

'IMOGEN! WHAT A lovely surprise.' The receptionist looked up from her desk. 'I didn't expect to see you again.' She paused, her smile fading. 'I was so sorry to hear about your mother.'

Her voice held a note of sympathy that stirred grief, even after four months. It was like pressure applied to a bruise that hadn't faded. The pain was more intense today because coming here, doing this, was so difficult. Imogen laced her fingers together to stop them trembling.

'Thanks, Krissy.' The staff here at the specialist's consulting rooms had been terrific with her mum and her.

Imogen swept her gaze around the familiar space. The soothing sea-green furnishings, the vase of bright gerberas on the counter and the waiting room of people apparently engrossed in their magazines. She recognised their alert stillness—a desperate attempt to pretend everything would be all right. That they'd receive good news from the doctor, despite the fact he had a reputation for dealing with the most difficult cases.

Her stomach swooped in a nauseating loop-the-loop. A chill skated up her spine to clamp her neck.

Swiftly, she turned back to the desk.

'What brings you here?' Krissy leaned in. 'You just can't stay away, is that it? You love our company so much?'

Imogen opened her mouth but her throat constricted. No words came out.

'Krissy! That's enough.' It was Ruby, the older receptionist, bustling in from a back room. She wore an expression of careful serenity. Only the sympathetic look in those piercing eyes gave anything away. 'Ms Holgate is here for an appointment.'

There was a hiss of indrawn breath and a clatter as Krissy dropped the stapler she'd been holding.

'Please take a seat, Ms Holgate. The doctor is running a little late. There was a delay in surgery this morning, but he'll see you shortly.'

'Thanks,' Imogen croaked and turned away with a vague smile in Krissy's direction. She couldn't meet the other woman's eyes. They'd be round with shock. Perhaps even with the horror she'd seen in her own mirror.

For weeks she'd told herself she was imagining things... that the symptoms would pass. Until her GP had looked at her gravely, barely concealing concern, and said he was sending her for tests. Then he'd referred her to the very man who'd tried to save her mother when she'd suffered exactly the same symptoms.

Imogen had had the tests last week and all this week she'd waited for a message from her GP saying there was no need to see the specialist, that everything was clear.

There'd been no message. No reprieve. No good news.

She swallowed hard and made herself cross the room, taking a seat where she could look out at the bright Sydney sunshine rather than at the reception desk.

Pride dictated she play the game, hiding her fear behind a façade of calm. She took a magazine, not looking at the cover. She wouldn't take it in. Her brain was too busy cataloguing all the reasons this couldn't end well.

A year ago she'd have believed everything would be okay.

But too much had happened in her twenty-fifth year for her to be complacent ever again. The world had shifted on its axis, proving once more, as it had in childhood, that nothing was safe, nothing sure.

Nine months ago had come the news that her twin sister— flamboyant, full-of-life Isabelle—was dead. She'd survived paragliding, white-water rafting and backpacking through Africa, only to be knocked over by a driver in Paris as she crossed the street on her way to work.

Imogen swallowed down a knot of grief. Isabelle had accused her of being in a rut, of playing safe when there was a wide world out there to be explored and enjoyed.

Her twin had followed her dream, even knowing the odds of her succeeding were a million to one. Yet she *had* succeeded. She'd moved to France and through talent, perseverance plus sheer luck had snaffled a job with a top fashion designer. She'd had everything to look forward to. Then suddenly her life was snuffed out.

Soon after had come their mother's diagnosis—a brain tumour. Massive, risky to operate on, lethal.

Blindly, Imogen flipped open the magazine on her lap.

When the news had come from Paris she'd protested that there must have been a mistake—Isabelle couldn't possibly be dead. It had taken weeks to accept the truth. Then, as her mother's headaches and blurry vision had worsened and the doctors looked more and more grim, Imogen had been convinced there would be a cure. Fatal brain tumours just didn't happen in her world. The diagnosis was impossible.

Until the impossible had happened and she was left alone, bereft of the only two people in the world who'd loved her.

The past nine months had shown her how possible the impossible actually was.

And now there was her own illness. No mistaking this for anything other than the disease that had struck down her mother. She'd been with her mum as her illness had progressed. She knew every stage, every symptom.

How much longer did she have? Seven months? Nine? Or would the tumour be more aggressive in a younger woman?

Imogen turned a page and lifted her eyes, scanning the room. Was this her destiny? To become a regular here until they admitted there was nothing they could do for her? To become another statistic in the health-care system?

Isabelle's voice sounded in her head.

You need to get out and live, Imogen. Try something new, take a risk, enjoy yourself. Life is for living!

Imogen snorted. What chance would she have for living now?

She thought of the dreams she'd nurtured, planning and carefully executing every step. Working her way through university. Getting a job. Building professional success. Saving for a flat. Finding a nice, reliable, loving man who'd stick by her as their father hadn't. A man who'd want a lifetime with her. They'd see all the things Isabelle had raved about. The northern lights in Iceland. Venice's Grand Canal. And Paris. Paris with the man she loved.

Imogen blinked and looked down. Open on her lap was a double-page photo of Paris at sunset. Her breath hitched, a frisson of obscure excitement stirring her blood.

The panorama was as spectacular as Isabelle had said.

Imogen's throat burned as she remembered how she'd turned down her sister's invitation, saying she'd visit when she had a deposit saved for a flat and had helped their mum finish that long-overdue kitchen renovation.

Isabelle had ribbed her about planning her life to the nth degree. But Imogen had always needed security. She couldn't drop everything and gallivant off to Paris.

Fat lot of good that will do you now you're dying. What will you do, spend your money on a great coffin?

Imogen gazed at the Seine, copper-bright in the afternoon light. Her stare shifted to the Eiffel Tower, a glittering invitation. *You'd love it, Ginny—gorgeous and gaudy by night but just so...Paris!*

She'd spent her life playing safe. Avoiding risk, working hard, denying herself the adventures Isabelle revelled in, because she planned to do that later.

There'd be no later. There was only now.

Imogen wasn't aware of getting up, but she found herself striding across the room and out into the sunlight. A voice called but she didn't look back.

She didn't have much time. She refused to spend it in hospitals and waiting rooms until she absolutely had to.

For once she'd forget being sensible. Forget caution. She intended to *live*.

CHAPTER ONE

'TELL ME, *MA CHÉRIE,* will you be at the resort when we visit? It would be so much more convenient having the owner on the premises when we do the promotional photo shoot.' Her voice was intimately pitched, reaching him easily despite the chatter of the crowd in the hotel's grand reception room.

Thierry looked down into the publicist's face, reading the invitation in her eyes.

She was beautiful, sophisticated and, he guessed by the way she licked her bottom lip and pressed her slim frame closer, ready to be very accommodating. Yet he felt no flicker of excitement.

Excitement! He'd left that behind four years ago. Would he even recognise it after all this time?

Bitterness filled his mouth. He'd been living a half-life, hemmed in by conference-room walls and duty, forcing himself to care about minutiae that held no intrinsic interest. *Except those details had meant the difference between salvaging the family's foundering business portfolio and losing it.*

'I haven't decided. There are things I need to sort out here in Paris.'

But soon… A few months and he'd hand over the business to his cousin Henri and, more importantly, the managers Thierry had hand-picked. They'd guide Henri and maintain all Thierry had achieved, securing the Girard family fortune and leaving him free at last.

'Think about it, Thierry.' Her lips formed a glossy pout as she swayed close. 'It would be very…agreeable.'

'Of course I will. The idea is very tempting.'

But not enough, he realised with abrupt clarity, to drag

him from Paris. These meetings would bring him closer to divesting himself of his burdens. That held far more allure than the prospect of sex with a svelte blonde.

Hell! He was turning into a cold-blooded corporate type. Since when had his libido taken second place to business?

Except his libido wasn't involved. That was the shocking thing. At thirty-four Thierry was in his prime. He enjoyed sex and his success with women showed he had a talent, even a reputation, for it. Yet he felt nothing when this gorgeous woman invited him into her bed.

Hadn't he known taking on the family business would destroy him? It was sucking the life out of him. It was...

His gaze locked on a figure on the far side of the room, and his thoughts blurred. His pulse accelerated and his chest expanded as he hefted a startled breath.

His companion murmured something and stretched up to kiss his cheek. Automatically, Thierry returned the salutation, responding to her farewell as she joined a group who'd just entered the hotel ballroom.

Instantly, his gaze swung back to the far side of the room. The woman who'd caught his eye stood poised, her weight on one foot, as if about to leave.

He was already pushing his way through the crowd when she straightened and drew back her shoulders. Delectable, creamy shoulders they were, completely bared by that strapless dress. The white material was lustrous in the light of the chandeliers, drawing a man's eyes to the way it fitted her breasts and small waist like a glove before flaring in an ultra-feminine swirl to the floor.

Thierry swallowed, his throat dry despite the champagne he'd drunk. A familiar tightness in his groin assured him that his libido was alive and kicking after all. Yet he barely registered relief. He was too busy drinking her in.

In a room packed with little black dresses and sleek, glittery outfits, this woman stood out like *grand cru* from cheap table wine.

She turned her head, presenting him with an engaging profile, and Thierry realised she was speaking. He halted, surprised that his walk had lengthened to an urgent stride.

Her companion was a gamine-faced woman, pointing out people to the woman in white. The woman in white and scarlet, he amended, taking in the pattern of red flowers cascading around her as she moved. There was white and scarlet on her arms too. She wore long gloves to her elbows, reminding him of photos he'd seen of his *grand-mère* at balls and parties decades ago.

Thierry's gut clenched as the woman lifted one gloved hand to her throat in a curiously nervous gesture. Who knew gloves could be erotic? But there was no mistaking the weighted feeling in his lower body. He imagined stripping the glove down her arm, centimetre by slow centimetre, kissing his way to her fingers before divesting her of that dress and starting on her body.

Why was she nervous? A shy woman wouldn't wear such a glorious, blatantly sexy concoction.

Heat sparked. His gaze roved her dark, glossy hair swept up from a slim neck. She had full red lips, a retroussé nose and heart-shaped face. Curves that made him ache to touch.

She wasn't just pretty; she was sexy on a level he couldn't resist.

The old Thierry Girard wasn't dead after all.

'You're sure you don't mind?' Saskia sounded doubtful.

Imogen smiled. 'Of course not. I appreciate all you've done these past few days but I'm fine. I'll drink champagne and meet interesting people and enjoy myself.' If she said it enough she might stop being daunted by the glittering crowd long enough to believe it. 'Now go.' She made a shooing gesture, nodding towards the knot of fashion buyers Saskia had pointed out. 'Make the most of this opportunity.'

'Well, for half an hour. I'll look for you then.'

Imogen blinked, overwhelmed anew by the kindness of her sister Isabelle's best friend. Saskia had not only shown her where Izzy had worked and lived, but shared stories about their time together, filling the black well of Imogen's grief with tales that had made Imogen smile for the first time in months.

Saskia had even presented her with the dresses Izzy had made for herself, eye-catching outfits Imogen would never have considered wearing. But here, in Paris, it felt right, a homage to her talented sister. Imogen smoothed her hand down the fabulous satin dress.

'Don't be silly. Go and mingle, Saskia. I don't expect to see you again tonight.' She smiled, making a fair attempt at Izzy's bantering tone, even tilting her head to mimic her sister. 'Since you snaffled me an invitation, I intend to make the most of my only society event. I don't need you cramping my style.'

'Isabelle said you weren't good with lots of new people but obviously you've changed.' Saskia's lips twitched. 'Okay. But join me if you want. I'll be around.'

Imogen kept her smile in place as Saskia left, ignoring the trepidation that rose at being alone, adrift in this sea of beautiful people.

Stupid. This isn't alone. Alone is discovering you're dying and there's no one left in the world who loves you enough to feel more than pity.

Imogen shoved aside the thought. She refused to retreat into self-pity. She was in Paris. She'd make the most of every moment of the next six weeks—Paris, Venice, London, even Reykjavik. She'd wring every drop of joy from each experience before she returned home to face the inevitable.

She swung around, her full-length skirt swishing around her legs, and refused to feel out of place because other women were in cocktail dresses. Isabelle's dress was too wonderful not to wear.

'Puis-je vous offrir du champagne?' The deep, alluring voice sent heat straight to the pit of her stomach, as if she'd inadvertently taken a gulp of whisky.

French was a delicious language. But surely it had been designed for a voice like this? A voice that sent shivers of sensual pleasure across her skin.

She jerked her head around and then up.

Something she couldn't identify slammed into her. Shock? Awareness? Recognition?

How had she not seen him before? He stood out from the crowd. Not just because of his height but because of his sheer presence. Her skin prickled as if she'd walked into a force field.

She met eyes the colour of rich coffee, dark and inviting, and her pulse pounded high in her throat as if her heart had dislodged and tried to escape. Deep-set eyes crinkled at the corners, fanning tiny lines in a tanned face. A man more at home outdoors than at a fashionable party?

Except his tall frame was relaxed, as if he wore a perfect dinner jacket every night to mingle with a who's who of French society. His mouth curled up in a tantalising almost-smile that invited her to smile back. Was that why her lips tingled?

Dark hair, long enough to hint at tousled thickness. A determined chin. Strong cheekbones that made her think of princes, balls and half-forgotten nonsense.

Imogen swallowed, the muscles in her throat responding jerkily. She cleared her throat.

'Je suis désolée, je ne parle pas français.' It was one of her few textbook phrases.

'You don't speak French? Shall we try English?' His voice was just as attractive when he spoke English with that sensuous blurring accent. Pleasure tickled Imogen's backbone, and her stomach clenched.

'How did you guess? Am I that obvious?'

'Not at all.' His gaze did a quick, comprehensive sweep

from her head to her hem that ignited a slow burn deep inside. A burn that transferred to her cheeks as his eyes met hers and something passed between them, as tangible as the beat of her heart. 'You are utterly delightful and feminine but not obvious.'

Imogen felt the corners of her mouth lift. Flirting with a Frenchman. There was one to cross off her bucket list. Back home she hadn't been good at flirtation, but here it seemed she didn't have to do anything at all.

'Who are you?' Funny the way dying helped you overcome a lifetime's reserve. Once she'd have been too overawed to speak to a man who looked so stunningly male. He was one of the most attractive men she'd ever met and despite that aura of latent power he was definitely the most suave. Even that prominent nose looked perfect in his proud face. Just as well his eyes danced or he'd be too daunting.

'My apologies.' He inclined his head in a half-bow that was wholly European and totally charming. 'My name is Thierry Girard.'

'Thierry.' She tried it on her tongue. It didn't sound the same as when he said it. She couldn't quite get the little breath of air after the T, but she liked it.

'And you are?' He stepped closer, his gaze intent. She caught a scent that made her think of mountains—of clear air and pine trees.

'I'm Imogen Holgate.'

'Imogen.' He nodded. 'A pretty name. It suits you.'

Pretty? She hadn't been called that in ages. The last person to do so had been her mum, trying to persuade her into bright colours, saying she hid behind the dark suits she wore for work.

'And now, Imogen, would you like some champagne?' He lifted a glass.

'I can get my own.' She turned to look for a waiter.

'But I brought it especially for you.' She looked down and realised he was holding two glasses, not one. This stranger had singled her out in a room of elegant women and brought her champagne? For a moment she just stared. It was so different from her world, where she paid her way and never had to field compliments from men about anything other than her work.

He raised the other glass, giving her a choice of either. His eyes turned serious. 'Whichever you prefer.'

Her cheeks flushed. He thought she was stalling because she didn't trust him. In case he'd slipped something into one of the glasses.

It was the sort of thing that would have occurred to her once, for in her real life she was always cautious. But right now she was struggling to absorb the fact she was with the most charming, attractive man she'd ever met. The fact that he offered both reassured her.

She took a glass, meeting his eyes, ignoring the tingly sensation where their fingers brushed. 'Is it champagne from the Champagne region?'

'Of course. That's the only wine that can use the name. You like champagne?'

'I've never tried it.'

He blinked, astonishment on his face. *'Vraiment?'*

'Really.' Imogen smiled at his shock. 'I'm from Australia.'

'No, no.' He shook his head. 'I happen to know the Australians import French wine as well as exporting theirs. Champagne travels the world.'

She shrugged, enjoying his disbelief. 'That doesn't mean I've drunk it.' She eyed the wine with excitement. What better place to taste her first champagne than Paris?

'In that case, the occasion deserves a toast. To new friends.' His smile transformed his face from fascinating to magnetic. Imogen inhaled sharply, her lungs pushing at her ribcage. Her fingers tightened on the glass. That smile, this man, made her feel acutely aware of herself as a woman with desires she'd all but forgotten.

Stop it! You've seen men smile before.

Not like this. This was like standing in a shaft of sunshine. And it was an amazing antidote to the chill weight of despair. How could she dwell on despair when he looked at her that way?

She lifted her glass. 'And to new experiences.'

She sipped, feeling the effervescence on the roof of her mouth. 'I like that it's not too sweet. I can taste…pears, is it?'

He drank too, and she was riveted by the sight of his strong throat and the ripple of movement as he swallowed.

Imogen frowned. There was nothing sexy about a man's throat. Was there? There never had been before and she worked surrounded by men.

But none of them were Thierry Girard.

'You're right. Definitely pears.' He watched her over the rim of the glass. 'To new experiences? You have some planned?'

Imogen shrugged. 'A few.'

'Tell me.' When she hesitated he added, 'Please. I'd like to know.'

'Why?' The word shot out, and she caught her bottom lip between her teeth. Typical of her to sound gauche rather than sophisticated. She just wasn't used to male attention. She was the serious, reserved sister, not the gregarious one with a flock of admirers.

'Because I'm interested in you.'

'Seriously?' As soon as the word escaped heat scalded her throat and face. She squeezed her eyes shut. 'Tell me I didn't say that.'

A rich chuckle snagged at her senses, making her eyes pop open. If his smile was gorgeous, his laugh was… She couldn't think of a word to describe the molten-chocolate swirl enveloping her.

'Why don't you tell me about these new experiences instead?'

Imogen opened her mouth to ask if he was really interested in hearing about them then snapped it shut.

Here was a wonderful new adventure, flirting with a gorgeous French hunk over champagne. She wasn't going to spoil it by being herself. She was going to go with the flow. This trip was about stepping out of her shell, tasting life's excitement.

Chatting with Thierry Girard was the most exciting thing that had happened to her in ages.

'I've got a list. Things I want to do.'

'In Paris?' She loved the way his eyes crinkled at the corner when he smiled.

'Not just here. I'm away from home for a month and a half but I'm only in Paris a fortnight.' She shook her head. 'I'm already realising my plans were too ambitious. I won't fit everything in.'

'That gives you a reason to return. You can do more on your next visit.'

His eyes were almost warm enough to dispel the wintry chill that descended at his words. There'd be no return visit, no second chance.

She had one shot at living to the max. She'd make the most of it, even if it meant stepping out of her comfort zone. She tossed back another mouthful of champagne, relishing the little starbursts on her tongue.

'This is delicious wine.'

He nodded. 'It's not bad. Now, tell me about this list. I'm intrigued.'

She shrugged. 'Tourist things, mainly.' But she refused to feel self-conscious. 'See those Impressionist masterpieces at the Musée d'Orsay, visit Versailles, go for a boat ride on the Seine.'

'You'll have time to fit those in if you have two weeks.'

She shook her head. 'That's only the beginning. I want to attend a gourmet cooking class. I've always wanted to know how they make those melt-in-the-mouth chocolate truffles.' The ones that were exactly the colour of his eyes.

Her breath gave a curious little hitch and she hurried on. 'I'd hoped to eat at the Eiffel Tower restaurant but I didn't realise I needed to book in advance. Plus I'd love a champagne picnic in the country and to go hot-air ballooning and drive a red convertible around the Arc de Triomphe and… Well, so many things.'

His eyebrows rose. 'Visitors are usually scared of driving there. Traffic is thick and there aren't lane markings.'

Imogen shrugged. She was scared too. But that was good. She'd feel she was really *living*.

'I like a challenge.'

'So I gather.' Was that approval in his expression? 'Have you been hot-air ballooning before?'

'Never.' She took another sip of champagne. 'This is a trip of firsts.'

'Like the champagne?' There was that delicious crinkle around his eyes. It almost lured her into believing Thierry Girard was as harmless as her work colleagues. Yet every feminine fibre screamed she was out of her depth even looking at the ultra-sexy Frenchman. Everything about him, from the breadth of his shoulders to the intriguing dark shadow across his jaw, signalled he was a virile, powerful man. 'Imogen?'

'Sorry, I was distracted.' Her voice was ridiculously husky. The way he said her name turned it into something lilting and special. She lifted her gloved fingers to her throat, as if that could ease her hammering pulse.

The glint in his eyes warned that he understood her distraction. But she refused to be embarrassed. He must be used to women going weak at the knees.

'Tell me about yourself,' she said. 'Do you live in Paris?'

He shook his head. 'Occasionally. I'm here for business meetings over the next week or two.'

'So while I'm out enjoying myself you'll be in meetings? I hope they're not too tedious.'

Nonchalantly, he lifted those impressive shoulders, and a wave of yearning washed through her. She wanted to put her hands on them, feel the strength in his tall body and lean in to see if he tasted as good as he smelled.

Imogen blinked, stunned at the force of her desire. She didn't *do* instant attraction. She didn't fall in a heap in front of any man. But her knees were suspiciously shaky and her instincts urged her to behave in ways that were completely out of character.

Was it champagne or the man? Or maybe the heady excitement of Paris and wearing Isabelle's gorgeous gown. Whatever it was, she approved. She wanted to *feel*, and from the moment her eyes had locked on Thierry's she'd felt vibrantly alive.

'You sound like you have experience of boring meetings.'

Imogen sipped more wine, enjoying the zing on her palate. 'Definitely.' She rolled her eyes. 'Our firm specialises in them. I'd bet my meetings are more boring than yours.'

'I find that hard to believe.'

Thierry took her arm and guided her away from an influx of newcomers. Even through the satin gloves his hands felt hard, capable and incredibly sexy. Trickles of fire coursed from the point of contact then splintered into incendiary darts that trailed through her body to pool down low.

How sad that she could be so turned on by that simple courteous gesture. But that wasn't surprising, given the state of her love life. Or her lack of one.

'Believe it.' She dragged herself back into the conversation. 'I'm an accountant.' She waited for his eyes to glaze over. 'A tax accountant. I know tedious.'

His lips twitched but he didn't look in the least fazed. If anything there was a spark in his gaze as it swept her from head to toe. Did it linger here and there on the way? Imogen's stomach tightened and her breasts swelled against the satin bodice as she drew a sharp breath. Strange how the lace of her strapless bra suddenly scratched at her nipples when it had been perfectly comfortable before.

'You're not acquainted with French property and commercial law, are you? The phrase "red tape" was invented to describe them. And the meetings…' He shook his head.

'You're a lawyer?' He didn't look like any lawyer she'd seen, except in some high-budget courtroom film with a smoulderingly gorgeous hero.

Thierry laughed, that rich-as-chocolate sound doing strange things to her insides. 'Me, a lawyer? That would be a match made in hell. It's bad enough being a client. My first meeting tomorrow will go all morning. I'd much rather be out of the city.'

'Really? You look like right at home here.' Her gaze skated over his hard body in that made-to-measure dinner jacket. When she lifted her eyes she found him watching her, his quirk of a smile disarming.

'This?' One casual hand gestured to his impeccable tailoring. 'This is camouflage.'

'You're saying you don't belong?' Her pulse raced at the idea of finding another outsider. For, try as she might, she couldn't feel at home in this sophisticated crowd, despite her sister's clothes.

He shrugged, and Imogen watched those wide, straight shoulders with something like hunger. She'd never felt *needy* for a man. Not even Scott. Was it this man or the unfamiliar setting that pulled her off-balance?

'I've been forced to adapt. Business means I need to be in the city. But I prefer being outdoors. There's nothing like pitting yourself against nature. It beats meetings hands-down.'

That explained those eyes. Not just the creases from sun exposure, but his deceptively lazy regard that seemed at the same time sharp and perceptive. As if from surveying distant views?

'Each hour behind a desk is pure torture.'

'You poor thing.' Impulsively, she placed her hand on his arm, then regretted it as she felt the tense and flex of sinew and impressive muscle. There it was again, that little jolt, like an electric shock. Imogen jerked her hand back, frowning, and looked at her glass. Surely she hadn't drunk enough to imagine it? Just enough to make her do something out of character, like touch a stranger.

Yet she couldn't regret it. That fierce flick of heat made her feel more alive than...

'You'd like another?' Thierry gave their glasses to a waiter and snagged two more.

She took the glass he offered, carefully avoiding contact with his tanned fingers.

'To red convertibles and champagne picnics and balloon rides.' His eyes snared hers and her heart thumped. When he looked at her, the way she imagined men looked at truly beautiful women, she almost forgot what had brought her to Paris. She could lose herself in the moment.

Imogen raised her glass. 'And to meetings that end quickly.'

'I'll drink to that.' Thierry touched his glass to hers, watching her sip her wine. She took time to taste it. Her lips, a glossy bow, pouted delectably. Her dark eyelashes quivered, and he knew she was cataloguing the prickle of bubbles on the roof of her mouth. She gave a delicate shiver of appreciation, and he found himself leaning closer.

She was so avid. So tactile. Touching her through those long gloves had made his hand tingle! From anticipation and excitement, something he usually experienced while risking his neck outdoors.

Imogen Holgate was an intriguing mix of sensuality and guilelessness.

And he wanted her.

'I can help with the ballooning.'

'Really?' Her eyes widened and he saw flecks of velvety green within the warm sherry-brown of her irises. It must be a trick of the light but her gaze seemed to glow brighter. 'That would be marvellous.'

She took a half step closer, and his breathing hitched. He inhaled the scent of vanilla sugar and warm female flesh. His taste buds tingled and his gaze dropped to her lips, then to the faint, fast pulse at her creamy throat.

He wanted to taste her, right here, now, and discover if she was as delicious as he expected. He wanted to sweep her to some place where he could learn her secrets.

Hazel eyes and vanilla sugar as an aphrodisiac?

His tastes had changed. She was completely different from Sandrine and all the women since her. Yet sexual hunger honed his senses to a keen edge. He searched out the nearest exit, the part of his brain that was pure hunter planning how to cut her from the crowd when the time was ripe.

'I'd appreciate it if you could.' Her words interrupted his thoughts, or maybe it was that excited smile making her face glow. 'I should have researched it earlier but this trip was on the spur of the moment. Can you recommend a company I could contact?'

It took longer than it should have to remember what they were talking about. 'Better than that. A friend runs a balloon company outside Paris. We used to make balloon treks together.'

'Really?' Her eyes widened and there again was that trick of the light, for they seemed almost pure green now. How would they look when ecstasy took her? The tension in his lower body ratcheted up too many notches for comfort. 'You've been ballooning? Tell me all about it. Please?'

She clutched his arm and that shimmer of sensation rippled up it.

Over the next twenty minutes she peppered him with questions. Not the usual *What's it like up there?* and *Aren't you afraid of falling?* but everything from safety procedures to the amount of fuel required, from measuring height to landing procedure. All the while her expression kept shifting. He didn't know whether he preferred her serious, poutingly curious or dreamy-eyed excited.

She was enchanting. Refreshingly straightforward, yet complex and intriguing. And passionate.

He watched her lips as she spoke and desire exploded.

How long since he'd felt like this?

How long since he'd met a woman fascinated by him and his interest in adventure rather than money, social status or his reputation as a lover?

Plus she was passing through. She'd have no aspirations to tie him down.

Imogen was the perfect short-term diversion.

CHAPTER TWO

THE LIGHTS DIMMED and at the far end of the room a band struck up. The swell of the bass was incongruous in this ornate setting, but no one seemed surprised, even when beams of purple, blue and white light shot across the crowd.

A spotlight caught Imogen's eyes and she flinched, moving closer to Thierry. Instantly, his arm curved protectively around her. She liked that too much, but she had no desire to pull away. Not when every nerve screamed at her to lean into him.

His arm was hard and reassuring as the band's volume rose to a pounding beat. Imogen relished the unfamiliar thrill of being close to all that imposing masculinity. For, despite his perfectly tailored suit, there was no disguising that Thierry was all hard-muscled man.

His hands were a giveaway too. Neat, clean nails, but there were tiny, pale scars across his tanned skin, hinting he did more than wield a pen.

Imogen wondered how they'd feel on her bare flesh.

He said something she didn't hear over a crescendo of music. At the same time the light show became more frenetic, a staccato pulse in time with the drums. Imogen felt it all swirl and coalesce like a living thing. Light stabbed her eyes.

Not now. Please not now!

Just a little more time. Was that too much to ask?

Her stomach cramped and her breathing jammed. She blinked. It wasn't the light from the stage blinding her, it was the white-hot knife jabbing inside her skull. Her vision blurred, pain sawing through her.

'Imogen?' That arm at her back tightened. She caught

a drift of something in her nostrils, some essence that reminded her of the outdoors, before the metallic taste of
pain obliterated everything. Sheer willpower kept her on
her feet, knees desperately locked.

'I…' It came out as a whisper. She tried again. 'I'd like
to leave.'

'Of course.' He took the glass from her unresisting hand.
'This way.' He turned her towards the exit but she stumbled, her legs not obeying.

Music shuddered through her, a screaming beat, and in
her head the jab, jab, jab of that unseen knife.

Warmth engulfed her and it took a moment to realise
it was from Thierry's powerful body as he wrapped his
arm around her waist and half carried her from the room.

Imagine what he could do with two arms.

*And those hands. You've always had a thing for great
hands.*

That was her last coherent thought till they were in the
peace of an anteroom. She couldn't recall exactly how he'd
got her there but the lean strength of his body made her
feel anchored and safe, despite the lancing pain.

'Imogen? What is it? Talk to me.' His accent was more
pronounced, slurring the words sexily. Even in her dazed
state she heard his concern.

'Headache. Sorry.' She tilted her head up, trying to bring
him into focus through slitted yes.

'A migraine?' Gently, he pulled her to him, resting her
head on his shoulder and palming her hair in a rhythmic
touch that amazingly seemed to make the pain recede a
little.

She wanted never to move, just sink into his calm
strength. The realisation she'd never be held like this again
by anyone brought a sob rushing to her throat. She stifled
it. Pity wouldn't help.

'Sorry.' She sucked air through clenched teeth as she
straightened. 'Enjoy the rest of the party. It's been—'

'Where are you staying?' His voice was low, soothing.

'Here. Three-hundred and five.' She fumbled in her purse, dragging out her key card. All she had to do was get to her room.

Had he read her befuddled mind? One minute she stood on trembling legs, the next she was swept up in his embrace. She felt bone and muscle, the tickle of his breath on her face. She should have objected. Breathing through excruciating pain, she merely slumped against him, grateful that for once she didn't have to manage alone.

This past year she'd had to be strong, for her mother and more recently for herself. Leaning against Thierry, feeling the steady thud of his heart beneath his jacket, she felt a little of the tightness racking her body ease. Was it her imagination or did the pain pull back a fraction? She shut her eyes, focusing on his iron-hard arms beneath her, the comfort of his embrace.

Another first. Being swept off your feet by a man.

Warm fingers touched hers as he shifted his hold and took the card from her hand.

'Here we are.' His deep voice wrapped around her. 'Not long now.' A door snicked closed and soon she was lowered onto a mattress. Smoothly, without hesitation, his hands withdrew and Imogen knew a moment's craziness when she had to bite back a plea that he not let her go. There'd been such comfort in being held.

Her eyes shot open and she winced, even in the soft glow from a single bedside lamp. Thierry towered above her, concern lining his brow.

'What do you need? Painkillers? Water?'

Gingerly, she moved, the smallest of nods. 'Water, please.' While he got it she fumbled open her bedside drawer and took out her medication with a shaking hand.

'Let me.' He squatted, popped the tablet and handed it to her. Then he raised her head while she swallowed it and sipped the water, his touch sure but gentle. Stupidly, tears clung to her lashes. Tears for this stranger's tenderness. Tears for the extravagant fantasy she'd dared harbour, of ending the night in Thierry's arms, making love with this sexy, fascinating, gorgeous man.

Fantasy wasn't for her. Her reality was too stark for that. She'd have to make do with scraping whatever small pleasures she could from life before it was too late.

Defeated, she slumped against the pillow, forcing herself to meet his concerned gaze.

'You're very kind. Thank you, Thierry. I can manage from here.'

Kind be damned. He looked into drowning eyes shimmering green and golden-brown and his belly twisted. This woman had hooked him with her vibrancy, humour and enthusiasm, not to mention her flagrant sexiness. Even her slight hesitancy over his name appealed ridiculously. Her vulnerability was a punch to the gut, and not just because he'd aimed to spend the night with her.

'Shut your eyes and relax.'

'I will.'

As soon as you leave. The unspoken words hung between them and who could blame her? He was a virtual stranger. Except he felt curiously like he'd known her half his life or, more correctly, had waited that long to meet her.

A frisson of warning ripped through him but he ignored it. She was no threat. With her tear-spiked lashes and too-pale face, she was the picture of vulnerability. There were shadows beneath her eyes too that he hadn't seen before.

'What are you doing?' Her voice was husky, doing dangerous things to his body. Thierry had to remind himself it was from pain, not arousal.

He put the house phone to his ear, dialling room service. 'Getting you peppermint tea. My *grand-mère* suffers from migraines and that helps.'

'That's kind but...' Her words petered out as he ordered the tea then replaced the phone.

'Just try it, okay? If it doesn't work you can leave it.' He straightened and stepped back, putting distance between them. 'I'll stay till it's delivered so you don't have to get up.'

She opened her mouth then shut it, surveying him with pain-clouded eyes. Again that stab to his gut. He frowned and turned towards the bathroom, speaking over his shoulder. 'You're safe with me, Imogen. I have no ulterior motives.' *Not now, at any rate.* 'Trust me. I was a Boy Scout, did I tell you?'

When he returned with a damp flannel, he caught the wry twist of her lips.

'I'm to trust you because you were a Boy Scout?' Her voice was pain-roughened but there was that note of almost-laughter he'd found so attractive earlier.

'Of course. Ready to serve and always prepared.' He brushed back a few escaped locks of hair and placed the flannel on her forehead.

She sighed, and he made himself retreat rather than trace that glossy, silk-soft hair again. He pulled up a chair and sat a couple of metres from the bed.

Shimmering, half-lidded eyes met his. 'Are all Frenchmen so take-charge?'

'Are all Australian women so obstinate?'

A tiny smile curved her lips, and she shut her eyes. Ridiculously that smile felt like a victory.

The musical chimes of a mobile phone grew louder, drawing the attention of other café patrons. It was only then that Imogen realised it was her phone chirping away in her bag. In a fit of out-with-the-old-Imogen energy, she'd decided the old, plain ring tone was boring, swapping it for a bright pop tune.

'Hello?'

'Imogen?' His voice was smooth and warm, deep enough to make her shiver.

'Thierry?' The word was a croak of surprise. She'd berated herself all morning for wishing last night hadn't ended the way it had.

The fact Thierry had stayed so long only showed how dreadful she must have looked. And that he was what her mum would have called 'a true gentleman'.

'How are you today? Are you feeling better?'

'Good, thank you. I'm fit as a fiddle.' An exaggeration—those headaches always left her wrung out. But she was perking up by the moment. 'How are you?'

There was a crack of laughter, and Imogen's hand tightened on the phone. Even from a distance his laugh melted something inside. She sank back in her chair, noticing for the first time a blue patch of sky through the grey cloud.

'All the better for hearing your voice.'

She blinked, registering his deep, seductive tone. Her blood pumped faster and she tried to tell herself she imagined it. Nothing, she knew, put men off as much as illness. Even illness by proxy. For a moment Scott's face swam in her vision till she banished it.

'How did you get my number?'

There was a moment's silence. 'Your mobile was on the bedside table last night.'

'You took the number down?'

'You're annoyed?'

Annoyed? 'No. Not at all.' Surprised. Delighted. *Excited!* A little buzz of pleasure zoomed through her.

As she watched, the blue patch of sky grew and a beam of sunlight glanced down on the wet cobblestones, making them gleam. The café door opened behind her and the delicious aroma of fresh coffee drifted out.

'What's on your agenda this evening? Night-time bungee jumping? Motorcycle lessons? Or maybe that ghost tour?'

She smiled, enjoying his teasing. 'I'm still deciding be-tween a couple of options.' Like a long bubble bath, paint-ing her nails scarlet or gathering her courage and finding the dance venue Saskia had mentioned.

'How would you like dinner at the Eiffel Tower? There's an unexpected vacancy.'

'There is?' She sat up. 'But I couldn't get a reservation when I tried.'

'There's one for you now if you want it.'

'Of course I want it!' She squashed a howl of disap-pointment at the idea of dining in such a romantic setting alone. But she was a pragmatist. She'd learned to face hard truths. Thierry felt sorry for her after last night and had arranged this treat. 'It was kind of you to do that, Thierry. Thank you.'

'Excellent. I'll collect you at eight.'

'Eight?' She blinked, dazed. He was collecting her? He was taking her to dinner?

'Yes. See you then.'

He ended the call, and Imogen stared at the phone. Thierry Girard, the most drool-worthy, fascinating, charm-ing man she'd ever met, was taking her to dinner? She didn't know whether to be stunned or nervous.

She settled for thrilled.

Imogen felt like she floated on air as they drove back to her hotel. The evening had been perfect. The food, the wine, the company, the weight of Thierry's gaze on her like a touch.

When he surveyed the dress of green and bronze her sister Izzy had created, his eyes lingered appreciatively. But when his attention roved again and again to Imogen's bare throat and shoulders, and especially her lips, heat coiled inside, like a clock wound too tight.

It made her laughter at his outrageous stories die, replaced by a hunger that no food could remedy. Was it possible to explode with sheer longing for a man's touch?

Did she have the nerve to follow through? Casual sex wasn't in her repertoire. Yet there was nothing casual about how Thierry made her feel.

The question was, what did he feel? Was tonight a random kindness to a stranger or something else? Imogen wished she knew. She had absolutely no experience of high-octane, sophisticated men like Thierry Girard.

He stopped the car before her hotel and she turned towards him, only to find he was already out the door, striding around the car. A moment later her door swung open and he was helping her out.

Now. Ask him now before he says goodnight.

But her throat jammed as he hooked her hand over his arm and led her into the grand hotel—her big splurge on this end-of-a-lifetime trip. His heat, his scent, fresh as the outdoors, and the feel of his body against hers, made her light-headed. He led her through the luxurious foyer, past staff who stopped to greet them, to the bank of lifts.

'I—' Her words died as he stepped into the lift with her and hit the button for her floor.

So, he was seeing her to her room. She shot him a sideways look, discovering that in profile his features were taut, as if his earlier good humour had faded.

Abruptly, her anticipation drained away.

Had she misread him? Perhaps he didn't feel that hum of sexual arousal, that edge-of-seat excitement. Maybe he'd used up all his charm entertaining the unsophisticated tourist over dinner. She'd known last night she was out of place at that glamorous party, despite the wonderful dress she wore. Maybe after hours in her company he'd realised it too. Did he regret asking her out?

'You...?' Eyes of ebony locked with hers, and she sagged in Izzy's green stilettos.

Izzy would have known what to say. How to entertain

and attract him and, above all, follow through. Imogen's only intimate experience had been with Scott, cautious Scott, who never acted on impulse, never broke rules or took a chance. He'd never made her feel the way Thierry did.

But, cataloguing the tension in her companion's shoulders and the pronounced angle of his strong jaw, she realised her mistake. Thierry's was a casual charm. Of course he didn't want more from her. He was French. He was being polite. And those heavy-lidded looks that stopped her breath? They probably came naturally to him and didn't mean anything.

'It's kind of you to see me to my room.'

The doors slid open, and he ushered her down the hall to her room, her arm clamped to his side.

Probably afraid you'll collapse like you did last night.

'That's the second time you've accused me of being kind.' His voice sounded tight, but she didn't look at him, delving instead into her purse for her key card.

'You've been wonderful, and I appreciate it. I—' She frowned as he took the card and opened the door.

Did he have to be so eager to say goodnight?

But, instead of saying goodbye, Thierry stepped over the threshold, drawing her in. The door closed behind them and, stunned, Imogen turned. His tanned features looked chiselled, uncompromising, and those liquid, dark eyes…

'I'm not good at "kind".' He stroked a finger down her cheek in a barely there touch that rocketed to the centre of her being. 'In fact, I excel at doing exactly what pleases me most.' His head dipped, and Imogen's breath stalled as his breath caressed her lips. 'And what pleases me most is to be with you, Imogen.'

Imogen swallowed hard. It was what she wanted, what she'd steeled herself to ask. Yet part of her, the cautious, reserved part that had kept her safe for twenty-five years, froze her tongue.

Safe? There was no safe, not any more. Not when she could count the future in months, not decades.

'Or am I wrong?' His hand dropped, and still she felt his touch like a sense memory. 'Do you not want…?'

'Yes!' Her purse tumbled to the floor as her hand shot out. She clutched his fingers, threading hers through them. The flash of heat from the contact point was like an electric charge. 'I want.'

How badly she wanted. Need was a shimmering wave, engulfing her.

He didn't smile. If anything his features grew harder, flesh pulling taut across those magnificent bones. His fingers tightened around hers.

'I can offer you short-term pleasure, Imogen. That's all.' His eyes narrowed as if he tried to read her thoughts. 'If that's not what you want—'

Her finger on his mouth stopped his words and sent another ripple of sensual awareness through her. Despite his honed, masculine features his lips were surprisingly soft. She felt light-headed just thinking about them on her mouth.

'That sounds perfect.' She drew a breath shaky with grim amusement. 'I'm not in the market for long term.'

The words were barely out when his head swooped and his mouth met hers. Firmly, implacably, no teasing, just the sure, sensual demand of a man who knew what he wanted and, Imogen realised as her lips parted, who knew how to please a woman. The swipe of his tongue, the angle of his mouth, the possessive clasp of his hand around her skull were so *right*; she wondered how she'd gone her whole life without experiencing anything like it.

Whatever she and Scott had shared, it was nothing like this.

Thierry circled an arm around her, pulling her against his hard frame. Everywhere they touched, from her breasts to her thighs, exploded into tingling awareness, as if she'd brushed a live wire. Darts of fire shot to her nipples, her pelvis, even up the back of her neck as he massaged her scalp, and she heard herself moan into his mouth.

He tasted better than chocolate, rich, strong and addictive. She slid her arms around his neck and hung on tight as her knees gave way.

Instantly, the arm at her back tightened. He swung her off the ground, high in his arms, making her feel precious and feminine against his imposing masculinity. His mouth devoured hers, seeking, demanding, yet giving so much pleasure that exultation filled her.

This was a kiss. *This* was desire.

She was greedy for him, hungry for the passion he'd stoked so easily. She pushed her fingers through his hair, its soft thickness enticing.

'More,' she mumbled against his lips.

For answer she felt movement. Then she was on the bed and he over her, his weight pressing her down, his long legs imprisoning hers. She'd never felt anything as erotic as his hard length pinioning her, his breath hot on her neck as he grazed her with his teeth, making her jolt and squirm.

'Thierry!' That scraping little nip at the spot where her neck met her shoulders had her shuddering as great looping waves of delight coursed through her. They swamped her body, arrowing in to concentrate at the sensitive point between her legs.

He shifted his weight, settling low in the cradle of her hips, and she throbbed deep inside.

Urgently, Imogen arched, feeling the strong column of his arousal between her legs, and her brain shorted. She slid her hand down, wrapping around the solid weight of him, needing that contact. Desperate for more.

His breath hissed as he lifted his head. One large hand covered hers, holding her palm against him for a moment then dragging it away.

'Patience, Imogen.' She barely comprehended. His accent was so thick and her ears so full of her pulse pounding like the thud of a hammer on metal.

'Yes, now.' Was that reedy, desperate voice hers?

His eyes looked smoky, on the edge of focus, as he forced her arm wide, imprisoning her hand. When she shifted and brought her other hand down to touch him he pulled that arm wide too, so she lay spread-eagled.

The action pressed his groin against her pelvis, and her eyelids fluttered. Circling her hips, she moved against him, and to her amazement almost tipped over the edge into ecstasy. How could pleasure be so intense? So instantaneous? With Scott...

Thought died as Thierry murmured something in that lush, deep voice and lowered his head again. His breath feathered the sensitive flesh of her neck and then warm lips pressed just there and... Oh, yes, just there.

Again that powerful pulse through her pelvis, making every muscle clench and every erogenous zone shiver in anticipation.

'No. Don't!' It was a gurgle of sound, a hoarse whisper scraped from the back of her throat, but he heard it. Stilled.

She felt him draw a deep breath, his chest expanding. His hands tightened as if in spasm before loosing their hold. Then he pulled back, lifting his head.

Gone was the urbane sophisticate. Gone was the man in control. The glittering eyes that met hers held an unfamiliar wildness. His lips were a twist of what looked like raw pain.

Imogen watched him open his mouth. He shut his eyes and swallowed. Fascinated, she followed the jerky movement of his throat. Then blazing, dark eyes met hers again. 'You've changed your mind?' Even his voice was unfamiliar.

'Of course not.' How could he even think it? 'But I can't wait. I need you *now*.' Already she was running her hands over him, revelling in the heat of ridged muscle beneath his fine shirt. One hand dipped to his belt buckle and her fingers fumbled in their haste.

Thierry's eyes widened, his body rigid, as if he couldn't trust her words. Hadn't he ever met a woman so eager for him? Impossible!

What was impossible was that she, Imogen Holgate, was so desperate she didn't think she'd survive another minute of his seduction.

He was going to kiss and caress her, taking his time, and she'd self-combust at any moment. She'd never known anything like this spike of arousal.

'Please, Thierry.' Finally, she got his buckle undone and slid the belt free with clumsy hands. 'You can seduce me later. Whatever you like. But I need you inside me now.'

Fire washed from her throat to her hairline. But she didn't care about embarrassment or appearing unsophisticated. *Desire* was too tame a word for this urgent, visceral need. Nothing mattered but being one with this man.

Imogen bit her lip as her fingers slipped on his zip. She tried again and heard his sharp inhale. Hard fingers closed around hers.

He wasn't going to stop her, was he? Not now. She almost sobbed with frustration, her whole body burning like a single, vibrant flame that would at any minute consume her.

'Let me, *ma chérie.*'

Thierry kept his eyes on her face as he shucked his shoes and grabbed one of the condoms he'd brought.

She was glorious, her skin flushed with sexual arousal. Her eyes were bright as stars, veiled by long black lashes. Her reddened lips were plump and inviting, but not as inviting as the rest of her. His movements quickened, sheathing himself as his gaze dropped to proud breasts straining against that tight bodice. A surge of hunger hit and he drew an uneven breath. Despite what she said he needed to rein himself in, not surrender to hunger and take her with no preliminaries. He needed to…

Thierry's thoughts spun away as she reefed up the hem of her dress. Long, pale, toned thighs. Skimpy, emerald-green lace panties. The subtle, enticing scent of vanilla sugar and feminine arousal.

Slender fingers hooked the green lace and she arched her hips up, wriggling, to pull it away.

His hands tangled with hers, stripping the lace off. Then his hands were on her, skimming satin-soft flesh, stroking the dark silk, already damp, at her core.

He didn't register moving closer. But an instant later he was there, pressing against her softness, his hands planted beside her on the bed. Her skirt was up around her waist and her hair had come down on one side, dark tresses curling to her breasts.

A shudder ripped through him. He wanted to feast on her, take his time to build their pleasure, but he couldn't.

It wasn't the tug of her fingers digging into his shoulders that shattered his control, or the tiny, throaty purring sound she made. It was simply that he'd never wanted a woman so urgently.

His hand shook as he lifted her to him. Then in one sure, glorious stroke he surged home, high and hard, till he felt nothing but her, knew nothing but her liquid heat, sweet scent and indescribable pleasure.

Tawny green eyes snared his. Her head pressed back, baring that delectable throat. He heard his name in a throaty, broken gasp. It was the sexiest thing he'd ever heard, and to his amazement was all it took for him to lose the last of his control.

She quivered, jerking and shaking around him, drawing him into the most mind-blowing climax he'd ever experienced.

It was a long, long time before his brain functioned again. Imogen shifted drowsily, and he found himself quickening into arousal again. His immediate thought was to wonder if he'd brought enough condoms.

His second, when her eyes fluttered open and her tentative smile hit him square in the chest, was to congratulate himself on finding her. He'd never known a woman so unstinting in her passion.

Two weeks would barely be enough to enjoy all she had to offer. Yet that was all they had. She'd be gone in a fortnight.

Thierry felt a flicker of something almost like regret. But it would dissipate. A temporary lover was all he wanted. A couple of months and he'd be free of the shackles that had tied him down for four years. Then he'd leave, ready for adventure and the physical and mental challenges he missed. Which was why Imogen, who could only ever be temporary in his life, was absolutely perfect.

CHAPTER THREE

IMOGEN STARED FROM her hotel window at the London square with its communal garden and neat Georgian buildings. A couple strolled by hand in hand and her stomach did a little somersault. She looked away, lifting her peppermint tea to her lips.

She'd developed a taste for herbal tea since that night in Paris when Thierry had ordered it for her.

Turning, she found her gaze following the couple and felt a pang of regret. They were in their seventies, she'd guess, yet they held hands, heads turned towards each other as if in conversation.

What would it be like to grow old with the man you loved? The question wormed into her brain and she had to slam down a protective portcullis before her thoughts went too far.

Thierry Girard had been a revelation. Any woman would have been in heaven experiencing Paris with him, even if she hadn't spent years buried in a half-life of tedium, hemmed in by caution. Was it any wonder Venice, Reykjavik and London hadn't seemed quite as fabulous as Paris? He'd brought the city alive.

He'd brought *her* alive.

But she couldn't give in to romantic fantasy.

What they'd had had been wonderful and she'd lingered over each memory, loving the hazy sense of wellbeing they brought. But their passion, the romance and sense of connection had been illusory, the product of an affair that could only be short-lived.

She sipped her tea then grimaced as her taste buds did that strange thing again, turning a flavour she enjoyed into a dull, metallic tang. She put the cup down then realised she'd turned too fast, for the nausea rose again. Imogen gripped the table, taking slow breaths.

Her mother hadn't had these symptoms. Did it mean Imogen's condition was different after all? If anything the headaches had eased a little and were less frequent. But the nausea worried her. It was so persistent.

Reluctantly, she turned towards the bathroom. It was silly to consider the possibility of it being anything else. There was no chance a woman in her condition…

She shook her head then regretted it as the movement stirred that sick feeling again.

Clamping her lips, she headed to the bathroom. Of course it was absurd. This must be a new symptom of her deteriorating condition. Though, with the exception of the nausea, she felt better than she had in ages.

What was the point of second-guessing? She needed to see the specialist back in Sydney. He'd explain what was happening. How long she had.

Imogen drew a slow breath, deliberately pushing her shoulders down as tension inched them higher. Whatever the future held, she'd meet it head on.

She crossed the bathroom and reached for the test kit she'd left there. She hadn't had the nerve to look at the result before, telling herself it was nonsense and she'd be better having tea and biscuits to settle her stomach.

Now, reluctantly, she looked down at the indicator.

The world wobbled and she grabbed the counter.

Had her illness affected her eyes? But the indicator was clear. It was only her brain that felt blurry.

Pregnant.

She was expecting Thierry's child.

It was harder, this time, to contact him. He had a new PA who seemed dauntingly efficient and not eager to help.

No, Monsieur Girard wasn't in Paris. No, she couldn't

say where he was. Her tone implied Imogen had no right to renew his acquaintance. Had she been placed on some blacklist of importunate ex-lovers? Imogen imagined a throng of women trailing after him, trying to recapture his attention.

Was she to be so easily dismissed? Embarrassment and anger warred, and her grip tightened on the phone.

'When will he be back? It's urgent I speak with him.' She'd taken the first train from London to Paris, checking into a tiny hotel with the last of her travel money.

'Perhaps you'd like to leave a message, *mademoiselle*? He's very busy.' The cool tone implied he'd never find time for her again. Was that an overprotective assistant or a woman acting on orders?

Her crisp efficiency and Imogen's realisation she could only contact him via this dragon brought home the glaring differences between them. Thierry was powerful, mixing in elite social circles and living a privileged life. Employees protected him from unsolicited contact. She was working class and unsophisticated, more at home with a spreadsheet of numbers than at a glittering social event. Only the bright passion between them had made them equals.

Imogen set her chin.

'I need to speak with him in person. It's imperative.'

'As I said, I can take a message…'

But would it be delivered?

Imogen gritted her teeth, staring over the slate-grey roof of the building across the lane. It seemed close enough to touch in this cheap back street. A far cry from the magnificent hotel she'd splurged on during her first stay in Paris.

'Please tell him I need to see him. Five minutes will do.' She bit down grim laughter. How long did it take to break such news? 'I have…important information for him. Something he needs to hear as soon as possible.'

'Very well, *mademoiselle*.' The phone clicked in her ear.

* * *

'That's all now.' Thierry looked at his watch. 'Finish those in the morning.'

Mademoiselle Janvier primmed her mouth. 'I find it more efficient to complete my work before leaving and start fresh tomorrow.'

Thierry forbore from comment. His temporary PA took efficiency to a new level. At least these notes would take no more than half an hour.

He should be grateful. When there'd been that recent glitch in his plans to take over a rival business, her hard work had been invaluable. She'd even tried to match his eighteen-hour work days till he'd put a stop to it. Dedication he appreciated, but sometimes she seemed almost *proprietorial*.

If only she'd smile occasionally.

His lips twitched. That was his unregenerate, unbusinesslike side. The side that preferred being outdoors on a clear evening like this, rather than cooped up with a sour-faced assistant.

That part of him would far rather share a champagne picnic with an intriguing dark-haired beauty whose enthusiasm, sensuality and unexpected flashes of naïveté intrigued.

That couldn't be regret he felt? There'd be excitement enough in his life once he cleared this final hurdle. He'd given up four years of his life and wrought a small miracle, wresting the family business from the brink of disaster. Soon...

He rolled his shoulders. Soon he could take up his real life again. The one that defined him, no matter how irresponsible his *grand-père* branded it. But his *grand-père* had never understood it was the rush of adrenalin, the thrill of pitting himself physically against the toughest challenges, that made him feel *real*. These past years he'd been condemned to a half life.

Adventure beckoned. What would it be first? Heli-skiing or hot-air ballooning? Or white-water rafting? Orsino had mentioned a place in Colorado...

'By the way, there's a woman waiting to see you.'

'A woman?' Thierry checked his diary. He had no appointments.

'A Mademoiselle Holgate.'

'Holgate?' Something inside his chest jerked hard. 'How long has she been waiting?'

His PA's eyes widened as he shot to his feet. 'I warned her she'd have to wait. You had a lot—'

'Invite her in. Immediately!'

Mademoiselle Janvier scurried out, shock on her thin features. It was the first time she'd seen him anything but polite and calm, even when it had looked like his expansion plans, so vital to the solidity of the company, had unravelled.

The door opened and his breathing quickened. He stepped around the desk, elation pulsing.

Elation? He halted, a prickle of warning skating through him.

He and Imogen had enjoyed themselves but Thierry wasn't in the habit of feeling more than casual pleasure at the thought of any woman. Not since Sandrine, a lifetime ago.

He'd learned his lesson then. Women added spice and pleasure, especially now his chance for serious adventure had been curtailed. But none lasted. He made sure of it. Women fitted into the category of rest and recreation.

Thierry frowned as a trim, dark-haired figure stepped into the room and an unfamiliar sensation clamped his belly.

He almost wouldn't have recognised her. Those glorious dark tresses were scraped into a bun that reminded him of Mademoiselle Janvier with her rigid self-control. Imogen wore jeans and a shirt that leached the colour from her face. He'd never seen her in anything but bright colours. And there were shadows under her eyes, hollows beneath her cheekbones.

Again that inexplicable thump to his chest, as if an unseen hand had punched him.

'Imogen!' He started forward but before he reached her she slipped into a visitor's chair.

Thierry pulled up abruptly. It wasn't the reaction he got from women. Ever.

'Thierry.' She nodded, the movement curt, almost dismissive. And her eyes—they didn't glow as he remembered. They looked…haunted as they stared at his tie. Yet there was defiance in the set of her chin. Belligerence in her clamped lips.

What had happened? He'd seen her ecstatic, curious, enthralled. He'd seen her in the throes of passion. His lower body tensed. Those memories had kept him from sleep too many nights since she'd left. He'd even seen her in pain, with tears spiking those ebony lashes. But he'd never seen her look like this.

He grabbed a chair, yanked it around to face her and sank onto it, his knees all but touching her thighs.

She shifted, pulling her legs away, as if he made her nervous. Or as if his touch contaminated.

Something jabbed his gut. Deliberately, he leaned back, gaze bland, his mind buzzing with questions.

'This is an unexpected pleasure.'

'Is it? That's not the impression I got.' Her chin lifted infinitesimally and colour swept her too-pale face. That was better. The woman he knew had sass and vibrancy.

'You've just walked in the door.' He gave her the smile he knew melted female hearts. Despite her tension it was good to see her. He'd missed her more than he'd expected and—

'I suppose I should be grateful you found time out of your busy schedule to see me.'

* * *

Imogen bit her lip. This wasn't going right. She'd let fear and anger get the best of her. Anger at how long it had taken to see him, only then to be kept waiting for an hour. And fear. Fear that even with his help, assuming he would help her, the new life growing inside her was likely in danger.

She threaded her fingers together, trying to hide their tremor.

It didn't help that one glance was all she'd needed to fall under Thierry's spell again. He looked wonderful. Strong and fit, so utterly masculine that just sitting beside him was a test of endurance. She wanted to touch him, feel that strong life-force, remind herself there was some hope in this bleak situation.

'I'm sorry you had to wait. I didn't know you were there.'

Imogen waved a dismissive hand, her gaze skating across the huge office with its expansive, and expensive, views over one of Paris's most prestigious neighbourhoods.

'It doesn't matter.' She drew a breath, trying to slow her racing heart, only to discover she'd inhaled his distinctive scent—warm male flesh and clear mountain air. It teased her nostrils and set up a trembling deep inside.

For one self-indulgent instant she let herself remember how glorious it had been between them. How perfect.

But that was over. He'd moved on and she, well, she had more important things to worry about than her attraction to a heartbreaker of a Frenchman.

'I thought you'd be in Australia now. Wasn't it Venice, Reykjavik, London and then home to Sydney?'

He remembered. A tiny curl of delight swirled inside. 'That was the plan.' Her voice emerged husky, not like the firm tone she'd aimed for. 'But things have changed.'

'I'm glad.' His voice caressed. 'I've been thinking of you.'

Surprised, she jerked her head up, their eyes meeting.

Instantly, sultry heat unfurled in her belly like coiling tendrils. Her skin drew taut.

She didn't know how Thierry did that. She didn't know whether to be shocked, stoic or despairing that absence hadn't lessened his impact. Even with so much on her mind, that low voice, that slurred ripple of accented sound, made her body hum.

He leaned close, and she sat back, seeing the moment he registered her withdrawal. A frown puckered his brow.

'I came because I had some news.'

He stilled, and she sensed a watchfulness that belied his air of unconcern.

When they'd been together all that powerful energy had been focused on pleasure. Now, in this vast office that screamed authority, with those unblinking eyes trained on her, she saw how formidable Thierry was. Not just as the sexiest, most charismatic man she'd ever met, but because of the power he wielded with such ease.

She swallowed, her throat suddenly parched.

'News?' The word was sharp.

'Yes.' She swiped her top lip with her tongue and a flicker of something crossed his proud features. 'Yes, I…'

Spit it out! How hard is it to say? You've had a week of waiting to get used to it.

'You…?' He leaned forward, and she knew an urge to slide onto his lap and burrow close.

As if Thierry's embrace would make everything right! *Nothing* could make this right.

Again she licked her lips. 'I'm pregnant.'

For what seemed a full minute he said nothing, merely looked at her with a face frozen into harsh lines that emphasised the chiselled hauteur of those superb features.

'You say the baby is mine?'

Mistake number one, Thierry realised when Imogen snapped back in her seat as if yanked by a bungee cord.

Ice formed in her hazel eyes, turning them from warm and a little lost to frozen wasteland. Then there was the taut line of her mouth, the hurt in the way she bit her lip.

He hated it when she did that. He always wanted to reach out and stop her. And she…

Belatedly, he yanked back his thoughts. Pregnant. With his child?

His breath disintegrated and a sense of unreality engulfed him. Like the day, as a kid, when he'd learned his parents had died in a crash outside Lyon. Or four years ago, when his indomitable *grand-père* had had a stroke.

Was it possible?

Of course it was possible. He and Imogen had spent every night for almost two weeks together, insatiable for each other.

He'd never known any woman to test his control the way Imogen had. He'd plan some outing to tick off her bucket list—a visit to a dance club, or a moonlight picnic—and all the time she was beaming at him, laughing and thrilled at the novelty of new experiences, he was calculating how long before he could get her naked and horizontal. Or just naked enough for sex. As for horizontal…the missionary position was overrated.

Molten heat coiled in his belly.

'There's been no one else. Just you.'

Stupid to feel that punch of pleasure. Thierry forced himself to focus. This was too important.

'Since when?'

'That's not relevant. I—'

'Since when, Imogen?' Stranger things had happened than a woman trying to pin an unexpected pregnancy on some gullible man.

Her chin rose and the expression in her eyes could have scored flesh. 'Seven months.'

So long between lovers? Did that make him special, or a convenient way of ending the drought? Or maybe a target?

'That's very precise.'

'I don't make a habit of sleeping around.'

He'd worked it out. He vividly recalled her charmingly unpractised loving, the shock in her eyes at the ecstasy they'd shared.

'Pregnant.' He paused, frustrated that his brain wouldn't function. Now it had side-tracked into imagining Imogen swollen with his child, her hands splayed over her ripe belly. He'd never lusted after a pregnant woman yet the image in his head filled him with all sorts of inappropriate thoughts.

Diable! He should be concentrating, not mentally undressing her.

He dragged his attention back to her face. 'We used condoms.'

Jerkily she nodded. 'It turns out they're not a hundred percent effective.'

'You're sure about this?' He searched her features. She looked different—drawn and tired. And...was that fear?

'I wouldn't be here if I weren't. I took the test in London. That's why I came to Paris, to find you.'

Thierry stared into those haunted eyes and told himself the sensible thing would be to insist on a paternity test. He had only her word the child was his.

Yet, crazy as it was, he was on the verge of believing her. He'd been with her just two weeks, but he felt he knew her better than any of the women he'd dated.

Even better than Sandrine.

The thought sideswiped him. He'd grown up with Sandrine and had loved her with all his youthful heart.

The memory served its purpose, like being doused in a cold mountain stream. He needed to think critically. He straightened.

'What sort of test was it? One from a pharmacy?'

She nodded. 'That's right.'

Thierry stood, relieved to have a purpose. He strode

around the desk and reached for a phone. 'Then the first thing to do is get this confirmed by a doctor.'

The flare of relief in Imogen's eyes intrigued him. She didn't look like a woman trying to catch a man by getting pregnant.

She looked scared rigid.

'Well, that settles that.' Thierry's voice was as delicious as ever, the silky burr a ribbon of warmth threading Imogen's ice-cold body as they left the doctor's rooms.

She'd felt chilled and resentful all through the consultation. Perhaps because Thierry had insisted he remain, as if he didn't trust her. Perhaps from embarrassment, because she couldn't shake the idea the doctor, for all his professionalism, was quietly judging her and sympathising with Thierry. He'd continually addressed Thierry rather than her. As if she didn't have the wit to comprehend her condition.

Or as if she was an inconvenient problem.

'What does it settle?'

Thierry didn't answer. She darted him a sideways stare and guessed he was brooding over his own thoughts. That wide brow was furrowed, his eyes focused on the glistening cobblestones as they walked.

Yet, distracted as he was, his hand was reassuring in the small of her back. It felt…protective.

Imogen was needy enough right now to appreciate that.

Since the realisation of her fatal condition, she'd felt separated from the world by a wall of glass. Only her brief time with Thierry had seemed *real*. But the news she was pregnant… She'd never felt so frighteningly alone in all her life. Being responsible for another life as she faced the end of her own—how was she going to manage it?

She stumbled, and Thierry's arm slid around her waist, holding her upright and safe. She stopped, her heart hammering high in her throat.

What if she'd fallen? Would such a simple tumble be enough to dislodge that tiny life? Surely not? Yet Imogen's palm crept to her abdomen as fear spiked.

Her baby. She'd never get to see it grow. Never have the opportunity to be a real mother to him or her. But she knew with a sudden fierce certainty that she'd do anything to protect it. Anything to ensure her baby had a good chance at life.

'Here. It's okay. We're at the car.' Thierry clicked open the lock and ushered her into the gleaming sports car that looked like something out of a glossy magazine and which she knew rode like a growling beast eager for the open road.

Suppressing a sigh of relief, she sank into the moulded leather and shut her eyes. The car dipped as he got in then he started it and swung out into the traffic.

Minutes later she opened her eyes and stared glassily at the congested traffic.

'Where are we going?'

'To your hotel. You look like you need rest, and we have to talk.'

Imogen frowned as she recognised a landmark. 'I'm not staying in the centre of the city this time.'

'Then where?'

She told him and his ebony eyebrows slashed down in a frown. 'What on earth are you doing there?'

She shrugged. 'I'd spent all my holiday money. I was due to go home, remember?' She didn't add that she'd been loath to dip into the last of her savings. She'd kept some in the bank in Australia, figuring she'd need something to cover her last months.

'Money didn't seem to be a problem before.'

Was that accusation in his voice? 'Believe it or not, I didn't stay in a five-star hotel to catch myself a rich man—'

'I didn't say that.' The wrinkle on his brow became a

scowl and it hit her that Thierry wasn't used to having his intentions questioned.

'I told you before.' She struggled for an even tone, though she felt like shouting or maybe smashing something. It was hard enough to deal with the impossible hand fate had dealt her without coping with his doubt, however reasonable. Imogen dragged in a sharp breath and tried to ignore the twin scents of luxury leather and earthy male that filled her nostrils. 'The trip was a once in a lifetime experience. I splurged on things I'd never normally afford.' She laced her fingers together in her lap. 'Now it's back to reality.'

She pursed her lips to restrain the burst of hollow laughter that threatened. If she gave in to it she feared she'd never stop but hysteria wouldn't help.

They finished the rest of the trip in silence. It continued as he unlocked the door to an apartment in a prestigious old building looking out over the Seine. One glance at the spacious living room with its view of central Paris glittering in the twilight told her she'd stepped into another world. One where wealth was figured in numbers with far more zeroes than she'd ever see.

'Please, take a seat.'

Imogen settled onto a vibrant red lounger that toned with the slash of grey, red and yellow abstract art over the fireplace. A moment later Thierry passed her a tall glass. 'Sparkling water, but I can make tea or coffee if you prefer.'

'This is fine.' Gratefully, she sipped, watching as he strode to the bar in one corner, downed a shot of something then poured himself another before turning towards her.

'Are you all right?' As soon as the words escaped, she firmed her lips. What a stupid thing to say. Of course he wasn't okay. She was still in shock and she'd had seven days to get used to her pregnancy.

Yet his eyebrows rose in surprise. Because he hadn't expected her to notice he wasn't utterly in control?

Looking at him now, at those broad shoulders that seemed capable of withstanding any weight, at the glinting dark eyes and firm jaw, she realised that, no matter how surprising her news, Thierry Girard was more than capable of handling it.

Exactly the sort of man she needed. For the first time today she felt herself begin to relax, just a little.

'You're absolutely sure it's mine?'

Imogen stiffened, her fingers gripping so hard the water in her glass threatened to slop over the side.

She met searing eyes that probed her very depths. 'For all I know there could have been a man in Venice, one in Reykjavik and one in London too.'

Imogen swallowed hard, tasting indignation. 'You think that was on my must-do list? A lover at every stop?' Despite the harshness she heard in her voice, she couldn't quite keep the wobble from it. Maybe if she was the sort of woman to fall into bed with a stranger so easily she wouldn't have expected so much from Thierry.

She gnawed her lip and dragged her gaze from his. Was she stupid, hoping he'd help? They'd had fun together but she'd been what—a diversion? An easy lay? Certainly something different from the women he was used to in his rarefied world of wealth and privilege.

With careful precision she put her glass on a nearby table and scooted to the edge of her seat, grabbing her bag from where she'd dropped it.

'Where are you going?'

Imogen blinked, sanity returning.

She didn't have the luxury of pride. This wasn't just about her. She had a baby to consider.

'Stop it.' He crossed the space between them in a couple of long strides, making her crane her neck to look up at him.

'What?' Even as she said it his thumb brushed her bottom lip, making her register the salt tang of blood in her mouth. And more, the heady taste of his skin. Imogen had to fight not to dart out her tongue for a better taste.

'Stop torturing that lovely mouth of yours.'

The unexpectedness of that made her blink and sit back. *Lovely mouth?*

'I don't...' She shook her head.

Abruptly he dropped his hand and nodded, and Imogen was horrified at her sense of loss. Surely she was stronger than this?

Her mouth trembled, and she grabbed her glass, taking a long draught of the sparkling water, telling herself the sting of it where her teeth had grazed her skin was a timely reminder that she needed focus.

She straightened her shoulders and looked at a point near his perfectly knotted tie.

'I'm happy to take a paternity test if you like.' She paused, letting that sink in. 'Then, when you believe me, I need your help.'

CHAPTER FOUR

Help?

In the form of money, he assumed.

Thierry hadn't missed her wide-eyed appraisal of his apartment, the way her hand lingered on the plush fabric of the designer-original lounger and her eyes on the masterpiece of Modernism over the fireplace.

But, if she carried his child, why shouldn't she expect support?

He could afford it. He'd worked like the devil to turn around the family company, not just for his ageing grandparents and cousins, but for himself too. Duty had driven him, but he'd benefited. It had stunned him to discover the wealth he'd always taken for granted was in danger of slipping away while he travelled the world, following his own pursuits. Years of poor management as his grandfather's health deteriorated had taken its toll on the family fortune.

But it was safe now.

Unlike Imogen. The sudden thought disturbed him.

Pregnancy wasn't an illness. It was surely the most natural thing in the world. Yet the sight of her tension, the dark circles beneath her eyes and her pallor drew at something inside him, making him tense and restless.

He turned to stand by the windows. But it wasn't the lights of early evening that he saw. It was her wan reflection. Her shoulders hunched again and she seemed to crumple. Not at all like the vivacious Imogen he'd known.

'What sort of help do you want? To arrange an abortion?' Alone in a foreign country, she could well ask for that sort of assistance. Especially if, as she'd said, her money had run out.

Thierry knocked back a slug of cognac, surprised to discover its taste had unaccountably turned sour.

He scowled at the glass, slamming it down onto a nearby table. He still reeled from the idea of her being pregnant. He hadn't had time to begin imagining an actual child. Yet out of nowhere anger hit him. Anger that she could consider disposing of her baby. *His* baby, if his instincts were correct.

Her equanimity at the thought of a DNA test was convincing, as was his memory of her untutored loving. Imogen wasn't a woman who flitted from man to man, no matter how easily she'd fallen into his arms.

He spun around. 'Is that it? You want to get rid of the baby?'

It would solve his problems, remove any inconvenience. Yet his stomach twisted at the thought. He found himself looming over her, watching the convulsive movement of her pale throat.

'I suppose that would be a solution,' she whispered, looking down at her twisting hands. 'Maybe it's selfish to try…'

'Try what?' He hunkered before her, confused by his desire to take her in his arms even as he wanted to shake her for even considering destroying their baby.

Their baby! Was he really so easily convinced?

Perhaps he was. Adrenalin made his heart pound, just like it used to as he'd waited for the starter's signal at the beginning of a downhill race, his eyes fixed on the treacherous snowy slope before him.

He sensed, with a marrow-deep instinct he didn't even begin to fathom, that the child was his.

Imogen lifted her head and his pulse tripped. Her eyes, more green than brown, glistened over-bright and huge in her taut face.

'I'd hoped…' She shrugged. 'I want to give my baby a chance to *live*. Is that so wrong?'

'Of course not.' Her hands were cool and slight in his. He chafed them gently, telling himself relief was a natural response. 'So you want to keep the child.' He made it a statement.

'Yes. I do.' Her hands gripped his, and he was surprised at her strength. 'I want to keep it.'

'Good. That's one thing sorted.' He made his voice businesslike, as if dealing with unexpected pregnancies was no more difficult than the business challenges he handled daily.

Thierry disengaged his hands and stood. It was hard to think when Imogen clung to him, her eyes devouring him as if he were her last hope. That muddled his brain and he needed his wits.

He sank into a nearby armchair and surveyed her, wondering what it was about this woman that evoked such strong protective instincts in a man who'd spent his life avoiding any form of commitment. He'd perfected the art of being unencumbered until his *grand-père's* illness and the realisation he couldn't avoid the yoke of duty any longer.

'You want my help.'

'Yes. Please.' But instead of meeting his gaze she focused on sipping from the glass of water he'd given her. Suspicion feathered through him, an inkling she was trying to hide something.

'And what form would this assistance take?' Now would come the appeal for money. It was only natural.

She studied the glass in her hand, one finger stroking the condensation on the outside as if it fascinated her. 'I want your help if anything goes wrong.'

Thierry straightened, his hands gripping the plush arms of his chair. 'Wrong? What could go wrong?'

She shrugged, an uneven little movement. 'Things do.'

'Not often. Not with good medical care.' He frowned. Was she scared by pregnancy?

The idea confused him. Where was the woman who'd planned to skydive, climb a glacier and see volcanoes in Iceland? Who'd shown not one hint of fear as he'd taken her hot-air ballooning outside Paris?

Still she stared at the tall glass in her hands.

'Do you need money for health care? Is that it?' He'd assumed she was well-off, given where they'd met and where she'd stayed on her first visit to Paris. Now she seemed skint.

She shook her head. 'No. I should be all right once I'm back in Australia. There's comprehensive health care, plus I have some savings I haven't touched.'

Once she returned to Australia.

So, she didn't intend to stay here through her pregnancy. Thierry ignored the unfamiliar hollow sensation in his gut. It couldn't be disappointment. His lifestyle, and especially the lifestyle he was about to return to—never in one place longer than it took to conquer the next challenge—left no room for a baby. Besides, children were better off with their mothers; everyone said so. If he really wanted he could visit after it was born.

Yet discontent niggled.

And surprise. She didn't want to be with him. She didn't want his money. She only wanted his help if things went wrong.

Common sense told him he was getting out of this lightly. Most men would jump at the chance to divest themselves of such responsibilities.

But Thierry couldn't feel relief. He felt curiously deprived.

'What, exactly, do you want from me, Imogen?' At her name, she looked up, meeting his eyes squarely, and he felt a curious little thump in his chest, as if his heart had thudded too hard against his ribs.

Again that uneven little shrug. Her gaze swerved away, fixing on the view as if it fascinated her. 'I want to know you'll be there wh— if—something happens to me. I want to know you'll take care of him or her.'

She shifted in her seat, skewering him suddenly with a look he could only describe as desperate. Thierry felt the slow crawl of an icy finger up his nape, each individual hair on his neck and arms rising in response.

Not just desperation but fear. What was going on?

'I'm alone, you see. My mother and sister are dead. So if anything were to happen to me...' She swiped her bottom lip with her tongue. 'I know there are some wonderful foster parents out there, but I can't bear the thought of my baby being put into care.'

'It won't come to that. You and the child will be fine.' Thierry leaned towards her, willing her to think logically, despite the panic edging her husky voice.

He hated hearing her so desperate and fearful.

Then the full implication of her words sank in. 'You've got no one back in Australia? No family?'

'No. But I'm used to looking out for myself.' This time her jaw angled higher, as if daring him to feel sorry for her.

Thierry frowned. He might not be accustomed to taking responsibility for others—he might have spent years perfecting what *Grand-père* called his 'damned selfish bachelor lifestyle'—but the idea of Imogen, pregnant and alone, disturbed him. More than disturbed. It sent a shock wave tingling through him as if he'd touched an electric current.

'What about your father?' She'd said her mother and sister were dead but she hadn't mentioned him.

Her lips pulled taut in a grimace. 'I don't know where he is. He used to move around a lot, working in outback mines. And even if I did know how to contact him I wouldn't expect him to raise his grandchild. Not when he walked out on Mum the day he found out she was expecting twins.'

Diable! Thierry's hands closed into fists as he read the careful blankness on Imogen's face. It was the sort of blankness that hid pain, despite her matter-of-fact tone.

What sort of man deserted a woman pregnant with his children?

Then he remembered that moment of relief when he'd entertained the possibility this wasn't his baby. Or that Imogen might get rid of it and make things easier for them both. A shudder of revulsion ripped through him at the idea he had anything in common with a man like her father, even if only for a split second.

'You needn't worry about that.' His voice sounded harsh and he saw a hint of surprise on her features. 'I won't run scared.'

It was one of the things he'd always prided himself on—his ability to face fear. In his youth he'd stared it down on neck-breaking black ski-runs while the hopes of a nation weighed down his shoulders. Later there'd been adventure sports and his treks into inhospitable territory with his friend Orsino Chatsfield. More recently he'd confronted the ultimate horror: a desk job, hemmed in by solid walls while he came to grips with the ailing Girard business interests.

'You'll take care of our child if I die?'

Thierry surged to his feet. 'You're not going to die.' Years ago he'd been first on the scene in a desert car rally after a crash. The other driver had died in his arms while they'd waited for an airlift and Thierry had never felt so helpless. He refused to countenance such talk from Imogen. 'You're going to have an uneventful pregnancy, a healthy baby and a long, happy life as a mother.'

And, most probably, as someone's wife.

The realisation sent a twang of discontent through his gut.

'You sound so sure.' This time the curve of her lovely mouth, though tiny, was a real smile.

'I am.'

'Thank you, Thierry.' She looked away, but not before he saw her blink back what looked like a glimmer of moisture. Her lashes clumped as if wet, and the sight filled him with unfamiliar feelings.

'Don't.' He leaned down, taking the glass from her hand and putting it aside. Then he tugged her up till she stood before him, shorter than he remembered in her flat shoes. The scent of sweetness and vanilla filled his nostrils as he leaned close. 'There's nothing to cry about.'

Her mouth twisted in a crumpled sort of smile and her palm grazed his cheek. 'You're a good man, Thierry Girard.'

He blinked, transfixed by the mix of emotions flitting across her features. Or perhaps by the strange sensation in the pit of his stomach, as if he'd gone into freefall.

A good man? Focused, yes. Selfish, yes. With a taste for adventure and good-looking women. And an astute business sense that had surprised everyone, himself included.

Her hand began to slide away and he grabbed it, clamping it against his jaw. He liked its soft warmth against his skin.

'What's going on, Imogen?' She was hiding something. He'd read that in her refusal to hold his gaze. The way she kept looking away, as if scared he'd see too much. But what could it be? He was ready to accept the child was his, even if his lawyers would probably advise a paternity test.

'Nothing.' Her laugh sounded forced. 'Apart from an unexpected pregnancy.'

'Imogen.' He captured the back of her head in his free hand, delving his fingers into the soft luxury of her hair.

Memory hit—of those dark, silky waves slithering over them both as they'd lain naked in bed. Of him tugging gently on her hair so she arched her neck back, exposing her creamy throat to his mouth. Of the taste of her, sweet and addictive.

Fire ignited in his groin and his fingers tightened.

She could break his hold. All she had to do was step back, or tell him to let go.

The voice of reason urged him to do just that. Not to complicate an already fraught situation.

But he didn't.

He stood, looking down, watching a delicate flush steal across her cheeks, turning pallor to peaches-and-cream loveliness. And still she stood, watching him through narrowed eyes, her long dark lashes veiling her expression. She was a contradiction, a conundrum. Vulnerable yet unwavering, alluring and intriguing, a mystery to be solved.

Her lips parted, and he leaned closer, needing to taste. It had been too long.

His lips touched hers, and he realised he'd made a serious error of judgement when sensation exploded, tightening his limbs, his belly, his grip on her. His mouth moved with purpose now. Not for a whisper-soft taste, but with a ravening hunger that hadn't been assuaged since the day Imogen had left Paris.

She tasted so sweet. Lush, feminine and delicious. The scent of her intoxicated him and he bowed her back, thrusting his tongue into her mouth, shocked at how the familiar taste of her blasted at his control. A tremor passed through him, a huge, curling wave of hunger and exultation as she kissed him back, just as ravenous as he.

Her free hand slid up his chest to cup the back of his neck, fingers tight as if defying him to break away. He felt another detonation inside him, her touch, her need, triggering his to even greater heights.

Imogen made a low humming sound in the back of her throat that sent him crazy. From the first he'd lusted after her enthusiasm, her passion. He needed it now. How had he gone so long without it? She was sweet rain after drought, ambrosia after starvation.

Thierry released her hand and wrapped an arm around her, hauling her in to him so she cushioned his burgeoning arousal with her soft belly.

Her belly.

His baby.

Realisation slammed into him. Tension crawled along his limbs to grab his neck and shoulders. A new sort of tension that had nothing to do with sex.

He dragged his mouth free, hauling in air.

Hectic colour scored her cheeks and throat, and her lips were red from his kisses. Her eyelids fluttered as if reluctant to open.

He wanted to grind himself against her, strip her clothes away and lose himself in her welcoming body.

The body that cradled a fragile new life.

The body of a woman who for some reason feared this pregnancy like a physical threat.

What was he thinking?

He wasn't thinking. He was doing what he'd always done—indulging in whatever pleasure beckoned.

Abruptly, he straightened, his hands dropping, engulfed in horror at his lack of control. You'd think that in his thirties he'd have conquered the impulse to act rashly.

But one touch, one taste of Imogen, and thought fled.

He stared into dazed eyes that glowed green and honey-brown and knew he teetered on the edge of control.

Deliberately, he stepped back, his movements stiff and reluctant, forcing his brain to function. There was more he needed to understand. Much more.

'Are you going to tell me the truth now?'

'The truth?' The words sounded like a foreign language. Imogen stared at that firm mouth, the sensuous bottom lip, the taut line it formed when he stopped speaking. 'What do you mean?'

It was all she could do not to sway as she stood, bereft of his touch, still feeling his body imprinted on hers. She bit her lip, silencing the futile plea that he gather her close again.

She wanted Thierry. Wanted the comfort of him holding her, the taste of him—cognac and that bitter-chocolate tang that was unique to Thierry. She wanted to be naked with him, losing herself to ecstasy.

But he looked distant, even standing so near. His eyes were unreadable, his face taut, prouder, harder than she remembered it. Suspicious.

'What don't you want me to know? You're not telling me the truth.'

Imogen jerked back an unsteady step. Her heart thumped harder. 'I know the pregnancy is a surprise, but it's real. You heard the doctor.' Pride came to her aid, stiffening her backbone. 'Or is it the idea you're the father that you doubt?'

Had she really believed he'd take her word it was his? She pulled her arms across her chest, holding in the welling hurt.

Slowly, he shook his head, his piercing gaze never leaving her face. 'It's not that. There's something more. Something you're hiding. I won't do anything until I know what it is.'

That powerful jaw took on an obstinate cast as he crossed his arms across his chest, reinforcing that aura of tough, masculine strength despite his suavely tailored jacket. His lips thinned and his nostrils flared.

He looked intimidating. Not like the easy lover she remembered, or the passionate man of seconds ago. There was passion still, but something formidable too.

'You're reneging on what you said? You won't step in if something…happens to me?' Fear clutched. She wasn't even sure if she could carry this child to term but she had to believe she could. And she had to believe there'd be someone to care for it when she was gone.

'Hey.' His voice was soothing, his fleeting touch on her arm gentle. 'Don't get worked up. All I want is the truth. Surely I'm entitled to that?'

'You have the truth. The baby is yours.'

He stood silent, his scrutiny like a weight pushing her down.

She spun away, turning to the windows, vaguely aware of the lights of Paris beyond. Once, a few weeks ago, she'd have revelled in being here, seeing this. Now she felt terrified, scared not so much for herself as for her baby. Despair hovered in the shadows at the corner of her vision, ready to pounce if she let her guard down.

'I can't help unless you tell me what's troubling you.'

She pivoted towards him. 'Help?' She'd wondered if he was looking for an excuse to wriggle out of that.

'I said I would and I'm a man of my word.' He spoke with such authority she couldn't help but believe him.

Imogen hadn't wanted to tell him too soon, scared the knowledge he'd definitely be responsible for their child might frighten him off. Yet surely he deserved to know? The sooner he came to grips with what was to come, the better.

'Whatever it is, I'm sure it'll be okay.'

A laugh ripped from Imogen's throat. The sound scared her—so raw and guttural. It betrayed the fact she clung to calm by the skin of her teeth.

Thierry's dark eyebrows shot up, his gaze interrogative.

'It won't be okay, that's the problem.' Her voice was harsh and raspy. She cleared her throat. 'I'm not going to be a mother and I'm not going to know my child.' Pain settled like a lump of cold metal in her stomach, its chill paralysing. 'I'm dying.'

CHAPTER FIVE

THE NEXT HOUR passed in a haze, for which Imogen was grateful. She'd had enough of pain and grief and though both still threatened like bullies hovering at the edge of a playground, Thierry's presence kept them at bay.

Two things stood out. First, the way he'd gone stark white beneath the bronze of his tanned olive skin when he heard her news. Even the laughter lines at the corners of his eyes had morphed into creases that betrayed shock rather than humour. Second, his gentle solicitude as he'd ushered her back to a chair and pressed a hot drink into her hands.

His touch had been impersonal, as far from his earlier passionate grip as it was possible to be. Dying did that—it distanced you from people, putting up an unseen but un-breakable barrier no one wanted to broach. She'd seen it with her mother—people keeping their distance, as if they feared her brain tumour might be catching.

In Thierry's case, the fire died out of his eyes as she told him about her condition, and that her mother had died of the same illness just months before. He hadn't protested in disbelief but his face had grown grimmer and grimmer as she'd spelled out what was in store.

'We need to get you to a specialist.' Even his voice had changed, the timbre hollow instead of smooth and rich.

She leaned her head against the back of her chair. 'I have another appointment in Sydney in a couple of weeks.'

'So far away?'

She shrugged. 'I'm not in a hurry, Thierry. I've been through it all with my mother and I know what to expect. Except…' She pressed a hand to her stomach, terror swoop-ing through her as she thought of the danger to her baby.

'Don't.' He hunkered beside her, his hand on hers firm and strong, calloused, as if he did more with his time than attend meetings. Heat seeped from his touch. She imagined it as warm tendrils shooting and unfurling, spreading through her chilled body. Was it imagination or did the tightness around her hunched shoulders ease?

Then he said something that threatened to undo her.

'You're not alone now, Imogen.'

He made no ridiculous promises to find a cure when there was none, to snatch her from the jaws of death. That would have meant nothing, just the bluster of someone unwilling to accept the inevitable.

Instead, his words pierced the shaky wall she'd built around her heart. They made her feel less desperate.

She opened her mouth to tell him how precious a gift he'd given her but found she couldn't speak. She gulped down a knot of emotion.

She'd known this man a few short weeks and yet for the first time since she'd lost her mother—in fact since Isabelle had died—she felt something like whole.

'You need to rest. You're exhausted.'

It was true. Sleep had eluded her this week. As if on cue, a mighty yawn rose.

'You're right. I'd better get back to the hotel.'

For answer Thierry slid his arms beneath her and hoisted her up in one smooth movement as he stood. His darkening jaw was just centimetres away and beneath the hand she pressed to his chest came the steady thud of his heartbeat.

Safe, it seemed to say.

For once Imogen let herself ignore the tiny voice of reality that sneered nothing could keep her safe now. Instead, she let her head sink against his shoulder. Just for a moment it was nice to be cared for. It was a novelty she could get used to.

Except she wouldn't have the chance to get used to it, would she?

He must have heard her hiccup of laughter.

'What is it?'

'Nothing. I'm just tired.'

'Which is why you're going to bed.' He turned and carried her from the room. To her amazement they didn't head towards the foyer but down a wide corridor.

'Thierry? I need to get back to my hotel.'

He stopped. 'Why? Have you got medicine there that you need?'

She shook her head.

'Good. You can sleep here. I'll lend you something to wear and bring you supper once you're in bed.'

Imogen knew she should move, knew she couldn't afford to get used to being cosseted. It would only make things more difficult later. But what woman would willingly give up the pleasure of being in Thierry's powerful arms, even for a short time?

The beautiful bedroom with its high ceilings, elegant doors and honey-coloured wood flooring spoke of the elegance of another age, even if the *en suite* bathroom she glimpsed was all modern luxury. One quick survey told her this was a guest room. No sign of Thierry's personal belongings. Nor could she imagine him choosing the delicate pale blue and cream bed linens for himself.

He lowered her onto a bed that her weary bones protested was just too comfortable to leave.

Would it be so wrong to stay the night? Independence warred with exhaustion as she sat, swaying.

'Here. You can use this tonight.' She hadn't even noticed Thierry leave but he was entering the room again. He pressed something soft into her hands, and she looked down, seeing a black T-shirt that she knew would look fantastic clinging to his hard chest. Her pulse did the funny little jig that had become familiar during her time in Paris. *He* did that to her.

She looked up into burning dark eyes. Concern etched

his face. She wanted to assure him everything would be okay, erase the pain that turned his mouth into a sombre line, but she couldn't find any words to make this right.

Instead, she conjured a half-smile. 'Thank you, Thierry.' She paused, letting herself enjoy the sound of his name on her tongue. Soon she'd have no reason to use it, once she was back home. She shifted, forcing her heavy eyelids up, squaring her shoulders. 'It's thoughtful of you. I'd very much like to stay the night.'

Her hands tightened on the T-shirt. So what if a night of being cared for made the solitude she faced later harder to bear? She'd rather experience these past couple of hours with him, even if only in his apartment, not sharing his bed, than the emptiness of that soulless hotel room.

But it was more than a couple of hours. When the sun rose so did Imogen, staggering a little, groping along the wall as she made her way to the bathroom.

The headache was back. Amazingly, it was the first in weeks, but it clawed at her skull as if some giant bird of prey dug hot talons into her brain.

She was back in bed when the bedroom door opened. Thierry's hair was damp and gleaming black. Tailored charcoal trousers clung to solid thighs and his crisp white shirt revealed a V of tanned flesh where the buttons hadn't all been done up. Despite the miasma of pain, Imogen felt a twinge of pleasure at the sight of him. She regretted now that she had no photo of him. Taking holiday snaps to pore over later hadn't occurred to her. She'd spent her time trying not to think about the future.

'How are you doing?' He sat on the bed and even through the light blanket she felt his warmth. She wanted to snuggle into him and hold him tight, never let go.

She snared a breath. She had to be stronger than that. She couldn't rely on him or anyone else.

Imogen looked up through slitted eyes and read worry on his broad brow.

'Fine,' she lied, loath to make that worry worse. 'Just tired.' That, at least, was true. A week of little sleep had left her on the edge of exhaustion.

A hand brushed the hair from her face, and her eyes fluttered closed. His touch was so soothing, so gentle. Yearning rose in a welling tide.

'Are you sure that's all? Do you need a doctor?'

Her eyes sprang open to find him leaning closer, the spicy fresh scent of his skin making her nostrils flare.

'No doctor. I've had enough of them for now.' Sydney would be soon enough. 'I'm fine, really, just tired.'

'I've brought croissants and juice if you're hungry.' She shook her head, and he frowned. 'I have appointments all morning. I could put them off.'

'Don't be silly.' She tried to sound firm and strong but she suspected her voice was too hoarse. 'I'll get up now and head back to my hotel.'

'You really think I'd let you?'

'Sorry?' Was the ache in her head making her hear things?

'What sort of man do you take me for?' Anger sparked in that gleaming gaze. 'You'll stay here while you're in Paris. I'm just trying to work out whether I can leave you this morning.'

'Of course you can leave me. I'm not your responsibility.' Her brain told her to move, not loll here basking in his concern. But her aching head and tired body didn't want to move. She forced herself to pluck at the blanket, lifting it, ready to get up.

A hard hand clasped her wrist, forcing it and the blanket back down.

'Don't.' His voice caressed rather than ordered, and to her shock, awareness, acute and devastating, jagged through her. 'We'll argue about it later, when you have more energy.' He stroked her hair again and there was magic in his touch. She felt the tension rolling away in little waves. 'For now you need sleep. Promise me you'll stay here till I come back.'

It was pure weakness, she knew, but Imogen was barely surprised to hear the whisper emerge from her lips. 'Just for a while, then.'

When she finally woke, late in a golden afternoon, she was surprised to find herself refreshed, without that horrible hangover feeling after too much pain. Thankful for small mercies, she headed to the bathroom, only to discover her toiletries bag sitting there, and her hair brush. Dazed, she swivelled, looking back through the door to the bedroom. Her suitcase lay, unzipped, on the other side of the room.

He'd gone to her hotel and collected her belongings?

How had he done it? Surely there were rules about not giving strangers access to other people's hotel rooms?

Imogen's brow pleated as she tried to work out how Thierry had done it. And why. It was high-handed, and she should be annoyed, but right now the thought of getting into fresh clothes was just too appealing.

Shaking her head, she stripped off, stepping into the marble-lined shower and a stream of blissfully warm water. She'd work it all out when she was fully awake. But she'd bet Thierry's ability to access her things had something to do with that combination of innate authority and his bone-melting smile. No doubt the hotel employee he'd approached was female.

The thought stirred unwelcome feelings. A jab of what felt like jealousy.

Imogen caught herself up sharply. She had no right to jealousy. Thierry had never been hers in any real sense. Anyway, she wouldn't be with him long enough to worry about other women.

Emerging from the bathroom, she automatically reached

for jeans, then paused as she noticed the gorgeous light of late afternoon slanting in the big windows.

She'd been too exhausted yesterday to worry about anything but confronting Thierry and breaking her news. Now she needed to book a flight to Sydney since she had Thierry's word he'd care for their baby.

Which meant this could be her last evening in Paris.

Firming her lips, she put the jeans down and delved into the big suitcase. If this was her last night here…

Fifteen minutes later she stared at herself in the mirror. Izzy's dress in uncrushable scarlet lace clung more than Imogen had anticipated. And it was more suited to evening than late afternoon.

But she didn't care. Red would give her energy and the bravado she needed. Besides, she'd always loved the colour, even though back home she would never consider it. It was so attention-grabbing. So not her.

She loved it. Her last night in Paris; she refused to spend it looking like some quaking little mouse.

Thierry looked up at the sound of footsteps. Not merely footsteps but the tap of high heels, if he was any judge, which he was. His lovers all wore heels. Except Imogen, he realised. She'd been just as likely to turn up wearing flats or tennis shoes, because she was as interested in hot-air ballooning and picnicking as she was in dancing and dining.

No tennis shoes now. His heart revved to a thundering roar as a vision in red appeared in the doorway. Voluptuous, glorious, sexy as hell. The colour was a perfect contrast to the creamy swell of her breasts above the low, square-cut neckline.

She'd left her hair down. It rippled in ebony silk waves around her shoulders.

Thierry's groin tightened. Imogen only wore her hair loose in bed. That had been his secret pleasure, inhaling its indefinable sweet fragrance, rubbing it between his fingers, feeling its caress on his bare skin as they made love.

His gaze dropped to the hemline above her knees and her long, shapely legs. To scarlet stilettos.

His breath rushed out like air from a punctured balloon. Arousal vied with disbelief.

How could she look this way when she was *dying*? The word hung like a dark stain on his consciousness, tearing at his innards, making his gut writhe in denial.

All night and day he'd fought to come to grips with her news. Even now part of him rejected the prognosis as impossible. *Not Imogen*.

'You look stunning.' The words jerked out hoarsely.

She stopped, eyes rounding. 'I do?' Something that might have been pleasure flitted across her face. 'Thank you. I needed something to give me courage for my last night in Paris. I wanted to look...' she shrugged '...well.'

Instantly, guilt rose. Because he was busy lusting after a fatally ill woman. Because he couldn't get up from the seat where he was working on a report for fear she'd see just how well he thought she looked. He scrubbed a hand across his jaw, trying to reorient himself.

'You look more than well. You look blooming.' The red brought colour to her cheeks and the long sleep had lessened the shadows beneath her fine eyes. Savagely he squashed the temptation to stride across and haul her to him, to claim those lips he knew would be soft and inviting, to explore that glorious body.

Because she was dying. The word scourged his brain.

'Sorry? I missed that.' He knew she'd spoken but the rush of blood in his ears had deafened him.

'I asked if you have wi-fi. I need to book my flight home.' She lifted one hand and rubbed her bare arm, as if to counteract a chill. 'I *should* argue about the fact you collected my luggage without permission. And I should move back to the hotel.' She paused, turning towards the window. 'But I don't want to waste time. This will probably be my last night in France and I've got other things to do.'

'Other things?' Dressed like that? He shot to his feet, his papers sliding to the floor. 'Like what?' The way she looked, she'd have men clustered around her the moment she stepped out the door.

A tiny, self-conscious smile lit her face, and Thierry felt as if someone had reached in and grabbed his innards. How much longer would she be able to smile like that?

'I was so busy when I was here last time, I never took one of those dinner cruises on the Seine, even though it was on my list of things to do.'

Was that a hint of a blush? Was she too thinking of all the things they'd done instead of cruising the river?

It was on the tip of Thierry's tongue to say those cruises were crowded with tourists, and the loudspeaker commentary would detract from the ambience of the evening, but he firmed his lips. He wasn't going to spoil it for her.

'So, wi-fi?' She moved farther into the room and Thierry had to force his gaze up to her face instead of on the undulating curves outlined in the tight red dress.

He dragged open his collar as heat rose. She looked so sultry and alluring it was hard to believe she carried a new life inside. Or that she was gravely ill.

Even his lawyer's dire warnings about paternity tests wouldn't stop him doing what he could for her. He'd been told he had no duty to her legally. But legalities weren't the issue.

'I can do better than that.' He cleared his throat, conscious his voice sounded gruff. 'I'll have my PA make the arrangements if you bring me your passport. She can book a dinner cruise too.'

'She's still working?' Imogen glanced at her watch.

'I usually keep much longer business hours than this.' He'd cut them back when she'd been in Paris last time, working like a demon all day so he could have his evenings free for her. He stooped to pick up the reports he'd dropped and put them on the table. 'Mademoiselle Janvier will still be at work, believe me.'

'As long as I can pay you for the air fare.'

Thierry looked at her, standing proud in her high heels. This woman admitted she needed courage to face her last night in Paris and that she was short of cash, yet she refused to take charity when it would be so easy and reasonable.

His heart dipped and skidded to a halt, only to start up again in an uneven rhythm.

She was a wonder. He'd never known a woman like her. Except perhaps his *grand-mère*, whose petite size and exquisite manners hid a spine of steel.

Would he exhibit such courage in Imogen's situation? It was one thing to risk his neck in some dangerous adventure, quite another to be stoic in the face of a steady, fatal decline. The thought of what she faced curdled his blood.

'I'll make sure you get the bill for any air fare.' As if that was going to happen. 'Now, if you'll get me your passport, I'll contact my PA.'

'I don't know which is better, the *tarte tatin* or the scenery.' Imogen sat back, replete, looking from her empty plate to the beautiful, floodlit bridge they were about to pass under. A series of pale, carved stone heads stared sightlessly out from its side, intriguing her. 'I knew the Eiffel Tower looked terrific lit up, and Notre Dame and all the other buildings, but these bridges are amazing.'

Silently she vowed to store the memory of this last night with Thierry to pull out and remember later, when her condition worsened and the shadows closed in.

'So…' Beside her Thierry lifted his glass and sipped. 'It's not the company you're enjoying?'

When he looked at her that way, his eyes gleaming and that hint of a cleft grooving his cheek as he smiled, Imogen's heart leapt. In the subtle light of the lanterns on deck he looked suavely sophisticated. Yet Imogen knew from experience that his rangy frame, which showed off a dinner jacket to perfection, was actually a symphony of lean, hard-packed muscle and bone. He might look indolent but the man beneath the sophisticated exterior had the body of an athlete, and such strength…

Desperately, she dragged her eyes away. Pregnancy, like illness, had no effect on her attraction to him. If anything her response was sharper, more urgent. Because she'd developed a craving for his love-making and, just as importantly, because he made her feel *special*.

'Are you after a compliment?' Imogen forced herself to smile, hiding her tumble of emotions. Desire, gratitude, piercing regret and that undercurrent of fear. Once she left him she'd face her future alone. She squared her shoulders. 'It's wonderful of you to make my last night in Paris so memorable. I can't tell you how much it means.'

'You already have.' A casual gesture dismissed what he'd done as negligible. But Imogen was no fool. She'd been about to use the last of her available money to pay for a package tourist-trip. Instead, she'd found herself on a private luxury cruiser where they were the only guests, waited on by superb staff and eating one of the best meals of her life. The cost must have been exorbitant.

She leaned forward, reaching for Thierry's arm, till she realised what she was doing and grabbed her water glass instead.

'Don't brush it off as nothing, Thierry. What you've done…' To her horror she felt her throat thicken. 'You should at least let me thank you.'

Over the rim of his glass, Thierry's eyes locked with hers and a tingle of sensation shot through her, spreading to her breasts before arrowing to her womb. Imogen sucked in a stunned breath. Her body's urgent response to him threatened to unravel her totally.

Even the knowledge her condition had apparently killed

his desire for her couldn't stop that throb of feminine wanting. She'd read his closed expression and understood he
saw her as a victim, a figure of pity, not a desirable woman.

'You want to thank me?' He put his glass down and
leaned close. Too close, but she couldn't seem to pull back.
'Good. Because there's something I want you to do.'

'There is?' She couldn't imagine what. Unless, of
course, it was the DNA test to prove paternity. She'd heard
there were risks involved with those during pregnancy but
if it meant giving her child a secure future...

'Yes.' He paused so long tension tightened the bare skin
of her shoulders. 'I want you to marry me.'

There was a thud and cold liquid spilled onto her thigh.
Vaguely Imogen was aware of Thierry reaching out to grab
her water glass before it could roll onto the deck.

She didn't move, just sat, goggling.

'Ah, thank you.' He spoke to the waiter who appeared
out of nowhere to mop the tablecloth and clear the plates.
All the while Thierry sat there, leaning back now, one arm
looped casually over the back of his chair, watching her.

The waiter left.

'What did you say?' Her voice was a croak from constricted muscles.

'I want us to marry. This week.'

He looked so relaxed, as if he'd merely commented on
the quality of the meal they'd shared, or on the beautiful
old buildings floodlit along the banks of the Seine.

Her pulse fluttered like a mad thing. 'You can't be serious.'

'Never more so.' They approached another bridge and
for a few moments were bathed in light. That was when
she saw it, the glint of determination in those espresso-
dark eyes. And the arrogant thrust of his chin.

Imogen wasn't aware of moving but she heard a scrape
and suddenly she was on her feet, stumbling for the deck's
rail. She clutched it with hands that shook.

She didn't know what she felt. This was one shock too many. Her legs wobbled and she had trouble dragging in enough oxygen.

'There's no need for that,' she finally gasped out. 'Is this you trying to be kind?' She didn't need pity, no matter how good his intentions.

Imogen spun around, only to find Thierry standing behind her, just a breath away. His clean scent filled her senses as she fought for air.

'Not kind. Just practical. Planning for the future.' His voice was smoothly persuasive. Dully, she wondered if he used this tone to broker his business deals. Yet, despite his calm demeanour, she sensed he wasn't as relaxed as he appeared.

Good! *Her* heart was racing like a runaway train.

Imogen shook her head. 'I don't see what's practical about it.' She licked dry lips, peering up into his shadowed features. 'When the time comes… I'll ensure you're named as the father and—'

'You think it will be that easy? Claiming the child from the other side of the world? No matter what the birth certificate says, I'll bet Australian law is every bit as complex as in France. There'll be one hurdle after another for me to claim the baby. It could take months, years.'

The baby. Not *his* baby.

What had she expected? That a mere twenty-four hours after learning he was going to be a father, Thierry would have the same powerful connection she felt for the tiny life inside her? Of course it was too much to ask. All she could do was hope that with time that would change.

'Do you want to risk the possibility your baby will be put in care while the legalities are sorted out?'

Pain scoured her, as if someone took a rusty blade and scraped it through her womb. Her palm found her belly, pressing tenderly as if to make sure that little life was safe inside.

A large hand, warm and callused, covered hers, splaying gently across her abdomen. She blinked and looked up into unreadable eyes.

'If we marry there will be no legal hurdles. I'll be responsible for our child. There will be no waiting, no complications. Only what's best for the baby.' Thierry's voice dropped to a low, crooning note that flowed through her like molten chocolate. Or maybe that was the effect of his touch, so real, so *sure*.

'You know there's a chance the baby might not survive?' She choked back the horror that had haunted her since she'd learned of her pregnancy. The fear that her child might die simply because she wouldn't live long enough for it to survive.

In the gloom away from the lights, she could just make out the fierce jut of Thierry's hard jaw.

When he spoke his voice held an edge she couldn't identify. 'As your husband, I'll be in a position to do everything possible for it. And for you.'

For one enticing moment Imogen let herself imagine leaning on Thierry as she had today, allowing him to take care of her. But ultimately they were strangers.

'I don't belong here, Thierry. My home is in Australia.'

'Yet you admit you've got no one to look after you there.'

'You think I came to Paris to find someone who'd look after me?' She tried to free her hand from his but he simply pressed closer, crowding her against the railing. 'I'm Australian. I belong there.'

'And who will care for you?' His words were like soft blows, hammering at her. 'You have no family. Have you close friends who'll be there whenever you need them? Have you got *anyone*?'

Said like that, he made her sound so pathetic. 'My really good friends have all moved away with jobs or family.' And, while she got on well with her work colleagues, this last year she'd been so wrapped up in grief after Izzy's death, then busy caring for her mother, that she'd got out of the habit of accepting social invitations. She'd effectively cut herself off. 'But I'll be fine. The health service—'

'I'm not talking about people paid to look after you.' His fingers closed around hers and he lifted her hand between them. To her surprise he planted her palm against his mouth and pressed a kiss to it. A kiss that sent heat and wonder coursing through her, reminding her she wasn't dead yet.

'I'm talking about someone who will be there for you. Someone who can deal with the medicos when you're too weary. Someone who'll be on hand to look after our child.'

Imogen's heart swelled. Put that way, the offer was irresistible.

'You know I'm right, Imogen.' His lips moved against her sensitive palm and the low burr of his voice curled around her like an embrace. And something inside, some selfish, needy part of her, urged her to accept.

Silently, she nodded.

An instant later his arms closed about her, pulling her against his hard chest.

Relief filled her. She just hoped she wasn't making a mistake they'd both regret.

CHAPTER SIX

By Saturday they were married.

Thierry steered his car through the congestion of central Paris, hyperaware of the woman beside him, her belongings stored neatly in the back.

He was a married man.

Married and expecting a child.

His hands clamped the wheel. Sweat beaded his hairline and something like panic stirred. Him—responsible for raising a child? The notion was so far out of left field, he still couldn't quite believe it. He could face any number of extreme sports with a thrill of anticipation, yet the idea of being solely responsible for another life filled him with trepidation. He had no experience with kids, no desire for...

He caught the direction of his thoughts and cut it off. Shame pierced him, curdling his belly. So what if he knew nothing about child-rearing? He'd adapt. He'd take it one step at a time, just as he had when forced by injury to give up competitive skiing, and when he'd taken charge of the ailing family company. He had no right to complain, not when Imogen...

No, he refused to go there, at least today. For now it was enough that she was here with him. He was doing what needed to be done, despite his legal advisor's warnings.

He'd never had much time for lawyers. But to be fair the old man had probably been as stunned by his news as Thierry's family would be.

Thierry was the bachelor least likely to tie the knot, much to his grandparents' despair. In his youth he'd vowed never to settle for any other woman since he couldn't have Sandrine. Looking back on that time now, he felt merely curiosity and a twinge of remembered disappointment at the hurt which he'd thought had blighted his life.

How naïve he'd been. Far from being destroyed, his life had been filled to the brim. He'd spent the intervening years doing exactly what he loved—feeding his appetite for pleasure: sport, women, adventure.

'You look happy.'

He turned to see Imogen scrutinising him, as if trying to read him. Why wouldn't she? She'd put her life in his hands, and their child's life.

She'd put on a good show of being indomitable these past few days, but her tiredness betrayed her. He couldn't bear to think of where that would inevitably lead. The knowledge had been like acid eating at him ever since he'd heard. He'd never felt so appallingly *useless*.

'Getting out of the city is cause for celebration, don't you think?' He forced a smile and was rewarded with a slight upward tilt of her lips.

He'd always liked the way she responded to his smile, even when, as now, he guessed she felt out of sorts.

Out of sorts! His smile twisted.

'You don't like the city? I think Paris is fabulous.'

Thierry shrugged, focusing his attention on the road and the van trying to change lanes into a non-existent space between a motorcycle and another car.

'To visit, perhaps, but where we're going there'll be pure air. No fumes or road noise. No crowds either.'

'I thought you enjoyed socialising.'

He shrugged, taking action to avoid a kamikaze motorcyclist. 'I love a good party, but after a while I've had enough of the chatter.'

'So what do you like, then?'

A sideways glance showed her turned towards him, her gaze curious, as if she really wanted to know.

It struck him that most of the women he'd known had had their own agendas—to be seen at the right parties or with the right people, the heir to the Girard fortune being one of the right people. They'd had fun together but how many had tried to know Thierry the man rather than Thierry the CEO or Thierry the scion of one of France's elite families? Or, in the old days, Thierry the famous athlete?

'Surely it's not a hard question?'

Not hard at all. 'Skiing. Downhill and very, very fast.' Once he'd thought that was his destiny. He'd been in the peak of his form training for the Winter Olympics before a busted leg had put an end to those dreams.

'What else?'

Another glance showed she hadn't taken her eyes off him. Of course she wanted to know. He'd be the one raising their child. His hands tightened on the wheel.

'White-water rafting. Rally driving. Rock climbing.'

'You don't like to be still.'

'You could say that. Except for hot-air ballooning. There's nothing quite like that for getting a little perspective in your life.' He didn't add that a lot of his balloon treks took him to inhospitable, often dangerous places where tourists rarely went.

'And when you're not outdoors?'

'These days I'm usually working.' In the past he'd have unwound in the company of some gorgeous woman but lately his interest had waned. Until Imogen. Even today, in jeans and a plain shirt, her lithe curves made his hands itch for physical contact.

Not even telling himself that it was wrong to lust after a dying woman, a woman relying on him, could kill that hot flare of hunger.

'What about you, Imogen? What do you like to do? I don't mean the things on your travel list.' It struck him suddenly that hers really had been a bucket list to be accomplished before she died. The realisation was like an icy hand curling gnarled fingers around his chest, squeezing till his lungs burned.

'You mean, in my ordinary life?'

Thierry nodded, not trusting his voice.

'The list is pretty ordinary, like me. No white-water rafting.'

'*Ordinary* isn't the way I'd describe you, Imogen.' Not with her zest for life, her sense of humour and that entrancing mix of pragmatism and wide-eyed enthusiasm. As for her body... He couldn't go there, not if he wanted to keep his wits on the traffic.

She laughed, but the smoky quality of her voice held a harsh rasp. 'I suppose you think I'm more like a walking disaster zone. Suddenly you've been saddled with—'

'Don't!' Thierry dragged in a breath that grated across his throat. This wasn't the place to rehash their debate about her being a burden. He knew this was the right thing and he refused to resile from that. He forced a smile into his voice. 'You don't get out of answering that easily. Tell me at least three things that make you happy.'

In his peripheral vision, he saw Imogen slump a little in her seat. Then she turned to stare out the window.

'Books. I love reading, anything from romance to history or biography.'

'And? That's only one.'

She hesitated. 'Numbers. I've always liked numbers. There's something...comfortable about working with figures and finding the patterns that create order out of chaos. I suppose that's why I went into accounting.'

Thierry nodded. His cousin, Henri, was the same. Give him a spreadsheet and he was happy. The trouble was, though Henri was a genius with figures, he showed little aptitude for management. Lately it had become obvious that Thierry's plan of leaving the family company in his charge was fraught with problems.

'And the third?'

'Baking. Well, cooking generally, but baking specifically.'

'What do you bake?' Thierry was intrigued. He didn't know anyone who cooked for pleasure.

He thought of Jeanne, who'd been his grandparents' cook as long as he could remember. She was fiercely protective of her domain, a dumpy little woman with arms as strong as any farm labourer, and fingers that could pinch a boy's ears painfully if he wasn't quick enough stealing fresh-baked pastries. As far as he could tell, she had nothing in common with Imogen.

'Anything. Kneading bread dough is therapeutic but I love making sweet things, like baklava or Danishes. I always get requests at work for my honey-chocolate sponge cake.'

How apt that she tasted like one of her pastries—of vanilla and sugar. Except Imogen was more delectable than any cake he'd ever eaten.

It had been days since he'd tasted her. Yet, despite his determination not to press her when she was unwell, Thierry's craving for her sweet lips had grown, not eased, with abstinence.

'So, I'm pretty boring, really.'

He flicked on the car's indicator and changed lanes, accelerating as they left the city behind.

'You're anything but boring.' Thierry paused, mulling over what she'd told him. 'You like being at home.'

'I suppose so.'

'Tell me about it. What's your home like?'

Imogen shifted in her seat. 'I was saving up for a place of my own when this… When I decided to come to France. I'd been renting, sharing a flat, but I moved back in with my mother while she was ill.'

In other words she'd nursed her mother through her decline. What must it be like, after watching her mother's fatal deterioration, to know in intimate detail what she herself could expect?

Thierry put his foot to the floor and for a short time focused on the satisfying distraction of speed. But it didn't work. His thoughts kept circling back to Imogen.

'Your family home, then. What was it like?'

Again that short laugh, a little ragged around the edges. 'We didn't have one. We moved too often.'

He shot her a questioning look.

'My mother worked hard to qualify as a teacher when Isabelle and I were little, but she had trouble getting a permanent position. She never said so but it might have been because of the demands of raising twins. Anyway, she worked as a casual teacher, filling in where needed, sometimes for a term at a time if we were lucky.'

'In Sydney?'

'All around the state, though in later years she worked in Sydney. By then she'd come to enjoy the challenge of dealing with new pupils and new surroundings all the time. She chose to keep working on short-term placements.'

'Maybe that explains the bond between you all.'

'Sorry?'

'When you speak of your mother or sister I hear affection in your voice. I get the impression you were close.'

She was silent for a few moments. 'I suppose it did draw us closer together in some ways.'

'But not all?' Thierry passed a slow-moving truck then rolled his shoulders. Already he felt a familiar sense of release at leaving Paris.

'Isabelle thrived on new places, making new friends, starting afresh. She was the outgoing one.'

'You're not outgoing?' He thought of her laughter the night they'd met in Paris, the confident way she'd bantered with him. Plus there was the enthusiastic way she embraced every new experience.

Out of the corner of his eye he saw her rub her palm

down her jeans. He jerked his attention back to the road, before his mind wandered to places it shouldn't.

'I'm the reserved one, the cautious twin. Izzy would walk into a new classroom and by the end of the day she'd have five new best friends. It would take me weeks or months, and by that stage we'd usually be on the move again. My sister thought it a grand adventure but I…suppose I just wanted more stability and certainty.'

Hence the affinity for creating order out of chaos with numbers. Thierry tried to imagine what it must have been like for such a child, averse to change, being carted around the countryside. It didn't escape him that her other interests—reading and baking—were home-based. It was a wonder she'd crossed the globe in search of adventure.

As if she'd read his thoughts, she spoke. 'My sister followed her dream and took the gamble of coming to France, hoping to work in fashion, though everyone said her chances were slim. I was the one who stayed where I was.'

'I was always looking for adventure,' he said then paused, surprised he'd shared that.

'What sort of adventure?'

'Anything to break the monotony of home.' He sensed her surprise and shot her an amused glance. 'My childhood was the opposite of yours. Everything in my world was so stable it was almost petrified. Things were done the same way they'd always been done.'

If it had been good enough for the Girards to dine in the blue salon a hundred and fifty years ago, the Girards would continue to do so, even if it was a cold room that missed the evening sun in summer. Male Girards entered the diplomatic corps or the military before taking their place managing one of the family enterprises and there was an end to it. Rules covered everything, from his choice of friends to his behaviour in public and in private.

His parents had died when he was a baby so he'd been brought up by his strict grandparents. A psychologist might say he'd rebelled against their outmoded rules and restrictions. But Thierry was pretty sure he'd simply been born with a thirst for adventure.

'We weren't big on family traditions.' Imogen's voice was soft. 'Except spending Christmas Day together, and Easter. Even in the last couple of years the three of us would have an Easter egg hunt in the garden.'

'Your mother too?'

'Of course. She loved chocolate.'

Thierry tried and failed to imagine his *grand-mère* hunting for eggs in their exquisitely kept grounds.

'That sounds like fun. I've never been on an Easter egg hunt.'

'You haven't?' Her face swung towards him again. 'It's not a French tradition?'

'For some. But not in the Girard family.' Easter had meant his best behaviour and, of course, formal clothes. He couldn't recall a time when he hadn't been expected to wear a tie to dinner. No wonder yanking his top button undone was always the first thing he did on leaving the office.

He saw her hand swipe the leg of her jeans again. 'You make your family sound a little daunting.' She paused. 'Are they?' Was that concern in her voice?

Daunting? He supposed his grandparents were, with their formality and strict adherence to old ways, but for all that he loved them.

'They'll welcome you with open arms. They've all but given up on the idea of me bringing home a bride. But you needn't worry for now. My grandparents spend the summer at their villa on the south coast. And my cousins, aunts and uncles live elsewhere.'

'You share a house with your grandparents?' Surprise tinged her tone. Who could blame her? Until four years ago he'd lived his own life, visiting the Girard estate only occasionally. But it was easier to manage the estate and the family's diverse commercial interests from there since that was where the main offices were located.

'You think it unusual for a thirty-four-year-old?' His smile was tight as he remembered how reluctant that move back home had been. 'My grandfather had a stroke a few years ago and they needed me. But don't worry; we'll be quite private. There's plenty of space.' Even when his grandparents were in residence the place was so big he could go for weeks without seeing them.

Thierry considered explaining to Imogen just what to expect. But she'd been pale today, admitting to a little nausea, which to his astonishment had evoked a visceral pang of possessiveness in him. As if it made the idea of their child suddenly more concrete. She'd been nervous too. Better not to overload her with details. He couldn't guess whether she'd be excited or retreat mentally, as she'd done a few times when unsure of herself.

'Why don't you close your eyes and rest? We'll be travelling for a while.'

The sun still shone brightly when Imogen woke. Her head lolled against the backrest. She hadn't slept well lately but the rhythm of the car had lulled her into relaxation.

She blinked. The rhythm had changed, as if the road surface was different. When she looked through the windscreen she realised they'd left the main *autoroute*. They were in what looked like a park. Great swathes of grass with tall, mature trees dotted the scene. They clustered close to the road.

She frowned. Though paved, it was a narrow road with no lines marked.

'Are we almost there?'

'Almost. You'll see it soon.'

It? Imogen felt befuddled, shreds of sleep still clinging. Presumably he meant the town where he…

She gasped as the car topped a rise and the vista opened up. Her eyes popped.

'You live in a castle?' It couldn't be...but the road they were on—a private road, she realised belatedly—headed straight for the next rise where the sun shone off massive walls of darkest honey gold.

She swung around to Thierry but he looked unmoved, as if driving home to a medieval fortification was an everyday occurrence.

She sat back in her seat, her brain buzzing.

'I don't suppose your place is off to the side somewhere? An estate manager's house or something?'

His mouth quirked up in a smile, and he slanted an amused look at her. She felt its impact deep inside as her internal organs began to liquefy.

He only has to smile and you lose it.

No wonder you let him convince you to go along with this absurd idea.

Even now, hours after the short civil ceremony, she had trouble believing she'd actually married Thierry.

'Are you disappointed? Would you rather live in a cottage?'

Slowly, she shook her head, drinking in his profile as he turned back to the road. A castle. Maybe that explained that air of assurance she'd noticed in him from the first. It was more than just the insouciance that came from looking staggeringly handsome in bespoke formal wear, or the comfortable-in-his-skin athleticism of his magnificent body. It was something bred in the bone. And then there were his strongly sculpted features. Were they the result of generations of aristocratic breeding?

'Imogen? You don't like it?'

She turned her head. The walls rose several stories and were punctuated, not with tiny arrow slits, but with large windows that must let in a lot of light. Yet at the corners of the building were sturdy round towers topped with conical roofs, like an illustration of Rapunzel's story.

'I don't know. I can't imagine actually living in a castle.'

'We call it a *château*.'

'Okay, then. I can't imagine living in a *château*.' Imogen half expected to wake up and find she'd dreamt it. A *château*! The word conjured images of royal courts and lavish indulgence. Could anything be more different from the two-bedroom flat she'd shared in suburban Sydney?

'It's like living anywhere else except it costs a lot more to heat and the maintenance bills are a nightmare. But don't worry.' Imogen heard the current of amusement in Thierry's voice. 'It's been modernised through the years. It's even got hot- and cold-running water.'

'I wouldn't expect anything less.' She recalled Thierry's Paris apartment where her bathroom had been expensively modern bordering on sybaritic decadence. He might have restless energy and a hard body sculpted into muscle, but he was a man with a strongly sensuous streak.

Imogen gave a little shiver and clasped her hands together, trying to evict memories of his sensuality and how he'd uncovered a purely hedonistic side to her she'd never known.

'Has your family owned it long?' Her gaze drifted from the fairy-tale towers across the impressive façade.

'A couple of hundred years.'

Tension clamped her shoulders. She'd realised she was marrying into money, but the aristocracy as well? She was going to be totally out of her depth.

Not for long, reminded that persistent inner voice. The reminder dampened her momentary sense of rising panic.

The car slowed and pulled to a halt in front of the imposing building, gravel crunching under the wheels. 'Welcome to your new home, Imogen.'

Her throat clenched. He really was a man in a million. He'd taken her news with something close to equanimity, only the occasional flicker of emotion in his dark eyes betraying his shock. More, he'd not only agreed to take care of their child, he'd taken it upon himself to provide for her too.

'You didn't need to do all this.' She waved futilely. She could have been back in Sydney by now, alone. Instead, he'd brought her to his family home. That meant so much.

'Of course I do. You're carrying my child.'

Of course. His child. She had to keep remembering this was about their baby. She was just along for the ride.

Imogen bit her lip, swallowing a laugh that held no humour.

'Are you okay?' His touch on her arm was light, but she felt the imprint of his fingers in each riotously sensitive nerve ending.

'Perfect.' She turned and gave him her best smile. The one she'd practised so often before heading out to some large social event. She must be slipping, for Thierry didn't look convinced, just sat, watching, as if he read the unease and dismay she tried to hide.

'What's wrong?' Those espresso-dark eyes saw too much.

A litany of worries ran through her head. Her baby's health, her own illness, staying in France for these final months instead of Australia, where at least she spoke the language. Being a burden to Thierry and an unwelcome surprise to his family. If she wasn't careful all those concerns would submerge her just when she needed her strength.

'Neither of us really wants this marriage.' She shook her head. 'It's not what you'd planned for yourself.'

Thierry's scrutiny sharpened and his eyes narrowed. She couldn't read his expression.

'Things don't always work out the way we expect but I'm a firm believer in making the best of any situation.' His hand closed on hers, long fingers threading through hers. 'This is the right thing, Imogen. Trust me.'

CHAPTER SEVEN

IMOGEN PUT THE wicker basket down and sank onto the garden seat. Typically, it wasn't a bare stone seat. Someone had placed cushions on all the outdoor seats, in case she or Thierry or some unexpected visitor chose to stop.

Everything at the *château* was like that—not just elegant and expensive but beautifully cared for. No detail was too small, no comfort overlooked, from the scented bath oils made from herbs grown at the *château*, to crisp white sheets that smelled of sunshine and lavender from the purpose-grown drying hedge. Even the discreetly efficient lift to the top floors was hidden behind ancient panelling so as not to interfere with the ambience.

Imogen closed her eyes, soaking up the late-afternoon sunshine, enjoying the sense of utter peace. There was no sound but the drowse of bees and in the distance a motor. A car maybe, or a tractor. She inhaled, drinking in the heady scent of roses, and felt herself relax.

She'd done the right thing.

Of course she had!

It didn't matter that she felt like she'd forced Thierry into a corner so he'd been obliged to take responsibility for their child. She'd had no other option.

Nor did it matter that she was an outsider here. What mattered was doing right by her baby. If that meant spending her last months in France rather than her own country, so be it.

As if it was hard, living here at the *château*!

For days she'd rested, sleeping more than she could remember ever having done. Jeanne, the Girard's formidable cook-housekeeper, seemed to have made it her mission to tempt Imogen's appetite with one delicious treat after another. And when, with a knowing look, she'd seen Imogen turn pale at the pungent scent of fresh coffee, she'd begun providing herbal teas and delicate, light-as-air crackers that had helped settle Imogen's stomach.

Her thoughts eddied as she drifted towards sleep. It was so easy to relax here. So very peaceful.

The crunch of footsteps woke her. And the murmur of voices. Thierry's voice, a low, liquid blur of sound that flowed through her like luscious caramel pooling deep inside. Imogen kept her eyes closed just a little longer, reluctant to move. Listening to his voice was one of her greatest pleasures. Thierry could read weather forecasts or even tax law aloud and she'd melt into a puddle of pure bliss.

'Imogen?'

She opened her eyes to find him standing before her. He looked every bit as delicious as he sounded. His clothes were plain, tailored trousers and a pale shirt undone at the throat, but there was nothing ordinary about the man wearing them. He looked the epitome of hard athleticism from his solid thighs to his straight shoulders and every hard inch between.

Imogen gave a little quiver of pleasure. Every time she saw him it happened, even now. He made her silly heart stutter.

'I'd like you to meet my grandmother.' He gestured to his side, and her gaze swung to the tiny, grey-haired lady she hadn't even noticed before. A lady with a capital L, Imogen realised in the split second it took to register her immaculate hair and make-up, the sophisticated dark suit that screamed couture and the lustre of elegant pearls at her throat. She wore stockings despite the heat and gorgeous black patent shoes that Imogen wouldn't dare wear on gravel for fear of scuffing them.

Imogen shot to her feet, managing to tip over the basket of roses beside her. Secateurs clattered to the ground.

Eyes as dark as Thierry's, but much sharper, surveyed her from head to toe.

Imogen felt a flush rise to crest in her burning cheeks. She knew her shirt was rumpled, her jeans faded and one canvas shoe had got caked in mud when she'd ventured too near an ornamental pond. Faced with the other woman's elegance, Imogen felt a complete frump. It was one thing to borrow her sister's creations and play at dressing up in Paris. It was quite another to achieve that bone-deep level of stylish sophistication.

'*Bonjour*, Madame Girard.' Imogen paused, searching for the words she'd memorised: *it's very nice to meet you… 'Je suis ravie de vous rencontrer.'* Unexpected nerves made her stumble over even that simple phrase. Quickly, she put out her hand, only to whip it back when she realised she still wore gardening gloves.

'It's a pleasure to meet you at last too.' The other woman's English was crisp if heavily accented. She leaned in and kissed Imogen lightly on the cheeks in a gesture that held no discernible warmth. A light fragrance, perfectly balanced and no doubt worth a fortune, wafted around her. 'We will speak in English, as it's easier for you.'

'Thank you. I'm afraid my French is non-existent.' Under the other woman's assessing scrutiny Imogen almost blurted that she'd learned Japanese and Indonesian at school, but stopped herself before she could babble. Instead, she pulled off the soiled gloves and dropped them on the seat where Thierry had righted the basket of cut flowers.

'It's important that we become better acquainted. You have married my grandson. You are part of the family now.'

Imogen searched her inflection for any hint of welcome. She found none.

'Which is why you left *Grand-père* in Provence and hot-footed it up here,' Thierry murmured. 'It's a delightful surprise to see you.'

Fine eyebrows arched. 'He wasn't up to the journey this time.' She turned to Imogen. 'My husband has been unwell and needs rest. But we felt it important that one of us came to welcome you into the family.'

If the gleam in those shrewd eyes was any indication, it was more a matter of sizing her up. Yet who could blame the older woman?

What had Imogen expected? To be greeted by Thierry's family with open arms? She suspected she was doomed to disappointment in that case.

It didn't matter what they thought of her, she reminded herself. Unless that affected her child's future. The thought stirred Imogen's protective instincts.

'It's good of you to come all this way, Madame Girard. I'm afraid the news of our marriage must have come as a surprise to Thierry's family.'

'And presumably to your own.' Those keen eyes roved Imogen's face, as if searching for clues.

'I don't have a family.' The bald statement sounded more brutal than she'd intended and she read the shock on the older woman's face. 'I mean—'

'Sadly, Imogen recently lost her mother and her sister.' Warm fingers threaded through hers, and Imogen looked up to find Thierry watching her, his smile reassuring. His hand squeezed hers, and she smiled back gratefully. She wasn't in this alone.

Nevertheless, she felt like an imposter, pretending to be his one true love, the woman he'd spend the rest of his life with.

'I'm very sorry for your loss. That must have been very difficult.'

'Thank you. It was…difficult.' Could she sound any less sophisticated in front of this stylish matriarch?

'But now you have Thierry.'

Imogen blinked. Did his grandmother think she'd married him because she was lonely? No, more likely trapped him because of his money. 'I'm a very lucky woman.'

To her surprise, she felt Thierry's warm fingers stroke her cheek. 'I'm the lucky one, *chérie*.' His voice dropped to that low, shivery note she hadn't heard in so long. Since they'd shared a bed on her first visit to Paris. Imogen swallowed hard, hit by a surge of longing so strong she found herself swaying towards him. Yet his affectionate display was obviously a show for his grandmother. Thierry didn't want to explain the exact circumstances of their marriage and nor did she.

'You always did have luck on your side, Thierry. Now, if you'll leave us alone, I'd like to get to know your wife a little better.' It wasn't a request but an order.

Thierry ignored it. 'Let's all go inside for coffee. I've no doubt Jeanne has been busy preparing something suitable from the moment you arrived.'

Imogen liked that he wanted to look after her. But she wasn't totally helpless, even if she *had* turned to him when she hadn't known what else to do.

'We'll come in soon,' she assured him. 'It would be nice if your grandmother could show me the garden. I'm sure she knows the name of those beautiful roses at the end of the walk.' The gardener had mentioned that Madame Girard herself had overseen their planting.

'You're sure?' His eyes searched her face.

She nodded.

'Then I'll see you both inside very soon. There's a call I need to get back to.'

'Go on, Thierry.' His grandmother made a shooing motion. 'I know I interrupted your work. We'll be fine. I don't intend to eat the girl.'

As soon as he was gone Madame Girard turned to her. 'I was surprised to find him in the offices. You didn't want a honeymoon?'

She didn't beat around the bush, did she? But Imogen

rather liked that. One of the reasons she felt uncomfortable at big social events was that she'd never excelled at meaningless small talk. Those nights in Paris with Thierry were an exception, when flirting with him had been as easy as breathing.

'He has a lot of work at the moment and he can do that here.' Imogen had been surprised to discover the rear of the *château* accommodated offices for staff involved in running the Girard family's commercial interests. It was there Thierry spent his days, often working late, though always coming to share meals with her.

'Nevertheless, a bride should expect more of her husband. I'll speak with him.'

Startled, Imogen saw a flash of something like disapproval in the older woman's eyes. On her behalf?

'No! Please, don't. We're content as we are.' The thought of Thierry's grandmother telling him he had to spend more time with her…

'Content? What is that? Have you no passion, girl? No fire?'

Imogen drew herself up. 'It's not a matter of passion. It's a matter of common sense. Anyone can see Thierry has a lot on his mind right now.'

And she'd added to his burdens. It was only since she'd returned to Paris that she'd begun to realise how hard he worked. When he'd been with her before, she'd seen only the carefree side of him, the man who revelled in seeing her pleasure at her first hot-air balloon ride, or tasting her first glass of champagne.

'You're willing to take second place to business while he does so?'

'I have no complaints. Thierry has responsibilities and I knew that when we married.'

'The marriage was very sudden.' Those dark eyes glinted. 'Thierry didn't tell me exactly how long you've known each other but I don't recall him mentioning your name in the past.'

Imogen stared straight back at her interrogator. 'It was a whirlwind romance.'

'I see.' She sounded as if she didn't like what she saw. 'So, perhaps you have mutual friends. Is that how you met? You moved in the same circles?' Her gaze skated over Imogen's rumpled clothes.

Imogen held the basket close, as if that could protect her from the other woman's curiosity. If only she'd been warned of the visit, she'd have dressed up. Which was probably precisely why they'd had no warning. Thierry's grandmother struck her as a very canny woman.

'No, we don't have any mutual friends. We met by chance at a party in Paris and…'

'And he swept you off your feet?'

Imogen shrugged, ignoring the trace of a blush she felt in her cheeks. 'Something like that.' Deliberately, she held the older woman's gaze.

'I see.' Madame Girard tilted her head as if to get a better view of her. 'And your work? Do you have a job?'

Imogen's hands tightened on the basket but she drew a slow breath and released it, reminding herself it was natural Thierry's grandmother wanted to know these things. Did she think Imogen was unemployed, looking for someone to sponge off? One thing was for sure, she wouldn't mistake her for one of the idle rich, not in these clothes.

'I'm an accountant. From Australia. I was visiting Paris on holiday.'

'Where you met my grandson, had a passionate affair and found yourself pregnant.'

Imogen's breath hissed in and for a moment she felt the world wobble around her.

'Come! You need to sit.' A surprisingly firm hand gripped her upper arm, guiding her back down to the seat.

'That's better.' Madame Girard took the seat beside her. 'I don't have any patience with this fainting nonsense.'

'Good.' Imogen lifted her chin. 'Because I don't faint.'

To her amazement the other woman chuckled. The sound was unexpectedly rich and appealing. 'I'm very glad to hear it.' Then she nodded. 'With some coaching, you might even do for him very well.'

'I beg your pardon?' Imogen stared, torn between relief and offence.

'Your clothes, your lack of French… We'll have to work on both if you're to take your place beside Thierry.'

Imogen blinked at the 'we'. His grandmother intended to coach her? Or had pregnancy hormones made Imogen lose the thread of the conversation?

'How did you know I was pregnant?'

'Jeanne, of course. She's been at the *château* for years. As soon as she realised…' Madame Girard gave a fluid shrug. 'Of course she contacted me.'

'Of course.' Imogen paused, caught up in an unexpected tide of relief that she had one less secret to keep from this formidable lady. More than that, sharing the news with another woman made her feel less alone. So often she wished her mother was alive to talk to about the pregnancy. She had so many hopes and fears for this baby.

She chewed her lip. Thinking about that only made everything more difficult. Instead, she should focus on politely declining any make-over attempt. It wasn't as if she'd be here long term, so there was no question of her becoming the perfect wife for Thierry.

The knowledge stabbed, the pain sharper than before. But Imogen kept her expression neutral. She wasn't ready to share *that* with Thierry's grandmother. She already felt like she'd been stripped bare.

Curiosity got the better of her. 'You don't mind that Thierry married so quickly, or that I'm pregnant?'

'I might have, until I saw the way you looked at him.' There was a glimmer of a smile in those eyes so like Thierry's.

'The way I looked at him?'

'Absolutely. The way a woman looks when she's in love.'

Imogen gave up trying to sleep. Instead, she perched on the window seat in her bedroom.

It was twilight and in the distance she saw the haze of indigo mountains. Closer to the *château* were verdant fields and she could smell that sweet scent on the evening air again. Meadow flowers or perhaps something growing in the formal gardens. To the right was a sprinkle of lights from the nearest town.

She lifted her feet, wrapping her arms around her knees, drinking in the view.

But Madame Girard's words stole her peace.

The way a woman looks when she's in love.

Had she really looked at Thierry that way?

Imogen told herself Madame Girard indulged in wishful thinking because she wanted to see her grandson happy.

The bond between the pair had been evident through the evening they'd all spent in *madame*'s apartments—in a wing of the *château* Imogen hadn't visited before. The old lady was shrewd, with a dry sense of humour that had grown on Imogen. But sentimental? Not enough to skew her judgement.

In love.

Imogen had never been truly in love. At the time she'd thought perhaps with Scott... But, though she'd been hurt by the callous way he'd dumped her, her heart hadn't broken.

She admired Thierry. She liked him and was grateful for all he was doing for her and their child. After Scott, who'd resented the increasing time she spent with her mother as she'd faded, Imogen knew how remarkable it was to find a man who didn't run from harsh reality, but helped shoulder her burdens.

How many men would have done as Thierry had?

He wasn't content simply to put his name on the marriage contract. He was meticulous about seeing to her comfort. He never missed a meal with her and his careful attentiveness should have put her at ease.

Instead, it made her restless.

Physically she felt better than she had in weeks. But emotionally? The unwanted truth hammered at her. It wasn't her luxurious surrounds that made her edgy, or meeting Thierry's grandmother. As for her illness—she hadn't precisely become accustomed to it, but she'd learned to live in the moment as much as possible.

It was Thierry who tied her stomach in knots.

She raked her hand through her hair, pulling it back from her face.

She didn't want Thierry's hospitality. Each time he solicitously held her chair at the table or opened a door for her, impatience gnawed. He was caring and charming but there was an indefinable distance between them now.

What she wanted, what she *craved*, was his touch, his passion. Not love, she assured herself, but intimacy.

When she'd had that in Paris she'd felt able to cope with the future. In some inexplicable way it had given her the strength to face what was to come. Even after all this time she still reached for him in the night, waking to a loneliness even more desolate for his absence.

Had his attraction for her been so short-lived? Or did her illness turn him off? Or her pregnancy?

Or did he hold back from her for some other reason?

A breeze wafted through the window, stirring her nightdress against her breasts and teasing her bare arms. Her eyelids flickered as she thought of Thierry and how sensitive she'd been to his lightest touch. He'd made her body come alive as never before. He'd awakened something in her that refused to go back into hibernation.

A sound drew her attention to the door connecting her room to Thierry's.

Imogen's lips firmed. She wasn't dead yet.

Thierry paused in the act of hauling off his shirt when he heard a tap on his door. Not the door to his private sitting room but the one connecting to Imogen's room. The one he'd tried to ignore since they'd arrived, knowing she slept just metres away.

He'd almost locked it so he couldn't be tempted to do something reprehensible like forget the state of her health and take what he hungered for.

He let his shirt drop back into place, even doing up some of the buttons again, which was when he noticed the tremor in his hands.

'Thierry?'

He swung around. The door was ajar, and Imogen stood there, her hair tumbling about her shoulders and breasts in shining waves of ebony.

His gut clenched and a hammering started up in his chest. It took a split second to realise it was his heart, throbbing to an urgent new beat.

'Are you okay?' He paced towards her then pulled up short. He needed distance. That pale nightdress revealed too much. Her nipples pressed, proud and erect, against the light fabric and his palms tingled as he remembered how they felt, budding in his hands. How they tasted, sweet as sugar syrup and warm woman on his tongue.

He tried but couldn't stop his gaze skating lower to the hint of the darkness at the apex of her thighs. Thierry swallowed at the memories of her naked in his bed. His lower body turned into cast metal. A film of sweat broke out across his brow and his throat turned desert dry.

'What's wrong?' His voice was hoarse. 'Do you need a doctor?'

She shook her head and, mesmerised, he watched the way those dark locks slid and separated around her pouting breasts. He knew Imogen had a body to please a man. It was only now, worn down by the weight of abstinence, that he realised it could torture just as well.

Never had he been as fervently eager for work as he had been since their wedding. He was actually grateful for the distraction it gave from his wife.

'No, I'm not sick.' Her words had that throaty edge she got when nervous or aroused. Adrenalin shot through him, and he had a battle not to cross the room and haul her close. Of course she wasn't aroused. 'I wanted to talk.'

'Talk?' The last thing he needed was an intimate chat here in his bedroom. 'Can it wait till tomorrow?'

She shook her head and his breathing stalled as he watched her hair caress and frame her beautiful breasts.

Resolutely, he reminded himself that Imogen now fitted under the category of 'duty'. She and their child were his responsibility. He couldn't let himself be distracted by selfish cravings when he had a duty to care for them both. He'd spent years in the pursuit of pleasure. He could be utterly single-minded when it came to doing what he wanted. He couldn't afford to lose focus now and give in to the urge for pleasure. He needed control, purpose, resolve.

Besides, he didn't like the morass of emotions that threatened whenever he thought of Imogen the woman, rather than Imogen his responsibility. He didn't deal in emotion, except for the frustrations and elations of his chosen sports.

'Now's not the time, Imogen. It's late.' He watched her stiffen and silently cursed his harsh tone.

He shoved his hands in his trouser pockets. As if that made it easier to resist the temptation to touch! An ache started in his jaw from clenching his teeth too tight.

'What's bothering you? Is it *Grand-mère*? I know she can be overwhelming at first but she likes you.'

'You can tell that?'

He nodded. 'I think she liked the way you spoke your mind. She isn't one for prevarication.'

'So I gathered.' Imogen gnawed the corner of her bottom lip, and he wanted to reach out and stop her.

'She offended you?'

'No. I rather liked her too, though she made me feel like a fashion disaster.'

'No one expects you to dress up all the time.' Imogen in high heels and that red, clingy dress was branded too clearly on his brain for anything like comfort. It had kept him awake too many nights. Besides, he liked her in jeans; liked the way they shaped her long legs and…

'Just as well.' Something like hurt glowed in her hazel eyes. 'I feel like a fraud going along with her plans to improve me.'

'She means well. And a tutor to help you with French is an excellent idea. I should have thought of it myself.'

'It's not that. I'd like to learn French.' Her gaze slid from his then back. The impact of those eyes on his should have knocked him back on his feet. There was so much *feeling* there. It was like looking into her soul. 'I just don't feel right, pretending I'm your wife for real.'

'You are my wife. Believe me, the ceremony was legally binding, even if it was brief.'

'But I'm not the woman who's going to be with you for the rest of your days. This is a temporary arrangement for my benefit.'

Thierry had never wanted a woman to be with him for the rest of his days. Not since Sandrine. But he couldn't say that to a woman whose life was measured in months rather than years. The truth was he'd do whatever it took to make her remaining time as easy as possible.

He didn't just lust after Imogen. He didn't just see her as a responsibility. He cared about her.

Which meant he had to keep his focus on her well-being.

'Don't forget the child is mine too. We're in this together, Imogen.'

A little of the tension eased from her features, and he was stunned at how good it felt that he'd been able to do that for her.

'You don't have to worry about anything.' He kept his voice soothing. 'I'll take care of everything.' He paused, wondering whether to tell her his news.

'What is it?' She moved away from the door, her nightgown drifting around her like temptation.

'Sorry?'

'There's something you're not saying.'

Thierry frowned. Since when had she been able to read him? He prided himself on his ability to keep his thoughts to himself.

'Nothing to worry about.' But he saw she didn't believe him. Perhaps she'd had so much bad news she now expected the worst. 'Just that I've managed to get you an appointment with one of the country's finest specialists. They're sending to Australia for your medical records.'

'I see.' Her mouth twisted, and he wanted to reach out and smooth those plump lips with his thumb, stroke her hair and tell her everything would be all right. But the hell of it was he couldn't.

'That's very good of you. Thanks.' The huskiness had gone from her voice, leaving it flat.

Thierry's muscles bunched as he fought the urge to reach for her. His embrace might soothe her temporarily but at the risk of him taking things too far. And her fragility was for once obvious in her delicate features.

'Was there anything else you wanted to talk about? My *grand-mère*, perhaps?'

'No. I just…' She paused so long he began to wonder what was wrong.

In a flurry of lace and cotton she crossed the floor, planting her hands on his tense shoulders. She was so close he felt her like the earth felt the sun, drawn to her magnetic warmth. Her lashes lifted to reveal eyes of sherry-brown spangled with green that made him think of mountain streams and ecstasy. She cupped the back of his head, narrow fingers sliding through his hair, sending rivers of molten energy straight to his groin.

'I needed to thank you.' She opened her mouth as if to say more then shut it again, her gaze zeroing on his mouth.

An instant later she'd risen on her toes, leaning in so her breasts pushed, soft and enticing, against him. Her lips were hot and sweet on his, seeking, torturing with the promise of delight.

A quake rocked him to the soles of his feet. His hands fisted in his pockets so hard he thought they might never loosen again. He breathed in her scent, tasting her on his lips, and almost lost his resolve. He wanted this so badly. He wanted so much more than he should if he was to look after her as she deserved.

A lifetime's experience in giving in to temptation had him dragging his hands out of his pockets, anchoring them at her sides where he felt the supple shift of toned muscle and the mind-destroying seduction of her in-curving waist.

Something like a growl erupted from the back of his throat and her tiny, answering moan just about undid him. All he had to do was open his mouth and…

With a surge of inexplicable strength he put her from him, stepping back so he held her at arm's length. His arms were shaking and his heart galloped out of control, but he'd done it. By the skin of his teeth he'd actually done what he should have done all along. She didn't have to thank him with the gift of her body. A better man wouldn't have countenanced it even for a second.

'There's no need to thank me, Imogen.' He barely recognised his voice as finally he managed to drag his hands away. 'Not like this.'

Something flashed in her eyes. Something swift and raw that he felt like a smack to the face. But it was gone in a second. Her flushed features set in an expression he couldn't read. Her lips were slightly parted as she dragged in air, and her hazel eyes looked past him as if the far wall fascinated her.

'Truly, Imogen, there's no need for that sort of thanks.'

Slowly, she nodded, then before he realised what she was about she was walking out the door, leaving his hands empty. 'I understand. Goodnight, Thierry.'

CHAPTER EIGHT

IMOGEN SAT STRAIGHT in her seat, braced for bad news. Hope for the best but prepare for the worst, wasn't that the adage? Right now she was hoping the doctor would confirm her child would be safe. The alternative…

A callused hand enclosed hers, long fingers gripping gently.

Startled, she looked around to Thierry beside her. He was watching the doctor pore over her scan results, yet he'd sensed her fear as if attuned to her.

He'd done that before, she remembered, the day his grandmother had arrived. His gentle touch on her cheek then had calmed her, made her feel he was on her side.

Imogen released a shivery breath, trying to find a place of calm amongst her whirling emotions.

Thierry's touch was a two-edged sword. Unashamedly she clung to his hand, grateful for the reminder she wasn't alone. Yet the poignancy of his touch lacerated something fragile inside. He hadn't touched her willingly since that day with his grandmother in the garden. The night she'd gone to him, eager to show how much she needed him, he'd stood aloof.

The memory of his beautiful, big body, so still and unresponsive when she'd offered herself to him, gouged at far more than her self-respect. It felt as if she'd swallowed a razor blade that cut her every time she breathed. The pain of his rejection rivalled even her blinding headaches at their worst.

Had she really invested so much in this man?

Imogen looked away to the framed diplomas on the wall. Thierry hadn't even bothered to take his hands out of his pockets that night she'd kissed him! So much for re-kindling the passion they'd shared. He'd stood there, en-during her touch, till finally he'd grabbed her and put her aside. No words could have made it clearer that for him the physical side of their relationship was dead.

She really had been a temporary fling.

'Imogen?' His low voice curled around her, beckoning, but she refused to turn. She had to hold herself together.

'Madame Girard.' At last the doctor spoke. Imogen squared her shoulders in preparation for the inevitable.

Yet, instead of the grave expression doctors usually re-served for delivering bad news, this man looked animated. Pleased. Her breath caught. Did that mean her baby would be okay? Involuntarily, her fingers clenched around Thierry's.

'You're something of a puzzle, Madame Girard.' The doctor shook his head slowly but there was no mistaking the hint of a smile at the corners of his mouth.

'I am?' Her voice was a husk of sound.

'Your symptoms fit a classic pattern and, combined with your family history…' He spread his hands as if to say there was nothing he could do for her.

Her heart dived and she bit down a gasp of distress.

A chair scraped and Thierry roped a long arm around her shoulders. Warmth enveloped her, the woodsy scent of the outdoors and something more, something beyond mere physical comfort. She leaned into him. No matter that she could do this alone if she had to. She'd never been more grateful for company in her life, even if it came from the man who saw her solely as a form of duty.

'Despite that, I'm pleased to tell you the headaches and vision problems aren't what you think.'

'Pardon?'

The doctor smiled, his eyes alight. 'Contrary to expecta-tions, you're not suffering the same disease as your mother.'

The air rushed from her lungs as if from a punctured balloon. 'I'm not?'

'Absolutely not. In fact, I can tell you there is no tumour, malignant or otherwise.' His smile became a beam.

Dazed, Imogen shook her head. 'I don't understand.'

'There was never a tumour, though it seems your general practitioner, like you, feared the worst.' He spoke slowly, glancing again at the test results. 'I've consulted with both your family doctor and my specialist colleague in Australia. The one you were supposed to see but didn't.'

She didn't miss the questioning inflection in his voice, or the tightening of Thierry's grip on her shoulder.

'There didn't seem much point. I knew what he was going to say. I just...' She looked up into surprisingly sympathetic grey eyes and found the words tumbling out. 'I couldn't bear facing the diagnosis so soon after losing my mother. I felt trapped.' She hefted a deep breath into too-tight lungs. 'I decided to get away, just for a while, before I had to face all that.' She waved a hand at the reports on his desk. 'But you're saying it's not a tumour? What is it, then?'

'I understand from your family doctor that you also lost your sister recently?'

Imogen could have howled with impatience. Why didn't he just tell her what was wrong with her?

Thierry's warm hand caressed her shoulder in a gesture of support that helped her gather her scattered wits.

'That's right. She died suddenly in an accident.'

'And then your mother became ill?'

Imogen nodded. 'Very soon afterwards. But I don't see how that's relevant.'

Sympathetic grey eyes held hers. 'Stress and grief can do amazing things, Madame Girard.'

'I don't understand.' She leaned forward, dislodging Thierry's grip. 'Please, just tell me what's going on.'

'I'm pleased to say that, on the basis of these very extensive tests, there's nothing physically wrong with you.'

'But that can't be! I'm not imagining those headaches. They're so bad they even affect my vision.'

The doctor nodded. 'I'm sure they are. Tell me, are they still as frequent?'

Imogen hesitated, calculating. 'No, not as often as before.' She spoke slowly. 'I haven't had one since Paris.' She couldn't remember the exact date and darted a sideways glance at Thierry but he wasn't looking at her. His attention was fixed on the doctor.

'So you're saying all this is the result of stress?' Thierry's voice held a note of disbelief that matched her own. 'There's no physical cause?'

'That doesn't make the pain any less real. I have no doubt the symptoms your wife has experienced were every bit as disturbing as ones caused by a tumour.' He looked down at his notes then up at Imogen. 'It seems to me that you've been through a very traumatic time, Madame Girard. The best remedy is rest, and…' a small smile played at his mouth '…something positive in your life. Like a baby to look forward to.'

'You're serious?' Imogen couldn't take it in.

'Absolutely. The symptoms you're experiencing will pass with time.'

A great hiccupping sob rose in her throat, and she crossed her arms around her middle, folding in on herself as shock detonated at her core. Through a blur of emotion she heard the doctor reassure her, telling her he'd be happy to see her again if she had any questions later, and more that she didn't really take in.

All she registered was that she was okay. She and her baby were going to live. Everything would be all right.

And one other detail. The fact that Thierry hadn't touched her again. She missed the warmth of his large, reassuring hand.

'I feel like such a fool,' she said again, watching the streets pass by as Thierry drove them out of the city. 'I just can't believe it. It seems so incredible.'

Thierry didn't say anything. When she turned to look, his profile was set in lines of concentration, his brow furrowed and his mouth firm.

The traffic was heavy, she told herself. Of course he needed to focus on that. Even to her own ears she sounded like a broken record, replaying the same phrases again and again. But she needed to talk about this to make it real. It was so unexpected, so much the miracle she'd never dared hope for, that she couldn't quite believe it.

Her palm covered her belly and gratitude overcame her. Her baby would be all right. She felt the weight of every anxious night ease from her shoulders as tears pricked her eyes. She let her head sink back against the headrest, relief vying with so many other emotions she couldn't get a grip on.

Just as well it was Thierry driving. She wouldn't have trusted herself.

'I still don't believe it,' she murmured. 'The one and only time I act on impulse.' She clasped her hands together. 'All my life I've been cautious, the one who never acted rashly, always considering the pros and cons before making a decision. Yet that one time I acted on the spur of the moment…'

That day in the Sydney waiting room, defeat had pressed down so hard, there'd seemed no room for doubt. She'd *known* she had the same fatal illness as her mother. 'I should have stayed for that appointment instead of haring off to the other side of the globe.'

But if you had, you'd never have met Thierry. You wouldn't be expecting this child.

Shocking as it was to find herself pregnant, Imogen couldn't wish that undone.

She turned and peeked at Thierry through her lashes. His jaw was hard-set, emphasising the strong thrust of his nose and the slashing lines of his cheekbones.

She dragged in a rough breath that didn't fill her lungs.

'All of this…us…' she waved her hand '…is because I acted impulsively. I should have waited and checked my facts.'

Still he said nothing.

'I'm sorry, Thierry. Truly sorry. You must be upset.'

'You think I'd prefer if the doctor had confirmed today that you're dying?' A muscle twitched in his jaw. 'What sort of man do you think I am? You think I'm upset that you're going to live?' Finally, he looked her way, his gaze piercing. 'What have I done to give you such an opinion of me?'

'You know what I mean. If I hadn't jumped to conclusions all this wouldn't have happened. We wouldn't be married. Because of that mistake, we're stuck with each other.'

Unless, of course, they divorced. But for the life of her she couldn't bring herself to mention it. Not yet. Not till she'd had time to absorb everything.

'What's done is done, Imogen. There's nothing to be gained in lashing yourself over it.'

'You think not?' Imogen stared. He seemed far too calm, though now she looked properly, the chiselled stillness of his profile hinted at fierce control. What was he holding back?

'I didn't do it deliberately.' She reached out and placed her palm on his thigh. Instantly, she felt the long muscle beneath her hand bunch tight and solid.

It was the first time she'd reached for him since that night in her room. Imogen looked at her pale hand against the taut, dark fabric of his trousers and wondered with a catch in her chest whether it would be the last time. 'You have to believe me. I wasn't lying or trying to trick you. I truly believed—'

'You think I don't know that?' Again, Thierry's gaze captured hers, shooting fire along veins turned frosty with shock.

'I don't know what you believe.' Thierry had been so good to her, so supportive, but she'd never been able to read him fully except when they shared pleasure. Right now he was giving a good imitation of a graven image. She felt none of the closeness she'd experienced before. She lifted her hand, warm from touching him, and tucked it into her lap.

'Your shock was obvious when the doctor told you the truth. I thought for a moment you might faint.'

Yet he hadn't wrapped his arm around her and hauled her close as he'd done before.

'I believe...' He paused and she could have sworn her heartbeat slowed in expectation. 'That, instead of apologising, you need to celebrate. It's not often a dying woman gets such a reprieve.'

Finally, his mouth curled up at the corner, and Imogen's heart gave a flutter of relief. It took a while to notice the tension in his neck and jaw hadn't eased.

They celebrated with lunch at the sort of restaurant Imogen had read about in guide books but never anticipated visiting. The service was impeccable, the food unlike anything she'd ever tasted and the ambience discreetly elegant. If the wine waiter was surprised they toasted her news with sparkling water, he didn't show it.

Thierry was charming, urbane and witty and, by the time the chef came out to greet them, Imogen felt more relaxed than she had in ages.

It was as she was coming back from the ladies' room that she saw Thierry in conversation with another diner, a fit-looking man with a shock of shaggy blond hair.

'A friend?' she asked as she sat down, watching the stranger walk out the door.

It struck her that she didn't know Thierry's friends. They'd spent all their time together, unless Thierry was working, as he did so many hours in the day.

'Yes, someone from the old days.'

'The old days?' She wished she'd returned to the table sooner.

'The days before I became a respectable businessman.' It should have been a joke but it didn't sound like it.

She tilted her head to one side. 'What did you do before you became respectable?'

'Whatever I pleased.' When he saw her watching, he continued. 'Skiing, parties, trekking, ballooning, more parties.' He swallowed the last of his coffee. 'In fact, I was just invited to a weekend climbing in the Alps.'

'And are you going?'

He shrugged, but she didn't miss the glitter in his eyes. It was the same look she'd seen when he'd told her about some of his far-flung adventures. 'I have too much to do. Too many responsibilities.'

You're one of those responsibilities.

You relied on him when you were desperate and look where that got you both—trapped in a marriage that should never have happened.

'I think you should go.' Imogen wasn't aware of formulating the words but suddenly they were emerging from her mouth.

'Pardon?'

'Look at the hours you work.' He might be meticulous about joining her for meals but he was usually back at work in the evening. When did he get time off? He'd made time in Paris but now his business seemed to consume most of his waking hours. That and being on hand for her.

'That's because I've got deadlines.'

'Can't they be put back a few days? Long enough for a short break?' She watched his eyes narrow on the coffee cup he twisted with one hand. 'Surely nothing will go wrong if you take a weekend off? What are two days?'

Besides, it would do her good to have a few days alone. She had a lot of thinking to do. After months getting used to the idea of dying, she had to get her head around the notion of living.

Then there was this situation they were in—man and wife in a marriage that now had no built-in end date. Marriage to a man who was protective and caring but no longer desired her.

'You should go,' she urged, her constricting throat making her voice husky.

'Two days,' he mused, frowning. 'I admit, it's tempting.'

Two days turned into four. In fact, it would be five by the time he returned. Tonight was his fourth night away.

After the freedom of the mountains, the thrill of pitting himself against the elements on some of the region's most treacherous climbs, Thierry had been only too ready to agree when his friends had suggested an extra night at the resort before returning to his normal life.

Yet maybe he was getting too old for this. The hot shower tonight had been bliss on his sorely tried body. He couldn't remember feeling this level of weariness after a few days' climbing. Or maybe he felt out of sorts because he still grappled with the bizarre soap-opera storyline his life had become.

He swirled his cognac, inhaling its rich aroma, then knocked it back in one. The shot of heat to his belly was satisfyingly definite, unlike so much in his life now. He looked up, ignoring the party going on around him, and caught the bartender's eye, gesturing for another.

Thierry rolled his shoulders but couldn't shift the tension that had settled there. The sense of being weighed down. But worse was the roiling morass of *feelings*.

Thierry grimaced. His life had been simple and perfect. Yes, he'd had a little heartbreak in his youth but that had merely left him able to play the field, enjoying freedom in the bedroom as well as in his sports. Even the yoke of the family business hadn't taken that away from him. He'd shouldered massive burdens but he was close to freeing himself of that.

His old life had beckoned. Until Imogen.

He lifted his glass and slugged back another mouthful, ignoring the fact this liquor deserved slow appreciation. He didn't have the patience for that. He needed something to cut through the web of emotions tangling his brain.

He'd never felt such relief in his life as when the doctor had said Imogen was safe. That she and the baby would live. But the news hadn't just brought relief.

Cool logic told him Imogen hadn't deliberately set out to trap him into marriage. He'd been the one to persuade her and there'd been no mistaking her utter shock at the doctor's pronouncement. It wasn't her fault.

Damn it all, he could even sympathise with her walking out of that Sydney waiting room and heading for adventure rather than facing more appointments and treatment. It was the sort of thing he could imagine himself doing.

Yet no amount of logic could shift the sensation that he'd got caught in a net, in a situation far more complex than he'd anticipated. Marrying for the sake of a child was one thing. Acquiring a long-term wife was another. Then there were these feelings that clogged his chest. Half-formed ideas and sensations that were totally unfamiliar.

Thierry wanted his simple life back. Even in the beginning when he'd had to work soul-destroying hours to salvage the business he'd been certain of his purpose, and what little free time he'd had was his own to use as he chose.

Now he felt tethered. Tangled. Worse, he felt… He didn't know what he felt. Just that he didn't like it.

After the wedding he'd put Imogen in that box labelled 'duty'. He'd been able to deal with her as his responsibility when she was off-limits. Now suddenly that label didn't fit and all sorts of insidious ideas were weaving their way through his brain.

The waiter returned, and Thierry gestured for him to leave the bottle. Helping himself, he poured a double. His mouth twisted. He never drank this much. He preferred to keep his wits about him. But that hadn't done much good lately. Maybe he'd find clarity this way. *Something* had to break this untenable bind he found himself in.

He'd lost count of his drinks when he heard a husky whisper beside him. 'Is there enough for me to have a sip?'

He turned and for a second the edges of his vision blurred. But he had no trouble focusing on the woman beside him. Tall, slim, with cornflower-blue eyes and hair the colour of sunlight. Her mouth was wide and her expression aware. Exactly the sort of beautiful woman he'd always preferred. Given her height, he guessed she had long, lissom legs.

Thierry smiled and her pout of enquiry turned into a smile that would have melted the snow off Mont Blanc.

She put a glass on the bar, and he swiped up the cognac bottle, pouring her a measure without spilling a drop. He was congratulating himself on that feat when she leaned in to pick up her drink, pressing against him from breast to knee.

He felt the subtle stretch and arch of her body as she knocked back her drink, her breasts thrusting into his torso. Heat shot through him at that deliberate invitation.

She put her glass down and, holding his eyes, slowly licked her lips. Her bottom lip shimmered, and Thierry felt a pounding in his head—or was it his chest?—as she slid her arms around his neck.

'How about a private party?' she whispered, her breath tickling his throat.

Then she reached up, pressing her mouth to his, and he found his hands clamping convulsively around her waist.

CHAPTER NINE

THIERRY DROVE ROUND to the offices at the back of the *château*.

He wasn't really in a fit state for work but there'd be crucial matters for his attention after five days away. Two property deals were nearing conclusion and he wanted an update. Plus there'd be the revised schedule for the new ski resort to check.

Besides, he wasn't ready to face his wife.

Wife. That word had become real in ways he'd never imagined when he and Imogen had married in that swift civil ceremony.

A wife was more than a temporary responsibility, a woman to be cared for in her hour of need.

Imogen had ceased being a responsibility and had again become a woman—with all the complications that entailed. Not a woman for a quick liaison but a woman with whom his life was now inextricably entangled.

Because he'd followed his instinct and decided on marriage. He'd spent his life acting on instinct, even in business, and it rarely let him down.

His mouth set. There was always a first time.

He parked and switched off the ignition. His head beat like a drum, the pounding an insistent, punishing beat reminding him how foolish he'd been last night.

As if alcohol would solve his problems! Not even climbing, one of his favourite sports, had cleared his mind. Instead of enjoying the challenge of the sport, he'd been distracted by thoughts of Imogen and the disturbing emotions she stirred.

As for that debacle in the bar last night!

He leaned back against the headrest, shoving his hand through his hair.

Even drunk, he'd known what the blonde wanted. How could he not? He was the master of the short-term affair.

Too much cognac was a convenient excuse for the fact he'd smiled right back and offered her a drink. As if tangling with one sexy woman would solve the problems he had with another!

He couldn't remember if he'd felt a sizzle of anticipation as she'd sidled up to him, or what, if anything, had gone through his brain. All he knew was, the moment she'd pressed her mouth to his, revulsion had knifed him. Revulsion at her touch and, more, at himself.

His hands hadn't been gentle as he'd shoved her away. He had a suspicion she might even bear bruises from his touch, though last night she'd looked too shocked to register pain.

Thierry scrubbed a hand over his face. It had just been a kiss, a split second of a kiss at that, yet for the first time in his life he'd felt guilty about being with a woman.

Guilt and anger, and that sick swirl in his belly he'd like to believe was the result of too much alcohol. Instead, he suspected it was due to something else entirely.

Shoving the car door open, he swung out, letting it slam, and strode to the offices. He needed an afternoon concentrating on reports, plans and the delicate power play of property negotiations. Anything to take his mind off personal matters.

He made it past most of the offices and had reached the threshold of his own when someone called his name.

Thierry paused, biting down an oath. He wanted privacy, but this was why he was here, to lead the team. He turned and saw one of the legal staff approaching, an envelope in his hand and an expression on his face that had Thierry instantly alert.

'Is there a problem?' Mentally, he flicked through the

current investments—commercial property, high-end re-
sorts, the Côte du Rhône vineyard and—

'No problem.' Yet the lawyer's smile looked forced. 'Just
tying up loose ends.' He offered the envelope and, to Thierry's
surprise, walked quickly away.

Thierry's fingers tingled as he surveyed it. His staff here
made a close-knit team, without the formality of the Paris
office. They were relaxed and friendly, even in times of
high workload. But his senior legal advisor was worried.

Thierry entered his office and shut the door. He strode
to the window and slid the contents of the envelope into
his hand.

It was just a few pages. Flicking to the back, he saw
Imogen's name and signature and a date two days ago,
all witnessed. Thierry frowned and flipped to the front.

Minutes later he stood, staring, his hand carving
through his hair to clutch his scalp. Dimly, he registered
a cramping in his chest that reminded him to suck in air.

This was what his legal staff had done while he'd been
away?

The paper crackled as it crumpled in his fist.

Imogen must have asked them to draw this up. No one
else would have dared consider it.

He dragged in another breath and searched for calm. It
eluded him. Why had she so ostentatiously cut herself off
from his wealth, the material support he could provide? It
should have felt like a reprieve yet in some obscure way it
was a slap in the face, made more insulting because of the
shame he felt after last night.

He told himself a single kiss with a stranger didn't taint
his honour, yet he felt…stained. It had to be because of this
indignity Imogen had engineered. No doubt his employees
were gossiping about the fiasco their boss's marriage had
become. Thierry had never in his life cared about gossip,
but to be made a laughing stock in his own home…

The papers fell as he marched across the room, wrenched open the door and strode out.

She wasn't in her room. A scan revealed nothing except her passport on the dresser beside her purse.

Thierry scowled. Why was her passport out?

The sound of running water penetrated and he stalked to the bathroom door, pushed it open and walked in.

Behind the clear glass of the shower screen, water sluiced down Imogen's lush body. Her head arched back as she massaged shampoo from her long hair. The pose thrust her breasts out, silhouetting them against the window beyond.

Thierry stilled, his hand on the door knob. Everything inside him collapsed in on itself. Arousal, strong as the tug of the ocean's inexorable current, dragged at his lower body. He didn't notice the pounding in his head any more, just his lungs' short, sharp grabs for oxygen and the thunder of his heartbeat rapping his ribs.

'Thierry?' Her eyes opened wide, and she stood transfixed, glistening and perfect. His gaze traced her raspberry-pink nipples that beaded as he watched, down the plane of her ribcage to her taut belly that showed no sign yet of his child inside.

His child.

His hand tightened on the door as she turned her back to wrench off the taps. The dip and curve of her glistening back was entrancing.

His wife.

The thought curled through him like a beckoning finger, inviting him into the room.

He scooped up a towel and pulled open the shower door. Amazingly, she crossed one arm over her breasts as she turned, her other hand covering her pubic area. As if he didn't recall every slick curve and plane of that gorgeous body!

That was the problem. All this time dealing with Imogen the duty rather than Imogen the sensuous woman had left him sleep-deprived. No wonder he was out of sorts.

'There's no need for modesty, *ma chère*.'

Her chin tilted and something hot jabbed through him. He'd always responded to a challenge.

'I'd prefer you to knock before you come in.'

'It's late for setting ground rules, Imogen. You're my wife and I have a right to be here.' The long walk through the *château* had fuelled his roaring indignation.

His eyes flicked down, taking in her pale skin, blush-pink from the shower, and her sinuous curves.

Reason and patience retreated. He was tired of being patient. More, he was tired of the bitter stew of emotions he couldn't banish. Emotions Imogen had created.

He didn't do emotion. Not with women.

He should have followed through that night she'd kissed him in his bedroom. She wouldn't be tying him in knots if he had. But telling himself his frustration levels were his own fault didn't help. He'd needed that mental and physical distance to keep himself sane and ensure he looked after her as she deserved.

Mouth setting in a crooked line, she snatched the towel from him. He had one last glimpse of tip-tilted breasts jiggling deliciously before she wrapped the massive bath sheet around her, even covering her shoulders, as if knowing how her bare skin inflamed him.

She stared straight back, her look all hauteur, as if he'd crawled out of a Marseilles sewer.

Instead of freezing him, that stare ignited something dangerous. Thierry felt it like a whoosh of flame, razing his carefully nurtured restraint.

No woman looked at him like that. Ever. Especially not the woman for whom he'd done so much!

Thierry's hands were hard and brown against the white towel as he grabbed her shoulders. He felt her fine bones, heard the flurry of her quickened breathing, and that sent fiery heat spilling through his veins.

'What did you think you were doing, drawing up that… that…?' Indignation stole his vocabulary.

'That post-nuptial agreement?' Her chin notched.

'Were you deliberately trying to insult me?'

Her eyes widened. 'Of course not. I don't see the problem.'

'You go to my staff and ask them to draw up a contract specifying you renounce any claim to my assets, weeks *after* we marry. You sign in front of witnesses, and you don't see a problem?' His voice rose and beneath his hold she flinched.

Good! How dared she make him an object of ridicule?

Yet if anything her mouth set tighter. Green fire sparked in her eyes.

'I was doing you a favour. Your lawyers thought so. You should have seen their relief when I explained what I wanted.'

'You think I live my life to please lawyers?' His fingers clamped harder.

'I was doing the right thing.' Her chin jutted and her brilliant eyes met his unerringly. 'You didn't want a permanent wife. If you had, I'm sure you'd have expected a pre-nup. Circumstances have changed and I wanted you to know I'm not hanging around, aiming for a share of your wealth.'

Not hanging around? Was that why her passport was out? Warning jangled, and Thierry yanked her body full against his, soft to his rigid frame. He let go of her shoulders and wrapped his arms around her, pinioning her.

Memory assaulted him. Of that woman last night, her body pressed to his, her lips against his mouth. And all he felt was disgust. Because she hadn't been Imogen.

It was his wife he wanted. No one else.

That truth had hammered at him all day. There'd been no evading it, no matter how he'd tried.

Imogen had burrowed under his skin, destroying his interest in other women. That was bad enough. Worse was the fact she now acted as if she didn't want him! She deliberately provoked.

'What did I ever do to suggest I believed you were after my money?' His words were sharp as a lash, and he felt her tense. He breathed deep, nostrils flaring as he dragged in the scent of damp, sweet woman. 'When have I *ever* insulted you as you've insulted me? You make me look like a mercenary, gullible fool, scared you're going to fleece me. A man who needs saving from his own decisions!'

'That wasn't my intention.' Her eyes widened. This close, he caught the shock in those sherry-brown depths.

'You think I'm so incompetent I need protecting from my actions?'

'I think you're overreacting.' Her finger jabbed his chest. 'I saw your expression after the doctor said I wasn't ill. I saw your doubts.' She tried to stare him down. 'You were wondering if I'd deliberately misled you, weren't you? You suspected I was some gold-digger who'd set up an elaborate scam.'

Fury spiked in Thierry's gut, because for a split second the question *had* surfaced. That was what his lawyer had warned. But Thierry had dismissed the idea. Instead, he'd trusted her, ignoring any such doubt as unworthy.

How many men would have done that?

Besides, Imogen's reaction at the doctor's news had been absolutely genuine.

'What you saw was shock,' he ground out between clenched teeth. 'You'll pardon me for that, given everything that went before. Or are you the only one allowed to be taken by surprise?'

'It was more than surprise. You were quiet. You weren't...' For a split second he'd have sworn he read vulnerability in her expression but then she shoved her finger into his chest again, as if *he* were at fault.

He, who'd done nothing but look after her from the start!

'Weren't what?' he growled.

She shook her head and a slick ribbon of dark hair slid over her shoulder. 'You're saying you weren't regretting this marriage? You weren't regretting *me*?'

'You think I'd rather the doctor had confirmed you were dying? *That's* what you think of me?'

Deliberately, he lashed his anger higher, ignoring the fact there was a grain of truth in her words—he'd never expected to have a real marriage, only a short-term solution to the problem of caring for Imogen and her child.

Her eyes held his. 'Why are you so angry, Thierry?' Her breath came in short bursts that pushed her breasts against his torso and sent need quaking through him. Being close to her spun him out till he teetered on the brink of control. 'I don't understand. I was trying to do the right thing, making it clear I didn't expect more from you.'

He stared down at the mutinous line of her mouth. The mix of anger and hurt in her eyes.

Why *was* he angry?

What she said made sense. Yet he didn't want that sort of favour. At some deep, primitive level her action carved at his honour, his masculine pride.

Was it the careless way she spurned the fortune he'd worked like a slave to secure that needled? Or that he couldn't conquer the unfamiliar mix of emotions she'd stirred?

Or was it that the gesture felt like a rejection of *him*?

He hadn't known rejection since he was twenty and Sandrine had chosen another man. Since then he'd ensured his liaisons were short and easy, ones he could walk away from without a backward glance. Always he was in control—the hunter, the seducer, the one to leave.

The thought of Imogen spurning him made him wild.

The fire spread from his belly, coursing out in molten waves.

'Why have you got your passport out?'

She blinked. 'I wondered if I should book a flight to Australia. Clearly, you're not going to want me here long term.'

'Clearly?'

Her eyes skated away from his, and he felt something loosen inside.

'I don't belong here, Thierry. That's obvious.'

He ignored the strange, queasy sensation her words provoked. 'You were going to run away?'

Her gaze met his again in a clash that should have struck sparks. 'Of course not. I was waiting till you came home to talk about it.' For the first time he read hesitation in her expression. 'Now you're here we can discuss it. Just give me time to get dressed.' She gripped the towel tighter and made to take a step back. But he didn't let her go. Instead, his arms closed hard around her.

Imogen's head jerked up, consternation battling something he couldn't identify in her expression.

Why was she worried? She wasn't afraid of him. She'd made that clear. She was ready to walk out on him.

'No.' The word emerged from his tight throat. 'You're not going anywhere.'

She scowled and shoved her hands against his chest as if to push him away. The movement shifted the towel, revealing a tempting sliver of peachy, pale skin. 'What's wrong with you, Thierry? I don't understand.'

Nor did he. That made his anger burn brighter. The fact that it was instinctive, uncontrollable, totally inexplicable.

He just knew that none of this was right.

He'd be damned if he'd let her leave before he worked it out.

'Then understand this.' Hauling her to him, he took her mouth in a swooping kiss that started as punishing but morphed in a heartbeat to urgent, hungry, demanding. Desperate.

A moment's hesitation, a stillness that made something like fear rise in him, then her lips opened beneath his like a fragile blossom responding to sunlight.

This was what he wanted. What he'd craved. Imogen's fragrance, her taste, invaded his senses, a sweet, addictive flavour that blasted the back off his head as she tentatively moved her mouth against his.

One arm lashed about her waist and his other roved up to cup the back of her neck, supporting her as he bowed her back. She clung to his shirt and he knew a surge of triumph.

A shudder racked her, and he felt it from his mouth, down all the places where their bodies melded, right to the soles of his feet, braced wide to support them both. His brain told him to pull back; he was being too rough. Then he heard her little throaty moan, tasted it in his mouth.

He knew that sound. Imogen losing control. Imogen turning to flame and rapture in his arms. Imogen abandoned and eager.

Thierry's anger drained and with it the fear he'd refused to acknowledge. Fear that he'd lost her. Energy coursed through him; arousal weighted his groin and turned his body from flesh and bone to forged metal.

In a single, unhesitating movement, he swept an arm beneath her legs and scooped her up against his chest. Still they kissed, their lips fused with a passion that obliterated all else.

Her arms crept higher till he felt her fingers against his neck, holding tight. He wanted to whoop in exultation. Except that would mean lifting his mouth from hers. And the way she was kissing him, as if she'd been starved of him, just as he'd been without her... He refused to give that up.

Thierry spun round, lifting his eyes just enough to navigate into Imogen's bedroom.

Six strides and he was beside the bed. An instant later

and she fell onto the coverlet, and he with her, arms around her, his body pressing her down. She hitched her arms tighter around his neck and pressed her mouth urgently against his.

With one hand he wrenched back the towel from her damp body, his fingers brushing soft flesh and dissolving his brain. Urgently, he fumbled at his belt buckle. He couldn't recall ever being this desperate, this uncoordinated.

He breathed hard through his nostrils, trying to find focus. He would have lifted his mouth but Imogen gripped his skull so hard he succumbed to mutual hunger and contented himself with fumbling one-handed.

One slim, bare leg slid alongside his, then folded over the back of his thigh, as if trapping him against her.

Did she really fear he'd withdraw now?

Not with the taste of her on his tongue, vanilla sugar and feminine spice. Not with her mouth demanding, playing, teasing his. And her body moving sinuously beneath him. Those tiny, circling movements drove him insane. He had to get naked, quickly, before he lost it.

He'd lost count of the weeks since he'd had Imogen. It felt like half a lifetime. The need for her rose, eclipsing all else. Finally, he wrenched his belt undone, then the button on his trousers. But in the process the back of his hand brushed the soft, warm skin of her belly.

A shaft of awareness struck him. Not sexual awareness but something new. Something powerful and tender. Bracing himself better on his other elbow, he turned his hand and spread his palm over her stomach.

There was a roaring in his ears, a pounding like a hundred horses behind his ribcage, and a strange new sense filling it. It was wonder, possessiveness and a fierce tug of protectiveness all rolled into one.

Imogen's head fell back and suddenly he could breathe again, though in rasping breaths so harsh they tore at his lungs. Or maybe that was because of the look in her eyes. It was something like wonderment and it erased his searing temper in an instant.

Thierry slid his hand lower, entranced by the incredible silky texture of her flesh and the fact that his child lay nestled there.

He wanted to pound himself against her, fill her hard and fast till they lost their minds in ecstasy. But thought of the child gave him pause. Exultation warred with caution—the primitive against the civilised.

'Our baby,' he murmured, stunned by the reality of it.

Imogen's hand covered his, gently pressing. Her eyes glowed as if he'd just given her the best compliment in the world.

'I thought you didn't really want it.'

He shook his head. In truth he hadn't thought too much about it as a living, breathing child. He'd focused on getting through the pregnancy, seeing Imogen cared for. Intellectually, he'd understood there was a baby, but touching her belly, knowing that new life lay just centimetres below his palm... It was a humbling experience.

He shook his head. 'I would never reject it.' That, at least, was the truth.

Imogen lay panting, watching expressions flicker across Thierry's strong features. He'd taken her from zero to two hundred in a heartbeat with that glorious, savage kiss that had melted her bones. Now his tenderness threatened to melt her heart.

Our baby. Finally, he'd said it. More than said it. He felt how special this was—it was there in his touch, his stillness, his expression.

Suddenly, he was moving and Imogen bit back a cry as he levered himself away. She had to clench her hands to stop herself reaching for him.

But he didn't go far, just pulling back far enough to strip

the towel wide, leaving her completely exposed. He bent, his mouth grazing her belly softly in a caress that drew her skin tight with wanting and wonder.

Imogen looked down at his glossy dark hair against her skin, that proud face, his large, capable hand clamping her hip while his lips skated across the place where their baby lay.

Her heart turned over at Thierry's tenderness, and stupidly, tears pricked the back of her eyes. Rapidly, she blinked them back.

'You really do care about the baby.' The revelation tightened her throat.

His eyes met hers and connection throbbed between them, strong as the beat of her heart. 'Of course I care.'

Imogen shook her head, confused by what she thought she saw in his eyes. 'There's no need for this...us.' She stumbled over the words, hating the idea that, for the sake of their baby, he might pretend to want her too.

'No need?' His dark brows scrunched together.

She tried to hitch herself higher in the bed but his weight imprisoned her.

'You don't want me. There's no need to pretend.'

'Not *want* you?' His eyes rounded.

Imogen looked away, too aware suddenly of her nakedness. 'When I went to your room, when I wanted you, you rejected me.' Sheer pride kept her voice steady when it felt like she was crumbling into a thousand humiliated pieces.

'Listen to me, Imogen.' His hand was warm and compelling as he cupped her chin, turning it so she was forced to meet his gaze. 'I never, not even for a moment, stopped wanting you.'

'But—'

'But I tried to ignore that because I needed to look after you. I thought you were too sick, too fragile—'

'Fragile!' Her eyes bulged.

Thierry nodded. 'I was trying to protect you from me.'

Slowly the grim line of his mouth eased into a rakish smile
that made her heart dance. 'But you're not ill now, are you?'
His voice grazed her nerves like suede on silk.

Imogen opened her mouth to argue, to probe, but
abruptly he was gone, sliding down her body. 'Thierry?'

He positioned himself low, his strong hands urging her
thighs up and out, leaving her wide open to him. Imogen's
breath stalled, her protest disintegrating as those midnight-
dark eyes snared hers. His mouth dipped to touch her in
that most sensitive spot and a shiver of powerful excitement shot through her. She'd waited so long for his loving. Wonder filled her at the idea he, like she, had suffered
from the careful distance they'd maintained.

Imogen swallowed hard, but before she could formulate
words his mouth caressed her again. This time the bolt of
pleasure rocked her to the core.

Seconds later, her heart quivering from the smoky expression in his eyes, the flames erupted and her whole
body lit up from the inside. The climax was more powerful than any Imogen remembered. She found herself sob-
bing his name, her hands biting his shoulders as waves of
pleasure rolled through her.

Afterwards he didn't smile. There was no satisfaction
like he'd shown in the past when she hadn't been able to
contain her response to him. His expression was serious,
completely intent as he gently lowered her legs, stroking
her thighs till the racking shudders of ecstasy abated.

Through half-closed eyes she watched him undress,
revealing the lean, powerful body that was so superbly
masculine and honed to perfection. His movements were
methodical and slow, as if he didn't understand how much
she needed him, even after that climax. No, because of it.
She needed Thierry, his body joined with hers.

Finally, he covered her with his hard frame, careful to
take his weight on his arms. Heavy thighs pressed against
hers, the rough silk dusting of his chest hair tickled her

nipples and she sighed, relishing his heavy erection nudging her.

Imogen clutched his shoulders, trying to draw him closer, but he resisted, his jaw locked in an expression of determination that flummoxed her. But soon she understood.

It wasn't enough that he'd already reduced her to white-hot ash with that blast of sexual release. He was determined to do it again, with his superb body and his hand between her legs.

'I want you. Now,' she gasped, letting go of his shoulder and reaching for him. But she'd barely brushed her fingers across that hot erection when he captured both her wrists and shackled them above her head with one hand.

'Thierry!' But his mouth met hers, stopping her complaints, and all the while he made love to her with a slow, sure eroticism that made her tremble all over again. Heat sparked anew and she jerked hard beneath his touch as rapture took her.

How long he pleasured her she didn't know but she saw stars over and over again. Her breathing fractured and her body was limp and boneless from an overload of delight.

All the while those dark eyes held hers, his touch sure and fatally sensual, dragging response after response from her. Imogen told herself she should have stopped him, demanded what she wanted. But how could she when it seemed he knew her better than she did? He played her body like a maestro conducting a symphony. A symphony that left her euphoric and sated.

She felt as if those caresses had indelibly imprinted him on her body, marking her as his, so that in future she'd respond to no man but him. She was lost in the heady delight of his touch, his slow, seductive kisses and the magic he wove.

Finally, he came to her, joining them with one slow surge that brought him right to the heart of her. For an instant he held steady there and she wondered if she'd ever know again such a sensation of being one with another being. It was wonderful and scary and, despite her exhaustion, arousing.

Wrapping her arms around his slick torso, she held him close. He was determined to take things slowly, his movements measured, despite the way his heart pounded. Looking up, she saw the sheen of sweat on his forehead and the grit of a jaw locked, as if in pain. His heat was like a furnace, branding her.

A flash of suspicion hit. Was he afraid he'd injure the baby? Was that what kept his powerful body so tight?

As soon as the notion surfaced she knew it was true. He'd been mightily aroused from the moment he'd confronted her in the bathroom and still he held himself in check.

Her hands slid down the sleek curve of his back and around the impressive, taut curve of his buttocks. They flexed at her touch, and she tightened her grip, hearing Thierry's breath hiss. She turned her head, stretching higher to touch her lips to his ear. Then she whispered to him, confiding exactly what she wanted him to do to her.

She'd barely begun when he lost his slow rhythm and a burst of hoarse French filled her ears. A large hand clamped her breast, kneading, as Thierry's hips jerked powerfully, rocking into her, filling her faster and faster.

Imogen held tight, revelling in his urgency. She nipped at his earlobe and suddenly there was a roar of sound, a fierce, undulating wave of delight as he powered into her, no longer in control, as vulnerable to ecstasy as she'd been.

Heat pumped into her, an unfettered liquid throb that she'd never before experienced.

Dazedly, Imogen realised it was the first time they hadn't used protection. Maybe that was why this felt so momentous. So starkly real as she held Thierry's shuddering body protectively close. Not just satisfying, but as if together they'd discovered some primeval secret that would bind them for ever.

Finally, he slumped in her arms, his mouth at her neck, his weight pressing her down as exhaustion and satiation claimed them.

Imogen's last thought was a hope that, whatever they'd just experienced, it would change everything between them.

CHAPTER TEN

'ARE YOU HUNGRY?' The warm rumble of Thierry's voice made Imogen stir and stretch. She'd been lying in a haze of wellbeing, her mind drifting.

She opened her eyes and discovered soft lamplight filled the room. 'How long did I sleep?' She rolled over to find him propped against the headboard beside her. He looked scrumptious with his rumpled hair, the dark shadow on his jaw, and a casual shirt and jeans.

'You got dressed!'

His chuckle was like honey, rich and enticing, and her insides curled. Delight feathered her spine and between her thighs she felt a pulse flutter into life.

Responding again to the sensual promise in Thierry's voice should have been impossible after all they'd just shared. Yet when her eyes met his the impact of that connection jolted through her. She watched his smile fade.

'I had to get dressed or shock the staff when I went to get us a snack. You might prefer me naked but they wouldn't.'

Imogen wouldn't bet on it. No woman in her right mind would object to seeing a man like Thierry in all his glory—beautifully proportioned, every muscle honed and full of lean power. Watching him walk naked across a room was one of the treats she'd most missed when they'd said their goodbyes in Paris. He was built like an athlete in his prime, moving with effortless masculine grace.

'What time is it?' Surely it had been early afternoon when he'd confronted her in the bathroom? After her long walk in the sun, grappling with her options for the future, she'd felt weary and hot, ready for a cool shower.

He shrugged. 'Late. I cancelled dinner while you slept but Jeanne insisted I bring a tray to you.'

Imogen rose on her elbows. 'You should have woken me.'

Thierry didn't answer. His gaze was on her breasts, uncovered now by the sheet that someone had pulled over her. Heat suffused Imogen. Because she was so exhausted by their love-making she didn't even remember covering herself? Or because of the jangle of excitement when he looked at her that way—as if she were some delicacy for his enjoyment? She was so weak where he was concerned. Look how she'd gone up in flames in his arms!

Imogen grabbed the sheet and pulled it higher.

'Don't.' His arm shot out, fingers circling her wrist. 'Please.' His deep voice grated.

She swallowed, a delicate shiver rippling through her as he let go her wrist to touch her breast with gentle fingers. Was it his touch or the pleading tone that made her hesitate?

A gasp caught in her throat as pleasure cascaded through her. Her nipple beaded to an aching pout as he circled her breast.

'Thierry.' It was half groan, half plea, and she didn't have time to feel self-conscious about it because in another second he was there, his breath warm on her flesh, his eyes glittering greedily.

One arm pulled her close while the other cupped her breast as he lowered his mouth. Her skin tingled as he blew over her nipple, creating delicious quivers of reaction that spread across her back, down her belly and straight to her womb. Then his mouth was on her, drawing her in, offering bone-melting delight.

Imogen cradled his dark head in her hands, holding him to her while her hips turned towards him, pressing close through the bedclothes. She loved the softness of his hair in her hands, such a contrast to the hard muscle and bone of his powerful body.

When finally he dragged his head up her breathing was ragged and needy and she had trouble focusing on his expression.

'I came here to talk,' he murmured. 'But that can wait.' Already, he was peeling the sheet lower, his big, warm hand smoothing down her ribs.

She covered his fingers with hers, stopping his progress. 'You want to talk?'

'Later will do.' A hungry smile curled the corner of Thierry's mouth, and Imogen knew a compelling temptation simply to lie back and enjoy his attentions. Nothing in all her life made her feel so good as when he made love to her.

Except ever since the doctor's news, she'd wanted to talk with Thierry. Not the casual chatter that he'd used to fill her 'celebration' lunch, but to sort out things between them.

Lustrous dark eyes surveyed her. Oh, the promise in that heated look! 'It can wait.'

How she'd craved that from him all this time when he'd been punctiliously polite, like a courteous stranger.

Nerves stabbed her. He'd said he still desired her, had already proved it, yet maybe she wouldn't like what he'd say. They needed to clear the air and decide where they went from here. It took all her courage to do what she knew she must.

'No, it can't.' She put her hand on his shoulder, stopping him when he would have bent again to her breast. She felt the bunch and flex of muscle beneath her hand and knew she didn't have the power to hold him off. Instead, he chose to respect her wishes.

Finally, she felt some of his urgency abate a fraction as he eased back, resignation on his face. 'You choose the damnedest times to chat.'

A bubble of laughter rose to her lips but she smothered it, realising it was generated by nerves, not amusement. 'You were the one who suggested we talk.'

'That was before.' He moved his hand to tweak her nipple. She gasped as a chord of erotic energy drew tight and alive to the core of her being. Slowly, Thierry smiled. 'Are you sure you don't want to talk later?'

Of course she wasn't sure. She was only human.

Too human when it came to Thierry. For a woman who had no trouble resisting men, she found herself totally unstuck with this gorgeous hunk of a Frenchman. Even the lazy satisfaction of her well-used body didn't prevent a quiver of anticipation at the look in his eyes.

'We need to talk now.' Her voice, throaty and full, gave her away but finally, after close scrutiny, he nodded and rolled away from her to sit up.

Imogen gnawed at her lip rather than howl her frustration at the distance between them.

This is what you wanted, remember!

Physically, she was besotted with the man. She yanked up the sheet, determined to cover herself, and almost groaned out loud at the sensual torture of crisp cotton against her aroused nipples.

Out of the corner of her eye she saw him watching. Was that a smirk?

Did he know how turned on she was after the way he'd fondled her? Of course he knew! He was enjoying her reaction.

Setting her mouth, Imogen let go of the sheet and wriggled up into a sitting position, propping a second pillow behind her. Warm air caressed her breasts but it was the heat of Thierry's gaze that she felt like a touch.

He wasn't smiling now. He was focused on every sway and jiggle of her bare breasts with an intensity that almost stopped her breath.

Good! Served him right.

Casually, she reached for the sheet, drawing it slowly over her chest and tucking it tight under her arms.

She turned to him. 'You're ready to talk?'

'Witch.' But there was amusement in his eyes despite the tension in his features.

If she was, then it was because of him. Thierry Girard had turned a cautious mouse of a woman into one more than happy to flaunt herself before her lover. One with more confidence in her body than she'd had before. One ready to take on the challenge of living instead of dying.

Imogen felt an answering smile tug her mouth. She loved it when he was like this—charming, fun and oh-so-sexy. Far better than when he'd been politely distant. Or when he'd looked grim and implacable.

'Thierry? We've got things to discuss.'

Slowly, he raised his gaze to hers and once more she felt that sensation of melding, of connection. It warmed her in places that had been too long cold.

'Let's eat first.' He swung away and lifted a tray from the bedside table, busying himself ensuring it was stable.

In any other man those quick, restless movements would have made her wonder if he was nervous.

But this was Thierry, über-confident and competent, literally the lord of all he surveyed from his ancient *château*. What reason could he have to be nervous?

She was the outsider, the unwanted complication in his world.

Thick, dark hair fell across his brow, giving him a casual, boyish look that tugged at her heart.

Imogen's breath caught as she remembered his grandmother's words. Did she really look at him with love in her eyes? Was that why she was so desperate for more than his polite goodwill? Why she craved his smiles and this precious sense of them sharing not just their bodies, but some other intimate connection?

The idea made her simultaneously ecstatic and horrified. Trepidation and tentative hope danced along her nerves. But she couldn't bring herself to believe it was true. It was far too dangerous a thought.

'Fruit, quiche or trout?'

Imogen made herself focus on the lavish spread between them. Jeanne had done them proud. She could barely see the tray for the luscious food piled upon it.

Suddenly she realised she was ravenous. 'Everything.' She plucked a gleaming strawberry from a bowl. Her eyes closed as she bit into it. It tasted of sunlight and sweetness. She'd never known food to taste as good as here at Thierry's *château*. Because it was locally grown and fresh, or because her new lease of life made her appreciate small delights even more?

When she opened her eyes it was to find Thierry staring at her mouth, his expression taut and hungry. She gulped down the rest of the fruit, her throat constricting.

They had so much to sort out, but at least on a purely physical level the connection was as strong as ever. The intensity of Thierry's love-making earlier had given her hope and relief after these lonely days when he'd been away. Ever since her doctor's appointment she'd felt strangely alone, even when he was with her. He'd withdrawn mentally.

Not even the fact her headaches were fading had made her feel better. The last one, the first night Thierry had been away climbing, had been a mere shadow of the previous piercing agony.

'You're sure you want to talk?' His voice was pure temptation and the look in his eyes told her she'd enjoy every moment of *not* talking. But they needed to clear the air.

'Why were you so angry earlier?' Imogen had never seen him in a temper and riding that lashing storm had been shocking. Yet on some level she'd thrilled to the vibrancy in him, excited by it.

Because he cared enough to be angry?

That sounded masochistic and she wasn't fool enough to want a man who took out his frustrations on her. Yet she sensed Thierry's anger was rare. After all, he'd taken in his stride all the complications she'd presented him with, never once blaming her or losing his cool. It was more that his flash of temper had broken down the wall between them, the wall she hadn't seen him build till it was too late.

'I apologise for that.' A pulse ticked in his jaw as he helped himself to cheese and home-made crackers. 'I over-reacted. I see now you were trying to make a point.' Suddenly, he looked up, his eyes, dark as bitter coffee, snaring hers. 'But there was no need to prove yourself.'

Imogen spread her hands. 'It was important to make it clear I didn't want any more from you. You've done so much, acted so...honourably.' That old-fashioned word seemed apt. For surely that was what Thierry's grave concern, his gentleness and the efforts he'd gone to on her behalf, amounted to?

'It's done now. I suggest we forget it.' Yet he hadn't. There was an edge to his voice.

'But there's something bothering you.'

He dropped his gaze to her breasts, and her nipples peaked against the crisp cotton. 'From here everything looks perfect.'

Heat crept from her breasts to her throat and face. She still hadn't grown used to such blatantly carnal looks. They threatened to turn her brain as well as her bones to mush. After all, she'd spent twenty-five years avoiding risk, playing safe.

Thierry and her—this connection between them—had been easier to cope with when she'd been able to write it off as a flare of passing attraction, a desperate fling of a dying woman. But she had a full life before her now. She had to come to grips with what was happening.

Her whole being lit up when he looked at her that way. Focusing was almost impossible.

'Why do I get the feeling you're changing the subject?'

Thierry blinked and for an instant she read tension in that powerful frame.

'Things have changed,' he said finally. 'You were right about that.'

Imogen's frustration levels rose when he didn't continue. If he wouldn't confront the elephant in the room, she would.

'I'm not dying. Which means we've saddled ourselves with marriage when we needn't have.' The words tasted bitter.

'Saddled?' His nostrils flared as if in distaste.

'Come on, Thierry. Don't tell me you wanted a permanent wife. Marriage made sense when I thought I was dying and it meant you could claim our baby. But now—'

'Now you want to back out of it?'

'It's not a matter of backing out. It's a matter of being sensible.' The thought of leaving him tore at something vital inside her. But she owed him. That knowledge threatened to shatter every certainty she'd once harboured.

All her life she'd been risk-averse, carefully building security for herself, keeping herself independent of any man, she realised. No wonder Scott had found it so easy to walk away from her, using the time she'd devoted to her mother as an excuse. Now it seemed her happiness was bound up with a man she'd met just months ago.

Yet she couldn't hold Thierry to this marriage, not unless they were both committed to it. 'You were kind to me when I most needed it. I don't want to repay you with a complication you never wanted.'

No matter how she yearned for him.

Sexual attraction alone was not a sound basis for a relationship. As far as she knew, that was all he felt for her, plus responsibility for their baby.

'You think of our child as a complication?'

She struggled to read his inflection.

'It was unexpected, but I can't regret it. I was referring to me being a complication in your life.' Why was he so obtuse? His quick understanding was one of the things she loved about him.

Loved.

Something clenched in the deepest recesses of her soul. It was true. It was really true.

Here she was, trying to convince him he didn't need a spouse, when all the time…

Imogen sucked in a deep breath, dizzy with the implications of the one crucial fact she'd been avoiding for weeks.

'Imogen?' Thierry's frown grew, lines ploughing his forehead and carving around his mouth.

Helplessly, she stared at him. She was in far too deep when the sight of his concern threatened to undo her resolve. She tried to tell herself that it was natural she'd grown fond of him when he'd been so wonderful.

But *fond* didn't go anywhere near describing her visceral need for Thierry. A need that was far more than physical.

Imogen crossed her arms as if to hide the tumultuous throb of her heart hurling itself against her ribs.

'I could be on a flight in a day or two.' She dragged the words out. 'There's no need for…' She waved her hand across the bed as words dissolved.

'You *want* to leave?' He leaned close, his finger stroking her cheek, pushing her hair back over her shoulder. It was all she could do not to turn into his touch and nestle her cheek against his palm.

She wanted so much. Thierry. This closeness. His passion—definitely his passion—but far more. She swallowed hard over a knot of pain.

Against the odds she'd shared a wonderful affair with a man who in every way the world counted was far out of her league. Now, when it should be over and they should be saying their goodbyes, it tore her apart.

Because it was true.

She'd fallen in love with Thierry Girard.

She wanted to be with him, not just now, sharing pleasure, but always, growing old together. Being a part of him just as he'd become a vital part of her.

'I'm trying to do what's right.' And it had never been so hard. To her horror her mouth crumpled with the effort of holding in so much welling emotion.

'I don't want you to go.' The words circled the still air and eddied deep inside her. Her head shot up, eyes locking with his.

'You don't?'

His smile was crooked and devastatingly sexy. 'I want you here, *chérie.*'

Imogen's heart locked in her throat. Could it be?

'Is it so bad being here with me?' he murmured, his hand trailing down her throat to her bare collarbone.

'Of course not. I…' She swallowed hard, trying to find her voice. 'I like it here.'

She'd like anywhere so long as Thierry was with her. The enormity of her feelings blindsided her. How had she gone from casual attraction to full-blown love in such a short space of time? Maybe because she wasn't made for casual affairs. That was why she'd been so cautious with her heart and her body before this.

'I'm glad. I'd wondered if it might be too quiet for you here.'

Imogen shook her head. She loved the peace of the estate. Besides, it was only minutes to the nearest town and a short drive to the nearest city. But what made it perfect was Thierry's presence.

'You really want me to stay?' Did he hear the longing in her voice? Hurriedly, she went on briskly. 'I'd rather you were totally honest.'

Thierry hesitated and there was something in his eyes that made her uneasy. As if he hid something.

Yet what could he hide? He had been trustworthy, honest and generous from the night they'd met. He'd even pulled back from her physically when he'd believed her ill, putting her wellbeing before his own sexual needs.

He wouldn't lie to her.

'I want you to stay, Imogen.' His gaze bored into hers, and she felt the impact right to her core. Slowly, he smiled and it was as if he'd flicked a switch, releasing the tension straining between them.

'Think about what we've got.' His hand dropped to the sheet covering her, his long fingers brushing her breasts in deliberate provocation. 'We like each other. We're sexually more than compatible.' He lifted his hand away and it was only then Imogen discovered how far she'd leaned forward into his touch. 'And we're having a child. Why not stay together?'

Dazed as much by his touch as his words, Imogen sank back against the pillows, her body heavy and lax.

'You want to stay married?' She needed to hear him spell it out.

'I do.' That smile devastated her brain, making logic almost impossible. 'It makes sense, Imogen.'

Part of her wanted to exult. He wanted her here, and not just as a temporary girlfriend. Imogen knew that a future with Thierry would be everything she'd never dared to hope for. Because when she was with him she felt...

'What we have is good, isn't it?'

Good?

Imogen's thoughts screeched to a halt.

Good. That insipid word couldn't describe how she felt when she was with Thierry.

She opened her mouth then closed it. Her neck prickled, the hairs standing to attention as finally her sluggish brain moved into gear.

She'd been on tenterhooks, wondering if he wanted her gone, but it was only now she realised what was missing.

Imogen met those gleaming eyes that she'd seen kindle with desire, crinkle with laughter or warm with concern. She took in those straight shoulders that she'd leaned on in moments of weakness and those capable hands that had helped her when she'd needed it. Thierry was caring, passionate and considerate.

But he doesn't love you.

There was no urgency in him, no desperation. Just calm logic and, yes, liking.

Imogen's heart skated to a bruising halt then lurched into a discordant rhythm so powerful she felt queasy.

Now she understood!

'This is you making the best of the situation, isn't it? Making do.' She recalled him talking in those terms in Paris, about not pining for the impossible, but adapting to whatever situation he found himself in.

'Why not?' That insouciant Gallic shrug made a mockery of her secret hopes and dreams. 'I'm expected to marry some time and here we are with a baby on the way.'

He must have noticed her breathless rigidity because he went on with a smile guaranteed to turn any woman to a puddle of pure longing. 'We like each other.' His hand settled on one of hers, lightly stroking an intricate scroll of desire from her wrist to her thumb. 'Sex between us is fantastic and we respect each other.'

'You said that before.' Her voice sounded scratchy. Were those the only reasons he could come up with for them to stay together?

'They're important.' The skin between his eyebrows pinched, as if he was surprised or annoyed she wasn't gushing with delight. 'I couldn't marry a woman I didn't respect.' His mouth curved in a way that devastated her resolve. 'As for the sex…' He shook his head. 'I can't remember it ever being so good.'

Imogen sat utterly still, scared that if she moved something, like her stupid heart, might shatter.

He wants to stay married to you because the sex is good. And because you're conveniently providing him with a child.

No doubt he wants one to inherit the estate and the villa

on the south coast, and all the other things the Girard family have amassed. He wants an heir.

She'd been dreaming of love but Thierry laid out their relationship as if it was a business merger.

Her lips flattened. That was how he saw this—a neat solution to a difficult problem. A way of keeping his child while getting companionship and sex into the bargain.

She had no illusions she was the sort of woman he'd marry in normal circumstances, but Thierry had proved himself a realist through and through. Why yearn for caviar when you have fish and chips already on the table?

Imogen felt her hair slide around her face and neck as she shook her head. 'I don't think that's a good basis for marriage.'

His hand tightened, long fingers shackling her wrist. Did he feel her pulse hammering? He leaned in, crowding her against the pillows. For the first time since this conversation began she felt disadvantaged, naked beneath the sheet while he was dressed.

'Of course it's a good basis for marriage.' His eyes narrowed. Fervently she hoped he couldn't read her thoughts. 'Unless you're after some fantasy of romance. Is that it?'

Self-preservation made her shake her head, even as her soul cried out that that was exactly what she wanted.

'I didn't think so.' His lips quirked up in the hint of a smile. 'You're like me, *chérie*—too practical to want hearts and flowers and sentimental protestations of undying love.'

Dry-eyed, Imogen gritted her teeth. Thierry couldn't know how she felt about him. He'd never deliberately trample over her feelings. Yet that didn't stop the pain from each dismissive word.

'You don't believe in love?'

His lips quirked. 'Once. I fell in love with a girl from a neighbouring estate. But she married someone else. At the time I thought my heart was broken but I'm old enough now to realise that's just a fiction. I've been happy with my life. It wasn't blighted by rejection after all.'

His expression was reflective as he stroked her palm, making her shiver. 'What we have is precious, Imogen, even if it doesn't go by the name of love. Respect, liking and a baby—those make a good starting point.'

'Don't forget the sex,' she said, hiding pain behind a twisted smile.

'Oh, I don't. Not for a moment.' He pressed his mouth to the spot below her ear where she was most sensitive. Instantly, tremors of heat racked her, and she shivered. Yet her heart ached.

'Let me warm you properly, Imogen.' He reached for the tray between them, made to lift it away, but she put a shaky hand on his arm.

'No. Don't. I'm hungry.' The food would be sawdust in her mouth but she couldn't have sex with him, not now. Not knowing she'd given her heart to him and he only saw her as a convenient solution to a problematic situation.

She didn't care about his wealth or his power. But she wanted to *matter* to someone, to be the most important thing in their life. And that someone was Thierry. Because that was how she felt about him. Once she'd have settled but now she didn't want to *make do*. She wanted *everything*.

But he didn't believe in love. Would he ever? If he did, would it be for her or some woman from his own set, privileged and sophisticated?

Bile rose, and she almost choked.

'Are you all right?' The concern in his eyes was real.

Thierry did care. Just not enough.

'Fine,' she croaked, reaching for the sparkling water on the tray. She had to hold the glass in both hands so as not to spill it, but at least that gave her something to concentrate on other than Thierry's piercing gaze.

She felt his scrutiny like a touch. He wanted an answer. What was she going to do? Flounce home and give up any chance he might, over time, begin to care for her as she did him? Or stay here like some charity case, making do with what he handed out, maybe breaking her heart little by little each day?

The mineral water tasted unbearably metallic, and she put it down with a grimace.

'Maybe I won't have anything to eat after all.'

'You're unwell? Morning sickness?' Thierry whipped away the tray, getting off the bed to put it on a nearby table. Imogen's breath eased out in a sigh of relief. She needed space to think.

'I'm a little out of sorts.' After one swift glance at his frown she looked away, watching her hands smooth the rumpled sheet. How had she gone from ecstasy to misery in such a short space of time?

It wasn't as if he'd led her on. He'd been marvellous. It was all her own doing, because she'd made the mistake of believing the fantasy. Because she loved him.

'I'll get you some herbal tea.'

'No. Nothing, thanks.' She doubted she'd keep anything down.

'Lie down then and I'll stay here till you sleep.'

'No!' Her head shot around to find him staring at her curiously. 'No, there's no need.'

See? He was caring. The sort of man any woman would want, even if he didn't love her. Was she crazy to wish for more?

She must be. Why would a man born to his world of privilege and power fall for someone as ordinary as her?

A warm hand closed around hers. He stood beside the bed, so close she had to crick her neck to meet his eyes. They were unfathomable, deep and steady, yet she felt the intensity of his stare through every part of her being.

'So you'll stay, Imogen? You agree?'

She imagined tension in his voice. Clearly, she was projecting her own emotions.

'I…'

'You won't regret it. We're good together; you know it.'

Good. There was that word again.

She didn't want good. She wanted spectacular, amazing, special. She wanted love.

She gnawed at her lip, torn between fighting for what she wanted and the craven impulse to take whatever Thierry offered. She wasn't sure she'd like the woman she'd become if she did that.

'Stay, Imogen.' His voice was compelling, his hold tight.

She swallowed hard. 'I'll stay. For now. Let's see how it goes.'

CHAPTER ELEVEN

SEE HOW IT GOES.

She was going to see how it went.

As if he were on probation!

Thierry frowned, flipping another page of the contract before realising he hadn't taken in a word.

Disgusted, he shoved his chair back from the desk.

His ability to concentrate, even in a crisis, had always been one of his strengths. It had saved his hide more than once on long-distance motor rallies and while climbing. It had been one of the few assets he'd had in the early days when he took on this business.

Until today concentrating on what needed to be done hadn't been a problem. Even when he'd yearned for the wind in his hair and a far more physical challenge than that presented by corporate negotiations. He'd always given his all to the job at hand, knowing the sooner he solved a problem and moved on, the sooner he'd be free.

Nowadays he even found satisfaction in developing and expanding the business, finding new opportunities.

Not today.

A month today since Imogen had agreed to stay and *see how it goes*.

A month and no resolution.

He felt like he was on trial.

He surged to his feet and stalked to the window, staring at the blue sky that mocked his mood. He felt dark, stormy and miserable.

Thierry folded his arms over his chest. Made miserable by a woman. It didn't seem possible. Never had it happened in all the years since Sandrine had rejected him and his volatile young heart had counted itself broken.

Since then he'd enjoyed women but never wanted or expected anything serious.

Naturally, that had changed with Imogen. She was his wife so they needed a secure, meaningful relationship. One based on respect.

That was what he'd offered her and still she refused to commit to staying.

What more could she want?

He spun around, his gaze driving unerringly through the office's glass wall to his cousin Henri's desk. There he was, his head bent towards Imogen's.

Heat blasted Thierry's gut as he watched the pair, so at ease, totally absorbed in the accounts Thierry personally found incredibly dull. But Imogen and Henri spoke the same language. The language of numbers.

When Imogen had complained she didn't have enough to keep her busy—as if she needed to work when he could provide for her!—Thierry had suggested she assist with the accounts. It had been a masterstroke and a disaster. Imogen was happy with the opportunity to work as an accountant again, her smiles becoming more genuine and frequent, at least in the office. More than that, she'd proved a valuable asset, her skills obviously top notch.

But her happiness at work only made him realise how rarely she smiled with him. He missed those lit-from-within smiles, so incandescent they were contagious.

His eyes narrowed as he heard a laugh and watched Imogen and Henri share some joke.

Thierry wanted to stride out and yank her away. Insist she share the joke with him as once she would have.

Except it didn't work like that. With him she was polite, friendly, as she was with Jeanne or his grandparents when they visited. But never was he treated to those delicious gurgles of pure joy that had entranced him when they'd met. Or those cheeky, teasing grins.

He missed that. Missed Imogen. It was as if the most vital part of her was locked somewhere he couldn't reach.

Sometimes when they made love he felt he'd almost breached that gap, reached the woman locked behind her reserve. For, despite initial protests, Imogen hadn't been able to deny the passion between them. They shared a bed and his one solace was that in his arms she went up in flames as surely as the propane that fuelled his balloon flights. She was mesmerising, her passion all he could ask for.

Yet afterwards a curious blankness replaced the smoky flare of rapture. She'd withdraw mentally. For the first time ever Thierry found himself wanting to dig deeper, even discuss her *feelings*!

She drove him crazy.

He wrapped a palm around the back of his neck. He was too close to the edge.

Thierry glared through the glass. *Diable.* He wasn't jealous of his cousin, was he?

Impossible. Yet he found himself striding across the office, only to slam to a halt, his hand on the door.

Think, man! What are you going to do? Go out and drag her off to your bedroom?

The idea appealed, especially when he saw her smile at Henri as the younger man touched her hand then pointed to something on the screen. Waves of heat battered at Thierry, turning his belly into a churning morass.

Okay, he admitted it. He was jealous. He knew there was nothing between them except liking and professional admiration but that didn't lessen his envy.

Thierry dropped the door handle as if it burned with an electric current. He took a step back.

What was happening to him?

He wasn't interested in examining his feelings. He

wanted action. But abducting his wife and ravishing her till she cried his name in rapture, while perfect in its own way, would leave him disgruntled when she withdrew again.

Sex wasn't the answer. Not alone. He had to find another way to connect with Imogen.

'Imogen.' She stilled, her heart pattering as that deep voice turned her name into a caress.

Would she ever *not* respond to it?

Slowly, she turned, willing her breathing to steady as espresso-dark eyes snared hers and she tingled all over. It was hard, sometimes, to remember Thierry saw her as a convenient wife, not the love of his life. That heavy-lidded stare sizzled with a promise she'd almost swear held more than physical desire.

Except she was done with fantasy. She was back into self-protection mode, carefully weighing her options for the future. She owed her baby that.

'Thierry.' She stumbled a little over his name. Last time she'd said it had been just hours ago, in that big, luxurious bed of his, and she hadn't said it: she'd screamed it in pleasure. 'Did you need this report? We're almost done.' Casually, she glanced at Henri, hoping he'd take up the conversation.

'It's not about the report,' Thierry said. 'I need you.'

Imogen's head snapped around. But the banked embers in his eyes had disappeared, or maybe she'd imagined that. Thierry looked all business.

'Of course. Excuse me, Henri?'

'Yes, fine.' He turned back to the spreadsheet. 'We've almost sorted this. You'll have it in ten minutes, Thierry.'

'No rush. So long as I get it by this evening.'

Imogen frowned. An hour ago the report had been urgent. But her thoughts frayed when Thierry put a hand under her elbow as she stood.

Once she'd loved those little courtesies. Now they were exquisite torture.

'You want me for something?' Her voice was only a little husky.

'I do.' To her surprise, he escorted her out to the car park where the sun shone warm on her face. 'I suppose I'll need to get another car,' he murmured as they approached his.

'You will?' The words flummoxed her. He adored his low-slung sports car.

'There's no room for a baby seat in this.'

The idea of Thierry replacing his streamlined beast with a family sedan stunned her. He really was serious about being an involved father.

If she stayed.

'Why are we here?' She stood back when he opened the passenger door. 'I've got work to do.'

'You've done your share today.'

Imogen shook her head. 'It's early—'

'You married the boss, so there are perks. Besides...' his expression turned serious '...you need to look after yourself. You're still getting morning sickness.'

'Only a little.' She found it better if she kept herself busy. Between the accountancy work, intensive French lessons and the hours she spent with Jeanne learning the secrets of French baking, every waking hour was filled. Soon she'd have to decide whether to leave, but having time on her hands hadn't helped her reach a decision. All it had done was depress her.

'Well, today we have somewhere else to be.' He held open the door. Imogen wavered, for suddenly it hit her—she'd deliberately arranged her days to spend as little time as possible with her husband.

Because she was afraid he'd convince her to stay?

'Please, Imogen. It's important.' His mouth flattened. Curiously, she read strain in his proud features and restlessness in the way his hand slid along the open door.

'What's wrong?' Anxiety leapt into her chest. She'd learned no one was immune to bad news and she'd never seen Thierry look this way, as if suppressing agitation.

'Nothing's wrong. Can't you just trust me?'

Imogen looked into the face of the man she loved and knew that was the one thing she'd always done. He'd never deliberately hurt her. He'd gone to remarkable lengths to protect her.

She laid her hand on his where it shifted along the door. Instantly, he stilled, and she felt the familiar thrill of connection. 'Of course I trust you.' Whatever Thierry wanted, she'd help him if she could. She owed him that.

Yet she was careful not to meet that gleaming gaze as she slid into the passenger seat.

'I can't believe it. This is amazing!' The wind caught her words as hair streamed across her face. Imogen laughed, lifting her free hand to pull her hair back.

The air rushed around her, skimming her body just as the small sailing boat skimmed the lake's sparkling waters. The sensation of speed, the huff and ripple of the wind against canvas and the joyous sense of adventure were like champagne in her blood. Her skin tingled, and her heart felt lighter than it had in months.

Thierry beamed, his face creasing into grooves that accentuated his devastating appeal. He looked totally at ease, his long frame swaying, adjusting easily each time the small boat shifted. Yet she'd seen how quickly he could move, coming to her aid whenever an unexpected change in conditions threatened her fragile confidence. She was a complete novice.

But he'd made sailing so easy.

Her hand clenched on the tiller. That was what he'd always done, wasn't it? Make things easy for her. Their affair. Their baby. Even dying. No matter what she'd faced, he'd been at her side.

Her heart lurched against her ribs. She loved him so much. How was she supposed to walk away? Was she mad, even considering it?

'I knew you'd take to it.' He linked his arms behind his head, stretching those long legs towards her till they almost touched.

'You couldn't possibly know that.'

'Of course I did. Face it, Imogen, we're the same. Both with a taste for adventure.'

Automatically, she shook her head. She wasn't like Thierry. Those extreme sports he enjoyed made her hair curl. 'You've got me wrong, Thierry. I'm ordinary and cautious. I'm an accountant, remember? Until recently I'd never done anything exciting. Only the threat of dying got me out of Australia.'

'But it did, didn't it? You didn't stay, waiting for the end, but went out and found your true self.' He sounded satisfied, almost smug, as if today's surprise sailing treat was a major win in some way she couldn't fathom.

'I'm afraid not.' How could he have got her so wrong? 'My true self belongs at home or in an office. This is just...' She shrugged. 'My sister was the courageous one, not me.'

The wind shifted and the little boat shivered as Imogen struggled to guide it. Instantly, Thierry was beside her, his shoulder against hers, his hand over hers on the tiller. Seconds later they were gliding easily over the water again. He lifted his hand but didn't move away.

A sense of wellbeing filled her, and for once Imogen didn't fight it, just accepted this glorious moment, with the rush of wind, the thrill of sailing and Thierry beside her.

'You don't think it took courage to look after your dying mother? Even though it cost you your lover? You don't think you were courageous when you faced what you thought was your own death? Or when you planned to face pregnancy alone?'

'I didn't have any choice. That wasn't courage. That was necessity.'

Thierry lifted her free hand to his lips and her heart sang. 'You're wrong, Imogen. You're exciting and marvellous and brave. We're well matched—because we both have a taste for *life*.'

She opened her mouth to disagree but his finger on her lips stopped her. 'We *are*, Imogen. Don't you feel it whenever we're together?'

The trouble was she did. But she told herself it was because she'd fallen for him, hook, line and sinker. Whereas he— Well, Thierry wouldn't fall for someone like her.

'You're talking to a woman who has just spent days learning how to make the perfect choux pastry. I'm no daredevil.'

Thierry shook his head. 'You think it's so black and white? That we aren't all complex? I might love motor rallies and alpine climbing but I never spent all my time doing that. Do you know how many hours I spent beneath the engine of my rally car, getting it tuned to perfection? Or planning the optimal route for a trek?' He slipped his arm around her, his embrace warming her in places she couldn't name.

'You don't understand. I'm not the woman you think I am. That woman in Paris wasn't the real Imogen.'

'Wasn't she?' His voice was a deep burr that did wicked things to her heart and her self-control. 'You've spent so long putting yourself in a pigeonhole you can't see that you're more complex than you ever imagined.' He paused. 'I think that's why you're afraid to take a chance on me.'

Before she could say anything he rose and took up a position just far enough away that she couldn't touch him. But his eyes held hers, bright and challenging.

'We have so much going for us, Imogen. Why won't you give us a chance? Us and our child?'

Because I'm scared. I'm terrified to love you when you don't love me back.

'Trust your instincts, Imogen. Think of the good times we could have together.' His was the voice of temptation, coursing through her like liquid chocolate.

Of course she wanted to stay. That was the trouble. It was too easy to imagine being with him, spending time together, not just at the *château* or in his arms, but *living*, sharing adventures like this.

'All you have to do is let go of your fear and trust in us.'

Let go of her fear! After living with fear so long that was easier said than done. Yet the temptation to trust in him was almost overwhelming. Only a lifetime's caution held her back.

But what was she holding back from? Fear of not being loved? If she walked away from Thierry she'd sever whatever bond they already had. Plus she'd destroy any chance that he'd ever love her.

Did she ask too much, expecting him to love after such a short time, just because she loved him? Imogen frowned. Looked at that way, she seemed impatient and greedy.

Imogen stared at his sprawled body, apparently relaxed, yet with eyes so watchful. He'd deliberately distanced himself when it would be easy to persuade her with his arm around her. Her mind always went to mush when he touched her.

He was being noble, damn him, and to her chagrin that only made it harder to deny him. But he wouldn't be the man she adored if he wasn't decent and caring. Look at today—giving her this first exhilarating taste of sailing.

Her thoughts stuck and circled. Thierry had shared his love of the outdoors with her, his delight in speed and adventure.

He wasn't blocking her out of his life, or taking her for granted like the convenient bride she'd imagined herself.

He was letting her in.

Imogen stared hard at the man before her, the tautness of his shoulders and hands revealing he was anything but relaxed. He wasn't cold-blooded. He might see marriage as a pragmatic solution to their situation but Thierry was passionate and caring. He didn't love her but surely there was a chance he might one day?

If she stayed.

Her heart pounded like stampeding wild animals and she blinked, blinded by the sudden brightness of sunshine on glittering water.

'Watch out!' A moment later he was with her again, his firm body hot beside her, his strong hand guiding hers.

The boat shifted, poised for a moment, then turned and caught the wind, flying across the water.

But it wasn't the speed that caught the breath in Imogen's throat.

She sank against him, her head against his chest, his tantalising scent stimulating her senses. She closed her eyes and felt the tension leave her.

Really, she had only one choice.

'You win, Thierry. I'll stay.'

It might be the biggest gamble of her life, the only gamble, but she'd play it to the end.

CHAPTER TWELVE

THIERRY'S HANDS CAME around her waist, pulling her back against him. In the mirror she read that familiar smile, and her stomach tumbled over itself as it had that first night in Paris.

'You look good enough to eat.' He pressed a kiss to her neck, and she shivered as desire spiked.

'Seriously, this dress is right for tonight?' It was her first formal event as Thierry's hostess and nerves had struck. When he'd mentioned it a month ago she'd told herself wearing one of Izzy's creations would be perfect. The full-length white satin with crimson flowers would give her confidence. It was the dress she'd worn the night she'd met Thierry and it felt like a lucky talisman.

Should she have taken his offer to buy something new?

'This dress is perfect.' He spread his palm over her belly, now rounded just enough that she'd had to find a dressmaker to let out the dress a little.

'Even if I'm making it strain at the seams?' Surely she'd put on weight in the past week? Soon she'd need new bras too.

Thierry's hand slid up to her breasts straining against the satin. His light touch made her knees quiver. 'The only problem will be the disgruntled women when all men watch you, *ma chérie*.'

Imogen's lips twitched. 'Sweet talker.'

'Siren.' His hand stroked her budding nipple, and she gasped in exquisite arousal. Pregnancy made her even more sensitive to his touch. And he knew it. In the mirror his smile was pure erotic invitation as she sank back against him.

It had been so easy to give in and agree to live as Thierry's wife. He made her feel desired, appreciated, supported. Even if he didn't love her, surely that was enough to begin a marriage? And their sex life just got better and better. She read familiar heat in his expression.

'Thierry! We don't have time. And I've got my make-up on.'

Firmly, she stifled a wish that he felt more than sexual attraction. She needed patience. One day surely…?

He pressed an open-mouthed kiss to her neck that made her shiver, then stepped back. Instantly, she felt bereft. She was as needy as ever and now she'd opened her heart to him too.

'I'll be good. Besides, I have something for you.'

'You do?' She made to turn but he stopped her.

'Stand there.' She watched, dumbfounded, as he lowered a magnificent necklace over her head. The dressing-room light flashed on brilliant gems and old gold that glowed with the patina of age. Imogen was dazzled as the weight of the necklace settled on her.

'I've heard of rubies the size of pigeons' eggs…' she said shakily.

'You think it too old-fashioned?'

'It's gorgeous,' she murmured. 'I just hope it's not as precious as it looks. Tell me it's costume jewellery.'

He shook his head. 'It's real. You're my wife, my hostess. You need to look the part. This has been in the family for generations. Besides, it matches your dress.'

He was right. The crimson glow of the central stone matched the flowers on her dress and the ornate necklace paired well with the simplicity of the strapless bodice.

Her fingers fluttered over it, her eyes wide. She looked different—not like the woman she knew.

Disquiet shivered through her, but she forced it aside. Naturally Thierry wanted her to do him proud tonight. The session he'd organised for her with a beautician had been a thoughtful gift. Thierry's grandmother had spent hours coaching her on the who's who of French society that would be at tonight's party. Plus, with her language tutor's help, Imogen felt reasonably competent with introductions and very basic conversation.

She smoothed her gloved hands down her dress, telling herself she'd be fine. It wasn't that she was scared of crowds, just that they weren't her thing. But with Thierry at her side she'd be fine. More than fine. She'd shine.

Only Thierry didn't stay at her side.

For an hour he was with her, his arm around her waist, greeting their guests, turning these sophisticated strangers into people she could relax and laugh with. Most of them, if curious about her, were friendly.

But after a while they got separated. Occasionally he'd turn his head to check on her, his eyebrows raised in question, and she'd nod, silently letting him know she was okay.

She was a professional woman, used to meeting strangers. She didn't need her hand held, even if some of the glitterati were rather daunting.

There was one woman in particular—Sandrine. A tall, slender blonde who looked like she'd stepped from a glossy magazine. She was the most beautiful woman Imogen had ever seen, with a long sweep of platinum hair, perfect features and an assurance that allowed her to wear backless silver lamé and a fortune in diamonds with casual insouciance.

But it wasn't the other woman's beauty that made Imogen stare, it was the realisation that this was the woman who'd broken Thierry's heart. Sandrine made it clear they'd known each other since the cradle. Several times in their short conversation she'd subtly reinforced the fact that Imogen was an outsider in this milieu.

When Thierry was beside Imogen that didn't matter. But as the evening wore on it was harder not to make comparisons between herself and the glamorous blonde so at home in these superb surroundings.

Imogen dragged her attention back to the couple talking with her about Australia, reminiscing about a trip to an exclusive resort she'd heard of but never visited.

'I was disappointed,' the husband said, 'not to see those dangerous snakes we hear about.' The twinkle in his eyes belied the complaint.

Imogen smiled. 'I can recommend some nature reserves for your next visit.' She glanced down and noticed their glasses were empty. Looking around, she couldn't see any of the waiters brought in for tonight's party.

'If you'll excuse me, I'll send someone over with drinks.'

'No, no, it's fine. It's no trouble.'

Nice as it was to chat, it felt good to do something practical, attending to guests' needs. It made her feel less of an imposter in this well-heeled crowd. To be fair, though, not all the invitees were rich. There were locals and friends of Thierry who shared an interest in extreme sports.

Imogen was moving to the end of the room where the bar was set up when a woman's voice slowed her steps.

'Of course she's pregnant, what other reason could there be? He's married her to make the child legitimate. She's not Thierry's type. When has anyone ever seen him with a brunette? And as for the rest... Thierry deserves someone with panache, someone who fits in.'

Pale blonde hair swung across the speaker's elegant bare back.

Sandrine. Thierry's old friend. His first love.

Imogen's chest tightened and she faltered to a stop. Was that why Thierry was adamant he'd never want a love match? Because he'd given his heart to this woman and no one else would fill her place?

It was one thing to know her husband had once been disappointed in love. It was quite another to discover the object of his affection was the most stunningly beautiful woman she'd ever seen.

Did she seriously expect him to love her when his taste ran to svelte goddesses?

'Oh, come on, Sandrine.' An American accent this time. 'You can't know that. I say it was love at first sight. You just have to look at her to know she's head over heels in love with him. I think it's sweet.'

Imogen pressed a hand to her suddenly queasy stomach. She needed to keep moving. She didn't want to hear the speculation about her marriage.

Before she could move, Sandrine shrugged. 'I couldn't agree more. I feel sorry for the poor little thing.' Her voice dropped and the woman with her leaned closer.

Despite her resolve to move on, Imogen found herself waiting with bated breath.

'Didn't you see the photo in that scandal rag a month or so ago? Thierry kissing some blonde in a hotel bar when he was supposed to be on a climbing trip? The way he held her, it was obvious they'd just got out of bed.'

'Imogen. There you are. I was hoping to find you.' Startled, Imogen swung round to see Poppy Chatsfield beside her. The tall, red-headed model was another of the sophisticated set but her smile was warm.

Imogen blinked, trying to focus. Her stomach heaved and she almost stumbled as the floor rippled beneath her. A chill clamped her spine, freezing each vertebra in turn.

Thierry kissing another woman.

Thierry holding another woman...

'Imogen?' A hand gripped her elbow and she found herself ushered to the side of the room. 'You need to sit. In your condition you shouldn't be standing so long.'

A ragged laugh escaped Imogen's lips as Poppy led her to an antique sofa. 'Does *everyone* here know I'm pregnant?'

'Of course not.' Poppy sat beside her. 'But Thierry and

Orsino are old friends; he just told us the news. I came to congratulate you.' She paused, her concerned gaze roving Imogen's face. 'Can I get you something? Water? I found sipping it slowly sometimes helped the morning sickness.'

'No. I'm okay.' Imogen felt her mouth stretch in a grimace. Okay? How could she be okay? If what Sandrine had said was true... She wrapped her arms around her midriff, holding in the searing hurt.

'If you'll take my advice, you won't pay any attention to Sandrine.'

Imogen's gaze met Poppy's and heat washed her face. How many people had heard?

Poppy went on, her voice soft. 'I don't know what she said but I have a good idea it's what made you feel sick.'

Despite the haze of hurt and disappointment, Imogen found herself liking this woman.

'That's better. You look less like you're going to faint.'

'That's not going to happen.' Imogen straightened, drawing breath and putting a hand to her hair. 'But thank you. I appreciate your concern.'

Poppy nodded. 'You should know, Sandrine is—'

'I know. Years ago she and Thierry were an item.'

'Actually, I was going to say Sandrine isn't a complete witch, even if she's not at her best tonight. She's piqued because you married Thierry.'

'Why should she be piqued? She rejected him. She's been married to someone else for years.'

'Yes, and in all that time she's had the satisfaction of seeing Thierry go from one woman to another, never settling. As if he couldn't get over her.' Poppy nodded. 'Imagine how she feels after years thinking his heart was hers. Now you come along, stealing him. It's obvious he's fallen for you.'

Imogen pressed her hands together, wishing she could take comfort in Poppy's words.

Thierry hadn't fallen for her. He'd told her they were

well-matched because neither expected hearts and flowers and declarations of love.

Did that explain the other woman? Imogen swallowed convulsively at the thought of them together.

That must have been the weekend after they'd learned there'd been no need for them to marry because she was going to live. Imogen had known Thierry was rocked by the news, as she was, but he'd denied it.

A blonde. Sandrine had said brunettes weren't his type. Imogen's stomach churned so hard she thought she'd be ill. His taste ran to blondes like Sandrine and the woman in that bar.

Imogen stared blankly at the chattering crowd. How many had seen that photo? How many knew he'd betrayed her with another woman?

Clearly, Thierry didn't think it a betrayal—because he didn't love her, or because such things were accepted here? Did he expect her to put up with his affairs? Was that how he saw their marriage working?

This time the pain was a piercing white-hot blade to the heart.

'Imogen? You're worrying me. Shall I find Thierry?'

She jerked her head around to meet Poppy's stare. 'No,' she croaked. She couldn't face that yet. She needed time to digest this.

'I'm just...' Dazed, she searched for words to reassure Poppy. 'It's so crowded and close. I just can't get my breath.' It was true as far as it went.

Poppy squeezed her hand. 'You poor thing. I was the same when I was pregnant with Sofia.'

'If you'll excuse me, I'll head outside for some fresh air.' Imogen stood, locking her knees when they wobbled. She wasn't going to collapse in a pathetic heap, especially amongst Thierry's friends.

'I'll come with you.' Imogen was about to protest when Poppy whispered in her ear. 'You won't get far alone. Everyone wants to talk with you. If you're with me, you've got an excuse not to stop and chat.'

Minutes later Imogen rested her palms on the stone balustrade of the terrace. The buzz of the crowd was a muted hum and the high-riding moon washed the scene silver.

Imogen made herself turn to Poppy. 'That's better. Thank you. I'm okay now, so you can go back to Orsino. He's probably wondering where you are.' She was desperate to be alone.

Poppy waved a careless hand. 'No, he won't. He and Thierry are busy planning their grand trip.'

'Grand trip?' Imogen hadn't heard anything about a trip. But then she was probably the only person here who hadn't known about his other woman. Her fingers clenched on stone as revulsion welled.

'Oh, just the usual. For years they've been planning their next big adventure—the one they'll take as soon as Thierry's free.'

'Free?' The word tore from Imogen's choked throat. Free of her? She frowned. But then why insist they stay married?

'Free of the business.' Poppy bent her head, tsking as she disentangled her bracelet from a sequin on her dress.

'What do you mean, free of the business?'

Poppy looked up, astonishment on her features. 'You don't know?' She paused. 'Maybe I got it wrong,' she said quickly. 'I—'

'Please, Poppy. I need to know.'

Did Poppy hear the strain in her voice? Finally, she shrugged but she didn't look comfortable. 'Only close friends know. Thierry wouldn't talk about it in public.'

Clearly whatever *it* was, he hadn't thought to share it with his wife.

Disappointment hammered at Imogen's heart. She'd been fooling herself that if she was patient one day things would change between them!

How many secrets did Thierry hide?

'Thierry was dragged kicking and screaming into the family business when his grandfather became ill.'

Imogen nodded. 'He had a stroke.' She knew that, at least.

'Thierry hates being cooped up behind four walls—says it will send him crazy one day, being tied down. He vowed to set the company on its feet then step aside, find some good managers and take up his old life. He and Orsino used to do a lot of balloon treks together, rally driving too, and climbing.'

She paused, her glance darting to Imogen as if for confirmation she already knew this. Imogen said nothing, just turned to look at the cold, moonlit garden.

'For ages they've talked about a big trek to celebrate his freedom when it comes. Last I heard, it would be whitewater rafting somewhere inhospitable. Somewhere you wouldn't catch me, ever. I'll stay where there are some creature comforts, thank you very much.'

Imogen recalled seeing Thierry across the crowd with Orsino Chatsfield. The two handsome, dark-haired men were easy to spot, given their height. But it was the animation on Thierry's face and the intensity of their conversation that she'd noticed.

Poppy turned towards her. 'Perhaps we could spend some time together when they're away? Get to know each other better?'

'That's a lovely idea.' Imogen forced the words out before her throat closed on a ball of wretched emotion. She liked Poppy. In other circumstances she could imagine them as friends. But it wasn't going to happen.

The pain morphed from a piercing stab to a heavy, slow-grinding ache pressing down, robbing her of air.

What more did she need to convince her this marriage was all wrong? He wasn't interested in settling down any more than he believed in love. He begrudged the time he spent in one place saving the family firm. How much more would he come to resent the woman and child who tied him down even further?

He'd put a good face on a bad situation. No doubt about it, her husband didn't shirk from what he believed to be his duty. Having met his grandparents, she realised he'd had responsibility drummed into him from an early age.

Something in her chest tore in an excruciating, slow-motion rip of anguish. Her heart?

'I'm afraid things are a little up in the air at the moment. A little…complicated.' She tried for a casual smile but knew it didn't convince, by the sombre way Poppy surveyed her.

'Of course. I don't mean to pressure you. A new marriage can be challenging as well as exciting.' Her laugh held a jarring note. 'Orsino and I went through hell before we worked out we loved and trusted each other.' She touched Imogen briefly on the arm. 'Just remember, if ever you need to talk, I'm available. I know how hard it can be, married to one of these take-charge men.'

'Thanks, Poppy. That's kind of you.' Imogen gulped, overcome by her empathy and kindness. She struggled for a lighter tone. 'I suppose we'd better get back inside before we're missed.' She couldn't think of anything worse. But she had her pride. She'd see the evening out then decide what to do.

Except she knew she'd run out of options.

She'd given her heart and soul to a man who didn't love her. Who could never love her. Who couldn't even give her his loyalty. He liked her, and he shared himself as much as he could with her, but ultimately she and their child were encumbrances, like the business he'd stepped in to save and couldn't wait to be rid of.

Her fond dream of him returning her feelings was just that—a dream.

There was only one thing any self-respecting woman could do. It was just a pity she hadn't done it months ago.

CHAPTER THIRTEEN

'IMOGEN?' THIERRY FLICKED on the light switch only to find his bedroom empty.

Where was she? She'd come upstairs when the last of the guests had left. There'd been fine lines of tiredness on her face yet that stubborn streak had seen her determined to play hostess to the end, despite his suggestion she retire early.

Thierry smiled. She'd been magnificent. He'd wondered if such a big function would be too much but she'd sailed through it with ease. Every time he'd looked over she'd been the centre of some eager group.

Afterwards he'd remained chatting with Orsino, who was staying with Poppy in one of the guest suites. It had been too long since they'd caught up. It was only now as work turned from manic to manageable that he realised how little he'd seen of his friends, as opposed to business contacts.

He marched across the room and opened the bathroom door. Empty. Where was she? His belly tightened in a premonition of trouble.

A few strides took him to the dressing room, but it too was empty. He scowled, thinking of her pale features as she'd headed upstairs and cursed himself for not seeing her to their room, despite her protests.

Thierry whipped around and back into the bedroom. Flicking off the light, he stepped towards the sitting room. That was when he noticed the strip of light under the adjoining bedroom door.

His heart slammed his ribs as he stopped mid-stride. What was she doing in her old bedroom? Incoherent thoughts jostled his brain. Was she ill? Was it the baby?

He wrenched open the door. The room looked peaceful in the glow of a bedside lamp and he heard water running in the bathroom.

He was almost at the bathroom door when he noticed the laptop open on the bed. One glance sent a sucker punch to the gut.

Thierry staggered, stared, and felt the world tilt.

Diable! Imogen had seen this? He went hot then cold as wave after wave of prickling remorse hit him.

He didn't want to, but Thierry took a step closer, then another. The photo was even worse close up. The blonde leaned into him, every line of her body taut and hungry as they kissed. From this angle, and with his hands at her waist, it looked like he'd been utterly lost to passion.

What had Imogen thought when she'd seen it? Flicking down the screen, scanning the snide little magazine commentary, he saw it was dated too. She'd have been in no doubt when this was taken.

His belly turned to lead. It was no good telling himself there'd been nothing in it. That didn't stop the guilt.

The door opened behind him, and his head flicked around.

'Hello, Thierry.' Imogen looked composed but pale.

'Are you all right?' He started towards her but stopped at the look on her face. Closed. Shuttered. Distant. He'd never seen her like that and it made something catch hard under his ribs.

'Why wouldn't I be?' She took off her watch and put it on the dressing table.

Thierry frowned. 'I was worried when you weren't in our room. What are you doing here?'

She shrugged as she moved things on the dressing table. Avoiding him? He stepped closer.

'I'm very tired and a bit queasy. I thought it better to sleep here.'

If she was tired, why wasn't she in bed?

The answer was easy: she'd been checking on him, trawling the media to find that incriminating photo. He tried to whip up indignation but found only regret.

'About that photo...' Her head swung round, her gaze meshing with his, and for a split second pure energy blasted through him, like he'd tapped into an electric current. 'It wasn't the way it looks.'

She walked past him and turned off the laptop, taking it to the dressing table.

'Imogen? I said it wasn't like it seems.'

'If you say so.'

'I do say so.' His fingers closed around her bare arm. The swish of her silky nightdress against his knuckles reminded him of the hours of pleasure they'd shared in his bed. It made her curious composure all the more disturbing. 'Why don't you say anything?'

Her eyes met his, more brown than green now and strangely flat.

'I'm tired. Can't we talk in the morning?'

'You've got to be kidding.' She'd seen that photo and withdrawn as if he were a stranger. Anger stirred. It was more palatable than the guilt lining his belly. 'We need to talk now.'

Her mouth flattened. 'I've had enough for one night.'

But instinct told him he couldn't delay. Keeping his hold on her arm, he led her to the bed. Her chin jutted mutinously but she said nothing as he sat beside her.

'Aren't you curious about the woman in the photo?' If he'd seen a picture of her in the arms of another man he'd have been more than curious. He'd want to rip the guy's arms off.

'Not particularly.' Her blank tone didn't match the fire in her eyes.

'She kissed me.' Thierry felt a shudder pass through her. 'I was drinking in the bar the last night of the climbing trip—'

'You don't have to justify yourself.'

But he did. He couldn't bear for her to believe he'd been with someone else. 'She asked for a drink then she kissed me.'

'I'm sure it happens to you all the time.' The hint of a snarl in her tone stirred tentative hope. Anger he could deal with. It was this...*nothing* that scared him.

'Nothing happened, Imogen. Just a kiss. What you saw was me pushing her away.'

Hazel eyes held with his, searching, then Imogen looked away. He felt her sag. 'If you say so.'

'I *do* say so.' How could he convince her? Her listlessness scared him. Where was his vibrant Imogen? Why wasn't she reacting? Even to hear her yell would be a relief.

'Right. Now that's cleared up, I'm going to sleep.'

Thierry stared. 'What's going on, *chérie*?'

'Don't!' She stiffened. 'Don't call me that.' She yanked her arm free and shuffled along the bed, putting distance between them. Her hand came up to cradle the spot where he'd held her, as if he'd hurt her, though his touch had been careful.

'I'm not your *chérie* and I never will be.'

'What are you talking about?' His pulse hammered a tattoo of fear. 'Of course you are. You're my wife.' He didn't like where this was going. He'd never seen her act so.

'A convenient wife—not your dear or your sweetheart, or whatever the translation is.' She waved her hand dismissively, and Thierry felt a plummeting sensation in his belly. 'I know it's just a word, a little nothing that slips out easily, but...' She turned her profile to him. 'But I don't want your casual endearments.'

'Imogen—'

'And since you insist on talking now...' she turned to him '...you should know I've decided to leave. This isn't working.'

Thierry shot to his feet, stalking across the thick carpet.

'Because of one stupid photo? I explained that. Nothing happened! I give you my word.' He squared his shoulders. A Girard's word was rock-solid, unquestionable.

She didn't look impressed. She hugged her arms around her, and he had to work not to let his gaze linger on her breasts, straining against her nightgown. 'It's not because of the photo.'

He strode across to loom over her so she had to arch her neck to look at him. 'Don't lie, Imogen.' Pain settled like a weighted blanket. 'We've always had the truth between us.' It was one of the things he'd most appreciated about her. She was direct and open, someone he could believe in.

'You want the truth?' Abruptly, the blankness was gone and heat shimmered in her eyes. 'The truth is marrying you was the biggest mistake of my life. I've had enough and I'm going home. I've booked a flight to Australia. Once I'm there I'll see about a divorce.'

The light dimmed and for a second Thierry's vision blurred, like the time he'd almost knocked himself out on a ski run in Austria. He braced himself, bending his knees slightly to counteract the sensation that he was swaying.

Yet nothing counteracted the horrible clogging in his chest, or the fierce pain slicing through his gullet.

'You're not going anywhere.' He didn't consciously form the words. They simply shot from his stiff lips.

'You're going to stop me by force?' Her eyebrows rose, giving her a haughty look that reminded him of his grandmother at her most disapproving. But his grandmother had never struck fear into him as Imogen did.

He stumbled back then steadied himself. 'I won't let you go.'

In a slither of fabric, she rose, standing toe to toe with him. 'You can't stop me.'

He shook his head, trying to fathom what had happened. Only hours ago everything had been fine.

'You know I can.' His voice was low and urgent and

when he touched her cheek he felt as well as heard her sudden intake of breath. 'We're good together, Imogen. You can't seriously want to give that up.'

Her head reared back and his hand fell. 'Sex?' She sneered. 'Yes, that's good. But why would I uproot myself just for that? It was a mad idea to think of staying in France.'

Thierry's eyes widened at her determination, and fear engulfed him. More than that. Fear was what he'd felt in the accident that had ended his Olympic skiing career. And the time his parachute had jammed before finally releasing.

This was more. This was on a level he'd never experienced. It was slow, grinding terror. Instead of creating a surge of defiant adrenalin that gave him courage to face danger, this weakened his very bones.

It made him feel…helpless.

'You think this is just about *sex*?' He saw her flinch and realised his voice had risen to a roar.

Thierry backed up, astonished at his loss of control. He never shouted. He never lost control. But he'd never felt anything like this visceral dread.

Before he could apologise she spoke, so softly and steadily the contrast with his own exclamation shamed him. 'If this relationship isn't about sex, tell me what it *is* about, Thierry.'

Her gaze held his gravely, and he swallowed. He flexed his hands.

'Our child…'

She dropped her eyes, her shoulders sagging before that bright hazel gaze met his again. 'Our child will do very well without this. It doesn't need us to live together in a farce of a marriage to be happy and healthy. I'd never try to cut you out of its life.'

So, he was to be a long-distance parent? Outrage flared.

'A farce? There's nothing farcical about this marriage, Imogen.' Fury leavened the horror. After all he'd done, all he offered, that was what she thought of them together? 'It's real. As real as French law can make it.' As real as *he* could make it.

'I don't care about the law, Thierry.' She folded her arms. 'I care about the fact I've married a man who doesn't love me. Who can never love me.' Her eyebrows rose as if in challenge. 'I want more. It was a mistake thinking I could settle for less.'

'I told you I didn't sleep with that woman.' This time, instead of anger, he felt desperation. Why wouldn't she believe him?

She shook her head. 'This isn't about her. This is about the fact you'll never really want *me*. Not for myself, just for the heir I'm providing, and because physically we're compatible.'

Imogen paced to the window, and Thierry tracked her with his eyes, willing down the need to haul her close and seduce her into forgetting this nonsense. Seduction wouldn't work this time.

His gut clenched in panic.

'We talked about this.' He kept his voice low and persuasive. 'We've got the basis of a great marriage.'

'No!' This time the shake of her head splayed dark tresses around her shoulders. 'I've changed, Thierry. Once upon a time I'd have been willing to put up with second best, with not quite achieving the dream. Once I didn't dare to dream because I was too busy being cautious. But thinking I was dying gave me courage.' She paused, a wistful smile curving her lips.

'So did you, Thierry. You helped me to be brave. You encouraged me to follow my dreams.' She hefted a breath that lifted her lovely breasts. 'My dream is to love and be loved. As simple and as huge as that.'

She rubbed her hands up her arms as if cold. Did she too feel the draught of icy air coursing around him?

'I understand you'll never love me, Thierry. You explained you don't believe in romance. Plus, I'm not the woman for you. I'm not blonde or sophisticated.' She shrugged. 'The woman you met in Paris wore borrowed plumage, just like tonight, and pretended to fit in, though she knew she was an outsider. I don't belong in your world, so it's better I go.'

'To find a man to love?' The words grated from his throat, leaving it raw.

Her face twisted with what looked like anguish. Except *he* was the one being torn apart.

'If I can.'

He stalked forward, grabbing her hands. They were cold. He looked down at her small, capable fingers in his and knew he couldn't bear to release her. It was asking too much.

'No.' His voice was a scrape of sound.

'Sorry?'

'You can't do that.'

Thierry watched his thumbs trace a possessive path across her knuckles. He imagined their hands together in twenty years, forty years, veined and wrinkled. The image made him feel…right inside. The idea of Imogen giving herself to another man, growing old with *him* instead, turned Thierry's stomach.

'You can't do it to me.'

'To *you*?'

Thierry met her questioning eyes. Instantly heat, recognition and emotion slammed into him. All those feelings that had been growing since the night he'd looked across a crowd in Paris and seen Imogen.

At first he'd thought it simple attraction, sexual desire with a dollop of curiosity and vicarious pleasure in watching her wide-eyed excitement at so many new experiences. But his feelings went way beyond that. They had almost from the first.

She tugged to free herself and his grip tightened.

'Let me go, Thierry.' Desperation laced her words. It gave him hope when moments ago there'd been none. There must be a reason she sounded as desperate as he felt.

'I can't.' It was the simple truth. How had she put it? *Simple and huge.* The truth was so huge it felt like he'd swallowed the sun.

Thierry met his wife's eyes, willing her to believe, to understand, to share what he felt. 'I can't, Imogen, because I love you.'

Thierry's hands on hers kept her standing as the room whirled. His arm came around her, strong and sure. Yet it was the look in his eyes that held her immobile. A look she'd never seen.

How was that for wishful thinking?

'Don't lie, Thierry.' She choked on the words.

He held her gaze, and she could almost believe she read desperation there. Enough to feign love now he realised it was what she wanted?

'I don't lie, Imogen.' He spoke gravely.

How badly she wanted this to be true! Enough to half-believe him, though it defied logic. 'I can't take any more, Thierry. Not tonight.'

'This can't wait.' Before she knew it she was high in his arms, cradled against his chest. She tried to be strong, but found her cheek nestling against him. His unique scent filled her. If this was the last time he held her she was determined to commit every detail to memory.

He moved, and her heart hammered, but he wasn't carrying her to bed. She was grateful. He'd be hard to resist if he tried to seduce her. Surely it was relief, not disappointment, she felt when he settled on the window seat, cradling her?

'I love you, Imogen.' The words vibrated through his body into hers. They wafted warm air in her hair.

'Thierry. Please.' She swallowed pain. 'Don't pretend. I won't stop you seeing our baby. You'll still have access.'

'This isn't about the baby. It's about us.'

Imogen turned her face into his chest, absurdly seeking comfort from the very man she shouldn't. 'It's not about us. This is pride speaking. You just don't want to let go.' Not after he'd shown his bride to his friends and all those society people.

'Of course I won't let you go. Not without a fight. It's taken a lifetime to find you.'

Shock caught her throat. Sincerity throbbed in every word. But it couldn't be.

Tilting her head, she leaned back enough to see him. Tension accentuated the planes and angles of that remarkable face. His mouth was grim, but his eyes looked lost. Surely not!

'Don't play games, Thierry.' Her voice scraped. 'It's cruel. That's not you.'

His arms tightened. 'What would be cruel is losing you. I love you, Imogen. Nothing matters but that.'

Her heart thudded in her throat and there was a rushing in her ears. 'You don't believe in love. You told me.'

'I was an arrogant, ignorant fool.' He brushed her cheek with a touch so tender it made her eyes well. 'Don't cry, Imogen. I want you to be happy.'

She opened her mouth to tell him she'd be happy if he released her. But it wasn't true.

'I'm not your type. I'm not tall and glamorous or—'

'You're so much my type I don't think I could live without you.' Her heart squeezed. 'As for me chasing blondes...' He shook his head. 'My tastes have matured. I never loved any of them.'

'Not even Sandrine?'

His mouth twisted. 'Does it make me sound old if I admit that was youthful folly? I was besotted but I'm glad she married someone else. We'd have made each other un-happy. We're too alike, too self-centred.'

'You're not.' His care for her had been anything but.

'I am. Now I've found you, I'll do anything to keep you.'

'Like pretend to love me.'

He cupped her cheek, holding her so she couldn't look away.

'There's no pretence. From the first you were differ-ent. I didn't know how or why but I felt it. Didn't you?' He barely paused. 'I told myself you were a breath of fresh air, a diversion, but you were much more. I was on the point of trying to find your address in Australia when you ap-peared at my office.'

'Really?' Her breath stilled.

'Really. I didn't know I was in love. Obviously I'm a slow learner. But it's true. I've been falling for you since that night in Paris.'

Hope vied with disbelief, stealing her words, jumbling her thoughts.

'But the woman you met in Paris wasn't the real me. I'm boring and—'

A crack of laughter stopped her. 'Boring? Anything but. You're more exciting than anyone I know.'

Imogen shook her head. 'You don't understand.'

'I understand. You're cautious, you like to weigh your options. You love numbers and order. But there's more. That woman in Paris is just another side to your personal-ity, even though you suppressed her for years. You weren't pretending, just letting her loose.' His smile was so tender her heart turned over. 'Your zest for life is contagious and you help me be the man I want to be. The thought of los-ing you...' To her amazement, his voice cracked.

'Thierry?'

'Don't ever say you're not glamorous.' The authorita-tive confidence was back in his voice. 'You're the most gorgeous woman on the planet, whether you're in a ballgown, or old jeans or nothing.' His voice dipped. 'Preferably nothing.'

'Now you're lying,' she gasped.

He smiled. 'You're the most extraordinary woman in the world. I love you, Imogen. Stay with me and in time maybe you'll love me back.'

Her heartbeat snagged. He truly didn't know?

'But you don't want a wife to tie you down. You want freedom. A life of adventures like the one you're planning with Orsino.'

He shook his head. 'Before you I pined for what I'd lost—the freedom to take off at a moment's notice. I told myself I hated the job I'd been forced to do and it was true in the beginning. But I've come to realise I enjoy commerce. I like the cut and thrust of it, sizing up opportunities and making the most of them.' His smile was self-deprecating.

'I've had to do a lot of growing up recently. From self-absorbed playboy to responsible adult. It was hard but I'm happy with the outcome.' Thierry's thumb stroked her cheek.

'I'd already decided I need balance in my life. Now the business is on track, I can step back a little and have a life outside the office. But I don't want to step back totally. I want to run the business and find time for a little climbing or ballooning. But what I want most of all...' His voice dipped to that low, earthy note that always thrilled her. 'Is to be with you and our baby.'

Thierry paused, his gaze meshing with hers. Imogen felt hope and excitement pound through her. 'That's going to be the most exciting adventure of my life. I wouldn't miss it for anything.' His thumb brushed her cheek.

'I'll give it all up, the treks, the business, whatever, if it means you'll stay with me. I'll move to Aus—'

Imogen put her hand to his lips. They were warm and soft, at odds with his harsh expression. 'You'd do that? Give up all this?'

'I love you, Imogen.' His lips moved against her hand, his words balm to her aching heart. 'All I want is to be with you. The rest is nothing.'

The *château*, the place in society, the birthright, were less precious than her?

'Ah, *mon coeur*, don't cry. Please, it breaks my heart.'

He leaned in to kiss the hot tears sliding down her cheeks, and she bit back a sob. Her heart felt too full, as if it were going to burst.

She clutched his shoulders, trying to reassure herself this was real. 'You mean it?'

'I've never been more serious about anything in my life.' His expression was so solemn, so earnest. 'Stay with me and I'll prove it to you. No man could ever love you more than I do and one day, I hope, you'll feel the same way about me.'

Fire caught Imogen's throat as she smiled through her tears.

'Not *one day. Now.*'

He stared blankly as if he couldn't make sense of her words.

She slid her hands up to cup the back of his head, a quiver of excitement filling her at the knowledge dreams really did come true.

'I'm in love with you, Thierry. I have been since Paris. Since that first night.' She waited for his satisfied smile. Instead, she read shock then wonder on his proud features. 'You swept me off my feet, my darling.'

He closed his eyes, murmuring something in French under his breath that sounded heartfelt and urgent. When he opened them again she caught the dark gleam of excitement she'd loved from the beginning.

'You truly love me?'

She nodded. 'That's why I was so miserable, so ready to leave. I thought I could love you and live with you even though you didn't return my feelings. But then—'

'Then you thought I was a selfish, ungrateful brute who didn't understand what a treasure I had in you.'

Suddenly he swooped her up in the air then deposited her on the window seat. Before she could catch her breath he knelt before her, drawing her hands into his.

'Thierry? What are you doing?'

Midnight eyes held hers, and she couldn't look away, for they were filled with love. The same love welling inside her.

'Imogen, will you make me the happiest man in the world? Will you marry me and live with me for the rest of our lives?'

'But we're already married.'

'I want to marry you again—properly this time. With us both giving our hearts. A marriage of love, not convenience.'

'Oh, Thierry!' She blinked back fresh tears.

'You don't like the idea?' He frowned.

'I love the idea! I can't think of anything I'd like more.'

His loving smile, his tender kiss on her palm, told her he felt the same, but there was a mischievous glint in his eyes. 'Women love shopping for wedding dresses and the trimmings for a big wedding.'

'A big wedding?' She pretended to pout. 'What if I want to get married in a hot-air balloon or—'

His kiss stopped her words. When he pulled back he was grinning. 'Whatever you want, *mon coeur*. Perhaps we could go somewhere more comfortable to discuss the options.'

Imogen felt that smile to the soles of her feet. 'You have the best ideas, Thierry.' She put her hand in his and let him draw her to her feet, knowing he was right. The future together would be the adventure of their lifetimes.

* * * * *